The
Cottage
by the
Loch

BOOKS BY KENNEDY KERR

MAGPIE COVE
The House at Magpie Cove
Secrets of Magpie Cove
Daughters of Magpie Cove
Dreams of Magpie Cove

A Spell of Murder

The
Cottage
by the
Loch

Kennedy Kerr

bookouture

Published by Bookouture in 2023

An imprint of Storyfire Ltd.
Carmelite House
50 Victoria Embankment
London EC4Y 0DZ

www.bookouture.com

ISBN: 978-1-83790-009-1
eBook ISBN: 978-1-83790-008-4

For all the romantics

PROLOGUE

Five Elms Hospice, August 2022

My girl Zelda,

The staff here at the hospice have suggested that I write you a letter. They say it's a thing people do at this stage of the illness, so that I can tell you everything I want to and get any last secrets out into the open.

They also said I could make a book of photos of me for you (like you don't already have them). Or maybe they think you'll forget what I look like. I'm not doing the photo book thing. It's just not my style, and I know you'll remember what I look like, because, girl, you look just like me.

I've told them that I don't have any secrets from you, but they still said I should write the letter. So, here it is.

I hope that, when you read this, you know that I love you and I am crazy proud of you. You are the best thing that I have ever done with my life. I am so proud to have been your mom. I'm just sorry that I have to say goodbye a little earlier than I hoped.

I did the best I could for you, and I know it was tough sometimes. Thank you for always being such a good kid and taking it on the chin. Your dad missed out by leaving us, I'll tell you that much. At some point, you may want to get in touch with him, and if you do, you have my blessing. Or, you might not, and that's okay too. I'm sorry, though, that I don't have any contact details for him and haven't for a long time, so you would have to find him some other way.

If I had one piece of advice for you, Zelda, it's to be strong. I always taught you to be independent and follow your heart, so keep doing that. And when life gets you down, remember what Maya Angelou said: *If you don't like something, change it. If you can't change it, change your attitude.*

I know you're going to be okay, but remember that, when I'm gone, you shouldn't grieve for me too much. Life is for the living – so, live it as best as you are able, my sweet girl. You may not think that I lived the life I wanted, but I made the most of what I had, and so should you.

May your days ahead be busy, and your nights filled with comfort.

I'll love you always, Zelda. I'll be watching over you.

Mom xxxx

ONE

'Scotland? Really?' Zelda Hicks had been leaning on the desk, looking at her colleague Emery's computer screen as he flicked through various websites belonging to Scottish castles. The white leather heeled boots she had worn to the office that morning were killing her ankles, so she sat down gingerly next to him instead.

'Afraid so, darling. The boss has her heart set on it: stone castle, brooding lochs, all the haggis you can eat. This whole collection's tartan.' Her British colleague, Emery, the photographer for *The Village Receiver* – a small but respected New York newspaper – tapped a pile of test shots on his desk.

Zelda flicked through images of red, blue and purple tartan pencil skirts, one-shoulder mini dresses and revealing bustier tops worn by models. She lowered her reading glasses onto her nose, pushing her black fringe out of the way. She'd just started wearing glasses for reading and screens, and tended to put them on her head when she was working, but then she'd forget where they were and spend ten minutes searching her desk until Emery or some other kind soul pointed them out.

'Shooting in Scotland's so unnecessarily *expensive*, though.

We could do it in Queens and it'd look just fine. Union Square. The lost and found office of the Empire State Building,' Zelda suggested. *The Village Receiver*, based in a slightly down-at-heel building just off Bleecker Street in the West Village, usually didn't have the budget for international travel: they were an artsy, local newspaper that generally featured New York artists, fashion, musicians and restaurants. However, since their new editor, Mira Khan, had been appointed, she had been spending money like it was going out of fashion.

Zelda had serious doubts as to whether Mira sending her and Emery to Scotland just for a fashion editorial was wise, but her opinion didn't mean much. Ultimately, she wasn't in charge; even though she'd worked herself up to the position of Features Editor from an entry-level position and Mira had come from a well-known fashion magazine where she was probably used to having more money for things like sudden trips to Scotland.

'Maybe. But may I suggest that you say yes with a bow on top? Sales are down for the fifth month in a row since she started and she's on the warpath.' Emery shot a glance at Mira's office, which sat at one end of the high-ceilinged loft space the newspaper occupied. Mira's was the only private office on the floor; the rest of the staff (Emery joked that she regarded them all as 'her minions') shared the open-plan space, which was draughty in the winter and boiling hot in the summer, but had a lovely view of a park below from its tall, loft-style windows.

'Do you really think she's going to send us to Scotland?' Zelda pulled a little at her neckline. She'd been trying to dress more smartly since Mira had started working at *The Village Receiver*, to create a good impression. But none of her pencil skirts or power outfits (vintage eighties numbers in electric blue or pink, with shoulder pads and big belts) had been clean that morning, so she'd come in wearing black jeans, a vintage Snoopy sweatshirt and the white leather boots, which were killing her.

'That's what she said, so, yeah. I'd have thought you'd jump at the chance for some free international travel. Personally, I like Mira's whole spendy vibe. Long may she reign.' Emery clapped his hands together enthusiastically. 'Oooh. I've got to think about what to wear!'

'So, we're going to Edinburgh?' Zelda thought about her choice of sweaters. She was prone to dressing for comfort at home, but she liked to dress up for work most of the time, apart from today, when just getting out of bed had been an effort. Usually, she wore a statement black eyeliner on her top eyelids, which suited her cat eyes and long, straight black hair. Often, she also wore a statement red lip. She was short, so she tried to wear heels when she could. Her mom had always told her that her hair was her best feature, but that she could make more of her mouth.

'Nope. We have the choice of... West Highlands. East Highlands. Midlothian.' Emery flicked through various web pages he had open and stabbed his finger on the screen each time, naming three different Scottish regions. 'All different castles.'

'Those words mean literally nothing to me. Just so you know.'

'Different parts of the mainland, but not in Edinburgh.'

'I thought there was a castle in Edinburgh?'

'There is, darling. Edinburgh Castle.'

'So, can we shoot there?'

'No, we can't shoot at Edinburgh Castle. It's like asking if you can do a shoot at Buckingham Palace.' Emery was indignant.

'Oh, jeez.' Zelda sighed. 'I have no idea why Mira thinks this is a good idea. So, Scotland has a couple of castles. So what? So does Germany. So does damn Transylvania, if she really has to send us somewhere.'

'Well, Scotland has hundreds of castles, actually,' Emery

insisted, a little doggedly. 'And are you really saying you'd prefer to go to Transylvania? Longer flight time, if nothing else.'

'Umm. No, I guess not. Though I've heard it's very beautiful.'

'Right. Scotland, tartan. Makes sense, even if some people might think it was an unforgiveable cliché. It sounds as though you don't want to go. What have you got against the place? Come on, be honest.'

'My dad was Scottish.' Zelda moved her chair for the office assistant who staggered past, dropping a pile of packages on Zelda's desk. 'Hey. Thanks, Midge.'

'Welcome, honey.' Midge was in her early twenties, wore her green hair in pigtails and had so many tattoos that Zelda wondered how she had ever earned enough money to afford them at such a young age. 'There's muffins in the kitchen, you guys. And Dave brought bagels.'

'Ah, great. Thanks.' Zelda smiled warmly. 'We'll be right there.'

'*What?*' Emery hissed, as soon as Midge was out of earshot. 'Your *dad*? As in, the dad you've never known?'

'Yep.' Zelda gazed at her pile of post. 'I did know him. Sort of. I just haven't seen him since I was three.'

'Jeez. "Hicks" doesn't sound very Scottish.' Emery frowned.

'No, that was my mom's name. His name was Mackay.' Zelda's stomach twisted. It had only been a few months since her mom had died from an aggressive cancer that had come out of the blue. It was difficult to talk about it without tearing up: in fact, Zelda tried not to talk about it at all, especially at work.

'Zelda Mackay. Who knew?'

'Not really,' she replied, shortly. 'I mean, I've never used his name, and I never will.' It had always been just her and her mom. Zelda had the sense of being unmoored from reality without her. Her mom had been her anchor. Now, she didn't know what she was doing with her life any more.

There had been many nights since her mom had passed away when Zelda had wondered what she was supposed to do. Work felt like a huge, elaborate circus with no meaning. For a long time, she'd been passionate about telling stories and loved the creative world that the newspaper brought her into contact with. But now, it felt meaningless. What point was there to an art gallery opening in the Village when her mom had passed away? It felt to Zelda that she had been skating on the surface of a frozen lake, blithely paying attention to what everyone else was wearing, when she should have been looking for the crack in the ice that had dragged her mom under with no warning. 'I never really knew him. I don't remember him, in any case. I have zero interest in him or my Scottish heritage,' Zelda snapped. 'Okay? Can we focus on work, please?'

'Fine, fine. No need to bite my head off.' Emery blinked.

Zelda felt awful: he had been nothing but kind to her when her mom died. He'd come around to her apartment, armed with a ridiculously large bouquet of white roses and two full bags of groceries, dropping it all at the doorway when Zelda opened it and enveloping her in a huge hug. Emery had been at the end of the line, late at night, when she'd needed someone to talk to. He'd listened to her, hugged her when she'd cried. He didn't deserve to be on the receiving end of her rudeness now.

'Sorry. It's just a sore subject.' She patted his arm awkwardly.

'It's okay. I understand.' He gave her his gentle grin and looked back at the screen.

'What about that one?' Zelda pointed to a picture of a grand-looking castle with lots of turrets. 'That's historic-looking.'

'Loch Cameron Castle,' Emery read aloud. 'It's lived in by the Laird... let me see. Okay, yes, it's available to hire for weddings and events, so we might be able to get it.'

'The Laird?'

'The owner. "Laird" is the Scottish word for "Lord". Usually, the title involves owning local land as well. A lot of these places have been sold off to trusts that look after them, or are ruins.'

'Huh. She doesn't want ruins, then? Wouldn't that be more atmospheric?' Zelda glanced over to Mira's office, where she could hear her boss berating someone on the phone.

'She told me she wants a Scottish castle with period interiors. This has interiors.' Emery flicked through a few unhelpful photos on the castle website, frowning. 'Though I do think this place would benefit from some better photography. I can't tell what condition the interior is in.'

'The gardens are good, though. We could shoot outside too,' Zelda observed.

'The gardens *are* nice. Shall I email and see what we can arrange?'

'Okay, sure. We're going to need to book it all in pretty quick, if she wants this for the next special issue.' Zelda went back to her desk opposite Emery's and opened her calendar. 'That's where we'd have space for something like this.'

'Think again, love. April, first week issue.' Emery flashed her an uncomfortable grin.

'April? You have got to be kidding!' Zelda covered her eyes with her hands, with a nervous laugh.

The girls on the other side of the office looked up, in case they were missing any juicy scandal.

'I'm deadly serious. We've got to shoot within ten days. You haven't read your emails yet, I take it,' Emery replied in a low voice.

'What's this replacing? We had all the April features planned out already. Oh, no.' The newspaper's features were a mix of things booked in way ahead of time, like exhibitions and author interviews for upcoming books, and some other bits and pieces that were dropped in more last minute, like reviews and local news stories.

Zelda opened her emails. She found one titled URGENT from Mira, read it and groaned.

'Seems like Mira wants to keep a big advertiser sweet.' Emery raised one perfectly plucked eyebrow. 'You know how this works, darling. Smile and say yes. Mira's way is the only way.'

Zelda sighed. This kind of thing was happening more and more frequently. She would sign off an issue in advance with Mira, and then Mira would either postpone or cancel her editorials altogether because she had met someone at a dinner who she thought was *the next big thing*, or had a phone call from an advertiser who harangued her into rearranging the issue.

As the Features Editor, it was Zelda's job to organise all the main stories – if it was fashion, she'd decide how to style the clothes, choose the models and the setting, call in the right jewellery and hairdressers, and a thousand other details. If it was a restaurant or an exhibition review, she'd find a time to visit the gallery or the restaurant with Emery, get the photos done, have a meal or look around the artworks and write up a piece for the paper. She also had to book in and write up interviews, attend book launches and parties. And, like everyone at *The Village Receiver*, she also did a million other little things: made coffee, tidied the office, kept the office birthdays calendar up to date and baked cakes when it was a special occasion. 'I was really proud of the New York fashion graduates story I had planned,' she muttered. The article, about graduates from some of the top fashion design courses in New York, had really made her feel like she was doing something important. 'We were profiling local young professionals. And she wants to replace that with...' Zelda read the rest of Mira's email. 'This designer's not even New York based!' she protested. 'These outfits... I mean, I don't mind tartan. But, it's kinda... cringy, don't you think? All these bodices and mini skirts?'

'I will pretend you didn't say that.' Emery faked a scandalised expression as he fluttered his hand over his chest.

'You know what I mean. What chance do young designers have nowadays?' Zelda sighed.

'Earth to Zelda. Like it matters what we do.' Emery sighed back at her. 'You know Mira by now. You know what she'll say if you go in there and try to argue. *If you don't want to do your job, there are a thousand Zelda Hickses out there, ten years younger than you, waiting to jump into those white leather boots and do it for less money and longer hours.*' He mimicked Mira's nasal twang.

'You're fun today.' Zelda pulled a face at him.

'I love you, darling. You know that. But you don't need me to tell you any of this.'

'No, but it's so great to hear it. As if I didn't already have nightmares about some twenty-year-old stealing my life,' she added, glumly.

What Zelda hadn't told anyone was that she was exhausted. She felt like she'd hardly slept for months, and she hardly ate. Grieving for her mom and working at the same time was harder than she would ever have expected. She knew she had lost weight, and there were grey circles around her eyes. She knew Emery and the rest of her friends in the office were worried about her, and she tried to keep it together. But, every day, it was more and more difficult to get out of bed.

'They wouldn't want your bunions,' Emery tutted. 'Or your roots.'

'I don't *have* roots! This is my natural colour! Look, I've got mere *days* to replan a whole story here.' Zelda plaited her black hair over her shoulder and tapped her phone. 'I need your help, okay? And I assume you're coming with me? To Scotland?'

'Wild horses couldn't keep me away, darling,' Emery drawled.

'Well, that's something. Let's talk hiring models in Scotland, whatever that involves.' Zelda reached for her cup, draining her coffee. On top of trying to deal with her constant, crushing sense of grief, an out-of-the-blue trip to Scotland with Mira breathing down her neck with regular calls and stressy texts was precisely what she didn't need.

She knew exactly how it was going to go: Mira would try to micromanage her from afar, then complain that Zelda hadn't got the shots she should have. There would be some kind of criticism about the choice of models, the location or the fashion itself, and how Zelda had styled it. Mira was notoriously hard to please, and Zelda couldn't think of a time when she felt she had actually had done so.

You know what, Zelda thought, as Emery clicked through a modelling agency website based in the UK. *I used to love this job. But I don't know if I still do.*

TWO

As Zelda and Emery approached the castle in a taxi, Zelda watched in awe as a long, winding drive took them through gardens filled with glossy dark green leaves. 'What are those?' she asked the taxi driver, pointing at the bushes.

'Rhododendrons,' he answered in his broad accent. 'Bonny, eh?'

'They certainly are,' Emery interjected. 'They won't bloom until summer, but I can imagine they'll be stunning when they're out.'

Zelda watched the skyline as they drove along; alongside them, a pine forest darkened the grey-blue horizon and made long, overarching tunnels of green that the taxi meandered through.

'O' course, most people say the best time tae visit the loch an' the castle's summer, but winter's ma favourite,' the taxi driver continued, switching on his windscreen wipers to clear the screen of the rain that had started to fall. 'More atmospheric.'

Zelda's window started to mist up, and she rubbed her hand

on it to see the view outside, pressing the button to open it a little and let the air in.

She didn't think she'd ever seen this kind of continuous green lushness: it felt unnatural to her eyes, used to wide streets and skyscrapers. Even in the rain it didn't seem dreary. In New York, when it rained, it just transferred the dirt of the city onto the streets and streaked the walls grey. Here, the moment she opened the car window, she realised that the rain made everything smell like a designer-scented candle: cedar, pine and an indescribable freshness.

Loch Cameron was, she had to admit, the kind of stunning rural beauty spot that everyone dreamt of visiting: purple heather-topped hills rose up behind the castle as if framing it, and a rocky stream led down to the loch below, following its path through lush green forest. The castle was like something out of a fairy story: tall turrets topped an imposing grey stone frontage, with long windows and a huge double-door entryway opening onto a gravel drive.

When they arrived at the castle's imposing front doors, Zelda and Emery were met by the housekeeper, Anna, a middle-aged, quietly spoken woman with a soft Scots accent and a warm smile.

Anna led them into the magnificent entrance hall, which featured a vast, dark wood staircase. The same wood panelled the walls, and was carved throughout with patterns of fruits and leaves.

Zelda gazed up at the carvings and the high, vaulted ceiling in wonder. 'This is amazing. I kinda thought all castles were ruined stone things,' she admitted.

'Ah, there's a great variety,' Anna explained, kindly, as she started up the stairs. 'Of course, there are plenty of those about. But this one has had a Cameron living in it for many hundreds of years. And a staff, obviously, to keep it all going. Far fewer now than there was once.' She smiled.

'Like that movie? With, like, hundreds of maids and butlers?' Zelda ran her hand along the carved wooden bannister as she followed Anna, imagining all the people who had run their hands along it over the years.

'Ah, well, maybe not hundreds. But, yes, butlers, drivers, maids, that kind of thing. Nowadays it's me, the Laird, a couple of cleaners who come in a few times a week, and a few other professional staff, but they work outside the castle. Groundskeepers, mainly.'

At the top of the stairs, Anna led them past a beautiful sitting room, panelled in wood and featuring an extensive library, and several bedrooms.

'Four-poster beds.' Emery nodded sagely. 'You know, at some of the old English castles like Hampton Court, they still have the beds that belonged to the kings and queens. They're so tiny! People were so small back then.'

'I have legit never slept in a four-poster bed.' Zelda sat on the edge of one that was covered in a dustsheet, and sneezed. 'So, did you, like, draw the curtains around you? What if the curtains had spiders?'

'A good housekeeper would beat the curtains soundly with a broom to ensure there were no spiders,' Anna answered, straight-faced.

However, some of the rooms seemed rather dusty and uncared for. In a large drawing room, Zelda pointed out the corners to Emery, where the wallpaper was peeling away.

'Needs a bit of TLC,' Emery whispered. 'No wonder. These old piles need so much maintenance. They're basically money pits.'

'Ugh. Look. Mouse droppings,' Zelda whispered back. Not that she wasn't used to that: she'd lived in New York most of her life, where rats, mice and cockroaches were commonplace.

'But isn't the Laird completely loaded? He has to be, right?'

'Oh, probably not. Most of the aristocracy aren't, nowadays. And, as I say, this place will take so much money to maintain.'

'Hmm,' she replied, thoughtfully. 'It just seems uncared for, you know? It's mostly cosmetic stuff; most of it would be easy to put right. So why isn't the Laird bothering with any of it?'

'Keep your voice down,' Emery whispered, letting Anna walk ahead. 'Don't be rude.'

'I'm not being rude. I'm genuinely curious.'

At the end of the top floor, there was a roped-off area. 'This is the Laird's private quarters,' Anna explained. 'Off limits.'

Emery walked on with Anna to the end of the hallway, but Zelda's hand lingered on the cord rope that hung between two hooks at the end of the hall. She had a sudden impulse to slip under the rope, just to see what a modern Laird's life looked like. Were his rooms as old-fashioned as the rest, or were they something entirely more modern? Did *they* have mice?

She was surprised by her own curiosity. She was supposed to hate Scotland, wasn't she? When she thought of the place at all, Zelda thought of what her mom told her about the time she visited: the Mackay family were rude and inhospitable, lived in a cramped, cold house and ate only over-boiled vegetables. But this wasn't anything like her mom's memory.

Emery and Zelda fell in love with the castle's large kitchen, which was decked out with gleaming copper saucepans and a huge, old black range oven. There was a room that Anna called the larder, filled with hanging hams, an extensive yet dusty wine rack, and rows and rows of tinned peaches, corned beef and tinned peas.

'The Laird isn't much of a one for cooking,' Anna explained, as she led them around, seeing Zelda bemusedly pick up a tin of corned beef. 'Not any more, anyway.'

'At least he has good taste in wine.' Emery pulled a bottle

from the rack and held it for Zelda to see. 'This bottle alone is worth more than I earn in a month.'

'Huh.' Zelda replaced the can and took the bottle from Emery, imagining an elderly Laird with a paunch and the red nose of a drinker. She felt sorry for him: living alone in his roped-off area, eating tinned food. Still, there were worse things than being a wealthy landowner.

'How come it's all a bit... you know...' Zelda met Anna's questioning expression. 'Uncared for?'

'Well, it all takes time, keeping a castle up to date,' Anna explained. 'When there was a Mistress of the castle, it was better.' She lowered her voice. 'But when the Laird was widowed... I think he stopped wanting to do it all.'

'Oh. I'm sorry.' Zelda imagined that the 'Mistress' had probably died of old age: she felt even more sorry for the old guy, living there, missing his wife. Now that she had experienced that kind of loss herself, she understood how deep it went.

Anna cleared her throat. 'Also, it's money. You wouldn't believe what this all costs to run, and maintaining the rest of the land.'

'I can imagine.' Zelda raised her eyebrow. 'The utilities alone must be insane.'

'Still, it's beautiful,' Emery added, as Anna led them into a long, magenta-carpeted hallway.

They inspected a billiards room, containing a drinks cabinet, leather sofas and leather-bound books, and two large lounges. Down a hallway, double doors led out to a large patio and extensive, manicured gardens.

The view down to the loch was breath-taking; Zelda took in a lungful of the clean, cold, misty air that hung over the loch and felt it sink into her bones.

The garden itself was unlike anything she'd seen before. Sure, Zelda had read celebrity and home décor magazines like everyone else, and marvelled at the places some people lived.

But, as a New Yorker, she'd never had this kind of access to a real-life castle, never mind the private grounds of a place like this.

Before her, rows of sharply trimmed privet hedges reached down towards the loch, in intricate patterns. In the squares and triangles created between the hedges, topiary trees in the shape of animals dotted the view alongside evergreen trees that spread their branches in the soft rain. Wide stone steps led down from the terrace outside the patio and, at the bottom of a grassy hill, joined a long stone wall that ran around the whole edge of one side of the castle.

Before she could chastise herself for thinking it, Zelda was imagining herself as the Lady of the manor, standing where she was but dressed in a vintage ballgown, her hair in an elaborate chignon.

She'd never thought of Scotland in this way, though it was probably the way that most people did: rolling hills, misty lochs, brooding castles. This was a world away from the cold, unpleasant place Zelda had imagined. Now, she could see what all the fuss was about. She still didn't feel like she belonged there: she was Zelda Hicks, from the Bronx, not a Lady of the manor in a voluminous tartan dress. Nonetheless, she forgave Scotland a little. It wasn't the country's fault that her dad had left her, after all. Or that her mom had passed away.

THREE

'Okay, so we're thinking kings and queens here. Regal. Chins up. Slow movements. You're the reigning monarch, but you're out for a walk in your country estate. And, go. Yeah. Great!' Zelda called out, following two models as they posed coltishly on a series of stone steps. 'Yep, yep, yep. Think Princess Margaret, but she's Lady Gaga. Establishment rebel. She's gone out to find somewhere to smoke, in secret. Away from the... what d'you call it? Servants?'

'Ladies-in-waiting,' Emery corrected her, from behind the camera. 'And Princess Margaret wasn't Scottish.'

'Who, then?'

'Mary Queen of Scots? Not with a cigarette, though. Maybe going to meet her lover,' Emery prompted. 'Since we have Greta and Austin with us. We talked about that as a story.'

'Okay, secret Scottish lovers,' Zelda agreed. Privately, she was thinking, *Let's just get this done so we can go home.*

Admittedly, Zelda's knowledge of Scottish history was patchy at best, and mostly informed by the film in which Mel Gibson had played William Wallace. If anything, she'd made an effort to know as little as possible about Scotland as she'd grown up, in a kind of rebellion against her dad, Robin Mackay.

All she knew about him was that he had come to America in the eighties to work on the stock market, and met her mom in a club. He'd left when he'd lost all the money he and Zelda's mom had saved: it'd turned out that the stock market wasn't the only place that Robin Mackay liked to gamble. They'd had to sell their nice house to pay off his debts, and Robin had gone back to Scotland, leaving Zelda and her mom with her mom's family business – the dry-cleaning shop – and the small apartment above it.

Zelda had seen pictures of that house: the one in the suburbs her mom and dad had had to sell. It was nice. There was a white fence. A tiled roof. A front door – painted red – that belonged to them alone. Much nicer than the tiny apartment she'd grown up in, despite how hard her mom had worked to make it home for her.

She had one memory of the house with the red roof: a summer day, playing in the yard outside with her toy car. Running it along the grass, and seeing a bee flying towards the red door. Zelda remembered trying to tell her mom, *There's a bee, there's a bee flying in!* She had been afraid that the bee would sting her mom. But her mom had laughed, picked her up in her strong arms and just repeated, *Bee, bee, bee*, not understanding why Zelda was crying.

Growing up in the tiny apartment above the dry-cleaning shop, Zelda's bedroom had been one side of her mother's bedroom, separated by a thick curtain. Finally, when she was a teenager, her mom had bought a sofa bed for the main living room and Zelda had slept in there, pulling the bed out every night and putting it away in the morning.

She'd loved her mom so much. But she had mourned the house she barely remembered, where she could have had a childhood room of her own, filled with toys. Where she could have had friends around and not had to explain the smell of the dry-cleaning chemicals that filled the apartment on hot, airless afternoons. Where she could have had a mom and a dad and all the normal mom and dad things.

She had been angry for a long time. She was still angry at her dad for leaving, and, somehow, even more so now that her mom had died. Maybe it was something to do with the fact that, without her mom, he was all she had left in terms of family. That made her mad. She had no desire to depend on him in any way.

So, Zelda had sworn she would never go to Scotland because presumably that was where her dad lived now. She didn't want to be on the same continent as him, never mind potentially twenty miles away. Yet here she was.

Emery had told her to pack practical clothes, and was himself dressed in a warm, waterproof jacket like the kind hikers wore, as well as jeans and hiking boots. Zelda had ignored him, partly because she hated being told what to do in general, and partly because she hadn't wanted to think about Scotland at all. It felt like a betrayal of her mom and her childhood self to even be there. Dressing appropriately for Scotland had felt like *giving in* to it somehow, so she was wearing one of her standard power-dressy work outfits: heels, a sharply tailored pencil skirt and a vintage band T-shirt under a tailored jacket.

Scotland wasn't going to take her outfits away from her.

Zelda Hicks was not about to let the drizzly, misty country of the father she pretended didn't exist infringe on her identity, not even so much as with a three-day outfit change, thank you very much. *Are you proud of me, Mom?* she wondered, remembering what her mom had written to her in that letter: *Be strong. If you don't like something, change it. If you can't change it, change your attitude.*

Zelda thought that her mom probably would have told her to put some flat shoes and a thick sweater on, but at least she had *changed her attitude* from dreading her trip to Scotland to stubbornly resisting its considerable charms.

However, this intransigence also meant that she'd almost killed herself twice by falling over on the stone walkways outside the castle in her heels. It also turned out that Scottish castles *were* pretty cold and wet, just like Emery had warned her, and she was freezing in her jacket.

'Zelda? I need a break. I need to call my agent.' Greta Zo, one of the models Zelda had booked for the two-day shoot pouted. 'And I need maybe some vitamin D serum. I'm dying with this lack of sun. Can we get heat lamps or something? Or supplements. Zinc, also, and Lion's Mane. I need a green smoothie.' She pronounced it 'smoozie': Zelda had used a UK-based modelling agency, but apparently Greta came from Switzerland originally.

Zelda smiled brightly. 'Sure, Greta. I'll see what we can source. Let's have a ten-minute break and then push on for an hour if we can. I think we've almost got pretty much everything we need.' She took out her phone and posted some moody pictures of the castle to Instagram and tagged them #fashion-shoot and #livingmybestlife.

If only the people looking at her Instagram posts knew that it was freezing cold, rainy, and that Zelda felt like she was swallowing her heartbreak every moment. She just wanted to go home.

The other model they were shooting that day, Austin Spencer, immediately walked off without a word, into an open door in the castle where they had a room to stash all their belongings. He came out, vaping, and looking at his phone.

'Man of few words.' Emery handed Zelda a bottle of local spring water. 'This fog's playing havoc with my lenses. Reckon we've got about an hour or two left of this light, then that'll be it.'

'Thanks.' Zelda took the bottle and unscrewed it. 'Did it

ever really get light today? What time is it? It's like a weird, in-between world,' she added, frowning up at the cloudy sky. 'I'm getting an energy bar. Want one?'

'No. I had a full Scottish breakfast, remember?' Emery patted his stomach. 'I could go for two days and not eat now.'

'Ugh. I don't know how you could eat all that meat.' Zelda shook her head as she walked back towards the open door to the castle. The little inn where they were all staying was very charming, and the proprietor, Dotty, had offered them a range of hearty breakfasts. Zelda had refused everything but a bowl of fruit and a black coffee, but she was regretting it now.

'Don't forget that vitamin D serum,' Emery called after her; she made a face at him in return.

Perhaps it was the way that she half-turned to Emery, or perhaps it was the slick soles of her four-inch heels on the wet stone of the paved path, but Zelda was suddenly aware she was slipping. She tried to rebalance herself, but the wet stone underfoot was having none of it. She reached out a hand to break her fall, and felt something snap in her wrist as she made contact with the earth.

Owwww! She wasn't sure if she actually said the words or whether they just reverberated in her brain, but damn, her wrist really hurt.

Zelda let out another cry as she crumpled in a heap, banging her head on the stone as she went down. Things went fuzzy for a while. She found herself thinking how tragic it was that she might die in some remote Scottish village, and how ironic that she'd avoided the country all her life, only to fall to her death more or less as soon as she stepped foot onto Scottish soil.

I was right, she thought. *I should never have come here. Scotland is cursed.*

She didn't know if she imagined it, but she felt strong arms picking her up, and being laid gently somewhere. She thought of her mom carrying her back into the apartment when she was a kid and she'd fallen over and grazed her knee really badly one time.

'Mom,' she murmured, dreamily. It was as if she was just close by; if only Zelda could reach just a little further, she would be back in their old apartment. Her eyelids fluttered. *Mom, I hurt my wrist.*

The memory morphed into the one with the bee. *Bee, bee, bee.* She remembered her mom laughing, picking her up.

'She's out cold. Get me a glass o' whisky,' she heard a gruff Scottish voice order before she sank back into her confused dream. She was running in the grimy streets where she had been a child, towards a castle in the distance.

And when she reached it, she awoke.

FOUR

'You're all right,' a man's voice reassured her as she blinked open her eyes. 'You were only oot for a minute or two. Dinnae try to sit up.'

Instinctively, Zelda tried to sit up, and the act of putting weight on her wrist made her cry out in pain.

'Told ye,' the man said, standing over her like a giant. He was dressed in paint-spattered work trousers and an old check shirt covered by what looked like a handknitted, brown cardigan with some buttons missing. He spoke with a soft Scottish accent, and his curly brown hair looked like it could do with a comb. His beard suggested that he hadn't been near a barber for some time.

'Who are you?' She leant on her other arm to push herself up this time, and propped herself up on the mustard-yellow sofa she was lying on. It too seemed rather worn, and Zelda frowned at the seventies-era tassels that hung from the bottom of it. Worse, some were missing.

'I work here,' he answered, turning his back to her and pouring a glug of amber liquid into a crystal glass. 'Who're you?' He offered the drink to her carefully. 'Drink that.'

'What is it?' She frowned at the smudge left on the glass from his fingers.

'Whisky. Do ye right.'

'Oh. I don't really drink whisky.' She took the drink with her good hand, though it trembled a little, and sipped. It made her cough.

'Medicinal. Drink it all,' the man advised, frowning.

Zelda took another sip and set the glass down on the table. 'I'll have some more in a minute. Did you carry me in here?'

'Aye. Couldn't very well leave ye out there on the slabs.'

'Oh. Well, thank you. But I think I'm fine now.' She tried to stand up, and the room spun around her. The man stepped forward quickly and caught her in his arms. Zelda got a brief impression of soap, wool and something else that she couldn't quite describe: a pleasant smell, a warmth of skin and closeness. The brown cardigan scratched her cheek, but there was a moment where she felt hard muscle underneath his clothes. The man was tall, too: Zelda, now without her heels, only came up to his chest.

'You are *not* fine!' Emery flew into the room. 'I'm so sorry, darling. I was just placating Greta and Austin. They were traumatised from watching you fall.' He rolled his eyes. 'How are you? You took quite the fall... Oh. Hello. I don't believe we've been introduced.' Emery's eyes widened as he took in all six-feet-something of the Scottish workman.

'Hal Cameron. Sorry I wasnae here to welcome ye when ye arrived, but I had somethin' tae attend to on the other side of the loch.' The man gently lowered Zelda back onto the mustard sofa and shook Emery's hand. 'I hope Anna's been looking after ye?'

'Oh, no problem at all. We've been fine,' Emery gushed. Zelda watched them, confused. Why was Emery being so nice to this guy? He was just some random workman. 'Emery Black. We emailed.'

'Oh, hallo. Of course, Emery.' The man – Hal – nodded politely. 'How's the shoot been?'

'It was all going marvellously until Zelda frightened the dickens out of me just then.' Emery fanned himself with his hand and sat down by Zelda's feet on the sofa. 'Zelda, dear. Are you hurt?'

'Zelda, is it? We were a little busy tae be introduced.' Hal gave Zelda a sudden warm smile that lit up his features in a most surprising way. Zelda realised that his eyes were a deep blue, and his face, though half-covered in a scraggly beard, had a strong bone structure. 'I think she's broken her wrist. I'm goin' tae call the doctor.' He went to a corner table which was covered in lace doilies and held an old-fashioned black rotary telephone. He picked up the receiver and started to dial.

'Hal Cameron? Is everyone called Cameron, then? Because of the castle?' Zelda picked up the glass of whisky again and took another sip. The fire of the liquid traced heat into her belly. She coughed again and put the glass back down. How had the Scots made this their national drink? It was like drinking fire.

'No, just me. And my kin, no' that there's many left,' Hal replied, having overheard. He then started talking into the phone. 'Oh, hallo, Jim. I wonder if ye could pop up to the castle when ye have a minute? I've a young lady up here wi' what looks like a broken wrist. Aye. Okay then. Bye.'

'Zelda, Hal is the Laird of the castle, and the village.' Emery gave her a meaningful look. 'Remember, we talked about it. Hal Cameron of Cameron Castle.'

'At ye service.' Hal Cameron made a formal bow.

For once, Zelda Hicks couldn't think of anything to say.

FIVE

'Ooh, ye poor bairn. What happened to yer wrist?' Dorothy Ballantyne, or Dotty, as everyone in the village called her, looked up from the Loch Cameron Inn's reception desk as Zelda edged carefully through the wide front door.

The Loch Cameron Inn had been the only option Emery and Zelda could find to stay in at the last minute. Indeed, there didn't seem to be many hotels or bed and breakfasts in the village at all, which Zelda had thought was odd until they got there and she realised just how small the village was. Still, she would have expected there would be more general places for tourists.

Fortunately, the inn itself was cosy, clean and, importantly, warm. Although the décor was a little dated – *traditional*, Emery insisted – Zelda liked it. There was a lot of mixed floral fabrics and fabric-upholstered chairs, with some distinctly chintzy, flowered curtains in her bedroom, but it made her feel at home, even though her apartment with her mom had never been like this, and her own apartment was all modern greys and minimal lines.

Downstairs, the inn opened into a friendly sitting room with dark varnished wooden tables and chairs and tartan tablecloths. A wooden bar ran along one side, and the kitchen lay behind it. To the other side of the bar there was a small snug with an open fire where you could watch TV on an ancient set that only picked up a few channels. Breakfast, lunch and dinner were served in the sitting room, either at the tables or in one of the comfy sofas.

Zelda's bedroom looked over the loch, and was spotlessly clean as well as having a surprisingly capacious baby-pink-enamel bathroom. There was a cupboard full of neatly wrapped bars of soap, spare toothbrushes, shower caps and small tubes of toothpaste in there too, and a pile of clean, fluffy towels. In the bedroom, Zelda had an easy chair like the ones downstairs, a retro-style radio and a more modern TV than the one in the snug. Her bed was king-size, with a thick, snuggly duvet and plump feather pillows that she'd sunk into on the first night with a sigh of relief.

The inn was run by Dotty, with her husband Eric manning the bar in the evenings and, as Dotty explained, 'Doin' all ma odd jobs.' Dotty was perhaps in her mid-sixties, and smartly turned out in what Zelda assumed was classic Scottish older lady attire: tweedy skirt, cream blouse, with a brooch pinned at the neck, and her hair tastefully ash blonde. Today she wore a lavender wool cardigan around her shoulders and a lavender and purple scarf featuring a Scottish thistle print, along with her usual skirt and blouse. It wasn't what Zelda was used to in New York, but, nonetheless, she liked Dotty's style.

'Hi, Dotty. Would you believe I broke it?' Zelda gave her a wan smile, showing Dotty the cast that Jim, the local doctor, had put on for her. Emery followed, carrying the camera kit.

'Doin' what? Not up at the castle?' Dotty gasped.

'Yeah. I fell over, held out my hand to break my fall.'

'Oh, dear me. Very bad luck. Though I must say, in this dreich weather, it can be lethal on the ground.' Dotty tutted.

'Now you tell me.' Zelda smiled grimly. She guessed that 'dreich' meant wet or rainy, or something along those lines. *Bad weather, anyway.*

'It's going to be tight getting to the airport, hon,' Emery warned. Their turnaround for the trip was quick; Mira didn't want them staying any longer than necessary. 'Want me to pack your stuff up?'

'Ach, no. Tae have tae get on a plane straightaway doesnae seem right,' Dotty clucked. 'Can ye even get on a plane wi' a cast? I've got the feelin' ye can't.'

'That's a good point,' Emery said. 'I think you're right. Here, let's check the airline's website.' He got out his phone and tapped at the screen for a minute, then showed it to Zelda.

'Oh, no. You're right.' Zelda felt her heart sink. 'But I've got a million things to do when I get back to New York!'

'You can't hold your phone. Or type,' Emery pointed out.

'I can talk. And walk. That should be enough,' Zelda insisted, but she had to admit that the thought of being jostled on a busy plane was not appealing in the slightest. Not least the risk to her blood pressure, which the airline website explained could be dangerous.

'Well, your room's free another week or two, is all I'm sayin'.' Dotty raised an ash-blonde eyebrow: Zelda wondered if there was a beauty salon in the village. There had to be, to maintain Dotty's perfect shade. 'Why don't ye let Emery go back, and take a few days' break? The forecast says we're goin' tae get some sun next week,' she added, in a hopeful tone.

'Mira would kill me.' Zelda shook her head. 'Our boss doesn't approve of last-minute vacations. Or, vacations at all, in fact.'

'It's not a vacation, babe,' Emery said in a weary tone. 'It's the rules. You are literally not allowed on the plane.'

'He's right, dear.' Dotty nodded sagely. 'Ye dinnae want a heart attack on yer hands. That's all I'm sayin'. Eric broke his leg before we had tae fly tae Spain for a cruise two years ago. Turned us away at the airport, aye. Had to rebook.'

'Call her and explain,' Emery suggested. 'I agree with Dotty. Take a few days. I'll call you if I need anything, and Midge can sub for you. You don't really have a choice.'

'I'm not sure about that,' Zelda protested. 'Midge has enough going on.'

'She's more capable than you think. Give her a chance. And call Mira now. I'm gonna pack up my stuff.' Emery waved his hand at her. 'Go!'

'Fine, fine. But she'll say no,' Zelda conceded. Secretly, she loved the idea. She was desperate for a break. But she was convinced Mira would definitely refuse: she'd allowed Zelda a week's compassionate leave when her mom had died, but that was only because Emery threatened her with a staff walk-out if she didn't.

Having some time away from everything – from her job, from New York, even – might be just what Zelda needed. She had to admit that just being at the inn was comforting. In New York, she had started feeling on edge; maybe it was the city itself? Maybe she'd always been on edge and just never realised it.

But, she didn't really think that. New York was her home, but it was losing her mom that had made her feel different, like she was lost on that frozen lake. She couldn't shake the feeling that she should have seen the crack in the ice coming. That she could have done something.

She needed time away from New York. And, somehow, being in Loch Cameron soothed her jangled nerves.

Zelda settled into one of the easy chairs in the cosy lounge area of the inn, just to the right of Dotty's ancient-looking wooden reception desk that held two large floral mugs containing a jumble of pens and pencils and a crystal vase of flowers. She got her phone out of her bag with her left hand, balancing it on her lap, and tapped in Mira Khan's direct number at *The Village Receiver* office.

She'd be there. She was always there.

When Mira finally answered the phone, she sighed when she heard Zelda's voice at the other end. 'Zelda. Aren't you supposed to be on a plane back home about now?'

'Hi, Mira. How's things?'

'Dreadful. How did the shoot go?'

'Good. However, I broke my wrist.'

'Oh. Did you get the shots you needed, though?' Mira Khan's lack of sympathy was already legendary at the newspaper, even though she hadn't worked there that long. She didn't accept physical weakness of any kind, or illness. She kept a drawer full of painkillers and various other prescription medications so that anyone who felt ill could continue to work.

Worse than that, though, while she was legally obliged to make every employee take their two weeks' vacation every year, Mira had prevaricated about approving leave applications since she'd started as Editor in Chief. In fact, Zelda hadn't had any time off work for two years apart from that one week of compassionate leave; anyway, she preferred to work. She'd been at the newspaper for six years, working her way up to Features Editor, and part of her success there was that she never said no to overtime and she never took holiday.

Mira had told her, more than once, that in her opinion Zelda's work was basically just one long holiday. *I wish I could go to parties at a moment's notice*, she'd sniff. *But some of us have real work to do.*

Zelda had chosen to smile and ignore that comment.

'Yeah. Greta and Austin were great. Listen, I've checked with the airline and I can't get on a plane tonight. It's a minimum of forty-eight hours before you can get on with a cast. So, I'm wondering if you could sign off on a few days' sick leave.'

'A cast?' Mira sounded dubious.

'I broke my wrist,' Zelda repeated, patiently. 'The rules are that you can't fly with a cast until at least forty-eight hours have passed, or my wrist could swell up and affect my blood circulation,' she explained. Not that she expected Mira to care, but there was nothing she could do about it. She was stranded there.

'You want to stay there for longer? A *vacation*?' Mira repeated. 'In *Scotland*?'

The irony was not lost on Zelda that she was begging to stay in the one place on earth she had been determined never to visit, but she persevered. 'I know, I know. I haven't had a vacation in two years, Mira. But this is sick leave.'

'We're not paying you sick leave,' Mira snapped. 'If you can walk, you're not sick.'

'I've broken my wrist,' Zelda repeated. *And I'm exhausted*, she wanted to add. She did everything Mira asked her to do. She had lost count of the all-nighters, the deadlines and all the times she'd missed out on a social life because of her job. 'Mira. I want some time off,' she added, seriously.

'In *Scotland*?' Mira repeated, incredulously.

'Jeez. You sent me here.'

There was a brief silence, and then Mira Khan sighed again. 'Fine. Take a week. But it's vacation, okay? HR is on my back because none of you ever take any time off, anyway.'

That's because you actively discourage it, Zelda thought. 'You're... you're saying yes?'

'Don't make a meal of it,' Mira snapped. 'And don't think the paper's going to pick up the tab for an extended hotel stay. You're paying for anything not included in the original three days.'

'That's fine. Mira, this is... very unexpected.' Zelda searched for the words. 'Thank you.'

'Don't thank me. I've got a lot to deal with right now. I can't spend any more time on this. Give my regards to Ireland.'

'We're in Scotland, Mira,' Zelda corrected her, but the line went dead. That was so typical. Mira had made such a fuss about them doing this shoot in a Scottish castle with a vintage interior, and now she couldn't even remember where she'd sent them.

Zelda looked up; Dotty was at the bar opposite, wiping some glasses.

'Hey, Dotty. I'm going to stay, if that's okay,' she called over.

'Oh, my dear! That's wonderful news. Yer scary boss relented, eh?'

'She offered me a week's vacation. I don't know why, but I'm not going to worry about that now.' Zelda came to sit at the dark wood bar on one of the tartan-topped stools. 'At least my wrist'll be in a better shape when I finally get on the plane, though. Dotty, can you make a cocktail?'

'Aye, lassie, I certainly can. How's an Old Fashioned for ye?'

'Sounds good.' Zelda took a deep breath and let it out again. A week in foggy Scotland wouldn't ever have been top of her vacation list, but she was there now and she should at least try to enjoy it. The prospect of a week in her comfortable bed, eating Dotty's meaty breakfasts and dinners, was not as unappealing as she might have thought.

Dimly, Zelda remembered a time before she had worked for the newspaper, when she'd relished weekend lie-ins and getting up only to eat her mom's comfort food. Beans and rice had been a favourite, with her mom's fried steak. Or mac 'n' cheese, with bacon, in front of the TV, watching a classic movie. Those were deeply happy memories. She had missed that, and it wasn't just because her mom had passed away. Once she had started working at the newspaper Zelda hadn't been able to spend that kind of quality time with her mom much. Her mom had understood; she knew Zelda was chasing her dream, but now Zelda missed those lazy weekends with a depth and ferocity of feeling that surprised her. A deep ache of loss bloomed in her stomach, and she wiped away a tear that threatened to spill down her cheek.

Zelda was tired, and the Old Fashioned made her head spin. It was probably just the drink, and the shock of her injury, making her emotional.

'Another?' Dotty watched her as she drained her glass.

'Why not?' Zelda cleared her throat, hoping Dotty hadn't seen her tear.

'Maybe some dinner too, aye?' Dotty suggested, gently. 'I'll see what we've got that ye can eat with one hand.'

Zelda shook her head. 'I don't need dinner. I tend to skip it.'

But Dotty frowned. 'Aye. I bet ye do. There's nothin' on ye. No one skips dinner under my roof, lassie. I'll get ye something, don't ye worry aboot that.'

Zelda felt her heart twist again, feeling the now-unfamiliar poignancy of being cared for. Her mom had been the same about food; as well as everything being comfort food, she was always worried that Zelda wasn't eating enough. *You're just skin and bone*, she'd say when Zelda visited.

Mom, I'm healthy, Zelda would argue, secretly glad to be harangued.

Dotty nipped out around the wooden bar and disappeared for a moment. When she returned, she was carrying a bowl of vegetable soup and a plate with thick, buttered bread.

'Get that down ye.' She set it in front of Zelda at the bar, and placed an ornate silver spoon and a thick linen napkin embroidered with a thistle next to the bowl. 'Homemade today.'

'Okay, okay. Thank you, Dotty.' Zelda picked up her spoon with her good hand, and met Dotty's gaze as she stood behind the bar, her arms crossed over her considerable bosom. 'You're going to make sure I eat it, aren't you?'

'I certainly am, dear,' Dotty smiled, and Zelda's heart clenched with the bittersweet memory of her mother's love.

SIX

Zelda stayed in bed for the first two days of her Scottish vacation. This was in no small part due to the painkillers that the local doctor, Jim, had given her, coupled with Dotty's 'medicinal' hot toddies that she brought up in the evening with more bowls of hearty soup and fresh bread. Plus, there was soft, creamy porridge in the mornings, which filled her up very well until lunch, which was a hearty sandwich or a casserole.

There were other easy-to-eat treats too, such as a silky, tangy lemon posset and something called a raspberry cranachan, which Zelda discovered was a traditional Scottish dessert, comprising oats, cream, whisky and raspberries. It was delicious. As Zelda licked the spoon after eating it on the second night of her recovery, she wondered if there was anything the Scots didn't put whisky in.

Still, she wasn't complaining. But, because she never took any time off, she wasn't sure she knew how to *be* on vacation any more. Feeling slightly sorry for herself, Zelda lay in her warm, cosy bed for those first two days and watched daytime TV from under the rose-sprigged duvet.

She had also discovered that the log fire in her bedroom was working, and after Eric had brought her up a basket of small logs and showed her how to get the thing lit, she revelled in its warmth and the pleasant, earthy smell of fragrant wood.

However, on the third day, Zelda hauled herself out of bed and ventured out into the small village. As Dotty had promised, the sun had come out and the fog had lifted, creating a totally different atmosphere.

Before, the loch had been misty, with a sense of foreboding. Today, the sun glittered on the flat water and the village bustled with activity. Zelda was surprised when people said, 'Hallo' and 'Guid mornin' to her as she walked around; they looked at her with curious interest, in her knitted monochrome dress, over-sized sunglasses and bright pink PVC jacket, as she tip-tapped down the somewhat uneven cobbled path of the small high street in a pair of designer stiletto boots.

She had, in fact, tried in vain to get the PVC jacket on over the cast on her wrist before giving up and draping it over her shoulders instead.

Loch Cameron village stretched along the opposite side of the loch to the castle, which stood on a hill, across a small, arched iron bridge which was painted blue. The village itself consisted of a small high street with perhaps ten or twelve shops, the inn, a hairdresser's that looked closed, and a friendly looking building with a noticeboard outside it, covered in notices on coloured paper. Zelda learnt from reading the notice-board that this was the community centre, which seemed to hold a lot of bridge competitions, a mother and baby group on Tuesdays and the occasional 'bring and buy sale', which Zelda guessed was like a yard sale type of thing.

Behind the high street, a number of white cottages stood in an elevated position overlooking the high street and the loch; the main road through the village ran along the edge of the loch with the high street next to it. Another narrow track ran behind the high street, to the houses. Behind the cottages, which looked like they had been there for a couple of hundred years at least, there was a newer development of red-brick houses that Zelda guessed housed the rest of the villagers.

She wandered into a bookshop, at the far end of the street from the inn. Zelda had always loved books. At *The Village Receiver*, some of her favourite jobs were going to book launches and interviewing authors. Romance novels were her favourite.

The bookshop itself was called 'Pageturner's', which was written in a slightly flaking gold italic script on the sign above the lead-lined windows. There was a wooden trolley of books on sale outside, covered in a plastic cover, and a black wooden sign with gold lettering that said:

NEW & SECONDHAND BOOKS
    WE BUY BOOKS

Inside, the shop was light and pleasant. Zelda sniffed the air; it smelt as though there might have been a log burner in there, as she could detect the comforting aroma of coffee mixed with woodsmoke. Tables were positioned at intervals on the small shop floor, covered in neat piles of colourful paperbacks, and a glass cabinet stood to one side, showcasing rare hardbacks. The shop was lined with dark wood bookshelves which were pleasingly irregular. A separate table carried glossy coffee-table books that Zelda would normally have looked at, but she feared her wrist wouldn't be able to take the weight of one of them today.

'Mornin'.' A man sitting behind the counter looked up and smiled. He had longish blond hair and a pleasant, open face; a light shadow of stubble covered his chin. He wore a grey sweater over a white shirt, with the sleeves turned up a little.

'Oh, hi. Morning.' Zelda was still trying to get used to the locals talking to her. No one talked to anyone in New York, unless it was to yell at you for being in the way in the street or catcall you as you walked past.

'Lovely day,' the man commented.

'Yup.' Zelda nodded. She walked to one of the tables and picked up a recent release, scanning the blurb on the back, before replacing it and picking up another with her good hand. Realising that the shop had a quaint cast-iron spiral staircase in the corner, she pulled out her phone and took some pictures, intending to share them on social media later. Going to stand under the staircase, she peered up to where it stretched, and caught sight of another room above, also lined with books.

'You can go up, if you want.' Having picked up a pile of books, the man walked around the counter and started shelving them. 'Just be careful. It's safe, but easy to slip on the steps.'

'Oh, wow! Thanks.' Zelda put her foot on the bottom tread of the staircase, then realised her heel had got stuck in it. 'Oh, damn,' she muttered, trying to work it free.

It stayed resolutely stuck.

'Hey. Are you okay?' The shopkeeper approached, and laughed when he saw what had happened. 'Wait. Don't move. I've got you.'

'I'm so sorry. I didn't mean to do that... Agh, I'm so embarrassed.' Zelda blushed. Again, her shoes had got her into trouble.

The man knelt down next to her, put both hands gently on her calf, and pulled. Zelda's heel popped out of the tiny hole in the cast-iron grating, thankfully without breaking.

'Not a problem. You'd be surprised how often that happens.' He grinned, and released her leg. 'So. You're not from around here, I'm guessing.' He smiled again, looking up at her from the ground, where he was still kneeling. *It looks like he's about to propose*, Zelda thought, the idea coming out of nowhere. *All the LOLs.*

'No. Just having a few days' R&R.' She smiled back.

He got up, dusting down his jeans. 'Ah, you're American. I can hear it in your voice now.'

'That's right.' Zelda really looked at him this time, and realised that he was actually very attractive. He had a sense of ease and grace about him, though he wasn't dressed up, and looked as though he kept in good shape. 'New Yorker. I actually just came here for work, and then I broke my wrist, so I'm taking a few days before I fly back.' She walked over to the table again and picked up a different book.

'Ah, bad luck.' He came to stand next to her at the table. 'Now. I can recommend that one. And this one's on the Booker Prize shortlist, if you like that kind of thing,' he added, pointing to the books on the table.

'Recommendations are always welcome.' She took the book with her left hand and scanned the back. 'This sounds great. I might browse for a couple more. Could you put it on the counter for me? I'm kinda not great at holding things right now.'

Zelda was thankful that she'd done her black flick eyeliner and red lipstick today. Even if she was wearing a cast on her wrist, at least everything else was as good as it could be.

'Ah, sure. No problem.' He took the book from her. Their fingers touched for a moment, and the man smiled, slightly bashfully, but it was a charming smile too. 'I'm Ryan, by the way.'

'Zelda.' She held his gaze for a moment; there was definitely some chemistry, or a snap of electricity in the air. She cleared her throat and changed the subject. 'Your accent's not from here either, right? Or am I getting that wrong? I can't always hear the difference, but you're not Scottish?'

'No. Irish.' He gave her that disarming smile again and took her book to the counter. 'Been here ten years, though. This bookshop was my uncle's, and he left it to me in his will. When I took over it was all musty second-hand editions of Keats and Blake. I thought it would be better to sell slightly newer books.'

'By people who are still alive.' Zelda nodded. 'Good thinking.'

'I know. Edgy, right?' Ryan laughed. 'So, what do you do? What made you break your wrist? What are you, like, a lady wrestler or something? A kickboxer? Oh, no. I've got it. You're a Navy Seal. Out here on top-secret manoeuvres.'

'Yup. Unfortunately, now you guessed, I'll have to kill you in the interests of national security,' she found herself flirting back a little. *What was that?* she thought. Zelda hadn't knowingly flirted with anyone since her mom died. She certainly hadn't been in the right space for it, mentally or emotionally.

It wasn't that there hadn't been opportunities; she was always at book parties and gallery openings and theatre shows. It was a given that there were usually more gay men than straight ones in her line of work, sure, but she still got asked out now and again. It was more that she hadn't had the energy to go on a date, or the time, since she'd thrown herself into her work. Plus, the thought of getting to know someone new filled her with fear. She didn't want to get close to someone, just so she could lose them too.

At that moment, the bell on the door tinkled and Hal Cameron strode into the bookshop. 'O'Connell! Here to pick up my order,' he said, rather brusquely, and approached the counter, not noticing Zelda.

'Oh. Hello, Hal. Yes, I've got it here.' Ryan rummaged under the counter and brought out a bag. 'That's thirty-four fifty.'

Hal reached into his pocket to pay, and half-turned as he did so, realising someone else was in the shop.

Zelda nodded to him. 'Hi again.' She didn't know whether she was supposed to call him Laird Cameron or Laird Hal or just Hal, as Ryan had done, so she avoided his name completely.

'Oh! Zelda. Hallo. You're still here? I thought you all flew back a couple of days ago.' For some reason, Hal seemed suddenly fidgety. Again, he was dressed like a pensioner in an old blue jumper and, today, what looked like tartan trousers.

Zelda thought that if he cut his hair or had a shave and put some nicer clothes on, Hal would be gorgeous: he was tall and powerfully built with broad shoulders and deep, dark blue eyes. He had that strong, muscular, healthy Scottish look, like you saw on calendars of sexy firemen.

Even with the old blue jumper and the overcommitment to tartan in the trouser area, Hal Cameron was surprisingly easy on the eye. She hadn't noticed that Hal was verifiably hot before, but that was probably because she'd been unconscious.

'I'm taking some time off. Haven't had a holiday for years, so here I am.' She made a *tah-dah* gesture with her hands and then wished she hadn't, in the face of Hal's serious gaze. 'I'm just browsing for books,' she said, clearing her throat.

'Aye, right. Ye ken, if you give it a wee chance, you'd find a lot to love here.' He smiled at her.

'Zelda's from New York, Hal. You've got to admit, Loch Cameron's not exactly what she's used to,' Ryan interrupted.

'Aye, well. Sometimes ye've got tae look past appearances.' Hal shot Ryan a surprisingly filthy look. *What's his beef?* Zelda wondered. Hal, it seemed, had woken up on the wrong side of his ancestral four-poster bed that morning.

Zelda picked up the book she was looking at and took it to the counter, brushing past Hal. She felt momentarily embarrassed by her designer outfit, after Hal's comment about appearances, but then she realised she was being silly to be so self-conscious. *The joke's on you, mister,* she thought, *because I bought these from a man selling knock-off designer sunglasses on a stall in Times Square.* Zelda did have a good eye for fashion, but anything designer she had was always sourced from one of the websites that offered eighty per cent discounts, or from thrift stores where, sometimes, you could find a buried treasure.

'Thank you, Ryan, for your hospitality today. I'll take these.

Oh, and that book you have in the window about King James, too.' She placed the books she was holding onto the counter, pleased that one of them was a literary prize winner and the other was a biography of Elsie Inglis, a Scottish suffragette who founded her own medical college and hospital for the poor. For the first time, Zelda felt like she wasn't a hundred per cent averse to knowing more about Scottish history and culture. Since she was here, she might as well learn something.

She opened her purse and took out her bank card.

'Well, then. Enjoy Loch Cameron, Zelda. Good-day.' Hal took his bag of books and walked out of the shop.

'Bye,' Zelda called after him, then turned back to the bookseller. 'Is he always like that?' she asked Ryan. 'He was a bit frosty.'

'Ah, sometimes. He can be bad-tempered. I generally stay out of his way; I'm not into that whole landowner, them-and-us thing, you know? But, I have to say, he is a good customer.'

'What d'you mean, them and us?'

'Ah, you know. Hal Cameron considers Loch Cameron his ancestral land. He really thinks he owns it. He might own it, on paper, but it's land. It doesn't belong to anyone. If anything, it belongs to the people who live on it, right?'

'Right. I guess I've never really understood that whole Lords and Ladies thing you have here.' Zelda put her purse back in her bag with some difficulty.

'Hey. Don't include me in that. I'm Southern Irish. No royalty for us.'

'Right. Socialist all the way, huh?' Zelda picked up the books in the brown paper carrier bag with its string handle. 'Ah. Y'know, I haven't thought this through. Can I, like, leave these here for a while? I need to go back to the inn, leave my handbag there and then I can come back for them.' Zelda briefly wished that she had a smaller handbag than her oversized bucket bag, but there wasn't much she could do about it now, apart from buy a bag from one of the local shops, but it didn't look like there was much choice. It was just a few more days, and then she'd be home. She could cope until then.

'I wouldn't hear of it. I'll carry them back for you.' Ryan picked up the bag.

'Oh, no. I couldn't ask you to do that.' Zelda was taken aback. 'You can't just leave the shop!'

'Ah, yes. The sprawling metropolis that is Loch Cameron can probably cope if I close the shop for ten minutes.' Ryan walked to the shop door, carrying her bag and miming swimming movements with his arms. 'If I can just... push... my... way... through... all these customers.'

'Okay, okay. Zelda laughed. 'You made your point.'

'Also, you know, it's almost lunchtime,' Ryan added, after he locked the shop door and they had started walking back towards the inn. 'Do you have any lunch plans?'

'Wow. Isn't it, like, eleven a.m.?' Zelda looked at her watch. 'I feel like I just had breakfast.'

'Eleven thirty. Legitimately okay for a drink as well.' Ryan looked at his watch. 'You're on holiday! I'd have had a drink by ten if it was me.'

'But you're Irish, though, right?' Zelda teased him, feeling like they'd known each other a long time already.

'That is an appalling stereotype!' Ryan pretended to be offended. 'Just for that, I'm only going to buy you two drinks and a packet of crisps.'

'That seems totally fair.' Zelda grinned.

'To be honest, I'm delighted to have some human company. Days can go by in the shop and it's just me and the mice,' Ryan added.

'Well, I am very happy to take you away from your rodent infestation.'

'Thank you. I've always dreamt that a woman would say that to me.'

'Do you ever stop talking?' Zelda giggled, enjoying the winter sun on her skin, the glint of the light on the loch and Ryan's company. On the loch, a fishing boat chugged past slowly, two bearded men standing on the deck, dressed in overalls and cable jumpers. Ryan waved to them, and they waved back. As they walked past the bakery, a delicious smell of freshly baked bread wafted past Zelda's nose and made her stomach rumble. Further along, they walked past a small primary school whose railings were festooned with laminated pictures of local birds.

'That's adorable,' she commented. 'How many kids even go to school here?' She thought of her own busy middle school in the Bronx.

'Oh, about twenty, I think.'

'Twenty? Two-zero?' Zelda did a double-take at the building. It was small, but still. Twenty kids at a school was unbelievable.

'Yup.' Ryan nodded. 'Small community.'

For the first time in years, Zelda felt like she was slowly relaxing. The tension she had brought with her was gradually ebbing away, thanks to Dotty's ministrations and the fact she was sleeping so well, too. With every moment, she felt the pressures of her job drift slightly further away. She knew it was temporary, but it was as if there were something in the clean air of Loch Cameron that was cleansing *her*, inside and out. There were no frantic work emails, just one or two check-ins from Emery, making sure she was okay. The rest, she was simply ignoring. The night before, she'd had a wonderful dream of her mom, revisiting a Christmas from years ago, when they'd gone for a walk on Christmas Day in the snow together, then home and made the obligatory turkey dinner. It was a simple dream – a memory, really – but she'd woken up happy.

Yet, at the same time, it was also true that the reason Zelda was so exhausted was that she had thrown herself into work after her mom had passed away. Mira had started at *The Village Receiver* just a few weeks before Zelda's mom had passed; when Zelda returned from the funeral, Mira had piled on the pressure with a raft of new responsibilities and projects for Zelda, and Zelda had taken it all on without question. Yes, she was exhausted. She would be in the office until midnight, some nights. But it was a way not to have to think about anything else.

Working was a way to ignore the fact that her heart was in pieces.

So it was almost surreal to Zelda that there she was, strolling along the side of a Scottish loch, chatting to an attractive young man without a care in the world.

The fact that her plan for the whole day was having lunch, possibly getting tipsy with an attractive Irish guy she'd just met in a bookshop and falling asleep in her insanely comfortable king-size bed overlooking a misty loch was weird, but nice.

Never say never, that's what people said. Whatever she thought about how she had ended up in Loch Cameron, Zelda rationalised that she was there now, so she might as well enjoy it.

Ryan held out a hand to help her up the steps to the inn, and she took it.

After a lunch of golden fried haddock and thick chips, lashed with vinegar – which Zelda had never tasted before but loved – they'd stayed in the cosy snug, playing checkers. Ryan called it 'Draughts'.

'I can't imagine a more British name for a game.' Zelda laughed, tickled at the idea. '"Checkers" makes far more sense. Look. Black and white checks on the board.' She pointed them out with a grin.

'Americans are so literal,' Ryan chuckled. 'It's Draughts! As in, it's draughty in here.' He gave a mock shiver.

'Get out. It's warm as toast in here, with the fireplace,' she argued; they were in the small snug with the old-fashioned TV, and Eric had lit the fire for them.

'May I remind you of the frequency of wind and rain in Scotland and Ireland?' Ryan asked, mock haughtily. 'There's probably a hundred English words for bad weather. And that's not even starting with Gaelic. Like how the Inuit people have a hundred words for snow.'

They managed to drink a lot of whisky while they were playing Draughts, to the point that Zelda could only blearily remember saying goodnight to Ryan and stumbling up to bed at around eight p.m.

I never realised Scotland would be this fun, Zelda remembered thinking as she spent the long afternoon with Ryan. *This isn't how I thought it would be. And maybe that's okay.*

SEVEN

A few days later, Zelda was in her room, one-handedly packing her bag to go home when her phone lit up.

It had started raining – *Just a smirr!* Dotty had trilled as Zelda had run into the inn with her blazer over her head, caught in a sudden downpour – and, despite Dotty's advice that it would clear up soon, it was now pouring. Or, as Zelda had ascertained in her brief stay in the village, *drookit*.

'Mira. Hi.' She frowned, answering the call. 'I'm coming back as agreed. Just packing now, in fact.'

'Don't bother. Newspaper's been bought. New team coming in. I'm letting everyone know.' Mira's voice was utterly matter-of-fact.

'What do you mean, bought?' Zelda sat down on the bed, in shock. She knew what it meant, but she couldn't believe that Mira was saying the words.

What it meant was that another company – most likely a rival publisher – had bought *The Village Receiver*, and had immediately sacked the existing team. They would bring in a totally new team, effective immediately: that was how it was in the media sometimes. Everyone knew it, but you never thought it would happen to you.

'*The News and Mail* bought us. It was on the cards for a while. I hoped it wouldn't happen, but it did.' Mira Khan sighed. 'You must have known that the last few months weren't great for sales. I tried a different tack with the features and stuff, but I guess it didn't work. Effective immediately. Sorry, Zelda. I'll have Emery clear out your desk and bring your stuff over when you get back.'

'I'm... sacked?' Zelda realised she was facing the antique mirror across the room. She stared back at herself, pale and glassy-eyed.

'Afraid so. Print media is struggling to stay relevant these days, you know that. We'll pay you until the end of the month. Best I can do. Anyway. I'll see you around, I guess. Take care,' Mira added, and hung up.

'What the...? Mira? Mira?' Zelda cried, but her phone had returned to the home screen. She looked at it in dismay. *What the hell had just happened?*

She sat on the bed and stared at the rain, which was now coming down in torrents. A low rumble followed a flash of lightning, and Zelda went to the window. A zig-zagging bolt of lightning lit up the grey clouds for a moment, appearing to lance the water of the loch, and the rumble repeated, much louder this time.

The light in her room flickered for a moment, then came back on. Like the call from Mira, the storm had come from nowhere. However, unlike being suddenly and unceremoniously sacked from the job she had done for more than six years, Zelda knew that the storm would pass.

She was officially unemployed.

The lightning flashed again, and Zelda jumped.

This time, all the lights went off and didn't come back on.

She flicked the light switch up and down: nothing

happened. Even though it was late afternoon, the weather had made it quite dark in the room.

'Halloo?' A moment later, after some banging and swearing from what sounded like Eric downstairs, Dotty knocked on the door and opened it. 'Blackout watch! Don't worry, dear. We get this all the time in storms. It'll come back on soon. Here's a torch and some candles.' She handed Zelda a penlight torch and a box of tea lights. 'Oh, and matches, of course. Ach, this weather keeps us on our toes!' she chuckled. 'If ye want a bit o' company, come down to the bar. The gas stove's working, and I've got oil lamps down there. We'll have a drink to pass the time, aye?'

'Might as well.' Zelda reached for a jacket and put it around her shoulders, picking up her phone with her good hand. She still couldn't quite believe she'd just lost her job. Just like that: no fanfare, no warning.

'Ye all right, lassie? Ye don't like storms?' Dotty led her downstairs. 'Watch ye step,' she warned.

'Storms are okay. I just got some bad news.' Zelda followed Dotty down to the bar, which was cosy with lamps that let out a golden glow. The fire in the snug was lit; Zelda could tell because of the pleasant smell of woodsmoke that filled the lounge area. The sound of a whistling kettle came from the kitchen area: she could see a faint blue glow in the background.

'At least the gas's still on,' Dotty tutted, going to the kitchen, presumably to lift the old-style kettle off the stove. 'Tea?'

'I wouldn't mind something stronger.' Zelda sighed.

'Drink?' Dotty's husband Eric was dragging a sack of wood towards the fireplace, presumably to make sure it kept going, but he stood up and wiped his hands on his cord slacks when Zelda and Dotty came in. 'Then we'll have a blether.'

Zelda had already picked up from her stay at the inn that *blether* meant *conversation*.

'Not sure I'll be much fun, but sure.' She slumped into one of the easy chairs.

Eric laughed. 'I'm sure ye will, lassie. Old Fashioned suit ye?'

'Perfect. Thanks, Eric.' Zelda picked up her phone and scrolled to Emery's last call, tapping out a text with her left hand.

You got the news?

She could see from the dots on the screen that Emery was typing out a reply.

Yep. It was a blast working with you, Zelda Hicks, he replied. *You got anything else yet?*

What, in the 15 minutes since I got the call? No, she answered, then added, *Sorry. Still in shock.*

It wasn't Emery's fault she'd lost her job.

You're a catch. Someone will offer, Emery replied. *You know how it is.*

Zelda texted back a *Yup.* She didn't have the energy to say much more.

Eric handed Zelda an almost full crystal tumbler. She sipped the amber liquid and felt it trace a line of heat into her belly.

Zelda had never been sacked before. She felt a horrible, stomach-churning feeling, as if she had done something terribly wrong somehow. Was it her fault? If she had been better at her job, could the newspaper have somehow stayed afloat? Could she have done anything different?

No. She knew, rationally, that the newspaper closing wasn't her fault. But, now, she felt hollow. Her job was the one thing she'd been holding on to since her mom had passed away. If she couldn't work, what was she going to do?

Outside, the thunder crashed. The storm was showing no sign of leaving.

EIGHT

Zelda was into her second Eric-sized Old Fashioned when the inn door banged open and Hal Cameron strode into the bar, a hail of rain flying in after him. The coats on the rack by the heavy oak door – mostly waterproofs and oilskins belonging to the inn, which Dotty lent to guests – fluttered wildly in the wind, and Dotty ran to the door to close it behind him as quickly as she could.

'Mind yer feet, Hal!' she tutted. 'Take yer boots off, as well. I willnae have ye trackin' mud all over ma nice hallway carpet.'

The carpet was, like most things in the inn, floral, and featured a pattern of large pink roses on a beige background. In the hallway that led into the lounge, Dotty had a series of large, oriental-style vases filled with dried flowers, which she also shooed Hal away from as he blundered in.

'Sorry, Dotty. Bloody weather!' the Laird exclaimed. 'Power's out here too, I see... Hallo, Eric. Oh. Hallo, Zelda.' He nodded politely to her and took off his hat and boots.

'Evenin', Hal. Driech, eh?' Eric welcomed the Laird in. 'Sit down, if ye've a minute.'

'Well, I'm doin' ma rounds, but ah dinnae want tae go

straight back oot, it has to be said.' Hal sighed and removed a waterproof rain cape, hanging it on a hook by the door. 'Power should be back once the engineers can get tae the site, but they're stuck in a mudslide ten miles away. Make sure ye've got ye blankets at the ready, is my advice,' he added.

'Right ye are, Hal.' Dotty buttoned up her cardigan. 'Fancy a dram while ye're here?'

'Aye, go on then.' Hal nodded. 'I'll get it myself, dinnae bother.' He walked behind the bar in his socks, reached for a clean glass from the shelf and took down a bottle of whisky. 'I'd ask if ye wanted one, but I see ye're well into it.' He nodded at Zelda's glass.

'I'm fine, thank you,' she replied, hoping she didn't sound tipsy. 'So. How're things at the castle?' she added, to avoid an awkward silence.

'Not bad. How's your wrist?' he asked, coming to sit in the easy chair opposite her. Today he wore a frayed green jumper over a cream-coloured shirt and black tartan trews. However, he had shaved and had a haircut, and Zelda noticed his cheekbones and strong chin. As he sat down, he pushed up his sleeves and revealed tanned, muscled forearms.

For a brief moment, Zelda wondered if the rest of him was as promising as his forearms, and then stopped herself. Clearly, the drink was having an effect. 'Getting better. Slowly.'

'Early in the day for a session.' He raised his eyebrow at the empty glass next to the one she was currently drinking. 'Or is this how all New Yorkers deal with a bit o' rain?'

'If you must know, I just had some bad news,' Zelda replied, resignedly. 'The newspaper I work on just got bought out. I've been fired.'

'Oh. I'm sorry tae hear that.' He leant forward in his chair, a concerned expression on his face. 'Can I do anythin' tae help?'

'Not unless you own an arts-focused newspaper that needs a features writer.'

'I don't, I'm afraid,' he said, sitting back in the chair.

'Yeah. Well. If I hadn't tripped on those lethal flagstones, then I'd have been back in New York to hear the news. And I don't know if that would be better or worse, really.' Zelda drank the last of her Old Fashioned. 'At least, because I broke my wrist, I was kinda forced to stay here and have some time off work. Away from New York. Maybe that's a good thing.'

'Aye. Maybe,' the Laird replied. 'I should probably put some signs up aboot the flagstones as well. Y'know, in case any other lassie comes along in four-inch heels, expectin' tae run all over a historic castle and not fall on her arse.'

'Wow. You're not suggesting that was my fault?'

'Not your fault, no. But it couldae been avoided, maybe.' He shrugged, smiling.

Zelda chuckled. 'I know, I know. I should have been more practical.'

'Mebbe wear some wellies next time, is all I'm sayin',' he suggested. 'Still, I guess they wouldnae look as nice.'

Zelda felt herself blushing. Had the Laird just paid her a compliment?

There was a pause in their conversation as Dotty brought in a bowl of crisps; Zelda was grateful for the distraction so that she could compose herself and stop blushing, which was just plain embarrassing.

It was just a throwaway comment, her mind argued.

From a hot Laird, though, another part of her mind argued back.

He's not that hot.

I don't know... the part of her mind that had noticed Hal's forearms replied, suggestively.

'Here y'are, my dears.' She set the bowl in front of them. 'Soak up some of that alcohol,' Dotty suggested, nodding at Zelda.

'Thanks, Dotty.' Hal reached into the bowl and took a handful. 'So, tell me what you thought of the castle?'

'I will.' Zelda frowned, willing herself to focus. 'But don't let me stop you if you're meant to be... doing your rounds, or something.' She gestured with her good hand. 'I don't know what responsibilities a Laird has in terrible weather. Do you need to check in with everyone?'

'That's kind of ye, but I'm okay for now.' Hal took some more crisps. 'When somethin' like this happens, I just like tae check everyone's okay. Particularly the older ones.' He lowered his voice, clearly not wanting to offend Dotty or Eric.

'Oh. Right. Well, your castle, apart from needing a full risk assessment and way better signage, is stunning.' Zelda took some crisps with her good hand.

'Oh. I'm glad you liked it.' He looked surprised.

'Of course I liked it. It's gorgeous, but you'd hardly know it from the website. Those pictures are so dark. And there's hardly any pictures of the interior. And the ones that are there don't show off any of the good features, like that big staircase in the entry hall, or the marble fireplaces. You could really put Loch Cameron on the map, but since I've been here I've seen hardly any tourists,' she finished.

'We're not set up for tourists.' Hal leant back in his chair. 'Loch Cameron's a nice little village. Why would we want tae change that? We dinnae want tae be overrun by strangers.'

'No. Heaven forbid you should earn enough money to... I don't know. Get an emergency generator.' Zelda gestured at the oil lamps that were giving the bar such a rosy glow.

'Well, it's not really as straightforward as that...' Hal frowned.

'Yes, I realise that. I was just making a point,' she interrupted. 'The point is, your website looks like it was designed with Word Art. Or by an overenthusiastic teenager in the nineties.'

'Hmm. I think the website's just fine,' Hal insisted, defensively.

'Please.' Zelda couldn't make out Hal's expression; he was deliberately stony-faced. 'You could do so much more with the castle. Does anyone ever have their wedding photos done there? Or the wedding itself? Parties? Fashion shoots? The possibilities are endless.'

'It's my home, Zelda,' Hal replied, slowly. 'Not a convenient backdrop for everyone else's lives.'

'But you need the money,' Zelda argued. 'And when I put some pictures of the castle on social media, everyone went crazy. People loved them.'

Zelda was not exaggerating about that: after a few posts of the castle, people had started asking her if she lived there and if they could come and stay with her.

'Hae d'ye know if I need any money or not?' Hal shot back. 'So I'm poor, am I?'

'Your housekeeper told me. I didn't say you were *poor*, just that the castle takes a lot of upkeep, and your other responsibilities to the village, I guess.' This time, she waved her arm expansively. 'Your castle has mice, and your website is appalling. Fix both, re-wallpaper some of the rooms, restore that lovely antique furniture and it could be beautiful. And then you could charge people serious money to see it.'

Hal stood up. 'Well, I won't tek up any more o' your valuable time, Miss Hicks,' he said, curtly. He strode across the snug, ripped his coat from the hook and picked up his hat, pulling on his boots too. 'Dotty. Eric.' He nodded briefly. 'Thanks for the dram.' Then he stormed out.

'Well, my goodness,' Dotty breathed, looking up from some knitting. 'He's pure grabbit the day.'

'Yeah. Wait, what?' Zelda did a double-take.

'Oh, lassie. Sorry. Ah meant, he's grumpy today. What did

ye say to him?' Dotty picked up the empty glasses from the table.

'Um. I may have been a little more honest about the castle than was necessary.' Zelda made an awkward face.

'Hmm. Maybe so.' Dotty gave her a wise look. 'Not tae worry, lassie. And I'm sorry about yer bad news.' She patted Zelda on the shoulder. 'Would ye like a sandwich? Or we've cheese and crackers. All cold until the power gets back on. Unless ye want more soup, but I think ye've probably had enough since ye've been here?' She smiled kindly at Zelda, who felt a little spinny. It was probably a good idea to eat, but she couldn't face any more of Dotty's questions.

'You know what, Dotty? I think I'm just gonna be on my own for a while,' she said, getting up a little unsteadily.

'Are ye sure, dear? Ah don't like tae think of ye, up there on yer own in the dark.'

'I'll be okay. I'll come down if I need anything,' Zelda promised.

'All right, darlin',' Dotty frowned.

Zelda made her way up the stairs to her room and flung herself on the bed. She was dimly aware of wrapping herself in the feather quilt before closing her eyes, and of a cheer downstairs a little later when the lights came back on.

Tomorrow, she would decide what she was doing next, but for now, she was going to allow herself to pull the quilt over her head, try to ignore the hollow pit of worry in her stomach that came with not having a job and being alone in a foreign country – and pretend her life wasn't falling apart.

NINE

Zelda woke up to golden light streaming through the curtains. She sat up, pushing off the quilt and yawning: it was still early. Her jetlag had more or less submitted to Scottish time, but it still meant she wanted to go to bed ridiculously early and wake up at dawn. *Like an old person*, she berated herself.

Maybe it was just the clean air and the food. Or the fact that she hadn't had a break from work in years.

Still, the sunrise that greeted her as she opened the curtains was a pretty good trade-off. Gold stretched across the morning sky, reflected like treasure in the still waters of the loch. At that hour, she couldn't see many people around on the road alongside the loch, but a single small van was trundling its way over the little arched bridge. A couple of men busied themselves alongside the fishing boats to the right of the inn, and Zelda could hear them call to each other, distantly, from her window.

Blearily, Zelda looked at her phone: it was plugged into the charger, and, mercifully, her bar was back up to a hundred per cent. She dimly remembered the power coming back on the night before, just as she was going to sleep. She tapped on a text message from an unknown number.

Since you have so many good ideas for the castle, I wonder if you have time today to come and talk to me about some of them? Hal.

Hal? Hal Cameron was texting her now?

Zelda squinted at the message again, putting on the reading glasses she'd left on the bedside table. She guessed he had her number from when they were doing the shoot at the castle, though until now she'd never texted with the Laird. Emery had done that.

Why did Hal Cameron want to hear her 'ideas for the castle'? And why did he think she even had any?

Oh. That was why. She remembered that she had been a little opinionated about what Hal could do to the castle if he wanted to earn more money from it. Had she been rude? She didn't think she had – not rude, perhaps, but maybe a little brash. Two-drinks-on-an-empty-stomach, in-shock-from-losing-your-job brash.

It was none of her business what Hal did or didn't do with his castle.

First, she had to make a plan about going back to New York. She would have to look for a new job. In fact, she could start doing that now.

But the thought of returning to New York filled her with trepidation.

She'd missed her flight again; fortunately, she'd changed it online last night before she went to sleep, paying a little extra to change it to an open return.

Don't make any crazy decisions right now, she berated herself. *For today, just get dressed, and go to see Hal Cameron at the castle. One thing at a time.*

· · ·

After the second time her heel stuck in between the cobbles, Zelda had to admit she really was woefully underprepared for the Highlands. She took a selfie with a frowny expression and added the caption *Ouchy turny ankle much? Cobbled streets = not built for a stiletto heel* before posting it to Instagram.

She was on her way to the castle, aiming to cross at the bridge and walk up through the private gardens on the other side. She hoped she could – Hal had texted her some directions and assured her that he would leave certain gates unlocked for her.

What else did she have to do today? Zelda would need to get in touch with her contacts and see if there were any opportunities at other magazines or newspapers, but she'd have to do that later because of the time difference.

She'd fired off a few emails over breakfast, managing to tap out the words with her good hand, and messaged Emery and some of her other journalist friends to see if anything was happening. So far, there had been no replies, but probably nobody was up yet. She had to keep reminding herself to stay positive. Something would come in soon. She had to believe that.

Being a journalist in New York meant she'd had to develop a thick skin. She'd had to be tenacious in going after some features, and deal with people who could be divas or just plain difficult. In short, Zelda had learnt over the years that if you didn't ask, you didn't get.

Zelda passed some parents walking along the high street, holding their kids' hands. The children wore a uniform, so she assumed they were heading to the tiny village school. She smiled at the little ones, carrying their book bags, buttoned up in their big coats. Along the street a little, the butcher's shop was just opening up, and the butcher was arranging pork chops in a wide glass counter alongside rows of huge sausages, thick steaks and all manner of other meats.

All the time, her thoughts were ticking over. She had enough savings to cover her rent for two months, and she had the credit card she was currently using to fund her impromptu Scottish holiday. But that was all. If she didn't get a new job in a couple of months, she'd have to move out of her apartment, and she didn't know what she'd do if both those things happened.

Zelda wasn't as fortunate as many of the people who worked at the newspaper: she didn't have parents she could move back home and live with; she didn't have a husband or a partner who could support her if she needed it. There was no safety net. All her professional life she'd felt like she was walking a tightrope. At least when her mom was alive, there had been somewhere she could go if she needed a hot meal and someone to listen to her.

Walking a proverbial tightrope was one thing, but Zelda realised that if she walked ten yards more on that cobbled street in her high-heeled boots, she was definitely going to fall over again. And she really didn't need another broken bone.

So, when she walked past a shop titled 'FIONA'S FASH-IONS' with thick Aran jumpers in the window, she sighed with resignation and walked in.

'Help ye?' a woman – Zelda estimated she was about thirty – looked over from where she was straightening a rail of waxed jackets.

'Oh, hi. Yeah. I was looking for some flat shoes or boots,' Zelda said. 'Your streets are killing my heels.'

The woman looked appreciatively at Zelda's black leather heeled boots.

'They're bonny, though. Armani?'

'Yeah, actually.' Zelda was surprised. She would never have expected anyone there to recognise designer wear. 'Seventy-five per cent off, last season. Still more than I could afford, but I loved them so much.' She sighed. If she didn't get a new job soon, then designer boots would be out of the question for a while, big discounts or not.

'Oooh. I'm so jealous. I'm studyin' fashion merchandisin'. Part-time, remotely. It's mostly online,' the young woman explained. 'An' I read all the magazines. I'm gearin' up to own a fashion empire.'

'A noble goal. You don't have any stylish flat boots, I guess?' Zelda asked, hopefully.

'Nope. Just wellies or hikin' boots. A few brogues, court shoes. No' much call for anythin' too fancy,' the woman answered cheerily. 'I'm Fiona, by the way.'

'Of Fiona's Fashions?' Zelda remembered the shop sign.

'Aye. It's ma shop. Boots're over here.'

'Wow. That's great.' Zelda followed Fiona over to the boot display. 'You're a real young entrepreneur, then? That's awesome.' She knew all too well what it was like to work hard to follow your dream.

'Aye, thanks. The way it works in the village, the Laird owns most o' the property, so he's my landlord. However, he supports small businesses. Withoot him, I wouldnae have been able to open.'

'That's very unusual. So, like, he gives grants or something?' Zelda picked up some hiking boots and examined them.

'Aye. An' he gives all the small businesses a huge discount on rent for the first two years. Still, even with that, I dinnae make a lot.' Fiona sighed.

'I can imagine,' Zelda sympathised.

'People say these are comfy.' Fiona offered her a heavy black walking boot with a thick rubber sole. Zelda took it in her good hand. 'Not very pretty, though,' Fiona admitted. 'What aboot these?' She picked up a calf-high boot with laces and a zip up the side. 'These come in purple as well.'

'Mmm. Anything else?' Zelda asked.

'Ah, not really. Unless you want wellies.'

'Patent black, maybe?' Zelda asked, hopefully.

'No, sorry. I've seen those online. They're nice!' Fiona looked rueful. 'But I don't stock them. I dinnae think anyone'd buy them.'

Zelda sighed. 'Okay. I'll take the second one you showed me. In black. I take a nine.'

'Right ye are.' Fiona beamed. 'Is that an American size nine? That would be... ah. I'll look at the size chart.'

'It's a UK seven. Sorry, I should have said that.'

'Oh, that's fine.' Fiona went into a back room and returned, carrying a shoebox. 'We don't get many Americans here, that's all.'

'You might be surprised. About what people will buy, I mean.' Zelda looked around at the shop. It was nicely designed, but the stock seemed completely aimed at people like the Laird, who seemed to dress only for practicality. 'Aren't there any young people in the village?'

'Aye. But they don't shop here.'

'They could, though. You know, even older customers might be interested in some different choices.' Zelda cast her eye over a nearby rail of tweed jackets. 'There must be some wealthy older women you could be targeting, if you don't want to reach out to the youth.'

'Mebbe you're right.' Fiona looked at Zelda curiously. 'You're the one who works for the newspaper, right? Dotty told me all about you.'

'She did, huh?' Zelda nodded, unsurprised. Small towns, lochside villages: they were all the same. In the Bronx, where she had grown up, everyone knew her mom because of the dry-cleaning shop, and so everyone had known Zelda too. That wasn't a small town, but it was the same principle: there was a community, and everyone knew your business. When she was younger, she'd hated it. But now, Zelda missed being a part of something.

Loch Cameron seemed to have a fairly thriving, if small, community. Zelda reflected on the way Hal had appeared at the inn in the power cut to check on Dotty and Eric, and the way he'd helped Fiona's shop be successful. She thought of the signs on the village noticeboard advertising baby clothes that were free to a good home, and the way that everyone stopped to say *hallo* to you in the street. It was a good feeling.

Being part of a team at the newspaper was a community, but that was more like a dysfunctional family with Mira Khan playing the role of Impossibly High Standards Mom. Zelda loved the art galleries and book parties but, even there, sometimes she felt like an impostor.

The dry-cleaner's was still there. Someone else had taken over the rent now. Zelda had been back a few times since her mom's death a few months ago. The current owners hadn't known who she was; she was just another customer, dropping in the occasional dress or jacket and picking it up a couple of days later.

It wasn't anything she ever talked about. But it was a way to come back home. Often, as she waited in line, the smell of the dry-cleaning chemicals and the sound of the trains rumbling in and out of Pelham Parkway station made her want to cry.

She missed her mom. She missed having somewhere to fall if the tightrope didn't hold.

'Aye. *The Village Receiver*. I looked ye up.' Fiona went to the counter and put the box down. 'I can't believe we've got a real-life New Yorker in Loch Cameron!'

'Well, not for too much longer. Oh, I'll wear them now, if that's okay.' Zelda pointed to the boots. 'I'll take the box, though, for these.' She sat down and started to unzip her Armani boots with her good hand. Laboriously, she shook one off and then the other, following them with the new, clunky walking boots.

'I hope we can chat before ye go, then?' Fiona said, hopefully. 'I'd love tae pick yer brains, all aboot the newspaper.'

'Sure.' Zelda recognised her own self, all those years ago, when she'd tried to break into features writing. It had taken years of working in dead-end jobs and building up her own blog before she'd finally got an apprenticeship at a small indie magazine, and worked her way up from intern to Assistant Features writer. From there, she'd found the entry-level job at *The Village Receiver* and worked her way up again from that. 'Give me your phone. I'll put my number in, okay? I've got to get to the castle, but message me later.'

'Oh, okay! Thank you!' Fiona handed Zelda her phone, and Zelda tapped in her number before paying for her boots. 'I'll be in touch, then.' Fiona looked a little starstruck.

Zelda gave her a wave as she left. It had been nice, chatting to Fiona; it also felt surprisingly good to walk in shoes that weren't trying to cut off her blood supply.

It was like Loch Cameron was deliberately trying to mess with everything she held to be good and true.

Maybe it was. But maybe that wasn't the worst thing in the world, either.

TEN

Zelda had turned up at the castle door half an hour earlier, secretly in love with her new boots, and taken some photos of the castle exterior, posting them on Instagram under #zeldasscottishlife. If nothing else, it would be a nice hashtag to look back on when she got back to New York.

The walk up to the castle had been unlike any other walk she'd ever had. First, she'd followed the cobbled high street to the little bridge, crossed that and then made her way through a field to the castle's grounds. Hal had described a series of certain gates that would be open for her, which she'd had to take quite a lot of care to find, almost getting caught up in a holly bush at one point. But, having passed through them, she'd followed a winding pathway through sun-dappled woods where she'd watched squirrels and even rabbits frisking around, like some kind of crazily idyllic pastoral scene.

Do people actually live like this? She felt like she was doing a double-take every five minutes as she walked along, taking in the olde-worlde charm of the woodlands. And then, when she got to the edge of the trees and the castle's gardens opened up in front of her, she actually gasped. She was immediately embarrassed at having done so, but fortunately there was no one else around.

She assumed the squirrels would keep her secret.

Climbing up the stone steps to the castle, Zelda had marvelled at the view that kept unrolling in front of her every time she stopped and turned around to look back out over the loch and the village.

It was a clear, sunny morning, though it had rained earlier, and the light over the loch was stunning. She felt like she could see for miles, out to distant mountains.

Reaching the huge oak front door at the top of the stone steps, Zelda had rung the old-fashioned doorbell, which could be heard reverberating through the house.

Hal had greeted her in a business-like manner and asked her in for tea, which they had in one of the downstairs lounges.

Zelda had begun by apologising for criticising him about the castle the night before, but Hal had waved her apology away.

'No' necessary.' He offered her a ginger biscuit from a plate. 'Have ye decided what tae do about a job now?'

'No. I mean, I've contacted a few people I know, to see what's out there. Newspapers and magazines are all pretty inbred. Everyone knows everyone. It's good on one hand, bad on the other.'

'What's the bad part?' he asked, smoothing down his jeans that, Zelda noted, seemed to be vaguely contemporary. However, if the Laird was making an effort to drag his style into the twenty-first century with a pair of jeans, the fact that he'd teamed them with a paisley-patterned shirt with a frayed collar underneath a nondescript navy blue cable-knit jumper meant he still had a way to go.

Admittedly, the blue jumper did bring out his eyes. Plus, now that he had shaved off his beard and actually had a haircut, she also saw that he had cheekbones to die for. Zelda cleared her throat.

Focus, she willed herself. She was suddenly vividly aware of Hal's powerful frame under those terrible clothes: his shoulders were broad and muscular, and she realised again as she sat with him just how big a man he was. She stole a look at his hands, which were so large that one of them would envelop hers totally.

Zelda had to admit that men's hands were big turn-ons for her. Hal's showed evidence of hard work, and he obviously wasn't one for hand cream as the skin on his palms was a little callused. However, there was no dirt under his fingernails, and no ragged nails.

She imagined what it would feel like to walk along with him, hand in hand.

A frisson of excitement shot through her, but it was also something else. There was something that made her feel safe in Hal Cameron's presence, and that in itself was attractive. His physical presence gave Zelda a sense of calm that she hadn't felt for a long time. She didn't understand it, but she liked it. Very much.

The journalist in Zelda imagined how Emery would arrange him on a shoot: against a moody backdrop, for sure, and ideally in a kilt with some kind of contemporary sportswear on the top. He was too big to model a suit effectively; those guys had to be tall, well-built, but a little slim, too. Zelda doubted there was any fat on Hal at all, but he was a big guy – more muscular and solid than a model usually was. Zelda got the impression he could pick her up and carry her the length of the castle gardens without breaking a sweat.

Okay. That was not focusing, she scolded herself. *Come on now.* She was surprised at herself; she hadn't quite anticipated the effect Hal was having on her.

'Sorry?' she asked, distractedly.

'I was askin' ye what the bad part was aboot workin' at a newspaper,' he repeated.

'Oh, right. Well, it's kinda gossipy. Everyone knows your business.' She shrugged. 'I don't mind that too much, I guess. It's kinda like family. Bitchy family, but family nonetheless.'

'D'ye have a family? I didnae see a wedding ring,' he asked, and then colour rose up in cheeks. 'Sorry. I dinnae know why I asked that. None o' my business.'

'That's all right. No, not married, no kids.' She thought again about the dry-cleaning store, back in the Bronx. 'I lost my mom recently. She was kind of all I had, so...' Zelda looked at his hands, taking a minute to make sure her voice didn't waver, though she felt the tears threatening. 'You don't wear a ring either.'

'I was married. She died,' he said, shortly.

'Oh, no. I'm sorry.' Zelda remembered now: Anna had told her and Emery when she guided them around the castle that time that the Laird was widowed. But she'd forgotten, because at that point she hadn't met Hal Cameron yet.

'She must have been young. That's so terrible,' she added, feeling sad on his behalf.

'Aye, it was.' He nodded. 'I'm sorry about your mother. It's hard when you're on your own.'

'Yeah.' She looked out of the window onto the ornamental gardens, searching for the right thing to say. 'Sometimes I feel as though it's crushing me, you know? The weight of the loss...' The lump reappeared in her throat, and she swallowed a few times. 'It's been six months. I know that's not long, but I keep waiting to wake up and feel normal again. Instead, I wake up every day, think of her and I feel like the bottom dropped out of the world.'

She thought again of the image she'd seen in her mind: of standing on a frozen lake, and it cracking, taking her mom under the water.

Hal took her hand; Zelda was surprised at the sudden contact, but touched at his gesture.

She was also surprised at how forthright she was being with this virtual stranger, but there was something in Hal that seemed to bring it out in her. Perhaps it was the fact that he had lost someone, too.

'I know. I feel the same way,' he murmured, gruffly. 'It's hard to go on, sometimes. Some days, there was nothin' I wanted tae do more than hide away. But I had to go on. It's so much work, managin' an estate this size. I have some help, but most of it I have to do myself.'

'Oh, Hal, I'm so sorry. That sounds awful. I'm not sure what else to say, apart from I wish it hadn't happened to you.' Zelda squeezed his hand. 'Did you have anyone to talk to? I mean, I had Emery, at least. The photographer who did the shoot with me,' she reminded Hal. 'He's saved my life more than once, probably.'

'Yeah, I've got some good friends. Thank God.' He gave her a small smile. 'Aye, well. Look at us. A right pair, eh?'

'I guess so.' Zelda smiled back; there was a quiet moment between them as their eyes met, and she felt a second of disappointment as Hal released her hand. She had liked the feel of her hand in his: his warm touch had been reassuring as well as containing a kind of electricity she would never have expected. She couldn't think of another person she had ever felt this safe with – as well as this excited just by his touch.

'Come on. Let's talk about the castle.' Hal patted the arm of the sofa as if to move the conversation on somehow.

Zelda poured herself some tea and sipped it. 'You wanted my help? I'm not sure what I can help with.'

'Aye. Well, you were right, last night. I could do with more income from the castle. I mean, it's ma home, like I said. I wouldnae mind hostin' a few more weddin's. So, I was thinkin', what with yer newspaper expertise, mebbe if ye could suggest a photographer, mebbe we could get some better pictures on the website, an' think aboot managin' the whole thing a bit better.'

'I think that's a great idea.' Zelda took another sip of tea. 'And you should have a social media presence. Instagram in particular would be perfect.'

'Ah dunno aboot that. Not my cuppa tea.' He frowned.

'It doesn't have to be your *cuppa tea*. Pay someone to do it for you.' She reached into her handbag, found a small tube of hand cream and squirted it onto one palm, rubbing it between her hands. 'Think of it as an investment in your future earnings.'

'Hmm. Well, this is the kindae thing I thought ye'd know aboot. Let's look around the house, anyway, and ye can tell me what bits I should show off more.'

Zelda had a momentary vision of Hal, bare-chested, in a kilt. *I can tell you right now which bits those would be*, she thought, making herself blush. *Oh, dear Lord. What's happening to me?* Maybe it was the sudden sense of being unmoored from her usual reality, or maybe Scotland was on some kind of sexy global energy line. Whatever it was, Zelda was not used to being so easily distracted.

'Sure. Lead the way.' She smiled, hoping she was projecting a veneer of professionalism and not giving away her smutty thoughts.

They walked through a different corridor than the one Zelda had been through before on her tour with Anna, which took them past a large storeroom filled with wooden barrels stamped with the name of the castle, and then up a small stairway that led on to another floor.

'What was in those barrels?' Zelda asked, as she followed him, curious.

'Whisky. The local distillery gives us a certain amount per year. It tends tae just sit down there,' Hal explained, carefully wiping dust from some gilded picture frames with his sleeve as they walked past. 'I don't get through much on ma own, as ye can imagine. We used tae get through them a bit more when we had parties.'

Zelda imagined a party here at the castle. It could be amazing, but there would be so much preparation. She wondered how many parties Hal and his wife had had, and what they'd been like.

'Oh. What are these rooms?' She peered into one as they passed; it was full of junk.

'Guest bedrooms,' Hal said, shortly. 'Unused.'

'I can see that,' Zelda replied. She could understand that there was no point in keeping everything operational and beautiful in such a big place: the cost would be enormous. Still, there was something sad about these unloved spaces. 'What about this one? Does it get used?' she asked, as they walked into the upstairs library she remembered from before. It had grand windows that looked out onto that glorious view of the loch and the distant hills, and she peeked under a dustsheet, finding an antique walnut writing desk. 'Because it could be beautiful. But no one will want to book a wedding here if everything's dusty and covered over.'

'No, it isnae used.' Hal answered brusquely. 'I think that should be obvious.'

'Why?' Zelda turned on her heel and looked around at the high ceilings, the coving, the rows upon rows of leather-covered books arranged neatly in series. 'This is such a cute room. Look!' She opened the long, heavy pink velvet curtains and sneezed as dust enveloped her in a cloud. 'Look at the view! And when the light comes through, it's so beautiful.'

Hal stood beside her at the window, looking out at the loch. Although it had been bright and sunny when Zelda had arrived, now it had started to rain. Still, the view stretched wide over the loch and the village, to the green and purple mountains on the horizon.

'It is beautiful,' he said, then pulled the curtains closed. 'But this room'll stay out of bounds to visitors. I dinnae mind the others. But nae this one, okay?'

'But why?' Zelda repeated. 'This room would be so—'

'Zelda. This room is out of bounds,' Hal repeated, and walked out of the room.

Zelda stared into the hallway from the library, wondering what she'd said to Hal that was so wrong. She went after him and found him on the landing at the top of the stairs. 'What just happened?' she asked, bluntly. 'You asked for my help, and then you just stormed out. If you don't want me here, then just say so.'

Hal stared at the deep-red carpet in the hallway. 'I think we should focus on the gardens and the ground level o' the property,' he replied. 'This level will be outta bounds.' He started walking down the stairs.

'All of it?' Zelda followed him. 'That seems a shame. Not least because if people book weddings here, you could give them the option to have accommodation too. Or at least somewhere for the bride to get dressed.'

'Well, that's what I've decided,' he said, stomping down the stairs.

'Are you always like this?' she asked, catching up with him.

'Like what?' he replied, gruffly.

'Do you always ask people for their professional advice and then completely ignore it?' Zelda followed the Laird into the hall. He opened a cupboard and shrugged on a black waxed overcoat.

'That isnae what I'm doin',' he replied, stubbornly.

'What are you doing, then?' Zelda insisted. 'Come on. Level with me.'

'That was her room. Where she went to read, play music,'

he said, quietly, after a moment. 'I just can't. Okay? I can't let strangers in there. Not yet, anyway.'

'Oh.' Realisation dawned on Zelda. 'Your wife's room?'

'Maggie's. Yeah.' He took a deep breath and met Zelda's eyes. 'I'm sorry, okay? I just can't,' he repeated.

'It's okay. Of course, I get it. I was being insensitive,' Zelda rushed, feeling awful. 'It's really none of my business, anyway. It's your house, not mine. Castle, I mean.' She smiled, wryly. 'Wow. I never thought I'd say that sentence.'

'Yeah.' He sighed. 'Sorry. I'm just nae good at explainin' myself, sometimes. I've got used tae bein' alone. If I turn into a miserable old hermit, ye've got tae tell me.'

'Deal.' She smiled up into Hal's eyes, and the grief that had lingered there just before seemed to clear.

He smiled back at her, this time with some of his previous jollity. 'Let's go outside.'

'Okay.'

He seemed as changeable as the weather, but Zelda was curious to see as much of the castle as she could. Even if just for her own touristy pleasure.

'D'ye want a coat? It's rainin' oot,' he asked.

'Ugh. I suppose so,' she replied, pulling a face to make him laugh, which he did.

'It's no' like ye dinnae have bad weather in New York.' He tossed her an identical coat to his own oilcloth monstrosity, but in brown. It was heavy, and huge. 'I've been there. It was awfa cauld.'

With difficulty, Zelda wrapped the coat around herself. 'Sure. We have snow in the winter and hot summers. We don't have this relentless rain all the time,' she protested.

'Just a bit o' a shower.' He squinted out of the window. 'I wanted tae show ye the gardens.' He shot her that sudden, twinkly glance again and Zelda felt herself go a little weak at the knees. *Why is this happening?* she berated herself. She had no way to stop it: it was as if her body was operating completely on its own, responding to Hal in some kind of ridiculously primal way.

'Well, we did shoot out there quite a lot, but okay.' Zelda followed him out of the front door, around the castle and down the sloping lawn towards the loch, making sure to give the impression that all this was super casual and that she absolutely wasn't *feeling things* about the Laird.

Yes, he was more attractive than she'd realised before, but today, there was something new in their connection: a shared understanding; a vulnerability that made her feel a little closer to Hal.

'Ye will nae have seen this part,' he called back to her, his voice buffeted by the wind that had sprung up from nowhere.

Aren't you just full of surprises, she thought to herself as she followed him to the stone steps that led down towards the topiary garden.

Get it together, Zelda, she disciplined herself. *He's just a man. That owns a castle. It was just a moment.*

But what a moment, said the voice in her head. And for the first time in a long time, she felt like she was having fun.

ELEVEN

'Wow.' Zelda edged past a large bush onto the wide beach where Hal stood, holding his hood under his chin.

'You'd never know it was here.' He nodded. 'Can't see it from the village side o' the loch, either.'

'This is amazing.' Zelda spun around, taking it all in. A grass lawn spread out alongside the loch, with the manicured gardens and topiary that she had seen hidden behind a tall stone wall. From this spot, you would never have known that the castle gardens were there at all; instead, a forest of pine led the eye down to a narrow, white-sand beach. Willows dipped their branches into the loch, further away. All in all, it felt like a secret garden where fairies might emerge from the trees on a moonlit night.

But Zelda's eye was caught most of all by the standing stones that formed a circle at the centre of it all.

'Is that... a stone circle?' she breathed. 'That is wild!'

The Laird followed her as she made her way over the wet sand and reached out a hand to touch an arrangement of ancient menhirs, standing up in the sand.

'Aye. Some o' the stones're missin' but the arch's still there.'

He gestured to three huge stones – two that faced each other and one that laid on the top like a lintel. 'This wouldae been a much bigger beach once, but time's brought the water line closer. I need tae move the stones, really. I just cannae quite bear to do it.'

'This is original, then? Like, Stone Age? Iron Age? I don't really know the right... you know.' Zelda waved her hands vaguely. 'Historical times. I've never actually seen one in person before, but I've always wanted to.'

'Iron Age, it would be. But no, they were put there by my ancestor in the seventeenth century sometime. Like a folly. I've always been fond of 'em, though. Time was, the villagers used tae have their weddin's up here, an' walk through the arch. Like a good luck charm.'

'Wow.' Zelda imagined men in kilts and leather boots, dancing with women in long, roughly woven tartan dresses as a fiddler played at the edge of the circle.

'Aye. There's pictures in an album somewhere. Drawin's, mostly. And then photos, in more recent times. Turn of the century onwards.'

'That must have been something.' Zelda gazed up at the lintel, her hand resting on the stone. 'What these stones could say, huh?'

'Aye.' He nodded, holding both hands behind his back and following her gaze. 'Ye know, there's plenty o' actual, original stone circles hereabouts. I could take ye tae see some, if ye wanted.'

'You would?' Zelda shaded her face with her hands from a sudden shaft of sunlight that lit up the lawn and the stones. 'I'd love that. I remember reading a book about them at school, and thinking I'd never get to see one.'

'Well, it's nae bother.' He looked pleased. 'What about Wednesday? I'm busy for the next couple o' days, but I could take you then. I'd have to drive. I could pick ye up, from the inn?'

'That would be great, Hal. Thank you.' Zelda didn't know where to look for a moment. Was he asking her on a date? She didn't know. She found that she wasn't altogether averse to the idea. Plus, she really had always wanted to visit a real-life stone circle. This one was beautiful and definitely old enough to impress her, but the thought of seeing one that could be thousands of years old blew her mind.

'So, do you still let the villagers have their weddings up here?' she asked. 'Because that would be an obvious win, publicity-wise, if you were looking to book more weddings at the castle from non-locals. Who wouldn't want to come up here and have their wedding at a stone circle at the edge of a Scottish loch?' She looked up and down the beach, her hands on her hips. 'Look! It's stunning! All you need is some flowers here and there, but the location does everything for you. Then it's back to the house for the reception. You'd be booked for the whole year, I guarantee it.'

'No one's got married up here for a while,' he answered, looking away. 'Not since Maggie died.'

'I'm sorry, Hal,' she said, quietly. She *was* sorry for him. It would be terrible to lose the person you thought you'd spend the rest of your life with – into old age – so young. Zelda doubted Hal was more than forty. It was no age to be a widower.

'Aye. She used tae get involved in organisin' the weddin's up here. She loved it.' He sighed.

'Did *you* get married here?' Zelda asked, imagining Hal in a formal jacket and kilt, with the sgian dubh tucked in his sock and the sporran at his waist. She'd done some hasty research before the shoot in Loch Cameron, thinking that they could accessorise the tartan bustiers and pencil skirts with some authentic Scottish items. So, she knew that the sgian dubh was a small knife worn in the sock, originally used to cut meat or bread or prepare other food, but also to be used in a fight if the occasion presented itself. The sporran, a pouch usually made of leather or fur, hung on a chain around the man's waist and hung at thigh level over the kilt, and acted like a pocket.

'No. Every Cameron Laird for hundreds o' years got married at St Giles' Cathedral in Edinburgh, an' I was a stickler for tradition. Still am, I s'pose.'

'And Maggie?' Zelda watched his face as he talked about his wife: there was a softness there when he did.

'Maggie wanted tae get married here. Damn the tradition, she said.' He smiled, nostalgia on his face as he remembered. 'She was right. It wouldae been lovely.' He sighed. 'Maggie was the one who liked parties.'

'You don't like parties?' Zelda raised an eyebrow. 'I thought all Scots were party animals. You guys certainly like a drink.'

'Aye, well. Some of us prefer a good book.' He gave her a half-smile.

'I'd actually consider getting married if I knew I could do it here.' Zelda peeled off the waxed overcoat and spread her arms out in the sun, flinching as her wrist tried to straighten. 'Ow. I keep forgetting.'

'Why did ye never get married?' Hal asked, leaning on the stone arch and shading his eyes from the sudden sun.

'Me? No time. And no one asked.'

'You couldae asked,' he said, giving her a sudden grin. 'Twenty-first-century women dinnae need permission, last time ah read a newspaper.'

'That's true. Well, no one that I wanted to ask, then. I forgot you were a book fan – I saw you that day in the bookshop.' Zelda changed the subject deliberately. Not letting anyone get close to her was as natural as breathing to her now: she'd had a boyfriend at college, who she'd loved. They'd talked about spending their lives together. But then he'd cheated on her with some girl on a different course and that had been that.

After losing her mom, Zelda didn't want to get close to anyone again, only to have to grieve for them when they'd gone. It was too painful. She'd spent months hardly sleeping; she'd thrown herself into her work as a distraction, but that had been taken away from her too, now. Grief felt like being disconnected from the world, being wrapped in a dark, still cloud of dust that choked her. She couldn't get free from it, and she couldn't breathe.

She was still in it, but she knew she was past the worst of it, and she never wanted to be there again – in that hinterland between life and death, where she felt she couldn't connect with the world any more.

'Aye, I always loved tae read. So dinnae judge a book by its cover, as they say. Unless it's one o' those romance novels with the lady with the heavin' breasts on the front, and the guy with the ripped shirt.' He chuckled. 'I give them a wide berth, I hafta say.'

'Come on. Those covers are so good!' Zelda giggled. 'There's a bar in New York and the ladies' room is plastered with those pulp covers and glamour girl adverts from the fifties. It's legit insanely cool.'

'I take it that means it's good.' He smiled. Zelda realised they had edged closer to each other as they'd talked, meaning they were now just a matter of inches apart. 'I dinnae always get what Americans are on aboot.'

'Yeah. Good. And I love romance novels. So shoot me.' She shrugged. 'Also, you Scots have some weird phrases. I don't understand half of what anyone says here. Yesterday Dotty found a dead mouse in the bar and she said it was "bogging".'

'A nod's as guid as a wink tae a blind horse,' he said, chuckling again. '"Boggin" means disgusting, filthy.'

'And the blind horse?'

'I'll tell ye another time.' He grinned.

Zelda laughed and looked up into Hal's deep blue eyes. He met her gaze, and the moment stilled between them. Zelda felt a pleasurable tension grow in her belly: Hal leant imperceptibly towards her. *Was he going to kiss her?*

In a panic, Zelda instinctively stepped back and made a *Hmm!* noise, as if to say, *Excellent, this has been an excellent meeting, definitely no awkward moments here.*

The softness that had returned to Hal's face in that moment of temptation or attraction – whatever it was – disappeared. 'Right,' he muttered, jamming his hands in his pockets.

'Yeah. Okay.' She cleared her throat again. 'You know, Hal, you really should go for it, with the weddings and stuff, at the castle. From what you've said, I think Maggie would want you to. And I don't think she'd want you to keep the upstairs closed off. I think she'd want you to open it all up. The parties, too. Whatever you used to do to make the castle feel alive and happy.'

She gazed back at the castle which loomed over the tall stone wall behind them. It seemed a shame that no one was enjoying the castle any more: it was a place that should be loved and appreciated.

Hal stared at her, and then took a deep breath and gazed at the stones. 'Mebbe you're right.' He sighed. 'Ye know, I think she wouldae liked ye. I think if she was still here, she'd tell me tae get my heid outtae my arse an' move on.'

'She does sound like my kinda woman,' Zelda agreed.

'Okay, well, let me think aboot it, okay? No promises.' He frowned at her.

'That's fair.'

'Right, then. We should be gettin' back to the hoose,' he said, gruffly.

'Yeah. I think it might rain again, anyway,' Zelda said, casting a glance at the now cloudless, stubbornly blue sky. *Typi-*

cal. The one time Loch Cameron couldn't be relied on to rain, storm or at least mist.

'Hmm. Possible,' Hal said, following her gaze at the now faultless blue panorama above them. He indicated the path between the bushes that returned to the gardens beyond. 'After you.'

TWELVE

The next day, Zelda decided to go for another walk, this time away from the village and along a rugged path that traced the edge of the loch and led past a few solitary cottages. Luckily this time she had borrowed a pair of wellies from Dotty who kept a few pairs for those tourists who had underestimated the muddy, stony ground around the loch.

She'd had a text from Emery that morning when she woke up:

> *How's the wrist, princess? Hope it's feeling better. I envy you your holiday. See you soon.*

She had used the voice function on her phone to dictate a suitably sympathetic reply.

Loch Cameron was long and wide, stretching alongside the village and around the castle, which almost appeared to be located on an island in the middle of it. It wasn't quite an island, as the castle's land was attached to the mainland behind. However, from where Zelda was standing now, she was reminded how much it looked like a fairy tale palace, surrounded by a mysterious body of water where sea serpents or dragons might live.

The small blue-painted iron bridge joined the village side of the loch to the castle; Zelda watched the occasional car drive carefully over it as she walked along. Once, a van approached on one side, and a car halfway over the bridge had to stop and wait for the van to reverse, so it could drive off on the other side.

The water of the loch itself shimmered blue-green in the late March sun. It was completely flat: an inland lake with no discernible tide, although Zelda had read online that it was fed by a number of small streams that ran down from the local hills, carrying fresh spring water. Scotland seemed to be a place where there were a thousand local springs, supplying the villages with mineral water.

Literally, these guys have Evian on tap, Zelda thought as she walked along the gravelly path that followed the line of the loch. Tussocky grass grew at the side of the path, and she had to step aside to avoid frequent puddles, but the view made up for it. The air was so crisp and fresh that Zelda thought pityingly of all the New Yorkers paying hundreds of dollars for their weekly oxygen beauty treatments. If only they knew that they could get all that for free in Loch Cameron.

She thought about her mom again as she walked along. Karen Hicks had not had a great experience of Scotland; the Mackays had been mean to her, probably aggrieved about the fact that she wasn't a Scot. It was such a shame. Zelda wished her mom had been able to come to a place like Loch Cameron and been welcomed as fulsomely as she had. Perhaps things would have been different between her and Zelda's dad if she had; perhaps Karen and Zelda could have had Scottish family to visit.

Walking past a pretty cottage on a rocky bluff, Zelda took out her phone and, rather clumsily, took some pictures of its whitewashed walls and blue-painted window frames. It was only then that she noticed an elderly woman standing in the overgrown front garden, feeding birds with bread she was tearing from a loaf.

'Morning,' she called out, trying to adopt the tradition in Loch Cameron of greeting people when you walked past them.

'It certainly is.' The woman shaded her eyes from the morning sun that was glinting off the loch. 'Haven't seen you before.'

'Oh, I'm just visiting.' Zelda stopped, watching the birds peck at the bread. 'Sorry. Do you mind me taking pictures of your cottage? It's for Instagram, that's all. Just my personal one.'

'Hmm. I'm sure I don't know what you're bletherin' about, dear, but I don't mind if you take a picture.'

'Thank you. I won't be a sec.' Zelda snapped pictures of the whitewashed cottage surrounded by pink and blue wildflowers, and then angled the camera to get some of the blue loch behind her too.

'No trouble. How d'you find it here?' the woman asked, not smiling, but not in an unfriendly way either. She was perhaps eighty, with white hair pinned in a neat bun and bright, intelligent blue eyes. She wore a colourful kaftan, with a loose scarf around her neck.

'Do you mean how did I find it, or how do I like it? I'm sorry. I can't always tell what people mean, here.' Zelda smiled politely, putting her phone in her bag.

'Ha. I mean, do you like it here?'

'It's nice. Quiet.' Zelda looked back at the loch. 'Not what I'm used to. I live in New York.'

'I don't doubt it. Not what many people are used to, these days.' The woman beckoned Zelda into the garden. 'Come in. I can't bear to shout across to you. Don't mind the birds, either. They'll desert me in a minute like they always do, once they've eaten all the bread.'

Zelda gingerly opened the wooden gate and made her way

into the cottage garden. 'Your house is like a movie set. It's gorgeous. Must be a hundred years old.' Zelda held out her hand. 'I'm Zelda Hicks, by the way.'

'You Americans. You think a hundred years old is old, and everything old is adorable. Still, it's been a good house. Gretchen Ross.' The woman shook her hand. She didn't have the same kind of accent as the other people Zelda had met in the village: Gretchen spoke in a clipped, English manner. It was more like what Zelda was used to hearing on English TV shows set in the roaring twenties, or featuring elderly lady detectives who lived in quaint English villages.

'Would you like some tea?' Gretchen asked. 'I was just about to boil the kettle.'

'Oh, okay. Sure. If I'm not interrupting you?'

'Well, I really do have a lot of old papers to sort, but I'm happy for that to wait.' Gretchen beckoned Zelda into the cottage porch, where pink and white roses bloomed over a wooden trellis. 'How do you like your tea?'

'I don't really drink tea,' Zelda confessed. 'So, however you make it.'

'Right you are.'

Zelda followed Gretchen into the cosy cottage. Inside the doorway, the cottage opened into a room with a large antique wooden dining table covered in piles of books and papers, some comfortable armchairs and a number of hanging plants. In the corner, a tall rubber plant had spread up to the ceiling and rather dominated the room.

'Ignore the mess. I'm putting the cottage up for rent soon, but it means I have to clear everything out, and it's a huge job.' She sighed. 'I wish I had some help, truth be told, but my only relative lives in Glasgow and he can't get off his bum to come and help me.'

'Can't get off his bum?' Zelda followed her into a sunny kitchen, where Gretchen pointed to a blue leather chesterfield-style chair by a blackened fireplace. She got the sense of the expression, but it was amusing to hear it.

'Yes. Bum. You know, bottom. Behind. Posterior. It's an expression.'

'I get it. I just don't hear the word very often, where I'm from.' Zelda laughed and sat down in the chesterfield, which was very comfortable, despite the fact it was losing some of its stuffing.

Gretchen filled a copper kettle with water and placed it on the old range cooker, flicking a switch as she did so. Then she bustled about, getting a floral porcelain teapot from a shelf, and some matching cups and saucers. 'Hmm. It's all "ass" in New York, I suppose.' Gretchen put on a sudden and unexpected New Jersey twang that made Zelda snort with laughter.

'Yeah. All about the ass,' she replied, as deadpan as she could.

'Figures. I watch TV, you know. I stay in touch with what the young people are doing.'

'Good for you.'

'I know.'

'I really don't want to be any trouble,' Zelda protested as the tea-making ceremony continued in the kitchen, but Gretchen gave her a dismissive wave.

'Don't be daft. I told you, I was about to make one anyway.' She set a plate of biscuits on a side table next to Zelda. 'Help yourself. They're from a packet, but that means you don't have to worry. My baking's atrocious.'

'Mine, too.' Zelda smiled, and took one. It was gingery and buttery and melted in her mouth.

'So, Zelda Hicks, what's your story?' Gretchen set a cup and saucer of amber-coloured tea next to Zelda, and carried her own over to a floral easy chair next to the kitchen table.

'Oh, wow. How much time have you got?' Zelda laughed.

'A lot,' Gretchen replied, straight-faced.

'Okay, well. I was born in Queens, but I grew up in the Bronx with my mom. She had a dry-cleaning business she inherited from my grandpa,' Zelda began, taking another biscuit from the packet. 'He had three dry-cleaner's but he lost the other two. My dad was Scottish but I never knew him.'

'Oh. Coming here must be strange for you.'

'It is, kinda. I wanted to hate it. But I don't.'

'Hmm.' Gretchen nodded. 'Go on.'

'My mom passed a few months back. Cancer.' Zelda tried to sound matter-of-fact about it, but her voice wavered.

'Agh. I'm so sorry, dear.' Gretchen let out a long sigh. 'That's a cross to bear.'

'That's all right. But thanks.' Zelda gave her a brave smile. 'I've pretty much thrown myself into my work. It helped.'

'Hmm. I know what you mean. I did the same, once upon a time. But it will catch up with you at some point. What do you do?' Gretchen asked, topping up her teacup.

Zelda realised as she chatted to Gretchen how much she had missed having an older woman to confide in. Emery was great, but Zelda kept her girlfriend group pretty small, and she hadn't talked to any of them about her mom passing away. She just couldn't, somehow: she didn't think they'd understand, and she didn't want to be a drag. She didn't want to be the sad friend who wasn't any fun and just brought everyone down.

Yet, being with Gretchen was easy, and Zelda didn't feel like the older woman resented talking about her mom passing away or her work, or anything. It was also nice to discuss it with someone who had already been there and done it. Gretchen had a kind of unshockable air about her, too. Like there was nothing Zelda could say that would provoke more of a reaction than 'Oh dear' or 'Hmm.'

'I'm a Features Editor for a small New York arts newspaper. It's called *The Village Receiver*. That's why I'm here: our new boss sent me and my colleague Emery to do a fashion shoot at the castle. We do fashion sometimes, if it's a hot New York designer or something. We don't usually come to Scotland, though.'

'I imagine not!' Gretchen laughed. 'You know, I think if your mum were here, she would want to tell you how proud she is of you. I can feel it.' She gave a small shiver. 'I don't mean I'm a clairvoyant or anything near as exciting. I just get feelings about people, sometimes. And I do think, dear, that your mum loved you very much. And she still does.'

Zelda didn't quite know what to say, but her heart ached. 'Do you really think so?' she croaked, hearing her voice catch, but not being able to control it.

'Of course, dear.' Gretchen stood up carefully and took the couple of steps to the other side of the table where Zelda sat, giving her a quick hug.

Zelda started to cry. 'Oh, I'm so sorry for crying,' she managed to get out between sobs. 'I'm so embarrassed.'

'Don't you ever be embarrassed for showing your feelings.' Gretchen hugged her tighter. 'You've gone through something terrible. Alone, by the sounds of things. You need to cry, and you need a lot of hugs. So, this is one.'

Zelda sobbed into Gretchen's wool-covered shoulder, a wave of gratefulness washing through her. 'I just miss her so much,' she mumbled.

'Of course you do, dear,' Gretchen crooned, stroking her hair. 'I missed my mother terribly when she passed, and I was older than you. It's terrible when they go when you're so young.'

'I just don't know how I'm going to get along without her.' Zelda took a deep breath and wiped her eyes on her sleeve. 'Ah, I'm so sorry, Gretchen. I wasn't expecting to do that today.'

'I told you: don't apologise.' Gretchen tutted kindly and returned to her seat. 'God obviously wanted us to meet. I'm pleased to have been able to help a little.'

'That's very kind of you.' Zelda took a few more breaths, and felt a little better.

'I'm not particularly kind. Don't kid yourself.' Gretchen sniffed. 'But I can recognise when a good person needs a little help.'

'Well, thank you.' Zelda felt mildly awkward, turning up at this random old woman's house and crying on her shoulder. They were still complete strangers, really, but sometimes that was how life was.

'So, did you hurt yourself at the castle?' Gretchen nodded to Zelda's cast, changing the subject, for which Zelda was grateful.

'Yeah. I fell over.' Zelda sighed. 'Couldn't get on a plane with a cast, so I'm staying for a week.'

'Well, a change is as good as a rest, so they say,' Gretchen said, thoughtfully. 'So, if you went to the castle, you've met Hal Cameron.'

'Yeah.'

'He's an interesting character, I'd say. I've known him all his life, and he can come across as rather gruff, but he doesn't mean it.'

Zelda pondered that. Hal had been distinctly unfriendly to Ryan in the bookshop, but she and Hal had bonded over their shared grief when she'd visited the castle. Plus, he was hot.

The jury was still out on Hal Cameron, as far as she was concerned.

'Tell me about this place. About your story.' Zelda sipped her tea, which she discovered she liked. 'Have you always lived in the cottage?'

'Ah, now then.' Gretchen got up for the teapot, refilling her own cup and then Zelda's. 'That's something. I've lived here for a lot of my life, though not all of it. That's a long time, but I won't tell you quite how long.'

'A lady never tells,' Zelda said.

'Quite. Well, where to start? I suppose you've heard about why the cottage is called Queen's Point Cottage?'

'Nope.' Zelda shook her head.

'Then that's a good place to start,' said Gretchen, sipping her tea.

THIRTEEN

'Legend says that Queen's Point – that's the piece of land we're sitting on here, Zelda – once held a smallholding where Mary Queen of Scots met her lover and soon-to-be husband Lord Darnley, in secret,' Gretchen said. 'Do you know your Scottish history?'

'Not really. But I have heard of Mary Queen of Scots,' Zelda admitted.

'Yes. Most people have. Oh, and when I say smallholding, I mean that there was likely a small house here, and the owners had a few chickens, a goat, some small crops. You know what I mean?'

'I can imagine.'

'Good. Well, in a nutshell, Mary had a difficult life. She was married at a young age to the Dauphin, in France, and when he died, she came back to Scotland. She was only eighteen, still. She fell in love with her cousin, Henry, Lord Darnley, and they got married. When they were courting, legend says that they used to meet here, in secret.'

'That's quite a story. Romantic.' Zelda leant back in her chair, imagining the young queen and her Prince Consort walking hand in hand along the edge of the loch. It appealed to her romantic nature, which she tended to keep secret but which manifested in her love of romance novels. Reading was safe, because no one would hurt you by leaving or dying, except fictional characters, and she could usually cope with that. But, even before her mom had died, Zelda had always been reluctant about getting involved with men, after the boyfriend who had cheated on her at university. She didn't trust them, after that, and so she didn't let them into her heart.

'Hmm. Yes and no. Unfortunately, Henry was a bit of a so-and-so.' Gretchen raised her eyebrows, and Zelda nodded. 'As soon as they were wed, he was off chasing other women, drinking and being a general pain in Mary's backside, poor lass.'

'Oh. Not so romantic.' Zelda also knew her distrust of men came from much further back than that university boyfriend: she'd been shaped by her mom's experience with her dad. Karen Hicks was a strong woman who had allowed herself to love Zelda's dad, and he had betrayed her. Karen had never allowed herself to love anyone else after that, except Zelda. Zelda wondered if that was really why she herself had never allowed herself to love a man, too. And, for the first time, she wondered seriously whether she was missing out.

'No. Still, he died in mysterious circumstances. Most people take the view that she either had her third-husband-to-be Lord Bothwell kill him, or Bothwell did it without her knowing.'

'Wow. Dramatic. And Elizabeth the First imprisoned her, right? Then she was put to death? I remember that, because we did a story a couple of years back about a Tudor-themed book,' Zelda mused.

'That's right. She had a tragic life, really.' Gretchen sighed. 'Strange that anyone finds it romantic, but they do.'

'So, your family have lived here for how long?' Zelda looked around at the quaint kitchen. A large wooden dresser stood at one end, showcasing a beautiful array of vintage crockery, and the large window overlooked a cottage garden full of bright wildflowers.

'Generations. Sadly, though, as I mentioned, I'm moving out. Bloody sheltered housing,' she grumbled.

'Oh. Don't you want to go?' Zelda felt awkward.

'Ah, don't worry. I do and I don't. I mean, it's probably time. This place needs a lot of upkeep, and I just don't have the energy any more. And I had a fall a couple of months ago. Scared me a bit. As much as I've loved this house, I think it's time to move on. Anyway, I've visited the place, and though it's annoyingly full of old people, the food was nice and they had a nice library room. I'm told it's one of the nicer homes.' She gave Zelda a sudden grin.

'Sounds pretty sweet.' Zelda grinned back. 'So, what's going to happen to this place? Will your ... you said you had a family member nearby? Will he live in it?'

'No, he doesn't want to. Too remote for him. Hal will let it, I think. I've rented it all these years, from him, and his father before him. That's how most of the houses are around here. Mind you, my family's lived here for a long time, as I said. I feel like we own the place, even if we don't.'

'Hal Cameron? This is still his land?'

'Oh, yes. Everything you can see and further. He'll find another tenant. Needs doing up before then, mind you.' Gretchen pointed at some wallpaper that was peeling off the wall a little in a small boot room adjoining the kitchen. 'Things like that. He'll probably come and do it all himself. Very practical, is Hal. Not that you'd have believed it when we used to have the old May Day fire festival. He used to love that. Every year, he recited Robert Burns, danced around the bonfire, the whole thing.' Gretchen smiled at the memory. 'Soul of a poet, that one. Hides it, nowadays, though.'

'What's the May Day fire festival?' Zelda was having a hard

time imagining the staid Hal Cameron dancing around anything, let alone a bonfire.

'Oh, it's an old tradition here. On May Day – that's the first of May every year – the village would build an enormous bonfire over in the castle grounds and have a huge party. May Day is the old farmers' celebration: the return of the sun, giving thanks for your crops and animals. People used to get married on May Day too, back in the old days.' Gretchen winked at her. 'Anyway, Hal used to organise a huge feast for everyone – a free bar, music, we danced, the lot. And he would recite some poetry. He was actually very good.'

'I find it pretty hard to imagine that, but, I guess, stranger things in heaven and earth and all that.' Zelda also couldn't imagine Hal Cameron reading poetry, no matter how hard she tried.

'People *are* surprising.' Gretchen got up and rummaged in a cupboard. 'Hang on. I've got it here somewhere.'

'What?'

'Aha. Here we are.' Gretchen walked slowly over to Zelda and handed her a small poster. The edges were a little tattered, but otherwise it was intact.

LOCH CAMERON MAY DAY FIRE FESTIVAL
DRINKS – FOOD – MUSIC – DANCING!
What is life, when wanting love?
Night without a morning
Love's the cloudless summer sun
Nature gay adorning
– Robert Burns
WELCOME THE SUMMER! SEVEN P.M. TO LATE,
Loch Cameron Castle

'So Loch Cameron's a party town, huh?' Zelda smiled. 'Now I wish I didn't have to leave so soon.'

'Ah, well. Perhaps you won't. Loch Cameron has a way of keeping the people who are supposed to stay.' Gretchen gave her a curious look. 'Now. You'll have to excuse me, but I'm meant to sort out all this paperwork, so I should really make a start.'

'Of course. Thanks for the tea.' Zelda got up to go, taking her cup and saucer and placing it near the sink. 'You want me to wash up?'

'Oh, no. You're a guest! But thank you for the offer.' Gretchen rested her hand gently on Zelda's arm.

'Okay. Well, thanks again. It was really nice meeting you.'

'Anytime, dear.' Gretchen nodded. 'Well. Anytime until next week, anyway. After then, come and see me where the OAPs go to die.' She laughed at Zelda's shocked expression. 'Oh, ignore me, honestly. You'll get used to my sense of humour.'

'I'm going back to New York soon, Gretch. But I'll definitely look you up if I ever come back,' Zelda explained kindly.

Gretchen nodded. 'We will let fate decide.' She walked Zelda to the front door, and gave her an unexpected peck on the cheek. 'Take care of that wrist, Zelda Hicks. And your heart.'

'Goodbye, Gretch.' Zelda was strangely touched. Sometimes you made a connection with someone and it felt like home. It had been years since she had felt that, but talking with Gretchen had been a little like talking to her own mom, if she'd been older, and British, and a little stand-offish at first. But rather than it being something sad, it was kind of heart-warming to connect to an older woman in that way. Zelda didn't need another mom. And she could never replace hers. But, still, it had been nice to connect with Gretchen.

She had liked Gretchen a lot, and she loved the little cottage with its country garden and cupboards full of history. It had been okay to open up a little to the older woman; Zelda had felt safe expressing her feelings, for the first time in a long time.

And as she walked back along the loch path, she wondered what it would be like to live in a cottage like Gretchen's: to wake up and look out at the loch, holding a warm mug of tea in her hands, with nothing but silence and the song of the birds as company.

She thought that it would be lovely.

As she followed the dirt path, Zelda realised that she felt a little lighter than she had before. She stopped for a moment and closed her eyes, letting the cool air off the loch tangle her hair and caress her face. *Mom, if you're listening, I love you,* she thought. *I miss you like crazy, but I'm okay.*

And, just for a moment, the breeze lightened, and Zelda could have sworn she heard her mom's voice in her mind saying, *I'll always be with you, Zelda girl. Be strong, remember. I love you.*

FOURTEEN

Myrtle's Café was the only option for lunch that Zelda had found in the village apart from the inn, and she liked the look of it straightaway.

After leaving Gretchen's place on Queen's Point, Zelda's first impulse on seeing the hand-painted sign above the café, and the chalkboard outside that advertised 'COFFEE – TEA – SANDWICHES – CAKE OF THE DAY', was to stand outside for a minute and admire the café's remarkable stained-glass windows.

She hadn't seen anything like it before. The wooden café door was painted red, but boasted a glass panel featuring a rising sun over water, and a rainbow beyond it. The café windows were a patchwork of coloured squares of glass, joined by black lead piping: cornflower-blue, rose-pink and bottle-green glass reflected Zelda and the loch behind her.

'Wow,' Zelda murmured, taking it all in. It looked more like a vintage boutique than a café.

She pushed the door, which opened into a cosy little space filled with knick-knacks, overflowing bookshelves, plants and the welcoming smell of coffee and baking.

'Mornin', dear. Come in, come in. I won't bite!' The woman behind the counter laughed at her own joke, gesturing at Zelda. 'Aye, ye must be the lassie stayin' wi' Dotty. She's told me all aboot ye.'

'Hi... yeah, I'm Zelda.' Zelda introduced herself, closing the door behind her and wondering at the local gossip network that meant this woman knew instantly who she was. 'This is some place.'

'Ah, well, it's nae much, but it's mine,' the woman replied. 'I'm Myrtle McGarry. A pleasure tae meet ye, Zelda.'

Zelda's gaze travelled over the walls, which were thoroughly covered in a variety of keepsakes and odd items. One wall was completely plastered in postcards, from locations as disparate as the North Pole to Barcelona. Another wall held bookshelves, with a hand-lettered sign: 'BOOK SWAP: TAKE ONE, LEAVE ONE'. Zelda peered at the titles on the shelf: again, they were a diverse collection, from old copies of *National Geographic* and saucy, bodice-ripping historical romances to a walker's guide to Fife, an old book of poetry and the memoir of a TV presenter she hadn't heard of.

The third wall showcased the oddest selection of all: a shelf of male and female mannequin heads wearing a variety of different kinds of hats. Bonnets, military-looking caps and a formal trilby sat on their respective heads, alongside a mannequin head with a beard wearing a straw boater, and a large teddy bear at the end of the row who wore a French beret.

'Admirin' me collections, eh?' Myrtle chuckled.

'They're quite something,' Zelda admitted. 'This whole place is quite something, Myrtle.'

'Thank ye, dear. All in a fankle, but there ye are.'

'In a fankle?' Zelda frowned.

'Aye. A tangle. Messy, really. But that's part of its charm,' Myrtle explained. 'Anyhow, what can I get ye?'

'I'd love a flat white, if you can do that? And something to eat.' Zelda scanned the handwritten menu on the board behind Myrtle. 'What do you recommend?'

'Hmm. I can do ye a toastie, or mebbe some sausage an' tatties if ye're hungrier,' Myrtle suggested. 'Nice sausages, fresh from the butcher today. In a sandwich, if ye prefer. An' a flat white is nae bother.'

'I'll go for the sausage sandwich. Thanks.' Zelda sat down at one of the four sets of mismatched wooden tables and chairs that made up the seating area of the café. It wouldn't take a lot to get crowded in here, but she guessed Loch Cameron didn't get a big lunch rush.

'So, how long has the café been open? And where did you get all that amazing stained glass?' Zelda called over to Myrtle, who was working a gleaming silver coffee machine.

'Oh, that's a story,' Myrtle said over her shoulder. She put some sausages under a free-standing grill, finished off the coffee with some steamed milk and brought it over to Zelda. 'Mind if I sit down? An' I'll tell ye.'

'Sure.' Zelda indicated the seat on the other side of the table. 'Be my guest.'

'Much obliged, hen.' Myrtle sighed, lowering herself gently into the chair. 'My legs aren't great at the moment. I should lose a bit o' weight, so the doc says. But I dinnae seem tae be able to.'

Myrtle was a larger lady, with a rough-cut auburn bob and an irrepressible glimmer of mischief in her brown eyes. She was wearing a bright pink knitted dress featuring a repeated pattern of black cats, heavy red hoop earrings and an orange scarf slung carelessly around her neck, which was pinned with a floral brooch. Zelda thought that Myrtle's overall impression was that of an older, more voluptuous Molly Ringwald from *Pretty in Pink*.

'Let's see. Well, the café used tae be a barber's shop, back in the day. The windae's all original from then. Auld Len, he used tae run it, he took over from his faither an' his faither before that. Family business. Rumour was that Len an' his kin used tae do a bit o' tradin' on the side, too. If ye know what I mean.' Myrtle winked.

'What? Drugs?' Zelda's eyes widened.

'No! Heavens.' Myrtle took a deep breath and fluttered her hand over her heart. 'My goodness, no! Drugs, indeed! I mean, black market goods,' she nodded conspiratorially.

'Oh, right. Sorry. It's just... that's what I expected you to say.' Zelda made an apologetic face.

'Ah, yes. Dotty said ye were from New York.' Myrtle said the city name in the same tone she might have said 'Hell'. 'I wonder ye manage tae get tae work and back without bein' mugged, from what I've seen on the TV.' She frowned. 'Give me Loch Cameron any day. Not that we dinnae have our share o' *goin's on*,' she added, a twinkle in her eye.

'What kind of black market goods was Len selling?' Zelda drank some of her coffee: it was strong and velvety, much better than she'd expected. 'And, what sort of *goin's on* are happening in Loch Cameron?' She mimicked Myrtle's tone.

'Ha. Yer a curious one, aye. Well, I think most o' the black market stuff was in the war. So, what people needed, I s'pose. Stockin's, drink, chocolate, that kind o' thing. But then, after, when Len was in charge, he used tae find things ye needed, for cheap. We didnae ask, he didnae tell.' Myrtle shrugged.

'Like what?' Zelda leant towards Myrtle.

'Jewellery. Cars. Furniture. You name it.' Myrtle lowered her voice. 'Many a lassie gone to the church on her weddin' day wi' a diamond from Len on her finger. No one could afford a real one.'

'Wow. So, he was a thief?' Zelda whispered.

'I wouldnae like tae say. There were no complaints, ever, that people were gettin' robbed. Len was the nicest of fellas. He was just well-connected, he liked tae tell ye.' Myrtle sighed.

'Anyhow, when Len died, he hadnae anyone to take over, so I took it an' turned it intae a café.'

'That's quite a story.' Zelda thought there was probably quite a lot more that Myrtle could tell her about Loch Cameron, too. She was intrigued as to what might constitute the *goin's on* that Myrtle had hinted at.

'Aye. People still come in from time to time, askin' for him. Sometimes they ask me, can I get them a sofa or a table or what have ye. I have tae explain I'm just in the sandwich business, no' the acquisitions business.' Myrtle stood up. 'Anyhow, let me get ye that sandwich, lassie. Ye must be famished.'

Zelda couldn't remember the last time she had been even close to famished, due to the almost constant food that was on offer in Loch Cameron, but her stomach growled nonetheless. 'Thanks, Myrtle,' she said, then began flicking through a cake-crumb-covered magazine that had been left on her table. On the cover, a woman in a riding jacket was pictured standing next to a sleek horse, with the subtitle 'SCOTLAND'S MOST ELIGIBLE HEIRESS? BELLA SUTHERLAND WOWS AT SANDOWN'.

As magazine covers went, this one wasn't particularly eye-catching, but she read the story anyway. Apparently, Bella Sutherland was a whiz on the racetrack, and looking for a husband: the article was mainly a gossipy comparison of some of the single Lords in the United Kingdom who, the magazine writer assured her, were looking for wives. The magazine had given them all horse-racing betting descriptions: 'THE ALSO RAN', 'THE OUTSIDER', 'THE LONG SHOT' – and their odds on being Bella's next squeeze.

As she turned over the last page in the feature, however, she let out an involuntary yelp of surprise. There, next to the words 'THE FAVOURITE' and taking up half of the page, was a picture of Hal Cameron.

FIFTEEN

'Gretch. What d'you want me to do with these hardbacks?'
Zelda called out as she knelt by Gretchen's ample bookshelves,
using her good hand to sort books into boxes. The next morning,
she had walked past the little cottage and, on a whim, knocked
on the door. Inside, she'd found Gretchen Ross pottering
around, trying to organise her acres of belongings for the move.

'Hardbacks go to Ryan. Paperbacks, I'll sort through,'
Gretchen called. 'Just make a pile of those somewhere. I can't
hold those big books any more with the arthritis in my wrists:
my grandson sent me one of those e-readers.' She appeared in
the doorway, dressed in green polyester slacks and a loud
paisley blouse, her hair in a tight bun. 'Did you know that you
can store hundreds of books on one little tablet? And it comes
with a light. Modern technology is amazing.'

'I know, they're great.' Zelda grinned and sat back on her
heels. 'Are you sure you want to get rid of all these hardbacks,
though? You've got so many. Lots of these are, like, first
editions.'

In fact, Zelda was fascinated by the many treasures
Gretchen had unearthed from various boxes under beds and in

cupboards: there were mint-condition promotional book posters, Lalique vases, vintage tea sets and at least a couple of designer handbags that Zelda coveted. Gretchen was piling things up rather unceremoniously on the dining table and, every now and again, Zelda would squeal and pick something up to examine.

'Gretch! You have amazing taste,' Zelda said, looking at a Clarice Cliff ceramic toast rack in bright orange, green and cream, with a matching cup and saucer set.

'I know, dear.' Gretchen sniffed. 'I always had a good eye. Most of this will go, though. I'll sell it to collectors, in the case of the Cliff, the Lalique. People love all that now.'

'It seems a shame.' Zelda sighed, packing the ceramics away carefully in a box. 'I wish I could buy it all from you. But I don't have a job or a home right now, after all.'

'Ahh. Not to worry, dearie. They're just things.' Gretchen gave her a quick squeeze around the shoulders. 'Not important, in the great scheme of life.'

Zelda had taken a picture of Gretchen's antique hardwood bookshelf, which was covered in carvings of vines, and posted it to Instagram under #bookshelfie and #zeldasscottishlife. She'd also posted pictures – with Gretchen's consent – of Gretchen sitting at the kitchen table with a cup of tea, looking imperious in her paisley top and slacks, and a selfie of herself and Gretchen in the lounge, sitting on Gretchen's flowery sofa.

Emery had commented, *Wow! Love this. Maybe a new life photographing rural cottages?*

In fact, Emery had been in touch fairly regularly, keeping an eye on her from afar, or so he said. He'd got plenty of free-lance work as a photographer and he'd already sent her a couple of leads for jobs. Zelda was anticipating that she'd have to fly home soon. She couldn't just stay on in Loch Cameron indefi-nitely: she didn't have a job, or somewhere to live apart from the inn, and that was slowly eating up her spare cash as the days passed.

'You don't want to keep any of these books?' Zelda checked, as she piled them into boxes.

'No. Sadly, I can't take it all with me to the retirement home. There's just no room. I'll donate a lot of the paperbacks to the library there, at least. But no one probably wants to read a biography of Tsar Nicholas nowadays. Ryan will take them, and give me a bit of money. D'you know Ryan at the bookshop?' Gretchen chatted as she pottered about.

'We've met.' Zelda had, in fact, really enjoyed her time with Ryan, getting tipsy and playing board games at the inn.

'Do you like books, dear? Take your pick of any you like.' Gretchen waved her hand at the towering bookshelf that ran along the entire wall of the sitting room. 'Not that you can probably hold any of the heavy ones either, with your wrist.'

'I do like books. To be honest, it's been nice having time to read them for once, since I've been here. And the wrist is getting better. Slowly.' Zelda sighed.

'And have you heard anything about a new job anywhere?' Gretchen enquired, lowering herself into one of her easy chairs. 'I'm going to take a breather. Put the kettle on, dear, would you?'

'Not yet. I need to get something soon. I'm not supposed to do any work for a UK company or person, though, so that presents a problem while I'm here,' Zelda said, getting up and moving into the kitchen where she found the kettle on the stove again, poured in water and lit the gas ring underneath it. She opened a couple of cupboards before she located the tea caddy she remembered from before. 'I need to go back to New York, really. I'm just hiding out here because I don't know what else to do.' Zelda spooned loose tea into the china teapot on the kitchen top and poured in the hot water when the kettle began to whistle.

'You have a flat in New York, don't you?' Gretchen raised her voice so that Zelda could hear her in the little kitchen. 'You'll be needing to get back to it, I suppose.'

'Yeah. I mean, I can't really afford to pay rent and stay at the inn for much longer, without a job. I mean, I'd love to – Dotty makes the best soups – but I have to go back. I'm just putting off the inevitable.'

'Hmm,' Gretchen said. 'And you really couldn't get any work here? Not in Loch Cameron, of course. I mean in Scotland. Edinburgh and Glasgow are fine cities.'

'I don't know, Gretch. I don't think so. And I'm an American anyway. I can stay here for six months as a tourist and not work, but a work visa is a whole other thing.' Zelda returned with the teapot and two cups and saucers on a tray.

'Seems a shame.' Gretchen sighed.

'Yeah. I do kinda like it here, you know. Despite the weather,' Zelda added, as she sipped her tea.

'Well, how about this? The cottage needs to be decorated after I leave. Hal said he can do it, but he's too busy to get to it for a couple of months. If you can decorate it for me and get it up to snuff, I'll ask Hal to let you live here rent-free until it's done. How's that? Means it gives you a little more downtime to work out what you want to do.' Gretchen sipped her tea, looking over the rim of the cup at Zelda.

'Gretch! You can't let me live here for free!' Zelda protested.

'Nonsense. I just told you, you'd be working. This place needs a lot of paint and repair, and it'd be Hal letting you live here, not me. I'd like to return the cottage to him in a good state, since he's been such a good landlord over the years.' Gretchen smiled. 'As long as your wrist is up to it, that is. Well. So, not doing a job, as much as helping out a friend.' She winked. 'I know Hal won't mind. You'd be doing him a favour.'

'Well, I guess I could.' Zelda thought of her apartment back in New York. She'd been planning to return and continue looking for jobs, but her rent was a concern if she didn't get anything soon. If she wasn't there, she could at least sublet her apartment for a while and make a little money. She knew it wouldn't be difficult – people were always desperate for apartments in New York. And she had to admit that the thought of living in the cottage had already crossed her mind.

Yesterday, she'd walked away from Gretchen's place and visualised herself standing in the doorway, drinking tea and watching the sun set over the loch. Had she somehow manifested this offer from Gretchen? She didn't know, but she did know that she wanted to stay.

'Yeah. Gretchen, I'd love to. I'm not doing anything else. And I can apply for jobs from here, do online meetings, that kind of thing.'

'Consider it a sabbatical.' Gretchen laughed. 'Who knows? You might fall in love, get married and stay here forever. I've got a feeling about you, you know, Miss New Yorker.'

'Not me, Gretch. Romance will never take me alive: it's strictly only for novels. But I'll gladly paint a few walls while I find myself. And a job, hopefully.' Zelda held out her teacup in a toast. 'To Loch Cameron! And to new friends.'

'Slàinte Mhath.' Gretchen tapped her bone-china teacup on Zelda's: the Gaelic phrase sounded like slanj-a-va when she said it. 'And, might I add' — she adopted a Scottish accent for a moment — '"What's for ye won't go past ye." That means, if it's meant to be, it's meant to be, Zelda Hicks. And no amount of denial on your part will make it otherwise.'

'Slàinte Mhath,' Zelda repeated. 'Let the good times roll.'

SIXTEEN

Zelda had called ahead to the bookshop so, when she pulled up in Gretchen's car outside, Ryan was waiting to carry the boxes into the shop. Zelda had managed to pack the boxes one-handed, but she'd had to ask the postman to load the boxes into the car at Gretchen's end. Fortunately, Loch Cameron was the sort of place where postmen didn't seem to mind doing odd jobs for injured women – especially when offered tea and biscuits afterwards.

The car came as part of the cottage package, at least for a month or so until it was due to be picked up by a charity that organised cars for elderly or disabled customers. Zelda had to admit that it was surprisingly fast, though she was taking it very slowly, driving on the wrong side of the road and using a stick shift. She'd offered to take the books over to Ryan as part of her new cottage duties, and Gretchen had been only too happy for her to do it.

'There're some real finds here,' Ryan cooed, peeking into the boxes as he carried them one by one into the shop. 'Wow. That's a first edition Angela Carter. Virtually perfect. Look at it!' He brandished a slim hardback in a colourful dust-wrapper for Zelda to see. 'And, look at this! Oh, my god! I think that's a UK first edition of *Carrie*. These things are like gold dust.' He flicked through it carefully and swore. 'This is signed! Zelda, this is worth thousands. Look.' He held open the inscription page where the author had written *To Gretchen, with best wishes*, followed by his signature.

'Jeez. I didn't really notice what I was putting in the boxes,' Zelda confessed.

'She really didn't want these?' Ryan gaped at the boxes: there were six altogether.

'She said she trusted you to give her a fair price for all of it. She's going into a retirement home, so I guess she could do with the money. Those places aren't cheap.'

'Right. Wow. Okay.' Ryan set the last box on the shop counter and shook his head. 'I'm so sorry. I didn't even say a proper hello.'

'That's fine. Book lust stole the show.' Zelda grinned. 'How are you, Ryan?'

'I am well, thank you, Zelda. You're still here, then?'

'I am.' Zelda brought Ryan up to date with her news. She hadn't seen him since their boozy lunch together; she'd expected it to be a one-off, and found that she was enjoying seeing Ryan again.

'Ah, well, there's nothing so bad it couldn't be worse.' He gave her a tap on the arm. 'That's what my mammy says. Since you're staying for a while, then, I think I should take you out to dinner to celebrate. There's a pub a couple of villages from here that has a stunning view, and chips to die for.'

'Oh. Okay, that sounds great,' Zelda accepted graciously. It was so easy with Ryan: he had that kind of pleasant affability that made everything seem like a good idea. Yet, she was conflicted. She had experienced a very strong physical attraction to Hal Cameron and though nothing had happened with either Hal or Ryan, she knew Ryan liked her.

She had an idea that Hal might too, if she was being completely honest: why else would he have leant in for a kiss when they were talking the other day? But Hal was hard to read, while Ryan wasn't. Hal could be spiky, and was clearly still dealing with his grief over Maggie's passing. Ryan was, as far as Zelda could tell, single and upbeat.

But Ryan didn't give her *the feelings* in quite the same way Hal Cameron did.

'Good. I'll need a day to sort these out and call Gretchen with a price for everything. So, you're at the inn? I'll pick you up at six, then?'

'I'm at the inn for another day or two, and then I'm going to live at the cottage for a while.'

'Wow! That's great news! How come?' Ryan looked pleased.

Zelda explained the situation briefly: that she still didn't know what she was doing, but that Gretchen had offered her a temporary solution, doing up the cottage.

'Sounds fun. I'll give you a hand with the painting, if you want,' he offered. 'Your wrist being less than perfect at the moment.'

'Oh! That's kind. Thank you.'

Her phone buzzed with a text: it was from Fiona at the shop.

Hi Zelda, I was wondering whether you'd like to come up to the shop for a cup of tea and a chat? Fiona xx

'Listen, I'll see you later, okay? I'm going to see Fiona for a bit. Come to the inn around five thirty?' She flashed Ryan her best smile.

'Fantastic. Make sure you wear your best ballgown, okay? These chips demand respect,' he mock-chided her.

'Luckily I have a gown with me for just such an occasion.' Zelda giggled.

'Perfect. I wouldn't want you to feel underdressed.' Unexpectedly, Ryan vaulted the counter in one coordinated, athletic leap and planted a kiss on Zelda's cheek. 'Until then, my sweet Yankee princess.'

Until then, Zelda thought as she left, a blush stealing its way across her cheeks. She hadn't expected anything to happen when she'd driven up to the bookshop, but now she had a date with a handsome Irishman.

She waved goodbye to Ryan through the shop window and headed towards Fiona's shop. Zelda felt excited about the date, but the notion that she could potentially be involved with two men in the same small village gave her a sudden, temporary moment of panic as she walked along.

Was it ethical to go on a date with Ryan, to the pub, and have another one planned with Hal, to a stone circle, in the same week? Would people talk? This wasn't New York, where nobody cared who you dated – and where it was far more usual to be dating numerous people at the same time.

What if the villagers – people she liked, like Dotty and Eric – judged her? What if they started gossiping about the American floozy who came to town and went through the single male population of the village like a stomach flu?

Zelda wished her mom was there with her to talk to. What would she say? She knew what Karen Hicks would say: *You don't need to feel guilty about it, baby girl. Take a breath. You're surely not the first woman to ever have two dates with different guys in a week in Scotland. Nobody's gonna gossip. And if they do, let them. So what?*

Zelda tapped out a quick reply to Fiona – *On my way now, if you're around?*

An answer arrived almost immediately. *Yes!!!!* Fiona wrote, adding on some emojis for good measure.

Zelda smiled. She was going to take her mom's advice and not worry; anyway, she had enough to think about for now, what with finding someone to sublet her apartment and looking for a new job. That would keep her busy enough.

SEVENTEEN

Zelda had spent an hour or two talking to Fiona in her shop, telling her about her job and how she'd started working at the newspaper. Zelda had given Fiona some useful connections – some UK-based fashion bloggers she'd been in touch with before, for the newspaper, and some PR companies that might be interested in hearing from someone with a cool little boutique in the Highlands.

It had been a nice afternoon: Zelda felt that she was, at least, being useful in some way. Fiona had seemed very impressed by Zelda's stories about New York parties and characters like Mira Khan, and Zelda left a couple of hours later, promising to go back another day to gossip more.

On her way back to the inn, Zelda got a text from Hal Cameron.

Okay. I think you're right about the website. Can you help me organise some better photos for it? Seeing as that's your area of expertise more than mine?

Sure, she texted back. *Let's do it. We can talk at the stone circle, if you want? Wednesday?*

Sounds good, he replied.

She was surprised and pleased; she hadn't thought Hal would ever agree to reopening the castle, but this felt like a positive step in the right direction for him, and a fun project for her while she stayed in Loch Cameron and tried to figure out what the hell she was doing with her life.

Since she'd lost her job, there had been frequent moments when Zelda had experienced a kind of vertigo. It was like falling: she felt as if the ground had been torn away from under her.

Still, tonight she had a date, and that was a good distraction from the general sense that her life was falling apart.

Getting ready for her date with Ryan, she put Hal out of her mind for the moment and assessed the suitcase of clothes she'd brought with her, deciding on a black pencil skirt and black heels with a baby-pink silk T-shirt. She plaited her long black hair and pinned it to the nape of her neck in a reasonable chignon. It would be good to get back to New York and get a proper blow-out done, she reflected. Most days in Loch Cameron, she'd scrunched her hair back in a ponytail or a bun, and it showed.

It would have been nice to go out on a date with sleek, glossy, straight hair, but she'd just have to live with a slightly messier style. She'd tried, repeatedly, to get an appointment at the only hairdresser in the village, but it was only open two half-days a week, and nobody ever seemed to answer the phone. When she'd gone to the salon on the two afternoons it had claimed to be open, it hadn't been. By now, she'd given up.

Is it a date? Zelda assumed that it was. She hadn't planned to date while she was away, but then, she hadn't planned any of this. It felt strange to be so unmoored from her normal routine, but she was trying not to let it freak her out, and just go with it. *Breathe*, her mom would have said. *Just go with it.* That was useful advice, especially in those moments of vertigo.

She had a moment of pause before leaving the inn, when her old feelings of grief resurfaced. Was she up to going out with a man? There was part of her that just wanted to hide out in her cosy bedroom, wearing pyjamas and drinking tea. She had briefly considered texting Ryan to cancel: he would understand if she said she just couldn't face it. And she could keep herself safe then, under the covers and away from anyone and everyone.

The feeling of falling threatened to rise up in her, but she choked it back.

Not now. I'm not falling. Not now.

Instead, she made herself go downstairs, and when she got to the bar, Ryan was waiting for her. The way his face lit up when he saw her made her glad she hadn't cancelled at the last minute.

'You were right – these fries are amazing.' Zelda bit the end off another golden, triple-cooked potato.

'Chips, Zelda. Not fries.' Ryan pretended to look shocked.

'No, "chips" are crispy and come in a bag,' Zelda protested, laughing. 'These are *not* chips.'

'No, *crisps* are crispy and come in a bag. Hence their name.' Ryan pointed to the bags of crisps behind the bar in the small gastropub.

'We're just going to have to agree to disagree.' Zelda ate another chip. 'But these *are* maybe the best thing I've ever eaten.'

'Glad to hear it. Potatoes are very dear to my heart.'

'Now that's just a stereotype. You'll be telling me next that you come from a long line of leprechauns.'

'Don't be silly. Leprechauns aren't real,' Ryan scoffed.

'No? You'll have to let everyone in New York know that next St Patrick's Day.' Zelda ate some of the juicy, mouth-watering steak that had come with her chips.

'I wouldn't dream of spoiling my American cousins' fun.' Ryan smiled, watching her eat. 'How is it? Good?'

'So good,' Zelda said, her mouth full. 'Thanks for bringing me here.'

When Ryan had picked her up at the inn, she had noticed that he had changed from his usual casual shop attire of scruffy jeans and jumper and was wearing a plain white shirt, open at the neck, with a navy blue blazer and smart jeans.

'So. Did you finish unpacking all Gretchen's books?' Zelda took a sip of her glass of red wine and looked around at the comfortable sofas and low tables in the pub; black wood beams striped the low ceiling, and a cosy log fire crackled away at the edge of the room.

'Yup. Some absolute gems in there. I'm gonna have to give her a good price.'

'I can't imagine you'll sell them that quickly, though? In the village?' Zelda raised an eyebrow.

'Ah, you'd be surprised. But, yeah. Most I'll sell online.'

'Oh, right. Of course.' Zelda nodded.

'So, tell me about you.' Ryan drained his pint of ale.

'What d'you want to know?' Zelda asked.

'Start from the beginning and end at the end.'

'That could take a while.'

'Okay, give me the abridged version, then.'

'I wouldn't know where to start,' Zelda hedged. She didn't want to share anything that personal.

'When's your birthday?'

'June eleventh.'

'Gemini, then.'

'Yup. Is that good?'

'Yeah, why not?'

'You hear about Geminis being pure evil.'

'Nah. Sagittarius here. We're good together.'

'Do you know a lot about astrology?' Zelda chuckled. 'I wouldn't have taken you for someone like that.'

'Someone like what? It's the twenty-first century. These things are normal now. And I read a lot.'

'Hey, I work for a New York liberal arts newspaper. We had an in-house astrologer. Or, I *did* work for one, anyway.' Zelda corrected herself. 'I can't get used to not having a job.'

'It must be really hard.' Ryan gave her a sympathetic glance.

'It is.' Zelda tried to sound upbeat, but she wasn't sure she was doing a great job of it. 'Agh. To be honest, I don't know what I'm doing, you know? I've agreed to stay at Gretchen's cottage and decorate it in return for rent. But what happens after that? What if I can't get another job? I'm gonna sublet my apartment, but long term, if I can't find a job, I'll have to give it up and move out of the city. It's too expensive.'

'No other newspaper'll have you?'

'Not so far. I mean, it's a tough time for print media. Places are closing down left, right and centre.'

'Can't you just reapply for your old job at *The Village Receiver*?'

'No. They'll bring in a new team. Clean slate.'

At that moment, Zelda's phone pinged, and she saw Mira Khan's name on the notification.

'Hmm. Speak of the devil.' She tapped on the message. 'I'm just going to look at this, if that's okay?'

Ryan made an open-handed gesture. 'Of course.'

Hi Zelda. Hope all is well. I'm working at The New Yorker *now and they're looking for new columnists. I was thinking*

*you could be good? Since you appear to be staying in the UK
for the time being, you could do a 'New Yorker in Scotland'
column. Talk about the terrible weather, the stodgy food, the
local theatre, practical fashion? Let me know?*

Mira Khan, you star. Zelda grinned. They followed each
other on Instagram, but since Mira had never commented on or
liked anything she'd ever posted, she'd had no idea that her old
boss knew anything about what she was doing or the #zeldass-
cottishlife hashtag she was using to record her stay in Loch
Cameron.

'What is it? Good news?' Ryan looked up.

'I think so. Look.' Zelda showed Ryan the email. 'I mean, it's
not full-time. But it's something.'

'That's awesome, Zelda! Congratulations!' Ryan hugged
her. 'C'mon, then. Let's take a selfie so you can put me in your
column. I'll be the hunky Irish bookseller you've developed a
crush on.'

Ryan's hug was warm, but Zelda couldn't help comparing
how she felt in that moment to how it was being with Hal. Hal
hadn't hugged her, but when she'd been close to his body, a
wave of sensation had washed over her. Hal made her feel
protected; he was, physically, much bigger than Ryan, but there
was also that underlying chemistry that raised the temperature
whenever she was near him.

It was nice with Ryan. But it just wasn't the same.

Zelda shook her head, but held up her phone. 'Agh. Can
you do it? My wrist still isn't right.' She handed him her
phone, ready to take a picture, and they posed, making stupid
faces.

'Come on. Serious now,' Ryan said, and took a few more of
them looking normal. 'Now, kissy face,' he insisted, and kissed
her on the cheek as he took the photo. He held on to the phone
for a little longer, tapping away at something.

'Ryan! Can I have it back, please?' Zelda held out her good hand.

'Fine, fine. And... posted!' He handed it to her.

'What did you post?' She scanned her social media accounts.

'Nothing terrible. Just that last one came out quite well. Thought it would be a good addition to your hashtag zeldasscottishlife posts,' he said.

'Oh, Ryan,' she tutted, finding the photo. Ryan had posted the picture of him kissing her on the cheek, and of Zelda laughing. He had written, *Chips, not fries, with local bookseller hunk Ryan O'Connell* and added a red heart after the post.

'What? Don't delete it. It's a nice picture,' he protested.

'I don't know if this news has reached bonny Scotland, but it's considered bad form to post on someone else's social media accounts without their permission.' Zelda went to delete the post.

'Sorry. I just did it for a joke.' Ryan sat back in his chair, still grinning. 'Ah, Zelda. Lighten up. It was just a bit of fun.'

'Please don't tell me to lighten up.' She placed her knife and fork purposefully onto the plate, feeling annoyed. It got her back up when men said things like that: being told to smile by random guys in the street was maybe the worst.

'Zelda, I'm sorry.' Ryan got up, switching his expression from one resembling a little boy caught out doing something wrong, to fully contrite. Zelda was a little alarmed at the sudden change in him as he knelt on the pub floor next to her chair and took her hand. 'Forgive me. It was stupid. You can delete the photo.'

'I know I can.' Zelda had developed an ability to be imperious when she wanted to be. Her mom had taught her well.

'Of course. I was wrong. I guess you just bring out the romantic in me.' Ryan twinkled a charming smile at her, and she felt herself being pulled into it.

'Don't try to pass it off as romance. You don't post on other people's socials. It's just rude.' She knew it wasn't that big a deal, but she was still annoyed and it felt hard to go back to being fun.

'Okay. Again, I'm sorry.' Ryan kissed the back of her hand. 'Please, delete the picture. Or, take another one of me looking terrible and title it "The worst kisser in Scotland".'

'Oh, my god. I will definitely not be doing that.' She shook her head, amazed at his confidence. Or, if it wasn't confidence, then whatever it was. 'Can we just move on?'

'Right you are. Shall we get the bill? And by "we" I mean "I", of course.' He returned to his seat and sat down, looking deflated.

Zelda felt a little bad for him: maybe she was overreacting. Ryan might well have just been being playful.

Maybe this is what I'll write my first column about, she thought. *Maybe men are different here.*

'We can split the bill,' she said. 'I insist.'

There was a silence as they finished their food. Ryan gestured to the waitress for the bill.

'I kind of feel like I ruined what should have been a lovely evening,' he said, after a long moment.

'You didn't ruin it. It's fine.' Zelda reached for her bag.

'I don't feel like it is fine. Can we start again?' Ryan reached his hand over the table. 'Ryan O'Connell. Nice to meet you.'

Zelda smiled, despite her earlier feelings. 'Zelda Hicks.' She shook his hand.

'Charmed.' Ryan bowed in his chair. 'May I say that you are looking lovely this evening, Zelda? And that I would love to buy dinner as a thank you for your company – and also purchase you the biggest dessert on the menu as an apology for my boorish behaviour tonight?' He held up the menu as the waitress approached the table. 'I've had the sticky toffee pudding and I can confirm it's the best in the world.'

'That's quite a claim.' Zelda took the menu and smiled, forgiving him. Anyone could make a mistake: it wasn't like she'd never regretted doing or saying something wrong. 'Okay. I'll have the pudding, and it's very kind of you to pay.'

'Excellent.' Ryan ordered two servings of the pudding, with whipped cream, and beamed at her across the table. 'I have a feeling this evening is going to progress much better now.'

'Whipped cream always helps an evening along,' Zelda commented, a smile at the corner of her mouth.

Ryan laughed loudly. 'There she is. Come on, let's celebrate your new column! To *The New Yorker*.' He held up his glass.

'*The New Yorker*.' Zelda grinned, clinking her wine glass on his pint. 'And to Mira Khan, who I used to call the worst boss in the world, but who turned out to be a lifesaver.'

'To Mira Khan, and to you.' Ryan held her gaze as she drank. 'I'm so glad you came to Loch Cameron, Zelda.' He reached for her hand. 'Even if I'm terrible at showing it properly. I really am, you know,' he added, softly.

Zelda's stomach did a little flip: was it confusion or attraction? She wasn't sure. She had thought, earlier, that Ryan was charming, and then that he was kind of an idiot. But the message in his eyes now was unmistakeable. Did she want that from him? Did she want it from anyone?

I guess I don't have to know right now, she thought. *It's just been one date.*

She thought of her mom telling her to *breathe* and *just go with it*.

She thought of Gretchen saying in her mock Scots accent, *What's for ye won't go past ye.* And she relaxed, and stopped worrying.

Whatever this was with Ryan, she didn't think she was going to be short of ideas for her new column.

EIGHTEEN

'So, here we are.' Hal stopped his battered green four-by-four at the edge of a narrow dirt track and grabbed his waxed jacket from the back seat. 'Let me get the door for ye. It's a wee bit tricky.'

He jumped out of the car and came around to the passenger side, opening Zelda's door for her. She stepped out gingerly onto a muddy verge, thankful she was wearing the new boots she'd bought at Fiona's Fashions.

It had started as a good day: Zelda had woken up to a message from a friend of Emery's about subletting her apartment for a month, maybe for longer, if they both wanted it. Though a month wasn't that long, it was better than nothing, and so she'd agreed. Emery had a spare key anyway, so she'd dashed off a message to him to say she'd call him later to organise everything. And, since it was a friend of Emery's, at least Zelda didn't have to worry about subletting her apartment to a serial killer.

'This way,' he said, leading her alongside the car to a stile in the nearby hedge. He climbed it effortlessly, swinging his long legs over with practised ease. Zelda followed, more cautiously.

'No' much call for stiles in New York, I'm guessin'?' Hal held out his hand to help her over the top, but Zelda made a point of showing that she could climb it herself.

'No,' she admitted. 'But I learn fast.'

They walked into a field of long grass, surrounded by trees that whispered in the breeze. It had rained earlier, but now the sun was out and had dried the ground underfoot, though Zelda could see that the grass still in the shade was dewy. She was surprised to see a number of shaggy-haired brown cows with huge horns watching them as they crossed the field.

'They're huge!' she called out to Hal, who was striding in front of her. 'In person. The cows. Well, they're not people. But, you know.'

'Ah. Aye, they are.' He grinned, and stroked a nearby cow on the nose. It snorted and shook its head. 'Highland cows. Their coats help them tolerate the cold,' he explained.

'They're cute.' Cautiously, Zelda approached the cow Hal was standing next to. The cow rumbled a deep sound in its throat, and she backed away. 'Uh-oh. I don't want to anger it.'

'She's nae angry. That's her saying hallo.' Hal scratched the cow's nose again. 'Ye can give her a scratch. She willnae bite.'

'Okay,' Zelda said, doubtfully, and very gingerly reached out her hand to touch the woolly hair on the cow's head. 'Oh! It's matted, kind of. But nice.'

'She likes ye.' Hal smiled. 'Guid girl,' he crooned to the animal.

'What's her name?' Zelda scratched the cow's nose gently.

'Dunno. They dinnae have names.' Hal shrugged. 'The herd's been on Cameron land for hundreds of years. There's hundreds, so we just number them.'

'Oh. Well, I'm going to call you... Joan,' Zelda mused.

'Joan?' Hal snorted with laughter. 'Joan the cow?'

'Yeah. Why not?' Zelda looked up at Hal, shielding her eyes from the morning sun.

'Well, it isnae a very cow-like name, that's all.' Hal chuckled. 'I thought you'd say somethin' like... Daisy. Or Betsy.'

'Oh, no. Those are clichés.' Zelda shook her head, seriously. 'This is a very beautiful cow, so she deserves a very beautiful name.'

'*Joan* is beautiful?' Hal did a double-take at the cow.

'Shhh. You'll hurt her feelings.' Zelda put both hands over the cow's furry ears. 'Yeah. Joan Collins. Joan Baez. Joan of Arc. Need I go on?'

'When ye put it like that, I see where yer comin' from.' Hal looked away, smiling. 'I suppose she is a nice-lookin' thing. Anyway. Get on with ye. It's the next field.'

'Okay.'

Zelda followed him to a wooden gate. Hal opened it and let her through.

'So, do we need to talk about the website?' Zelda asked him. 'You want to advertise the castle for weddings and stuff, right?'

'Aye. It is a good idea. I was just bein' pig-headed before,' he nodded. 'We should open the whole place up. You were right. If people can stay over, it'd be far more appealin'. We'd be able to put large parties up, an' that'd make us more money.'

'I'm very glad to hear it,' she said. 'In which case, what I suggest is that we do a day's photoshoot at the castle. Get some models in, and a professional photographer. We can get the models to act as bride and groom, so we show people looking at the site exactly what their wedding could look like. Really go mad on the romance.'

'Okay. Can you help me organise that? I'd have no idea where tae start.' Hal scratched at his stubble.

'Yeah. I can do that.' Zelda nodded. 'Luckily for you, I'm in town a little longer. Did Gretchen mention, she's letting me stay in the cottage for a few weeks if I can redecorate it for her? She said you were probably too busy to do it. Is that okay with you?'

'Oh. Aye, sure, that's fine. Nice tae know ye'll be here longer. How's the job-searchin' comin'?' he asked, politely.

'Well, I got a column job. My old boss got me a gig at *The New Yorker*.' Zelda was still amazed that Mira had come through for her. Mira Khan, of all people. 'It's not the same as having a full-time job. But it's something.'

'A column? On *The New Yorker*? That's huge!' Hal was visibly impressed. 'What're ye goin' tae write aboot?'

'Thanks. It's about being in Scotland, actually. My experiences in a tiny Scottish village. You'll probably be in it.'

Hal's cheeks reddened. '*The New Yorker*'s a big feather in ye cap, though, eh?' he said, still impressed.

'Yeah. It'll be about what the shopping's like here, the food, the weather – that kind of thing.'

'Ah, right. I thought fur a minute ye were goin' tae ridicule the auld Laird.' His eyes twinkled.

'Not unless you are terrible. So, be nice to me, I guess,' she joked. 'I mean, taking me out to see a stone circle's definitely a great way to start.'

'Ah, thank goodness.' He grinned at her. 'Well, in that case, here we are,' he said, gesturing to the sight that awaited her. 'The Seven Maidens.'

In the open field beyond the gate stood seven tall, thin, stone monoliths, arranged in a circle. Tall hedges grew along the far edges of the field, and a pile of rusting farm equipment was piled up in the corner.

'No one comes up here much,' Hal said. 'The occasional rambler, but technically it's private land. Not that I've ever minded anyone comin' up tae see the stones, but no' many do,' he added, taking off his coat in the warm sun, and pulling off his jumper too.

Zelda took in a deep breath of wonder as she caught sight of the stones, though she was also aware of the surprisingly intimate view of Hal's muscular torso that was briefly visible when he pulled his jumper off and his T-shirt rode up with it, briefly.

She looked away quickly, so he wouldn't be able to tell that she'd seen anything. *I didn't get caught with my hands in the cookie jar*, she thought. *Or, my eyes on the cookie jar. Whatever. He didn't see that I saw, and maybe looked for just a little too long.*

Hal smiled, now wearing just a black T-shirt and jeans.

'Amazin', isn't it?' he asked. Zelda knew he meant the stones, of course. And not his ripped torso. *But, oh my*, she thought. *Did it just get a little hotter out here?*

'Yeah. Amazing.' She let out a little laugh. She walked around the outside of the circle, reaching out to touch each stone. The total circumference was about the width of three large cars, nose to tail, she thought; she'd seen pictures of Stonehenge and she guessed that was bigger, but this was still a pretty good size.

'Wow,' she breathed. 'Oh, my... just *wow*.'

Hal let her explore; he stood leaning against one of the stones, drinking from a water bottle and gazing at the nearby trees. Zelda, knowing he wasn't looking at her, took a moment to admire his tanned, muscled arms as he drank. He was usually covered up in jumpers and coats, and Zelda had always known he was a big man, but his biceps were considerably larger than she'd expected.

Not that she had been thinking about Hal's biceps, or any other part of him. *Well... almost never.*

Smiling to herself, Zelda returned her attention to the seven standing stones. They were made of a light grey stone that seemed to almost sparkle in the sunlight, even though moss and lichen grew in their nooks and crannies, which must have been weathered by the rain and wind for hundreds, if not thousands of years.

Zelda closed her eyes, her hand touching the stone nearest

to her. *If you could speak, what would you tell me?* she wondered. *What have you seen? Who has touched you in all the time you've stood here?*

She could feel the sun on her hands, and smell the wet grass in the field. The air was clean and sharp, and birds sang in the trees. It was completely beautiful.

A perfect moment, she thought. *Elsewhere in the world, there's noise and pollution and chaos, but here I am, lucky enough to be standing here in a moment of pure peace.*

'What d'you think, then?'

Hal's deep voice surprised her, and Zelda opened her eyes to find he had come to stand next to her.

'Oh! I didn't hear you. Yeah. It's amazing.' She grinned up at him. 'Such a perfect day, too. Thanks for bringing me here, Hal.'

'My pleasure.' He grinned back. 'It's a bonny spot. Nice tae see it bein' appreciated.'

'I appreciate the heck out of it.' She looked back to the stones. 'So, how old is it?'

'No one knows, exactly. I think about five thousand years.' Hal put his hand next to hers on the stone. 'They've got a good feel, aye?'

'Yeah. They really do. Warm, somehow. Five thousand *years*? Are you kidding?'

'No, that's aboot right. Could be older. I've always liked it up here. Used tae come up as a kid wi' my dad when he was helpin' oot the farmers.' Hal's eyes met hers. 'I'm glad ye like it.'

'I love it,' she murmured, looking back into his deep blue eyes, and feeling herself getting lost in them. Zelda wondered what it would be like to kiss Hal. Without meaning to, she leant towards him a little more, their hands perilously close together on the stone in front of them.

He glanced at her mouth; was it her imagination, or did his lips part slightly? Was Hal thinking about kissing her too?

It was a ridiculously romantic setting, Zelda realised. They were alone, in the middle of the Scottish countryside, by a stone circle. It was the kind of situation that only happened in romance novels – at least, as far as Zelda was concerned.

'Zelda, I...' Hal murmured, not breaking eye contact. Then: 'Oh, damn.' He took his hand off the stone and pulled his phone out of his jeans pocket. It was ringing. He swore under his breath and looked at the screen. 'Ach. I have tae take this. Sorry.'

Hal turned away, holding the phone up to his ear, and walked off briskly to the edge of the field.

What just happened? Zelda wondered, taking her hand off the stone and watching him as he marched along, talking animatedly to whoever was on the other end of the phone. *Were we about to have a moment?*

Maybe it was just the crazily romantic setting that was doing things to both of them. Maybe it was the brief view Zelda had had of Hal's muscled stomach when he'd partially undressed, just earlier. Or, maybe nothing had been going to happen, and all of this was in Zelda's imagination.

I guess I'll never know, she thought, as she walked into the inner sanctum of the circle and stood there, basking in the spring sun. *And it doesn't matter, anyway, because I found this place. And I feel like I belong here, somehow. Like this old land has called me home.*

She couldn't explain it any more than that, but the feeling was real and true. Something in this wild land called to Zelda's soul, and she was grateful beyond words to Hal, who had brought her here.

Hal finished his phone call and returned to the stones. 'Sorry about that. I actually need tae head back, if that's okay with you? I thought I'd have longer, but there's somethin' I need tae attend to,' he said, apologetically. 'But I'm happy tae bring ye up here again another time. Or, ye could drive yerself, now ye know where it is.'

'That's okay. I can come back another time,' she agreed. 'Hal. Thanks for bringing me. This place is really magical.' She smiled at him, awkwardly. 'I really appreciate you showing it to me.'

'You're more than welcome, Zelda,' he murmured. 'Thanks for lovin' it.'

They made their way back to the car, not speaking, but it was a comfortable silence. When they got into the four-by-four, Hal started chuckling to himself.

'What?' Zelda clambered up into the passenger seat and put on her seatbelt.

'Joan the cow.' Hal giggled. 'I just remembered.'

'You're not going to forget that in a hurry.' She grinned. 'Joan is a very beautiful cow.'

'Sophisticated,' he agreed, turning the key in the engine. The jeep juddered into life. 'You know, I've got a whole new outlook on cows now, because of ye.'

'Happy to have helped.' She grinned, and watched the countryside start to speed past as they drove along. She wound down her window. 'Damn, but it's beautiful out here.'

'It certainly is,' he agreed, glancing at her and smiling.

NINETEEN

'Here. Put the rug here, with the trees in the background. And the picnic basket here.' Zelda took the props for the photoshoot from Hal and started laying them out on the lawn.

It was a week after Zelda's visit to the stone circle with Hal, and she'd been busy organising the day's photo shoot at the castle ever since – along with redecorating Gretchen's cottage. All in all, it had been pretty hectic, but everything seemed to be going to plan. She'd pressed ahead with the plan to get better photos of the castle as quickly as she could, having the feeling that Hal might change his mind any day; but, to his credit, he hadn't.

'I brought down the best crystal, as requested.' Hal set down a wooden box and opened it, revealing a set of intricately carved champagne flutes. 'These belonged tae ma grandmother. The crystal manufacturer closed down years ago, so they're irreplaceable,' he added.

'They're beautiful. And I'll be careful with them, I promise,' Zelda pacified the Laird.

'Okay.' Hal opened a bag and handed Zelda some tartan napkins. 'I thought these'd be good. And Anna's comin' down in a minute with the champagne and strawberries, as requested. She's waitin' for the photographer, and your male model.'

'Good.' Zelda had booked a fashion photographer she'd worked with before in New York who was, handily, now based in Glasgow, to take the new pictures for the castle website. To save money, she had agreed to be the bride in the photoshoot, and she had booked a male model from the biggest Scottish model agency to come along to play the part of the happy groom for the day.

Zelda had rented a couple of bridal gowns from a shop in Edinburgh and was wearing one now. Her favourite of the two, it was an elegant white silk evening dress with a low back. She had gone to the hairdresser's in the village that morning – unbelievably, they were actually open – and asked them to create a sophisticated, Audrey Hepburn-style updo for the shoot. She'd added her own pearl necklace to the ensemble, but otherwise was wearing no jewellery.

The dresses had arrived at the cottage the day before, when she was up to her eyes in cleaning down the walls in Gretchen's lounge before repainting the tired salmon-pink a fresh white. She checked her forearms again surreptitiously: she thought she'd got all the paint off.

Her wrist was healing nicely, and though the doctor had told her to rest it for six to eight weeks, it had been three weeks now and she had some mobility in it. She was using her left hand to paint the walls at Gretchen's cottage – fortunately, she'd always been ambidextrous – but she could now use her right hand to do small things like make a cup of tea and brush her teeth.

'May I say, Zelda... you look very nice.' Hal cleared his throat. 'Very... elegant.'

'Thank you, Hal.' Zelda shaded her eyes from the sun. 'Thank goodness we got good weather, huh?'

'Indeed.' He nodded.

'I have to make sure I don't get grass stains on this dress,' she added, turning around. 'Do I have any marks on the back?'

'Um... no, it looks fine.' Hal nodded and looked up at the house. 'I should probably give Anna a hand,' he added, and quickly strode off.

What spooked him? Zelda wondered, but her phone rang and distracted her from the Laird's retreating back. She answered it. 'This is Zelda Hicks.'

'Oh, hallo, Zelda. This is Nikki from Prime Models. I'm so sorry, but Bruce, the model you booked for today's shoot, won't be able to make it after all. He's just called us. Food poisoning,' the voice at the end of the phone told her. 'I'm so sorry.'

'He's just called you?' Zelda looked at the time on her phone. 'The shoot starts in, like, twenty minutes!'

'I'm so sorry,' Nikki repeated. 'Would you like me to send you out someone else? It's just that, as you're quite remote, I can't guarantee we'd get anyone to you before midday, but we could try and get someone to you for the afternoon.'

Zelda shook her head in frustration, looking up at the sun, which was blazing happily over the loch. There was no way that the weather could be trusted to stay good for another two hours. This was Scotland, after all.

'That's not ideal, Nikki. I'm literally standing here in a wedding dress outside a castle. I need someone now!' Zelda looked up and saw Hal returning across the lawn, accompanied by Brody March, the photographer. She watched Hal's broad, muscular shoulders flex as he walked, carrying a cool bag that presumably held the champagne and nibbles she'd planned. Today, he wore a plain white T-shirt and blue jeans. His curly brown hair had grown out a little, but not too much, and he was clean-shaven. He looked so good that she forgot she was on the phone for a moment.

'Hello?' Nikki said.

'Nikki, hold on.' Zelda put her phone down. 'Hi, Brody!

Listen, Hal, there's been a change of plan. Do you have a formal kilt, and the jacket, all of that?' she asked as he approached.

'Aye, of course. Why?' He frowned.

'I need a model, and you're it,' Zelda replied. 'The guy from the agency's cancelled, so you're going to do it.'

'What?'

'Be in the pictures with me. Okay?' Zelda gave him a strained smile. 'Look. The good light's only going to be with us for so long. We need to get these photos taken today. I'm not going to be lucky enough to find the hairdresser open again anytime soon, and these dresses are on a forty-eight-hour loan. So, let's get it done.'

Hal looked confused. 'But I'm no' a model,' he protested.

'No, but you are a real-life Scottish Laird, and this is your castle,' Zelda argued. 'Hal. You wanted my expertise. This is it!' She waved her hands, gesturing to the set-up. 'Or, you can pay all of us for not doing anything, and keep the crappy pictures on your site.'

'Fine, fine,' Hal acquiesced. 'I'll do it.'

'Great! Go get changed then.' Zelda shooed him away. 'Brody, you can get set up over there.' She picked up the phone again. 'Nikki, I've solved the problem. Thank you!' she trilled into the phone, listening to the woman at the other end apologise once again. 'It's okay. We found a solution.'

She hung up, and watched Hal climb up the stone steps to the castle. She had to admit that she was looking forward to seeing the Laird in his formal wear. *Purely for professional reasons, of course*, she told herself. For once she was thankful Emery wasn't with her, because she could just picture his sardonic expression if she said that out loud.

This was going to be interesting.

TWENTY

Twenty minutes later, Zelda was sitting opposite Hal Cameron on a picnic blanket, sipping champagne from his grandmother's ornate crystal flutes while Brody March snapped away with his camera.

Zelda hadn't quite been prepared for the vision of Hal Cameron striding down the lawn in full Scottish formal dress. His kilt was red with a thin yellow line and a black woven check, with a grey sporran. He wore a formal black jacket with tails, white socks with the sgian dubh tucked into one of them and black traditional lace-up shoes. Under his jacket, he wore a matching black waistcoat over a white shirt and black bow tie.

'Will this do?' he'd asked, slightly out of breath. 'If I'd had more time, I could have had my hair cut.'

'No, it's all... fine.' Zelda had looked him over with what she hoped was a professional manner, but inwardly she was think-ing, *Jeez, it's James Bond.*

'Okay, so, you need to sit closer,' Brody directed them. 'You've just got married. Let's do some linked arms, drinking from each other's glass. You know the kind of thing, you've seen it before.'

They had started shooting in various poses: standing together on the castle steps, outside the main castle door and, now, enjoying their faux-romantic picnic.

'Oh. Isnae that rather... a cliché?' Hal asked.

'It is, I agree. But Brody's right. Anyone wanting to book your castle for a wedding is kinda looking for as many romantic clichés as they can get.' Zelda sighed. 'Okay, wait, I need to make sure my dress is okay.' She manoeuvred herself carefully to sit close to Hal.

They linked arms, and Zelda twisted her good arm around Hal's so that her champagne glass was tilted towards his lips. He tilted his to her mouth.

'Great. Now, look into each other's eyes... yep, that's perfect.' Brody snapped away.

Zelda, forced to stare into Hal's deep blue eyes, felt a heat building between them. He was staring into hers with what seemed like a smouldering gaze. Maybe Hal Cameron was a natural at posing for romantic wedding shoots, or he was having some pretty X-rated thoughts right now.

Zelda blinked quickly, aware she was wearing fake eyelashes and some fairly smouldering makeup for the camera. A hint of a smile played around Hal's mouth; the tension between them grew.

How often is it that anyone – apart from models and actors – ever have to gaze unrelentingly into someone else's eyes? Zelda wondered. *It's unnatural. It's weird.*

And it was, also, both comforting and a little exciting to be this intimate with Hal Cameron.

Yes, it was sexy, but there was more to it than that. There was something about being so close to Hal's body that made her very aware of his strength, but Zelda felt comforted by it. There was a bear-like quality to him.

Zelda blushed and looked away. She wondered if he knew she was thinking about him as a bear. Well, not as a bear exactly. She wasn't *into* bears. *That really would be weird.* It was just that she'd never met a man before who made her feel sexy and protected at the same time. It was a heady combination.

'Zelda? You okay?' Brody called over.

'Perfect, thanks, but I could do with my wrist not being twisted up for much longer.' Zelda unlinked herself from Hal.

'Oh, is it sore?' Hal asked, a concerned look on his face.

'Oh. No, that's the other one. But, anyway,' Zelda answered quickly, eager to hide her awkwardness, 'you know what? We should shoot at the standing stones now.'

'Sounds good,' Brody said, hefting his camera onto his shoulder and picking up his bag. 'Let's do it.'

'That okay with you, Hal?' Zelda assumed her business-like tone again.

'It is,' he replied, and then his elusive smile broke out over his face, lighting it up. 'It's pretty fun, doin' this with ye,' he added shyly, as Brody walked away.

'Well, this is what I do,' she said, desperate to stay centred in her professionalism. She was here to do a job. She was not here to flirt with an attractive Laird, no matter how good he looked in a kilt. 'I mean, organise features, sometimes with photos. I don't usually model in them, though.'

'Well, ye do it very well,' he said, standing up and holding out his hand to help her up.

'Oh. Thanks.' Zelda could feel herself blushing, and looked away so Hal couldn't see. 'Come on, let's go.'

———

When they got to the standing stones, Brody suggested that he take some shots of Zelda and Hal under the arch, holding hands. Zelda ducked under the arch first, trying not to hit her head on the ancient stone. Hal – clearly forgetting he was much taller than she – wasn't as cautious, and banged his temple.

'Ow!' he shouted, swearing at the stone.

'Hold still!' Zelda remonstrated with him, reaching up to part his hair and check he wasn't bleeding. 'You're all right. How many fingers am I holding up?' She held up three fingers.

'Six,' Hal muttered, rubbing his head. 'That hurt, ye know. I might have tae go to A&E.'

'Probably a skull fracture.' Zelda nodded, faux-seriously. 'You'll pass out in a minute.'

'I appreciate the sympathy.' Hal chuckled. 'You'd make a terrible nurse, just so ye know.'

'Hey. I'm sympathetic when it's warranted.'

'My terrible head wound doesnae warrant yer sympathy?'

Brody called across to them again to hold hands and smile at each other.

'I don't think it's a cause for alarm,' Zelda said, from the side of her mouth as they posed. 'I mean, you're a grown-up. Deal with it.'

'I didnae tell ye te deal wi' it when ye broke yer wrist, Nurse Zelda,' Hal retorted, as he gazed faux-lovingly down at her.

'That's because it was a real injury.'

'Touché,' he muttered, a playful glint in his eyes.

'Okay, that's great. I've got some good shots,' Brody called out, interrupting the moment between them.

'We should go and shoot in the house, now.' Zelda looked away, keenly aware that things had heated up again between them. Hal was definitely flirting with her. *Wasn't he?* Surely calling anyone 'Nurse' *anything* had a hint of the flirtatious about it.

Admittedly, she'd flirted back. She couldn't help it, but now Zelda reined it in and got herself under control. *Be professional,* she reminded herself. *You're doing a job here.*

It wasn't a paid job, but Zelda felt that her professional pride was at stake nonetheless. It was important to her that she do a good job on the shoot, purely to prove to Hal that she was right: the castle would be hugely popular for parties and weddings, if only people could see it in all its glory.

And Zelda really wanted to help Hal. She knew what it was like, being inside grief, and how hard it was to pull yourself out of it. This was a way she could help Hal do that.

'We should shoot in Maggie's room,' Zelda suggested gently when they got to the house, holding up her dress so the hem wouldn't drag on the floor. 'You know. The one with the pink velvet curtains and all the books. We can take the dustsheets off everything.'

'I told ye, Zelda. We aren't goin' tae open that room up to the public, so there's nae point photographin' it,' Hal said, firmly. 'Anywhere else is okay. But no' Maggie's room.'

'But, Hal, it's such a pretty room,' Zelda said, knowing this was a sensitive matter for him, but also knowing how good the room would look in the photos they were taking.

'I appreciate that,' the Laird replied. 'But I'm nae changin' my mind, so drop it.'

'But don't you think Maggie would want you to restore that room? Make it as lovely as it must have been? It just needs a good clean,' Zelda repeated, not dropping it.

Hal turned away from her and took a deep breath. Brody busied himself with adjusting something on his camera, obviously finding the moment awkward.

'It's... it feels wrong if I clean it, wipe everythin' away. Okay? If I take it back tae bein' a functional room, then I've lost her forever. That's how I feel. That enough for ye?' Hal turned around and stared at her. His face was flushed.

'I get it, Hal. But she's already gone.' The words were out of Zelda's mouth before she could think twice about her lack of compassion.

Hal continued to stare at her.

'You told me aboot losin' yer mum, aye? Isnae that the same thing? I wouldnae ever be as insensitive tae suggest that ye should give up yer last connection to her, whatever that might be.' Hal raised his voice. 'Don't tell me what I should do about Maggie.'

Zelda's stomach sank. Of course, he was right. 'Oh, Hal. I'm so sorry.' She reached out for him, but he turned away.

He nodded at Brody. 'Ye can get some shots o' the downstairs withoot me. I've got work tae be getting' on with, so, goodbye.' He stormed up the ornate stairwell and left Brody and Zelda standing in the entry hall.

'Oh, I feel terrible.' Zelda covered her face with her hands. 'How could I have said that? I just... I guess I wanted to help him. In a really, really unhelpful and inconsiderate way.'

'Hey. I'm just here to work.' Brody was impassive. 'Anyway, we have loads of shots of you both. I can actually just take shots of the other spaces without you guys in them. They'll still be useful for the site.'

'Okay.' Zelda sighed. 'I'll come with you – move stuff around if it needs it or whatever. Let me change and I'll be right with you.' She left Brody in the hall and went to find her normal clothes in one of the reception rooms, her heart sinking. How could she have been so callous? Especially as someone who had been bereaved herself.

As she took off the wedding dress, checking it for marks, Zelda could have kicked herself for being so stupid. She'd enjoyed Hal's company today. They'd had fun. And she wasn't going to pretend to herself that she didn't still feel that sexy frisson in her belly when she remembered the way Hal had looked into her eyes.

But then she'd ruined everything.

Zelda hadn't meant to spoil things, but Hal could be so goddamned stubborn. It frustrated her, because she knew she could do great things with the castle. She just wanted Hal to trust her, and in her desire to help she had somehow forgotten that she was riding roughshod over Hal's grief. He was as heartbroken as she was but instead of treating him with the gentleness she had been so grateful to receive from friends like Emery, she had trampled all over his heart.

Zelda sighed. She would make it up with Hal. Maybe he would be happier when he saw the pictures.

She messaged a picture of herself in the wedding dress to Emery, who replied immediately with *OMG ARE YOU SERIOUS*. His reaction made her laugh, taking her out of her head for a moment.

No, I am not getting married, she replied to Emery. *Doing a romantic shoot at the castle with the Laird, though I think I just messed up big time.*

What did you do, Zelda Hicks? Emery asked, with a number of vegetable-based emojis and exclamation marks that made Zelda smile.

Not that, she answered, chuckling to herself.

What then?

Agh. I hurt his feelings. I was pushy.

Well, you're also a sweetheart, Emery replied. *Pushy how?*

Long story but I basically was a little too personal about his dead wife, she wrote, feeling awful all over again. *He's really protective of her memory. And I kind of trampled on his feelings. I should have been kinder, but I just really want to help him out. It was enthusiasm, gone wrong.*

So, think of a way to make it up to him, Emery messaged back. *You're creative. And kind, if a little... enthusiastic.*

Emery had a point. *If Hal needs anything, it's a friend*, she thought. Just like Emery was her friend. *I can make it up to him,* she decided, feeling a sense of resolve. *I can make this better.*

Okay. I'm on it, she replied to Emery, who responded with a smiley face.

Reassured, she went to find Brody in the castle to finish the shots.

TWENTY-ONE

'So, I was thinkin' aboot what ye were sayin' aboot stockin' some more glamorous options in the shop,' Fiona said, once they had settled down on an aged pink leather sofa by the shop's changing room with two mugs of tea and some biscuits. 'The thing is, I'd really love tae do it. I love fashion, as ye know. But the problem is how I get customers tae know what's here, and get customers tae come from farther afield as well. Loch Cameron's no' big. I mean, I can think of some well-to-do older ladies, but I could count them on one hand.'

'Sure.' Zelda sipped her tea. It was the national drink, if you weren't counting whisky. She'd lost count how many cups she was drinking now. Gone were the days of two litres of water and a green smoothie every day. She doubted Dotty would know what a green smoothie was. Secretly, Zelda found that if it was a straight-up choice between Dotty's raspberry cranachan and the green smoothie, she'd take the cranachan every time.

She had got up that morning and walked over to Fiona's Fashions in the village, in the mood to drop in on Fiona for a gossip. On the way, she thought about her mom's dry-cleaning shop. It had never been much, but it was central to their community in the Bronx. She liked the fact that Loch Cameron had little individual shops too: she'd discovered that there was a bakery, a traditional butcher, a fishmonger and a little shop that sold wool and dress patterns. Plus, there was Fiona's shop, the hairdresser's, a small local supermarket, an ironmonger's shop – which, Zelda had learnt, was a place where you could buy anything, from an individual two-inch nail to a length of electrical tape, a hammer, a dehumidifier and a tartan dinner service. Like her old neighbourhood, people greeted her in the street, although in Loch Cameron it was 'Hallo' or 'Guid mornin'.'

Thinking about her mom made her sad, but, weirdly, it also helped to ground Zelda. At least, if she thought about her mom, it was a way of steadying herself: of hanging on to who she was and where she came from.

'Well, you could advertise in some local newspapers to reach the older generation,' she suggested to Fiona. 'Maybe get the paper to come and do a story about your shop? And social media, to expand your customer base. D'you have an Instagram account for the shop? Like, you could post cute pics of you modelling the new stock, or get a friend to do it. Show people what you have, do discounts to get them through the door. That kind of thing.'

'I don't know how many people in Loch Cameron are on Instagram,' Fiona said, doubtfully.

'Yeah, but this is exactly the same conversation I had with Hal. You make Fiona's Fashions a destination shopping experience. People come to Loch Cameron just to shop here,' Zelda explained. 'I mean, you could still stock the practical stuff that people need. But also a selection of more glamorous pieces.'

'I like the idea a lot,' Fiona mused.

'I can hook you up with some more suppliers too, if you want.' Zelda got out her phone, tapped in a website belonging to a high-end fashion warehouse in Edinburgh and showed it to Fiona.

'How do you know all this? I mean, you work in New York usually.' Fiona flicked through the website on her own phone.

'I'm resourceful. You gotta be in my job. And, when I was planning the feature we got sent here to do, I had to research a lot of stuff.' Zelda grinned.

'How're you getting' on with the Laird, then?' Fiona raised an eyebrow. 'I heard you were up at the castle doin' a photoshoot.'

'Oh, right. Yeah, okay. I'm helping him out with the castle website.' Zelda sighed. 'He's a tricky one, though. Prickly. We're getting on fine and then, *poof!* I've offended him. Though, I fully admit that was my fault. I can be so blunt sometimes. It rubs people the wrong way.'

'Ah. He's deep, to be sure. But he's usually fair. And even if he seems gruff, you've got tae understand he's still recoverin' from what happened wi' Maggie.' Fiona lowered her voice conspiratorially.

'Yeah. Well, that's kinda where I should have kept my big mouth zipped.' Zelda frowned. 'It's so sad.'

'Aye, it was sad. Maggie was such a bright, bonny lass. Always cheerful. Always laughin'.' Fiona tutted. 'What happened between ye, then? Up at the castle?'

'Oh, Fiona. I basically told him he should just get over it. I was completely insensitive and tone-deaf. In my defence, I was only trying to persuade him to open up the castle more for wedding bookings. But I went too far.' Zelda still felt terrible about it.

'Ach, dinnae worry. He'll get over it, I'm sure. Still, it was terrible, what happened.' Fiona shook her head.

'What did actually happen? She got sick?' Zelda guessed. 'Or was it some kind of accident?'

'She got ill. One o' those rare inherited things.'

'That's awful.' Zelda sipped her tea.

'Hmm.' Fiona looked thoughtful. 'I havenae been up to the castle in a while, but I do remember when they had the last May Day party, they opened the whole place up. Maggie played the harp, an' she had it up in one of those rooms upstairs. She gave us a kind o' concert of sorts. It was pure brilliant.'

'Wow.' Zelda could only imagine what that must have been like.

'Aye. Hal's a private person, Zelda. You've got tae understand, when Maggie died, he changed. He was always the quiet one, but he also used tae be jolly. He'd have a joke wi' ye. An' Maggie was his whole world.' Fiona sighed. 'He hasnae been the same since she went.'

'It's a shame you don't have the May Day party any more,' Zelda said. 'What happened, specifically? Gretchen said he used to read poetry and there was a big bonfire.'

'Aye, all that. People got really dressed up too. Hal put on the food and drink. No one had tae pay for anythin' apart from their dresses.' Fiona smiled at the memory. 'At the last one, I hired a ballgown for the night from Jenners in Edinburgh. Posh as anythin'.'

'Now *that's* your event. If the May Day party happened again, you could be the official party gown supplier.' Zelda took a biscuit from the packet. 'People wouldn't have to hire dresses in. You could sell them. Or hire them. Point is, you'd be the official supplier.'

'I like that idea too. But I don't think the Laird's up for any more parties.' Fiona's expression was resigned. 'Sadly.'

'It does look that way.' Zelda dipped her biscuit in her tea and popped it in her mouth, thinking. She needed to convince Hal to trust her again and find a way to make things up to him. What better than organising a party at the castle? If she could remind Hal of all the good things that came with having people there, she knew he'd agree to opening the whole place up for weddings, and make a lot more money. Plus, she might even persuade him to clean up the rooms that had been so uncared for since Maggie's death and bring them back to their former glory.

Zelda knew she wasn't going to gain anything from being so invested in Hal's castle – he couldn't pay her. But, now, it was a point of honour. And, more than that, she'd realised that being up at the castle, feeling like she was doing something worthwhile, had stopped her feeling the horrible sense of falling she'd had ever since the phone call from Mira Khan telling her she was fired.

All her working life, she'd felt as though she was walking a tightrope. There was nothing holding her up, nothing supporting her. And when she'd lost her job at *The Village Receiver*, she'd felt as though she was in freefall.

She might not have a chance of being paid when working for Hal, but helping him organise a party at the castle and set up the place for weddings gave her something to focus on. And when she was focused, she didn't feel as lost.

On top of all that, she knew that Hal needed her help. After their argument she had seen the depth of his grief, and she knew what that felt like. If Zelda could help him pull himself out of the pit he'd got lost in, then she would.

In romantic novels, it was always the hero who saved the heroine. But, in real life, Zelda thought that even if there was no romance between her and Hal, then she could certainly be the one to do a little saving of someone else.

TWENTY-TWO

Zelda was sitting at her laptop at a majestic desk in one of the grand reception rooms at the castle, rearranging the photos that Brody March had sent over on the castle website.

She hadn't published the site yet: she was just trying out some various options to show Hal, who had said he'd meet her at the castle at noon. It was now twelve thirty, and there was no sign of him.

Still, Zelda was quite enjoying having the baronial room to herself: she felt like a Scottish Lady doing her correspondence at a great house. She was also thinking about one of her favourite novels, *Rebecca* by Daphne du Maurier, even though it hadn't been set in Scotland.

There was a scene in the book where the second Mrs de Winter – despite the fact that she loved the book, Zelda had always found it annoying that the reader was never given her name, like she should be some kind of anonymous, passive woman – had just arrived at Manderley, the huge house belonging to her husband. She had sat at the writing desk belonging to Rebecca, the infamous first Mrs de Winter. She had admired her personalised stationery, her book of appointments, her pens. Oh, right – that was it. She had broken a porcelain statue, and hidden it in the trash.

Zelda looked up from her laptop and took stock of the items on the red leather-topped writing desk. There was a copper pot with an assortment of pens, a plain notepad block of the kind where you could peel off squares of paper, and a small crystal vase holding a purple thistle. She reached out to stroke its spikiness.

'Sorry to have kept ye.' Hal strode into the room, a dog at his heels. 'The dogs went intae the neighbourin' fields and the farmer there got chatty. I got away as soon as I could.'

Hal had flung the double doors to the room open quite suddenly when he entered, making Zelda jump. She pinched the thistle tighter than she had intended to, and it was sharp.

'Ow!' she muttered, and dropped the thistle back into the small vase, which fell over and spilled water over the desk. 'Oh, no!'

Instinctively, she picked up her laptop and set it on the chair to avoid it getting wet, then looked around in vain for a cloth to soak up the water. Mercifully, the little vase hadn't broken.

'Wait there.' Hal went out into the hallway and returned swiftly with some old cloths which he used to mop up the spill. 'There. Good as new.'

'Jeez, I'm so sorry. That'll teach me to fantasise about being Mrs de Winter.' Zelda inspected the paper pad and peeled off a few damp sheets from the underside.

'What?' Hal looked at her, amused.

'Oh. I was just being stupid. I was thinking about that book, *Rebecca*. That's all.' Zelda dropped the wet paper into the bin, keenly aware that she sounded like an idiot.

'Daphne du Maurier? Great book. Although a wee bit dated now, eh?' Hal clicked his tongue to the dog, a silky-eared brown spaniel who came to sniff Zelda's ankles. 'Finnegan! Basket!' he added.

'It's okay, I like dogs.' Zelda was grateful for a distraction from her clumsiness. 'Hey, Finnegan. Who's a good boy?' She crouched down and scratched the dog's ears. 'You're a good boy. Yes, you are.'

Hal set the vase back upright.

'You like du Maurier, then?' he asked, with a smile. The dog padded over to a dog bed in the corner.

'Yeah. I guess *Rebecca* is dated in some ways. The sexual politics. The way Rebecca herself is demonised by the end. But it's also so romantic.'

'The guy murders his first wife, as I recall.' Hal walked to a bookshelf and pulled out a blue leather-bound volume. Returning to Zelda, he placed it in her hands. 'Isnae what I think of as romantic. But, if ye like it, and as a thanks for all ye hard work, ye should have this.'

'What's this?' Zelda turned over the book. She opened the cover and looked inside: *Rebecca* by Daphne du Maurier. 'I can't take this. It's a first edition.'

'Have it. I won't read it,' he insisted. 'That one belonged to my grandmother. She was kinda like ye. Feisty. She'd have liked ye tae have it.'

'Are you sure?' Zelda looked at the book again: it was in perfect condition. 'This is so sweet of you. And your grandmother.'

'Aye. Books're meant to be read. Anyway, I have tae apologise for last time I saw ye. It wasnae right o' me tae fly off the handle like that, about Maggie's room. I know ye were just tryin' tae help.' Hal sat down on the oxblood leather sofa next to the desk.

Zelda got up from the desk, and sat next to him instead. 'Oh, no, Hal. *I'm* so sorry. I should never have said what I did. It was so insensitive.' Zelda put down the book and took his hand, on instinct. 'More than anyone, I should have known how you feel. And you were right. Visiting mom's dry-cleaning shop, that's the thing that keeps me sane. It's not mine any more, but I still like to go back there. Just so I can stand where her feet used to stand. We lived in an apartment above the shop, too. I can't go into it any more because the new owners have moved in, but I sometimes stand outside it and wish I could. It's home, you know?' She wiped a tear from her eye. 'It tears me up that I can't go inside any more. I dream about it, all the time.'

'Ach, Zelda.' Hal took her hand in both of his. 'I know exactly how it feels. And at least I still live here, ye know? I can walk intae her room anytime I want. I cannae imagine what it'd be like not tae be able to any more.' He reached into his pocket and handed her a cotton handkerchief, embroidered with his monogram: HC. 'Go on. It's clean.'

Zelda took it thankfully, fighting the tears that wanted to burst out of her in a flood. 'I know. It's rough,' she croaked. 'I'm sorry. I didn't mean to come up here and cry all over you. Thanks, also, for this.' She gestured with the handkerchief.

'It's okay. Keep it. Look at me, I'm at it too.' He wiped his eyes, and laughed shakily. 'What a pair, eh?'

'Ugh. We're pathetic!' Zelda blew her nose in the handkerchief. She looked up into his eyes and, though they had both just been moved to tears, there was that sudden, electric connection again.

Zelda felt the strong urge to lean into Hal's craggy frame, thinking how much she could do with a hug, but she resisted. They really didn't know each other that well: she didn't want her intentions to be misconstrued. But, jeez, there was something so *right* about him. And these moments of pure electricity between them... she didn't know how to account for those. It went beyond Zelda's usual, rational world.

'All right, come on. Let's get back tae the real world, eh? Show me what ye've been up tae. Then I've asked Anna tae bring us in some lunch. All right?' Hal patted her shoulder awkwardly, but Zelda knew he was being kind and felt slightly mortified, but also touched.

'Oh, awesome. Yes. Thank you.' Zelda's stomach took that moment to rumble. *Jeez, stomach*, she thought. *What happened to the days of tomato salads and energy bars? Now you're making noise if no one's fed you every two hours.*

'Sounds like it can't come quick enough.' Hal leant towards her a little so that he could see the laptop screen.

'Okay, this is where I am.' Zelda started showing Hal the site. 'Your old site was impenetrable, so I made this new one. Look. It's super easy to manage. It's clean, professional...' Determined to focus on the task in hand and not get swept away in her emotions, she clicked through the pages she had built over a couple of days, copying most of the text from the original website and making some improvements here and there. 'We can still use your domain name if you give me permission to move it over.'

'Wow! Zelda, this looks amazin'.' Hal stared at the laptop as he flicked through the new website pages. 'You have my permission. I hated that auld interface.'

'Yeah. This one's way easier. See, you just drag and drop your page elements, like this.' Her arm brushed Hal's as she moved her finger on the mouse pad, and a shiver went up her spine.

She caught his eye, looking up in surprise at the electric connection. Hal had also felt something, she could tell: there was an expression in his eyes that belied his usual composure.

He cleared his throat. 'So, let's see these photos,' he suggested, moving his arm away from hers infinitesimally.

'Right. Photos.' Zelda clicked on the cloud drive Brody had sent her and started going through them.

'These're pure brilliant, Zelda,' Hal breathed, as she flicked through the images. 'The castle looks so bonny.'

'That's because it is bonny,' Zelda replied. 'Okay. Are we ready to see the ones of us being a couple?'

'Go on, then.' Hal put his hand over his eyes. 'I still cannae believe I did it.'

Zelda started clicking through the shots of them both in their fine clothes. 'It's cool. You can look. They're pretty good.' She gazed in astonishment at the pictures of them together. She knew that Hal was good-looking, but she hadn't realised he would be this photogenic. Not everyone was: some people were stunning in person, but it didn't translate onto the camera. But Hal was clearly a natural model: at the shoot, he had taken direction from Brody surprisingly well for a hard-headed Scotsman and Laird, used to being the boss.

It was only now that Zelda could see just how good the angles of Hal's cheekbones were for a photographer. How his smile smouldered as he looked at her in the photos. And the way his eyes never left hers as they linked arms, laughed and leant in towards each other.

'Wow. Ye look beautiful.' Hal leant in towards her, his arm brushing hers again. The same shiver resonated through Zelda's body. It wasn't just that: even without him touching her, there was a kind of energetic presence or link between them. Zelda was very aware of Hal's body; of the magnetic aura that surrounded him.

'Thank you. It was weird, wearing a wedding dress,' she said, talking to cover the feeling she had of being overpowered by whatever energy it was coursing between them.

Oh, Zelda, she thought. *Don't be coy. You know exactly what energy this is.*

'Well, ye look comfortable in it. Like it was made for ye,' Hal said, quietly, as Zelda came to stop on the last photo of them gazing into each other's eyes.

With her professional eye, Zelda could see it was the best of the bunch: Brody had captured a moment between them that felt authentic. They were the picture of the happy couple, and both of them looked good: no half-closed eyes, no double chins, no hair out of place.

As a woman, and without assessing the picture for its technical merits, Zelda remembered what that moment had been like: staring deep into Hal's eyes had been exposing and intimate. Feeling his eyes caress her with a depth of intimacy it was unusual to share with someone who was a mere acquaintance had been... erotic. That was the only word there was for it.

'You look pretty good too,' Zelda murmured, as they both stared at the picture. 'You... photograph very well.'

That same erotic current was there, again, between them. He could be infuriating, stubborn and stuck in his ways, but he also carried a deep pain that she understood intimately.

Perhaps, if there was a chemistry between them, it was connected to that, somehow.

'Thank you,' he replied huskily, as she turned her gaze upon him. 'Zelda, I...' Hal placed his hand lightly on her knee. 'I've wanted...' He leant in towards her.

He's going to kiss me, Zelda thought, every sense alert. Her lips parted and she leant in gently towards him, her body taking control. Every part of her wanted Hal. She wanted him to kiss her. To touch her. Instinct had taken over, and she wanted to be inside this zinging, warm energy for as long as she could.

Suddenly, the doors opened again and Anna swept in, pushing a steel cart. Finnegan barked at the sudden entry, and the moment between Hal and Zelda was broken.

'Lunch!' Anna called, brightly. 'Oh, there you are. I'll just lay it out for you. Hallo, Zelda,' she added. 'Good to see you.'

'Good to see you too, Anna.' Zelda stood up, dislodging Hal's hand from her knee. Anna didn't show any sign of noticing anything, and busied herself transferring plates to the dining table and chairs at the other end of the room.

Not that there was anything to notice, Zelda told herself.

Nothing had happened. There had been a moment, that was all. A badly judged moment of... what? Weakness? Lust? Sympathy?

It was all Daphne du Maurier's fault. Maybe Zelda had invoked the spirit of the romantic novel by talking about it, or imagining herself as the mistress of the castle. She'd even kind of re-enacted the scene of the broken porcelain figure, even though she wasn't Hal's new bride, and she wasn't (as far as she knew) being psychologically haunted by Hal's dead wife.

Did she want a romantic tryst with a Laird? *Hey, I wouldn't rule it out*, she thought. Trysts sounded like fun. What was a tryst, anyway? Like a fling? Or like a one-night stand? Maybe she'd write about it for her column: 'My Scottish Life: To Tryst or Not to Tryst'.

Zelda, you're spiralling, she thought. *Get a hold of yourself.*

It had just been a moment. That was all. Honestly, who wouldn't go a little weak at the knees, looking at photos of themselves posed in romantic photos with a hot Laird? Especially when they'd just bared their souls to each other. It was only natural that things might have felt a little... personal. But it was no more than that. Could she really see herself as the Lady of a castle in the middle of nowhere – no matter how charming it was?

No. Zelda, you're a city girl and you always have been, she thought to herself as she followed Hal to the table. *People have awkward moments where chemistry gets in the way. That happens. It's just pheromones. Chemicals in your brain. And the heady mix of wedding dresses, castles and romantic novels. You just got a little fried for a sec.*

'Well, this all looks yummy,' she said, sitting down at the table. *See, I'm making normal conversation. None of that eye-gazing, leaning-in-to-kiss stuff happened*, Zelda thought firmly. *Nothing to see here. All super normal.*

'Anna, why don't you get a plate and join us?' Hal pulled out a chair.

Anna looked surprised. 'Me? I... that's... very kind of you, Hal, but I have work to get on with in the kitchen,' she demurred.

'Please, Anna. Join us. It'd be great to get your opinion on the new website, and the photos,' Zelda added. Hal clearly didn't want to be left alone with her again, and she didn't want to have to sit through a lunch full of uncomfortable silences while he tried to pretend he hadn't just made a pass at her.

If Hal was going to ignore what had just happened, then so was she. Anna would make the perfect buffer.

'Oh... well, if you're sure.' Anna frowned, looking at them both. 'I'll... just get myself a plate.'

While the housekeeper went to a cabinet at the side of the room, Zelda lifted the silver tureen lid and peeked inside, keen to avoid Hal's gaze. 'Mmm. What's this?' she asked, sniffing a heady scent of curry.

'Coronation chicken and rice,' Anna replied, coming to stand next to her. 'It's a kind of British version of a curry. Created for the Queen's coronation in 1953. Not very spicy, but fruity. You'll like it.' She spooned a generous amount onto Zelda's plate, and pulled some cling film off a dish of white rice. 'Help yourself, dear,' she added, as she filled Hal's plate.

Hal cleared his throat. Silence filled the room, and Anna looked in confusion from one to the other.

'Thank ye, Anna.' Hal took his plate and helped himself to rice.

'This is really good,' Zelda said, to break the silence.

'Glad you like it.' Anna nodded, sitting down. 'So, how are the photos?'

'Perfect,' Zelda said, at the same time as Hal replied, 'Beautiful.'

'They're just what we need,' Hal said, looking uncomfortable at them speaking over each other. 'I must find a way to pay you, Zelda. Seeing as I can't pay you actual money, as per the rules of your visitor visa.'

'Yeah. I was going to mention that.' Zelda was grateful for the chance to change the subject.

'I cannae pay ye in rare books, I'm guessin',' Hal added.

'We'll think of something. I mean, I've got this writing gig now for *The New Yorker*, so things aren't as bad as they might have been.' Zelda spooned rice onto her plate. 'I tell you one thing that would be good, though. You should bring back the May Day festival. Party. Whatever it was.'

'Well, dinnae tek this the wrong way, but I'm nae goin' tae hold a huge party just because ye want me to,' Hal replied.

'Well, I was thinking I'd share some of the photos in the column.' Zelda chewed some chicken; it was delightfully tender. 'I thought I could start it with a kind of "Reader, I married him" joke, and then explain what we were actually doing. Like, actually, if I write something in the column about how we're trying to better promote the castle for weddings, people are going to be interested. And it'd be amazing publicity for Loch Cameron.'

'Oooh. That's a great idea!' Anna interjected. 'I love that.'

'I dunno.' Hal frowned. 'What if we get too much interest?'

'Hal – how much is too much? That you get booked out? Oh, no!' Zelda looked at him askance. 'That's what you wanted. Right?'

'Aye. I guess so.' Hal grinned. 'It's just all a bit... sudden.'

'Well, that's me. Making it rain.' Zelda rubbed her fingers together to indicate money. 'Though, here, that usually means actual rain. I could write a whole column about that.'

'It's part of Scotland's charm.' Anna laughed. 'Maybe don't mention it too much to your American readers after all, if we want those bookings.'

'Fair. But, listen, Hal – this May Day party. I'd really love to be able to write about it for the column. And the villagers really want it. I was just talking to Fiona the other day, at Fiona's Fashions? She was positively sad that there hadn't been one in the past couple of years. The whole village really wants to get together and have an opportunity to let their hair down.'

Zelda wanted to bring the castle back to life again, for him. Because she knew the hell he'd been living in, and she could see how much he deserved some happiness.

Hal was silent for a moment.

'That was Maggie's thing,' he said, quietly. 'I dunno if I want tae bring it back. It's been two years we've not done it: no' last year, as she'd passed, and the year before, she was too ill.'

'D'you think Maggie would want you to continue the tradition, in her honour?' Zelda asked softly. 'I don't mean to push you. It's your decision, and I'm definitely not trying to use Maggie's memory to get my own way here. I'm really not. But, from what I've heard about Maggie, she was really loved. What better way to remember her than to dedicate the party to her?'

'She's got a point, Hal,' Anna said. 'I agree. I'd love to see May Day come back. And the village hasn't been the same without it.'

'I'll think aboot it,' he said. 'That's all. Okay?'

'Okay.' Zelda nodded. 'That's fair.'

'All right, then.'

There was another silence, but not an awkward one. Anna caught Zelda's eye across the table and winked.

If Maggie *was* haunting the old castle, *Rebecca*-style, Zelda thought, then she'd probably be pleased about this development. And Anna, as housekeeper, seemed much nicer than evil old Mrs Danvers.

However, the whole setup *was* still very Daphne du Maurier, despite being in Scotland.

It was the perfect topic for her column.

A CASTLE, A LOCH AND ABSOLUTELY NO ROMANCE

By Zelda Hicks for *The New Yorker*

Use #zeldasscottishlife to share and comment

Daphne du Maurier's opening line in her most famous novel, *Rebecca*, opens with her narrator describing a dream of the hero's manor house, Manderley.

Like the unnamed heroine of the book, I too have found myself in an unfamiliar landscape, and discovered a local, pretty grumpy Lord (Laird, in Scotland) with a huge castle. However, his housekeeper is a delight, and none of us have fallen in love with each other.

Why am I here, you might ask? Well, I've temporarily found myself stranded here after a sudden change of job, and *The New Yorker*, in all its wisdom, saw my online posting about this tiny little Scottish loch-side community and thought you'd all be interested to know what life's like here. So, I'm going to do my best to paint as vivid and true a picture as I can for you from over here in bonny Scotland, home of haggis, thistles and an unreasonable amount of rain.

By the way, the very fact that anyone lives in a castle in the present day and is a real person, not a fictional paramour or a Disney prince/ss, blows my mind. I'm from the Bronx. Castles are not part of my mental landscape.

Sure, people have housekeepers. I've interviewed some pretty high-net-worth individuals in my time, so I know how these things roll. Lots of people have staff. Private chefs. Private security. Personal assistants. But pretty much none of the super-rich I've met are living in the castle that their ancestors have lived in for five hundred years, hung with portraits of their great-great-great-great-great-grandfathers and decorated with the swords, claymores (look it up) and daggers that their ancestors fought wars with other clans with.

Hal Cameron, the current Laird of Loch Cameron, tells me that he has one housekeeper, a staff of about five cleaners and a team of groundspeople. Other than that, he does everything alone, which is quite the flex for a visiting American journalist to get her head around. Wait, no below-stairs hordes of maids in white 'pinnies' whispering behind doors? No butlers?

I feel betrayed.

It's weird, being in Scotland for the first time. It's bringing up some stuff about family that I didn't know was simmering away in me, and it's also making me miss my mom a whole lot. She passed over a few months back, and I think this is the first time I've actually given myself time to take a breath and grieve for her properly. She wasn't from here: she was born and bred in the Bronx. But she was my rock, and I've felt unmoored from the real world since I lost her. If you're reading this and you've lost someone, then you know how it is.

It sucks.

However, there's something about being in this tiny Scottish village that's kinda... wholesome. Maybe it's the food (I've put on six pounds already; I actually don't hate it) or maybe it's living in a literal picture postcard with views to die for. And, the air's *clean*. Like, oxygen-bar clean. All that helps.

But, most of all, it's the community. People are like a family here. They care. When there was a power cut, the Laird walked around the village, checking to see if the old folks were okay. When I went to buy walking boots in the only shop here that sells clothes, the owner befriended me, and the next time I went in, we had tea and biscuits.

I love how nice people are here. And being among them is

somehow giving me the mental head space to remember my mom. And for that, I'm super grateful.

Anyway, maybe because I appreciate Loch Cameron so much (or maybe because I also love a good party), I'm trying to persuade the Laird to resurrect the annual May Day party at the castle: a traditional celebration held for the whole village. It's not going to be a costume ball (or 'fancy dress' as they call it here) but there would be a bonfire, dancing, food and drink.

Unfortunately, the Laird isn't on social media, so I can't ask you to @ him and persuade him to have the party. However, I'm going to try my hardest to get this to happen so that I can report back to you, dear readers – and because I genuinely think it would be a good thing for the village to get together and celebrate all their successes, mourn their losses and be grateful for everything they have here.

Lastly, if you have a moment, please take a look at Loch Cameron Castle's new website. I've been helping the Laird update it to showcase what a gem of a place this really is. Yes, that's me, with the actual Laird Hal Cameron, looking faux-romantically into each other's eyes. Yes, it was excruciating, but someone had to step in and help show the world what a great castle this truly is. Wedding bookings for all real couples are open.

Comments:

Zabarsloveme: You guys look like a real couple tho (smiling emoji)

NewYorkGal: We want to know more about the Laird, like is he single? I would live in a castle 100%

BrooklynBabe: Couple goals

Mets68: 'faux-romantically' (laughing emoji)

TWENTY-THREE

'You know, a man could die from thirst, painting this door,'
Ryan called to Zelda as he sat in the small hallway of Queen's
Point Cottage, paintbrush in one hand and a jar of white paint
next to him.

A paint-spattered tarpaulin covered the old rose-pink carpet
that Zelda had hired a standing carpet cleaner for. She had
asked Ryan to come over and help her with it tomorrow, but he
had offered to come today too, to speed along the painting in the
hallway.

'Cup of tea?' Zelda stuck her head around the door she was
painting at the opposite end of the hall.

'You're an angel sent from heaven, so you are.' Ryan sighed.

'Fair. And I could do with a break.' Zelda stood up,
adjusting the scarf she'd tied around her hair. Since it was so
long now, she'd tied it up in a bun – and found a drawer full of a
delightful array of Gretchen's retro floral scarves to protect it.
She doubted Gretchen would mind her borrowing one.

She went into the little kitchen and stretched both arms up
to the ceiling, adding in a few impromptu standing stretches.
She hadn't been able to do much yoga since breaking her wrist,

and her body was crying out for her normal routine. Zelda thought wistfully about the yoga studio she normally went to in New York; usually, she managed to go at least a couple of times a week before work.

Things sure are different here in Loch Cameron, she said to herself in a mock-country voice. For one thing, she hardly ever woke up before nine nowadays. Her new routine was pulling on the cosy bathrobe she'd bought at Fiona's Fashions – over her just-as-cosy pyjamas – and padding through to Gretchen's kitchen to make breakfast. Then, she'd either catch up with any messages or read – she was halfway through two of the books she'd bought at Ryan's shop, and had held on to a few paperback romances she'd liked the look of from Gretchen's books. Then she'd have a shower and spend the rest of the day painting and cleaning the cottage – or, as much as her wrist allowed, even though she was using her left hand for most of it.

As Zelda had been painting – plain white, as instructed by Gretchen, apart from a flash of pink in the sitting room – she had started thinking about how nice the cottage would be if it was redecorated properly. It would have to be sympathetic to the cottage and the area itself, of course: there was no point in doing a baroque makeover, or a Japanese minimalist approach. But Zelda had a great eye for interiors, and it had always been a bit of a passion of hers.

She selected a couple of mugs Gretchen had said it was okay to keep, filled the kettle with water and turned on the gas hob, placing the kettle on it carefully with her left hand.

Most of Gretchen's possessions had now either been taken into storage, sold or passed on to her grandson in Glasgow. Zelda wondered if there was anyone else, but Gretchen hadn't told her if there was. Zelda knew that Ryan had given Gretchen a cheque for several thousand pounds for her books, which would no doubt come in useful. Otherwise, there was a small double bed that Zelda was sleeping in, a sofa and the kitchen table and chairs. Other than that, it was all gone.

Zelda's phone rang, and she glanced at it. *Speak of the devil*, she thought, seeing Gretchen's name on the screen. She answered it and set it on speaker as she made the tea.

'Hi, Gretch,' she called out.

'Hallo, darling Zelda. I just thought I'd call to see how it was all going. Not too early for you, I hope?'

Zelda could hear voices in the background; she guessed Gretchen was in the lounge or one of the other communal areas of the care home.

'No, of course not. We're just taking a break from painting.' She poured the hot water from the kettle into the teapot. 'How are you?'

'Oh, all settled in, thanks. I've just had my hair done and I'm about to get a manicure. I just wanted to remind you that there are some spare brushes and rollers in the shed at the end of the garden, if you want them.'

'Oh, okay. Sounds like you're living the high life, Gretch.' Zelda grinned.

'Ah, well, mustn't grumble,' Gretchen muttered. 'The food is acceptable, though I'd kill for a filet mignon.'

'Just send one of your boyfriends out to get you one,' Zelda suggested. 'I know you've already got a harem going in there.'

'Zelda Hicks! I have no such thing.' Gretchen sounded pleasantly scandalised. 'I can't help it if these old duffers find me fascinating, somehow. Give me George Clooney any day.'

'Tea?' Ryan appeared in the doorway of the kitchen, side-stepping the wet paint on the door.

'Oh, who's that?' Gretchen enquired. 'Is that Ryan's voice?'

She doesn't miss a trick, this one, Zelda thought.

'Certainly is. Hi, Gretchen. How are you today?' Ryan enquired, his voice smooth and charming.

'Oh, all the better for hearing you, young man.' Gretchen giggled in a thoroughly uncharacteristic manner.

'Milk,' Zelda mouthed, pointing at the fridge.

Ryan took it out for her and set it on the side. 'I'm helping Zelda with the decorating,' Ryan explained, winking at Zelda and taking the mug from her when she'd poured the milk into the tea. 'Two hands are better than one, so they say.'

'Hmm. You just make sure that's all your hands are doing,' Gretchen chided him playfully. 'I don't want you distracting my Zelda from her work. I know what you Irishmen are like.'

'Gretchen. That is completely unfair,' Ryan protested, laughing. 'I'm helping out a lady. That's all.'

'Hmm. Very gentlemanly of you, I'm sure,' Gretchen teased him.

'Gretch? While I've got you, d'you think Hal might let me decorate in here?' Zelda looked around at the kitchen, and out into the hallway. 'Like, properly, not just making everything as plain as possible? This place has such a lot of character. It'd be amazing to bring that out, but in a way that a potential tenant would like. I'm thinking of whoever comes in after me, to rent it, y'know?' She'd been mulling over the idea all morning, while she and Ryan had been in the process of painting everything white. It seemed a shame not to bring out the cottage's own signature style a little more: she was imagining subtle florals, vintage pieces and cosy vibes.

'That's a nice idea, Zelda dear. Would you ask him for me, though? I've got so much to do, and I might forget.' Gretchen sounded distracted. 'Anyway, I should go. My manicure's waiting. I just wanted to check everything was okay, and remind you about the brushes.'

'All right, Gretch. Enjoy! I'll speak to you soon.'

'Goodbye, dear. And goodbye, Ryan.'

'Bye, Gretchen,' Ryan called out.

Zelda hung up. 'She's amazing. Sharp as a tack. I hope I'm like her when I'm old.'

'Yeah. They broke the mould when they made Gretchen Ross.' Ryan grinned. 'So, you want to make more of this place? Why? I thought you were just doing this so you could live here rent-free for a while.'

'I am. But I've got attached to the place. I thought it'd be nice, that's all. And it's a project for me. I've always been into interiors, and it'd be good experience for me, you know?'

'Sure, it'd be grand. But Hal's a grumpy bugger. He might say no.'

'Hmm. Maybe. I'll ask him when I see him. I was planning to pop up tomorrow.'

'You're seeing a lot of the Laird.' Ryan pouted. 'I have to tell you I was mortally offended you didn't ask me to come up and play weddings with you. I would have dropped everything.'

She'd texted Ryan after the day's shoot at the castle. 'Well, the model cancelled at the last minute. So, Hal had to step in.' Zelda rolled her eyes. 'I wish I had asked you. But Hal and I seem to be friends now.'

'Ah, Laird Cameron would have hated it if I'd modelled.' Ryan looked wistful. 'I would have loved to have seen the look on his face if we were canoodling for the camera.'

'Well, Hal and I weren't *canoodling*.' Zelda felt a blush creep into her cheeks at the suggestion: a sudden, visceral memory of Hal's smouldering stare flashed into her mind, followed by the moment at the castle when the Laird had leant in to kiss her. She cleared her throat. 'It was all very professional.'

'I'm sure, I'm sure.' Ryan held up his hands. 'And I loved your column, by the way. Really great.'

'Oh, thanks. It's my first one, so I was really kinda nervous about how it'd go down. People seem to like it so far, though, and my editor at *The New Yorker* was happy.'

Zelda had actually been quite worried about the column going live. She'd worked at *The Village Receiver* for some time, so she was used to having her name in the by-line for her stories, but that was a different kind of writing. Anything for *The Village Receiver* was always straight fashion, books, art or theatre: nothing personal.

The column was something altogether different. Zelda was being herself, on paper and online, for thousands of readers. She'd had a couple of nightmares about being trolled online for something she'd said, but so far, that hadn't happened. Instead, she'd got some more Instagram followers, and a lot more comments on her pictures of herself and Hal playing at weddings.

She hoped Hal didn't read the comments, because they were generally of the opinion that Hal and Zelda looked great together.

'Don't get me wrong,' said Ryan. 'I know you're helping him out. And it was all for show, right? Otherwise I'd be horribly jealous.'

'Of course it was.' Zelda knew that Ryan was naturally dramatic in the way he expressed himself; there was no reason for him to be horribly jealous, seeing as they'd only seen each other a few times. 'Biscuit?'

Ryan took a gulp of his tea. 'Perfect. I'm famished.'

'Hmm. I saw a packet of ginger nuts in the cupboard, whatever they are.' Zelda took down the biscuits from inside one of the kitchen cupboards and handed it to Ryan. 'What d'you mean, anyway, that he would have hated it if you were in the shoot? Don't you two get along?'

'Not so you'd notice.' Ryan shook his head. 'Safe to say that the Laird doesn't have much time for me.'

'Why?' Zelda thought back to the first day she'd walked into Ryan's bookshop and Hal had come in. He had been pretty frosty to Ryan. Yet, Fiona and Dotty seemed to think highly of him. And he could be charming when he wanted to be... Zelda was distracted for a second, then blinked. *Zelda. Quit it.*

'Agh. Long story.' Ryan made a face.

'Tell me,' Zelda insisted.

'Fine. You got it out of me.' Ryan put down his mug and looked out of the kitchen window onto Gretchen's overgrown garden. 'I was a good friend of Maggie, his wife. Well, you've probably heard by now that she passed away.' He looked sad.

'Yeah. She had an inherited condition, Fiona said.'

'Uh-huh. Huntington's disease. Poor lamb. Anyway, he nursed her for as long as he could, I'll give him that – when it got really bad, in that last year. But then he shut her up in one of the rooms in the castle, and she died there. No one was allowed to come and see her. No one was allowed to say goodbye. For months, all she had was him and a nurse. I know she would have wanted to see me. And the other people in the village. Hal Cameron denied us the chance to say goodbye.' Ryan's voice caught, and he took a deep breath. 'Sorry. It still hurts.'

'Jeez. That's awful. I'm so sorry.' Zelda laid her hand on Ryan's arm. 'I think I know the room you mean. I actually kinda had an argument with him about it. Pink velvet curtains? Lots of books.? All the furniture's covered over with dustsheets.'

'Yeah. That was Maggie's room. That was where she died.' Ryan shook his head. 'She loved it in there. But he made it her prison, and I will never forgive him for that.'

'I suggested we take pictures in there for the photoshoot. And that he should open the upstairs of the castle to the public. For weddings and parties,' Zelda explained.

'He doesn't want people going in there, I guess. Maggie was the one who made sure he looked after the village. Now, he just hides up there like some kind of B-movie villain.' Ryan sighed. 'He hates me because I loved Maggie. He wanted her all to himself.'

'Wow. I had no idea about any of this.' Zelda frowned. 'I just thought he was grieving.'

'Well, I guess he is. But Maggie needed us in those final weeks. We needed to say goodbye. He stole that from us.'

'I was up there earlier this week. I suggested he bring back the May Day party. He said that was her thing. He wasn't keen on the idea.'

'I bet he wasn't. Miserable sod.' Ryan shook his head. 'I just can't get past it, you know?'

'I'm so sorry, Ryan.' Zelda put her hand on his. There may have been some chemistry between her and Hal, but Zelda hated cruelty. Refusing Maggie her last days in the company of her friends and loved ones was controlling behaviour, and she hadn't known that about Hal.

Grief affected everyone differently. Maybe it had made Hal Cameron mean and isolated. Zelda didn't know what to think. She had felt such a connection with Hal, and she knew that he understood her grief for her mom.

'When you get under the skin of a place like Loch Cameron, you find a lot of secrets. This place probably has a lot of stories to tell, too.' Ryan waved his hand to take in the cottage.

'Gretchen's cottage?' Zelda was relieved at the change of subject. 'Oh, she told me that story about Mary Queen of Scots coming here to meet her lover. Lord something or other.'

'Lord Darnley. Yeah, I've heard that story too. I very much doubt it's true.'

'Maybe it is. I like the idea of it being a romantic rendezvous.' Zelda smiled.

'Yeah, I guess.' Ryan's expression softened. 'In which case, you know, we shouldn't disappoint the house.'

'Are we having a romantic rendezvous? Because I thought we were painting doors in an old cottage.' Zelda bantered back.

'We are.' Ryan leant towards her, setting his cup on the

table. 'But I've wanted to kiss you ever since you walked into my shop, Zelda Hicks,' he added, in a husky voice.

Zelda had a moment of panic. She wasn't averse to the idea of Ryan kissing her. He was good-looking and charming, and she knew he liked her. But she was conflicted. There was something between her and Hal, even though it never seemed to come to anything.

But Zelda didn't move away from Ryan. Yes, she was a little attracted to Hal. But Hal was still grieving for Maggie, and Zelda didn't want to get in the way of that. She doubted Hal had any room in his heart for someone new, even if she'd wanted to pursue something with him.

Ryan was uncomplicated; he had no ongoing romantic drama or lost love that Zelda was aware of, and she definitely knew that he liked her, because he had just told her. Unlike Hal.

Gently, Ryan's lips met hers: for Zelda there was something in the feeling of the kiss like diving into a sun-warmed swimming pool after a day lying on a sun lounger, reading a novel. It was sensuous, sweet and... *welcome,* somehow.

Ryan knew how to kiss a girl. After the first few seconds, Zelda knew she could relax and lean into it without worrying he was going to stab his tongue into her mouth like some guys did, or try to lick her teeth. Ryan didn't take the kiss as an opportunity to feel her up, either, which Zelda definitely appreciated. He smelt of clean cotton and paint. It was a good, wholesome kiss, yet with the promise of Ryan's ability to be distinctly less wholesome, if she wanted him to.

And, like the kiss, Scotland seemed to be one of those places that got better the more you leant into it. Zelda reflected that if the straight women she knew in New York found out there were men like Ryan here, there would definitely be an upswing in tourism to Loch Cameron. Because all women were looking for a man who could kiss like this.

In a world of tongue-stabbers, teeth-lickers, gropers and spiked drinks, a gentlemanly kiss from a charming Irishman was definitely very welcome.

A little later, after Ryan had departed for the evening, Zelda felt that he had left her with – though it was an unfortunate pun – a nasty taste in her mouth. She hadn't liked what he'd told her about Hal Cameron, and it played on her mind. Was Hal really the controlling Laird Ryan was making him out to be? Or was he simply a man lost in his own grief?

Zelda wasn't sure what to think, and she wasn't sure what to make of Ryan, either, only because he seemed like such a smooth talker. She found it very difficult to trust any man, and the idea that Hal might be hiding a darker side filled her with trepidation. Though nothing had happened with him, she felt her customary fears rising up within her at the thought of them getting any closer.

Her instinct was to keep both men at arm's length. That way, neither of them could hurt her. But as she got into bed that night, shivering with cold – the windows were open to let the smell of fresh paint subside – she thought about her mom, who had always taught her to be brave. Was it brave to keep a distance from Ryan or Hal? She didn't know. But she was unsure *how* to put her heart on the line for either of them, even if she wanted to.

Trust was so difficult for Zelda, and Ryan hadn't made it any easier for her to trust Hal Cameron. Yet, she found that she really *wanted* to, and she didn't quite know why. It was just a feeling, and Zelda had trained herself not to rely on her feelings for men.

Nevertheless, as she curled up under the thick goose-down duvet and the pile of blankets on top of it, she thought of Hal, and the moment they had shared that day at the stone circle.

She had felt she could trust him. And now, Ryan had made her doubt that, and doubt herself.

Yet, it was usually right for her to doubt her instincts when it came to men. Because she'd never met one she could really trust, apart from Emery. So, Ryan was probably right. And that thought made her deeply sad.

TWENTY-FOUR

The next day, Zelda started to clear out a storage cupboard in the corner of Gretchen's, and now her, bedroom.

Zelda adored the bedroom in the cottage. It wasn't huge, and it was sparsely furnished, seeing as most of Gretchen's stuff had gone into storage now. But there was something about the simplicity of the cast-iron bed frame with its curlicued iron and the cosy quilts on top that made Zelda feel like she was at home. In the corner, an old brass lamp with a pink tasselled lampshade threw a warm glow over everything, and she had got very fond of lying propped up in bed at night with a mug of tea, reading romance novels by its light.

The bedroom window looked out onto the loch. Zelda loved that she could lie in bed in the morning and listen to the birds circle the rocky outcropping of Queen's Point. She didn't know much about wildlife at all, not least whatever the local Scottish birds were, but she'd held on to a slim field guide of local birds when she'd been clearing out Gretchen's cottage. So far, she'd seen buzzards, gulls and she thought she'd spotted an osprey too, plus other assorted smaller birds that chattered and twittered in Gretchen's overgrown garden.

Zelda hadn't had a chance to do anything about the garden yet. Gretchen hadn't asked her to, but she thought it would be a kind surprise to sort out the outside as well as the inside of the old cottage. However, Zelda had been out there for an hour with a rusty pair of secateurs she'd found in an overgrown, spider-filled shed at the end of the garden before she admitted defeat. The garden remained wild. Zelda wasn't great at identifying flowers, but she'd downloaded an app that could do it if you pointed the camera at the plant. So far, she'd identified various shrubs as well as what felt like twenty or more wild rose bushes. She loved the colours and the intricate shapes of the flowers, and the sound of the bees droning around them in the evenings.

The cupboard sat behind a door painted blue; the same blue as the windowpanes and the front door, which contrasted with the white walls of the cottage. It stuck slightly when Zelda tried to pull it open, and then flung itself open suddenly, almost hitting her in the face. She swore, her heart racing.

Inside, boxes stuffed with papers vied with more old books, and the occasional blanket, for space. Zelda sighed, and started pulling the boxes out.

Gretchen had given her carte blanche to sort through any books or bric-a-brac she had left behind, but she'd asked that personal papers be set aside and brought to her.

Zelda started making a pile of books on the bed, wondering if Ryan would be interested in any of them. She picked up the lighter boxes of paperwork and carried them into the hallway, making a neat line of them by the front door.

One box was too heavy for her to lift, so Zelda crouched down in the storage cupboard and flicked through the contents to see what was in it. Inside was a series of photo albums. Zelda smiled and took one out, flicking through the black and white photos pasted carefully inside, separated by tissue-thin covering pages.

Zelda assumed the pictures depicted Gretchen as a young girl, but it was hard to recognise her in them: she had only known Gretchen the age she was now. However, one freckled girl seemed to feature in many of the photos. She was often pulling a cheeky face, or grinning from ear to ear. Zelda thought it might well be Gretchen.

As she ran a finger over the spines of the other albums, Zelda noticed a sheaf of papers sticking up between them and pulled them out, thinking she would add them to one of the paperwork boxes. Yet, when she worked them free – they were a little stuck to the old glue inside one of the photo albums – Zelda saw they were letters, brown with age and tied together with a frayed red ribbon.

Carefully, Zelda undid the ribbon. Realising it was quite hard to read the spidery writing on the fronts of the envelopes, she stepped out of the cupboard space and sat on the bed, where it was lighter. She spread the letters out in front of her on the pink wool blankets edged in an ancient, soft silk.

All the letters were addressed to the same person – Alice McQueen – at the cottage address: *The cottage, McQueen's Point, Loch Cameron*. Zelda stroked the old, brown envelope she held. Who was Alice McQueen, and why was there a bunch of her old letters in Gretchen Ross's cupboard? And how odd that Queen's Point had been called 'McQueen's Point' at some point in the past. Zelda guessed it must have changed over time.

She thought for a minute. She was curious to see what the letters said, but that would be intrusive, and she had promised to pass any paperwork she might find at the cottage to Gretchen.

However, the letters weren't addressed to Gretchen. Did that make it okay to read them?

Zelda sighed. It was still someone else's private stuff, so she shouldn't. Instead, she picked up her phone and called Gretchen's room in the nursing home, but no one answered.

Typical. Gretch was most likely playing dominoes, or having her hair done. She'd have to call later.

Or, you could just take the letters over, Zelda told herself. *Pay a visit to Gretchen at the same time. You haven't been yet.* That was a good idea. She could drive over: she still had the car a little longer.

Zelda piled up the letters together and put them on her bedside table, next to the reading lamp Gretchen had left for her. She called the main reception number at the care home and let them know she was planning to visit Gretchen the next day; the friendly receptionist confirmed that was fine, and that Gretchen was settling in well.

Zelda hung up, yawning. Cleaning up the old cottage was pretty tiring, and now she had a day of painting ahead of her. As she got changed into some old clothes Gretchen had left her to paint in, she thought about the letters, and all the people who had lived in the cottage over hundreds of years. There must be so many stories to tell; tomorrow, she hoped she would learn one of them.

TWENTY-FIVE

'Hallo. It's Zelda, isn't it?'

Zelda took a moment to recognise the woman next to her at the market stall, and then realised it was Anna, Hal Cameron's housekeeper.

'Anna? Hi!' Zelda was suddenly self-conscious about the large packet of fudge she was holding. 'Doing some shopping?'

'Aye. I like to come to the monthly market if I can. Support the small businesses. Plus, the bakery stall's amazing.' Anna pointed to a stall laden with loaves and shiny-looking buns halfway down the high street.

Zelda had been delighted to discover that Loch Cameron held a kind of farmers' market once a month, with all manner of local businesses coming to sell their local wares. The stalls all sported striped blue and white awnings that fluttered in the morning breeze, and the bright morning sun glittered on the loch behind them.

'It's really great. I love the local focus,' Zelda agreed. 'I wish I could buy more, but there's only so much I can carry,' she added.

Zelda had spent quite a few hours painting, but had had to

give up for the day when her wrist started complaining, so she'd walked down onto the high street and found the market.

'I'm glad I saw you.' Anna nodded. 'I've been meaning to talk to you about Hal. I agree with you, about the May Day party, you know. I've been trying to persuade him into it since you were up at the castle, but he's a stubborn so-and-so.' She broke off to smile at the man behind the stall. 'Hallo, Sandy. How's it going?'

The elderly man behind the stall beamed at Anna. 'Aye, no' bad, no' bad, Anna. And you?'

'I'm well, thanks. Sandy, this is Zelda Hicks. She's visiting us from America.'

'Ah, welcome, Zelda.' The man nodded shyly at her. 'Have ye tried the tablet?' Sandy picked up a plate filled with bits of a hard, crumbly-looking fudge and offered it to her.

'No, but I will.' Zelda took a piece; unlike the softer, chewy fudge she'd recently discovered, this was hard and very crumbly, and made her teeth ache from the sweetness. 'Wow. That's, like, pure sugar.'

'Aye. Lovely alongside a nice strong cup o' coffee,' Sandy beamed.

'Great. I'll take some.' Zelda passed him the bag she'd chosen earlier. 'And this one.' She handed over the money and stepped back to let a couple holding hands get closer to the stall. 'Thank you, Sandy.'

'Most welcome, Zelda. Nice tae meet ye.' The man nodded.

'I've emailed Hal some suggestions for decorations, fireworks, that kind of thing,' Zelda explained to Anna as they walked past other stalls selling local cheeses, the bakery stall and a lovely stall piled high with fresh organic fruit and vegetables. The next one sold jams, marmalades and chutneys, displayed in gleaming glass jars with red lids. Zelda wanted to buy them all; she imagined arranging them in a cosy cottage kitchen somewhere. 'But, no luck so far.'

'Hmm. Well, keep going,' Anna advised. 'I think he'll listen to you. I've talked about the old parties we had a few times; brought it up in conversation, that's all. Just reminding him about all the good times. But I agree, we should have it again. I'm concerned about Hal. He's virtually locked himself away in that castle since Maggie died. It's not healthy.'

'No, I can imagine.' Zelda stopped to look at a stall selling pretty scented candles, some poured into tea cups, and some traditional pillar candles. 'Look at these! Wouldn't it be amazing to have the whole castle lit by candlelight? Imagine that.'

'That would be lovely, though I'd worry about the fire risk.' Anna smiled wryly. 'But it would be very romantic. We used to have a hanging iron candelabra somewhere. An original one, from back in the day.' She looked thoughtful. 'Huge, it was. It used to hang in the great hall, before they had electricity at the castle. I bet it's up in one of those bedrooms. You saw some of those rooms, I think? Absolutely stuffed full of old treasures that he doesn't want to think about.' She sighed.

'Wow. That must have looked amazing.' Zelda tried to imagine the already grand great hall of the castle lit by candlelight.

'Yes. Smoky, though,' Anna added. 'I do remember my mother talking about having to strip down all the walls with sugar soap and then repaint everything. Honestly, that place is like the Forth Bridge. You finish painting it at one side, and it's time to start repainting it again.' She stopped when she saw Zelda's blank expression. 'Oh. The Forth Bridge? It's in Queensferry, near Edinburgh. Crosses the Firth of Forth. That's an estuary, going out to the North Sea. It's a red-painted iron bridge. Like the San Francisco Bay Bridge,' she added.

'Ah. Got it.' Zelda smiled. 'That's what they say about the Bay Bridge, too. And the Brooklyn Bridge. It's never finished.'

'Aye. Just the sheer scale of these things,' Anna replied. They turned back to the stalls, and Anna chose three loaves and a bag of glossy buns from the bakery. Zelda bought three, thinking she'd stash them in the cupboard at home for later.

'So, you should take my number,' Zelda suggested. 'And we can swap notes. You know, about the party and Hal. I think we can persuade him, between us. Like a pincer movement, or something.'

'Great.' Anna laughed. 'Give me your phone. I'll put my number in.' She tapped at Zelda's phone screen for a moment, and then handed it back to her. 'Okay. It was great to see you, Zelda. Let's keep in touch, okay?'

'Okay.' Zelda grinned. 'I'm totally not going to go and eat all this tablet in one go with a cup of coffee.'

'Oh, of course not!' Anna chuckled. 'I'd better get on. I'll see you soon, though? And stay in touch!'

'I will.' Zelda waved as Anna turned away towards the end of the high street, where the bridge led over to the castle.

Maybe this party is going to happen, after all.

TWENTY-SIX

'I'm so glad you came! I've been meaning to give you a call for a blether, but it's been chock-a-block since I got here.' Gretchen settled herself on the sofa in her room and arranged a blanket over her legs. 'Have a biscuit, dear. They're not bad.'

It was the next day, and Zelda had driven out to see Gretchen at the care home.

'No problem. Glad it's all working out.' Zelda sat on a chair facing her friend, the letters in her lap. 'Your hair looks gorgeous. And your nails. Hey, maybe I should move in here for a while. Look. I've even got paint in my hair.'

'It's very bohemian, dear. Suits you,' Gretchen sounded amused. 'Thank you for all your hard work. I do appreciate it, you know.' She sighed. 'Anyway, dear. How's the cottage? I do miss it.'

'It's coming along. Ryan's been giving me a hand here and there too.'

'So I gathered, when I called the other day.' Gretchen's eyes twinkled.

'*Gretch.* He's just being neighbourly.' Zelda hoped her tone conveyed that there was nothing going on between her and Ryan, because there wasn't.

Not yet, anyway.

'Hmm.' Gretchen pursed her lips. 'You make sure you keep an eye on that one, that's all I'll say. Pleasant young man. Very charming. A little *too* charming, I've always thought,' she added.

'Too charming?' Zelda ate a biscuit – by now she had learnt to call them 'biscuits' and not 'cookies'.

'Ah, well, let's just say Ryan O'Connell's had his share of girlfriends. And someone else's share as well.' Gretchen pursed her lips. 'And maybe there hasn't always been a lot of distance between one and the next, if you know what I mean.'

'Oh. I see. Well, nothing's happened between us, anyway,' Zelda said. They had kissed, and it had been nice. She liked Ryan, but keeping it casual was enough for her right now. She was still dealing with so much: her own grief, the loss of her job, and even her own identity, to some extent. Loch Cameron was bringing all of these things to the fore, and she knew it was helping her heal, slowly. But it was still painful.

'Hmm. You're a grown-up, so I'll trust your judgement,'

'Okay. Another thing: I was wondering if you'd given any more thought about me doing a bit more than just repainting everything and cleaning up. Remember, I mentioned it on the phone?' she reminded Gretchen.

'Hmm. I think you mentioned it.' Gretchen frowned.

'Maybe, I don't know – redecorating the place? Maybe styling it a little?' Zelda took out her phone and showed Gretchen some pictures of rooms styled in the simple but authentic cottage look she'd been thinking about. 'Look. Like, clean lines, but a little softness. Plants. Rattan. A few florals here and there, but nothing too girly. What do you think?'

Gretchen looked at the pictures Zelda showed her. 'I think it looks lovely, Zelda, but you need to ask Hal.'

'Okay. I'll ask him now.' Zelda tapped out a text to Hal and sent it.

Hi Hal. I know you're cool with me redecorating Gretchen's cottage, but I'm wondering if you'd let me design it a bit more than just repainting everything white? I promise I won't go crazy with the décor, but I thought it'd be nice to do something more stylish. At low cost, of course. Zelda x

Sure, he replied almost instantly. *Just no animal-print wallpaper. No neon-yellow sofas. I don't have a huge budget for renovations, so if you need new furniture, we could look at finding some second-hand.*

'See? He liked the idea.' Zelda was pleased.

'Ask Myrtle if you need furniture,' Gretchen suggested. 'She can get things.'

'Myrtle told me that was the guy who used to run the café before her. When it was a barber shop.' Zelda frowned. 'She doesn't do it. Anyway, that was the black market.'

'Eh. Myrtle's still our contact for things we need, as far as I know.' Gretchen blinked. 'She might've been a little economical with the truth with you.'

'Well, maybe. But I could source some stuff very low cost, or even free.' Zelda tapped her phone. 'You'd be amazed at the things people give away online. I've found a couple of apps where local people sell stuff or let you have it for free if you go and get it.'

'Wouldn't it just be rubbish, though, dear?' Gretchen looked at the app that Zelda showed her.

'One woman's rubbish is another woman's treasure, so they say,' Zelda replied.

'That's true. Goodness, look at those curtains! Ten pounds? I see what you mean.' Gretchen gave the phone back to Zelda. 'Anyway, it's not my place anymore.'

'No, but you can still help me, if you want. Just make sure I don't make it too New York.'

'Fair enough, dear.' Gretchen patted her hand. 'As long as Hal says it's okay.'

'Okay. So, anyway, my other reason for visiting.' Zelda handed Gretchen the letters that had been sitting in her lap. 'Not that I didn't want to come and see you anyway.'

'Of course.' Gretchen smiled, taking the letters. 'What are these?'

'I was sorting out the cupboard in the bedroom yesterday, and I found them,' Zelda explained. 'They kinda looked interesting, but I didn't want to open them without you saying it was okay. I mean, I assume they're addressed to a relative of yours, or something?'

'Oh! How intriguing.' Gretchen reached for her glasses, which hung on a beaded necklace around her neck. 'Hmm. Let's see. Alice McQueen... ah, yes, Alice was my great-great-grandmother, I think. Yes. My grandmother's grandmother.' She turned the letters over in her hands. 'How amazing! I had no idea they were there. Where did you find them?'

'They were kinda stuck half inside some photo albums. I brought some of them, actually. I couldn't carry the whole box but I pulled some out for you. I can bring the rest another day.' Zelda pointed to a pile of the photo albums she'd brought with her.

'Oh, how wonderful! Yes, I remember those albums. I haven't looked at them for years.' Gretchen gestured for Zelda to pass her one. 'Ha. Look at this! This is me.' She pointed to the photo of the girl with freckles that Zelda had seen the night before.

'I wondered if that was you. Same chaotic energy.'

'I'd prefer *"joie de vivre"*, dear, but yes.' Gretchen flicked the pages. 'Goodness, look. There're my parents.' She pointed to a couple, the man dressed in a military uniform and the woman in a 1940s-style high-necked dress. 'Aren't they stunning? You'd have loved my mother: she adored fashion. She made her own clothes, you know. People did, then.'

'It's a lost art.' Zelda nodded. 'My mom did alterations at the dry-cleaner's. She made my clothes when I was a kid.' She smiled at the memory. It was nice to think about her mom in a good way, rather than just focusing on the loss.

'How lovely! Did she pass the skill on to you?' Gretchen looked up owlishly from the photo album.

'A little. I mean, I couldn't make a dress, but I can do simple repairs. Put in a new zip, do a hem, that kind of thing. But I ended up working at a newspaper, so...'

'Indeed. Did I tell you that I worked in publishing for many years?' Gretchen smiled. 'The cottage was always our family home, but my parents made sure I went to university. Luckily, it was somewhat easier then – financially, I mean. The state helped. I pity the young people now.'

'That's why you had all those first editions.' Zelda nodded. 'I see.'

'Yes. I had quite the time when I was younger. I lived in Edinburgh for many years while my parents retired to the cottage. And then, when they died, it became mine, and I moved back into it.' She sighed. 'The circle of life.'

'You never married?' Zelda rested her broken wrist on her lap. It ached from the painting.

'No. There were some close calls, but none of them came to anything. I'm not sure I ever wanted it enough.'

'Fair. Me neither.'

'I recognised a fellow career woman when I saw you that first day, in the garden.' Gretchen nodded. 'You had the look of someone who wouldn't know one end of the kitchen from the other. I respect that.'

'Hey! I can cook,' Zelda protested. 'You can work *and* cook, you know, Gretch. Times have changed.'

'Tell me the last meal you cooked.' Gretchen looked her dead in the eye.

'Well, I can't remember *exactly*,' Zelda protested. 'I mean, I was well fed at the inn, obviously. Dotty's soups, casseroles and sandwiches are kinda legendary. But, no. I haven't cooked anything myself in a while.'

'My point exactly. It's not a criticism. I always preferred a novel to a cookbook.'

'So, there were men, then?' Zelda probed.

'Ah, yes. Ryan O'Connell's uncle ran the bookshop in the village for many years. We had a bit of a thing going,' Gretchen whispered, a glint in her eye.

'Gretch! Dish. Immediately!' Zelda giggled.

'Oh, it was all a long time ago.' Gretchen waved her away impatiently. 'Alexander. He was a good man. We had books in common, of course. That was how we got to know each other at first. I was always going in there, asking for books that had just come out. He had to order them because he didn't believe in new authors.' She laughed merrily. 'I used to tease him about it. There were no books in that shop published after the 1950s.'

'What was he like? Alexander?'

'Oh, handsome. Ryan has the look of him, a little. Bookish, obviously. Rather diffident, but romantic too. He wanted to marry and have children. I didn't. Not then.' She sighed again. 'That was that. I had a pregnancy scare when we were together. Obviously, we were sleeping together; Alexander thought that meant we had to get married. He proposed when I thought I was pregnant. I refused. I would have had the baby myself, but it turned out to be nothing.' A shadow passed over Gretchen's face. 'However, the fact that I turned him down pretty much ended our relationship.'

'You could have married him, though,' Zelda said. 'Didn't you love him?'

'Not enough to want to wash his socks for the rest of my

life.' Gretchen shook her head. 'Anyway. Let's look at who was writing to Alice McQueen.'

She opened the envelope carefully and withdrew a fragile letter.

'Oh. It's from... I can't make out the name. Is that a P or an R?' Gretchen passed the letter to Zelda.

'I think that's an R. Richard. Yes, I'm pretty sure it says Richard.' Zelda returned the letter to Gretchen. 'D'you have any ancestors called Richard?'

'I don't think so.' Gretchen frowned at the letter. 'Gosh. Well, it seems that my great-great-grandmother was having a romantic relationship with this fellow, nonetheless. Listen to this: *Dearest Alice, it has only been two days since our time together, but I am lost without you. Your kisses are like wine.*'

'Wow.' Zelda leant forwards. 'What else?'

'Hmm. Oh, gosh. *Your father may disapprove of me and our love, but I will not end this bond with you. Run away with me. I know a place where we can live freely without censure.*'

'Jeez. Intense.' Zelda blinked. 'What happened next?'

'I don't know. Let's find another dated after this one.' Gretchen peered at the date at the top of the letter. 'Fifth of June, 1855.'

Zelda took some of the letters and sorted through them, carefully opening them as she went along. 'Here's one. The third of July, 1855.' She handed it to Gretchen.

'All right... okay, here, he's saying, *You must come with me as I instruct. Soon we will not be able to conceal our love. My aunt has a smallholding in Dumfries where we can hide until the child is born.*' Gretchen looked up in surprise. '*Child!* Alice McQueen was pregnant, out of wedlock!' she exclaimed.

'Did you know that?' Zelda asked.

'No, not at all!' Gretchen scanned the letter in her hand. 'I mean to say, it was so long ago, there's no reason why I would know, really.'

'That tracks,' Zelda mused. 'So, that leaves the question of whether your great-grandmother was that baby, right?'

'I suppose so.' Gretchen flicked through the other envelopes. 'Here's another one, later again. Still addressed here, though, so I guess she didn't move with him to Dumfries. *Dear Alice. Though we are parted, I think of you and our child at every moment. Your father is a jailer and you are the prisoner. I walk past the cottage every night when the lights go out, willing you to appear and run away with me. Know that I will continue to walk past for as long as I am able. Your true love, Richard McKelvie.*'

'So did she ever go with him?' Zelda looked at the other envelopes. 'I mean, these are all addressed to the cottage, so it doesn't look like it. Unless she went with him after these were sent?'

'It's possible. But in those days, being unmarried with a baby wasn't accepted at all. They would have been pariahs in this community. Alice would have been thought of as mad, even.' Gretchen shook her head.

'Poor Alice.' Zelda felt the sadness of the love between the fated couple emanating from the letters. 'And poor Richard. Oh, wow. Listen to this. This is earlier. *Dearest Alice. I had always thought of the May Day celebrations at the stones as some pagan nonsense to be tolerated by us good Christians, but now my eyes have been opened. When we danced through the space between the stones, and when you took my hand, I knew that you were destined for me as clear as the stars in the sky.*'

'They danced around the stones on May Day! The old tradition!' Gretchen gasped. 'That must be when they first kissed, perhaps. Even in my time, the celebrations tended to get a little... enthusiastic.' She looked nostalgic. 'The combination of bonfires, free wine and dancing usually does it.'

'Clearly, that did it for Alice and Richard.' Zelda stared at the letter in Gretchen's hand. 'Do any of the other letters say what happened after they were forbidden to see each other?'

'Hmm. No, the letters stop after that one.' Gretchen let out a long breath. 'Damn. Now I really want to know what came next. What happened to Alice?'

'I guess she had the baby, and that was your great-grand-mother?' Zelda suggested.

'Perhaps. Perhaps not. It was common, in that situation in a family, for the parents to pretend that the baby was theirs. They may have done that, and my great-grandmother may have been another child Alice had later. I'm going to have to check.' She frowned. 'Though, I don't know who to check with now. Anyone who might have known is long gone.'

'You could look online. There are websites that can help you with this stuff,' Zelda offered. 'I can help you, if you want.'

'That would be wonderful, dear. If you have time, of course. I wouldn't want to take up your time.'

'Are you kidding?' Zelda laughed. 'This is a legit mystery. I want to know what happened.'

'Oh. Well, in that case, fire away with your websites.' Gretchen reached for a biscuit. 'I confess, I'm rather curious myself.'

TWENTY-SEVEN

Fine. I'll do it. But only if you organise it with me. I'm terrible at this kind of stuff.

Zelda was reading an interior decoration magazine with her feet up on the bed, her toenails drying from a fresh coat of polish, when her phone buzzed. She picked it up and looked at the text message from Hal.

Do what? she texted back. She was grateful that Hal apparently hadn't discovered video calling, because she'd decided to put on a face mask and go to town with some Sunday afternoon pampering.

We'll have the May Day party. But I need help to organise it, he replied.

Are you serious? Zelda let out a whoop. Clearly, her and Anna's gentle persuasion had worked. She didn't know what Anna had said to him, but Zelda was pretty sure it hadn't been her incessant emailing with links to local DJs that had done the trick. Or, maybe it had. Maybe he was just sick to death of being nagged.

Still, Hal was so stubborn that Zelda had expected him to refuse to comply, despite her and Anna's best efforts.

Yes, he replied.

Short but sweet, Zelda thought.

Okay. Should I come up to the castle? she replied. *I'm kinda busy here, but I can be there tomorrow, if that helps. Not much time to get it all done.*

In fact, when she looked at the calendar on her phone, Zelda realised that there were only four weeks until May Day – May 1st.

Sounds good, he replied.

Zelda's stomach filled with butterflies, all of a sudden. *It's just the excitement of organising a party*, she told herself. *This will be great for the column.*

However, after what Ryan had told her about Hal and Maggie, Zelda wasn't sure about Hal. She still liked him, and she felt for him deeply: losing someone so close to you was awful, like being thrown into a pit of despair. But, there was still a niggle of concern in her mind. Was Hal the controlling, mean-spirited man Ryan had described? He might have a dark side. People could and it wasn't always obvious.

She didn't trust Hal Cameron, though she wanted to. But she was happy enough to help him out with organising the party. It wasn't like her heart was on the line, just doing that. *And*, said the part of her brain that had noticed Hal's muscular forearms, *if you get to spend a little more time with a hot Laird, then what have you lost? Nothing.*

She didn't always like to listen to that voice, but she had to admit on this occasion that it was probably right.

———

'When you said we needed to look at flowers for the party, I thought you meant going to a florist,' Zelda confessed, slightly in awe at the sight in front of her.

A huge glass house filled with roses stretched ahead of her, the flowers arranged in neat sections. Blowsy pink blooms bordered rows of clean white rosebuds, with deliciously orange, sun-kissed roses beyond them. The smell was like nothing Zelda had ever experienced before.

'Why go to a florist when you own a nursery?' Hal replied, proudly.

When Zelda had arrived at the castle, Hal had been waiting in his mud-spattered green Range Rover, and had driven them down a succession of dirt tracks away from the castle, turning finally into a single-track road that had led them here. As well as the glass house, there were long polytunnels that Hal explained contained herbs and vegetables sold under the Loch Cameron brand.

'Aye. The estate owns a few businesses. We get income from fishin' on the loch, the roses, the organic herb farmin' an' there's the salmon business. Got tae diversify, in this day an' age.' He nodded.

'And there's the property in the village, right?' Zelda prompted him. 'You own all that. Got to be quite a value there.'

'Aye, but I'm also the landlord, so I'm responsible for the upkeep too.' Hal waved at a couple of gardeners in green overalls. 'Like Gretchen's cottage, for instance.'

'Ah, right. It's a great place.'

'Aye. It's been there as long as the castle. Maybe longer.' He smiled, watching as Zelda walked along a row of perfect white roses, touching the silky petals softly with her fingertips. 'The Ross family's been tenants as long as I can remember. They're an auld family in the village. Like a lot o' families.'

'I bet there's a lot of local gossip. Not just about the Ross family. I mean, all of them.' Zelda raised an eyebrow. 'I know what it was like in our neighbourhood growing up, never mind here, where people have lived for centuries. There must be a lot of long-running feuds, scandals, that kinda thing.'

'Diggin' for gossip, are we?' Hal grinned.

'No. Just curious,' Zelda replied, primly. 'Go on. Tell me. There must be some real zingers.'

Hal laughed out loud. 'Zingers? I dunno. I think ye'll be disappointed. It's all garden variety misunderstandin's, probably. No blood feuds. It isnae Sicily.'

'Really? Disappointing, Hal. Disappointing.' Zelda shot a playful glance back at the Laird as she walked along the rows of flowers.

'Ah, well. I guess I can tell ye one of the legendary stories of Loch Cameron. There isnae many – that I know, anyway – but...' He trailed off.

'Yes, please. What?' Zelda stopped, turning around expectantly.

'Well.' Hal lowered his voice. 'Legend has it that, many years ago, a local girl fell intae the loch. Hundreds of years back. No one knew her name. But she was famous for her beautiful, glossy black hair.' He touched the end of Zelda's ponytail, gently. 'Then, some years later, there were these disturbances.'

'What d'you mean, *disturbances*?' Zelda frowned, trying to ignore the electricity that had passed through her body when he'd touched her hair, so gently.

'Well, at night, there was somethin' in the loch, people said. Only on a night wi' no moon,' he added, his voice hushed. 'An' then, people started findin' their cattle dead, wi' big bites taken oot o' them.'

'What?'

'Aye.' Hal took a deep breath. 'Somethin' wi' great gapin' jaws had got 'em. Then, the sightin's started.'

'The sightings? Of what?'

'The WURM! The sea beast! Thirty feet long, an' crowned

wi' a head of glossy black hair!' Hal cried out dramatically, making a monster face.

Zelda jumped, emitting a little scream.

Hal bent over, laughing at her reaction.

'Oh, I'm not talking to you now.' She turned away, trying and failing to hide her laughter. 'You really had me there for a minute!'

'I know, I know. I couldnae resist,' Hal chuckled. 'Sorry.'

'The "wurm", indeed,' she muttered, trying not to giggle.

'Sorry. But there isnae much local gossip. I thought I'd make somethin' up for ye.'

'I kind of wanted it to be true,' Zelda confessed.

'Aye. Mebbe I should pretend it's true. We'd get more tourists,' he said, wiping his eyes with his sleeve. 'Ah, your face, though.' He started laughing again.

'*Hal.* Shhhh! People are looking!' Zelda shushed him, giggling herself.

'Ah, let them look.' He grinned. 'Anyway. Come on. We need tae go back tae party plannin'. For goodness' sake, be serious, Zelda Hicks.'

'Okay, okay.'

They continued in companionable silence for a moment. Zelda was thinking how different Hal was when he cut loose and allowed himself to have a little fun; he was so different to the serious Laird she'd thought he was.

'Can I just say, *wow*? About these roses?' she said, as they walked along. 'They are *gorgeous.*'

'Aye, of course ye can!' He looked pleased. 'It's nice tae see it bein' appreciated. My mother started the nursery when she was a young lassie. Keen gardener. My father built the nursery for her. So... what do you think we should have at the party?'

'Wow. I don't know. They're all so beautiful.' Zelda crouched down to sniff the pink roses, which smelt divine. 'Can you get a florist to make some arrangements? I could see you having an arch of white roses. And then maybe these pink ones for the tables inside, when you have the food laid out? And...' She straightened, then stepped across to the blowsy, sunset-orange blooms. 'Yes. Mixed arrangements, maybe, rather than all white. It's a celebration of the start of summer, after all, right?'

'Right. That makes sense.' Hal smiled, watching Zelda as she enjoyed the flowers. 'You like roses?'

'I love roses. They're my favourite flower.' Zelda sighed. 'I feel like you need to pinch me. I never imagined I'd be standing in the middle of so many of them. It's like a crazy romantic dream.'

Hal smiled, picked up some secateurs from a ledge nearby and cut one of the baby-pink roses, handing it to Zelda. 'Here,' he said, shyly. 'I'm no' gonna pinch ye. But mind the thorns.'

'Hal! Thank you!' Zelda took it and inhaled its lovely sweetness. 'Look how perfect it is. The shape of the petals. The way the colour fades out a little towards the edges. The feel of the petal. It's like skin,' she said, stroking it.

'It's beautiful,' he agreed, softly. But when Zelda glanced up, expecting to see Hal admiring the flower in her hand, he was looking at her.

TWENTY-EIGHT

'No, move the title up. There.' Zelda tapped her laptop screen, a little impatiently. Hal's document design skills left a lot to be desired.

'Ye do it. Yer better at this than me.' Hal turned the laptop to face her, giving her an angelic smile that Zelda strongly suspected was aimed at making her finish the poster they were working on for the party. He was clearly not enjoying the process, judging by the number of semi-audible swear words he'd muttered as he'd fought with the mouse pad.

'It's true, I am.' She grinned at him, rearranging the layout of the poster in the way she'd been trying to describe to him in a few moments, and adjusting the font size. 'There. That's what I meant.'

Hal leant over to look at the screen, brushing her arm as he did so. Zelda tried to ignore the electric feeling that zipped through her as he did so. She hadn't forgotten what Ryan had told her about Hal, and she still wasn't sure what she thought about it. Trust was always going to be an issue with her, but as long as she and Hal were just working together, then there wasn't a problem.

MAY DAY CELEBRATION
LOCH CAMERON CASTLE
MAY 1ST, 7 P.M. TILL LATE
DRINKS, DANCING, BONFIRE
What is life, when wanting love?
Night without a morning
Love's the cloudless summer sun
Nature gay adorning
– Robert Burns

'I like that quote,' Hal said, softly.

'I know. It was on the old May Day party poster. Gretchen showed me.' Zelda met his gaze, and then looked away, hurriedly. If she was honest, the problem was that it wasn't just work, with Hal. There was something else bubbling away between them, and she didn't know what to do about it.

She knew it was best not to encourage whatever attraction there was between her and Hal. It was too complicated, and, anyway, she had kissed Ryan now. She didn't know if she would go so far as to say they were dating, though. They had been out a couple of times.

But, knowing that she should keep everything about work with Hal, and actually doing that, were two different things. Sometimes, there were moments between them, and she always found herself responding to him. It was impossible not to.

And, yet, Zelda didn't trust Hal, because of what Ryan had told her about him.

'It looks good. I'll get a hundred printed. Put them up around the village,' Hal suggested. 'Or do you think we should get more?'

'That's probably enough. Think of the trees.' Zelda pushed her reading glasses onto her head and sighed. 'Tea? I think we deserve it.'

'Aye, go on then.' Hal sat back on the sofa and yawned. 'So, how're ye findin' it here? Comfortable?'

'Yeah, it's really cosy. I love it.' Zelda got up and went into the kitchen to put the kettle on to boil. Hal had offered to come to the cottage, since it had been raining hard all day and he'd imagined Zelda wouldn't want to walk over to the castle in the deluge. She had pointed out that she still had the use of Gretchen's car, but Hal had said he'd be happy to visit. Zelda wondered if he wanted to check she hadn't gone crazy and painted everything black or something.

'The decoratin's comin' on, I have tae say,' he called out to her, as if he read her mind. 'I like the wallpaper. An' the furniture's very nice.'

In fact, the cottage's small sitting room had undergone something of a transformation.

Zelda had covered the walls with wallpaper featuring wildflowers just like the ones in Gretchen's garden. She had removed the board that had once sealed up the fireplace, revealing an authentic Art Nouveau tiled fireplace inside. It had only needed a bit of a clean, and now the tiles – a light green with pink roses – acted as the centrepiece to the room.

She had also sourced a comfy upholstered chair with a hydrangea pattern, and a vintage pink chaise longue, which now sat at one side of the lounge. Zelda had also found a plain cream sofa online that she paid just fifty pounds for as part of a house clearance. The staff at the storage place had been very helpful and delivered the pieces to her at the cottage, moving them inside for her and positioning them exactly where she wanted them to go.

In fact, Zelda had really been enjoying redecorating the cottage. She'd started posting updates of her work on social media, just so that she would have a record of the changes, but she hadn't anticipated how many new followers she'd get because of it. Interior décor bloggers, stylists and homes enthu-

siasts commented on her posts, loving the fact that she was reno-
vating Gretchen's traditional Scottish cottage on very little
money.

Zelda really loved the creativity that a small budget
provided. She'd had to be canny, to use a Scots word, and find
bargains online and in the village.

'Glad you like it,' she called back. 'You know, I got that
chaise longue free. I just had to go and pick it up from a village
not far from here. Fortunately, I got it into Gretchen's car.'

'Very impressive.' Hall came to stand in the kitchen doorway, watching her as she busied around the kitchen.

'And I found a few very low-cost things elsewhere.' Zelda
pointed to some vintage china plant pots she'd left by the back
door, ready to fill with soil from the garden. 'Look at these plant
pots! Only two pounds for all four.'

Hal glanced at the pots. 'Plant pots?' He gave her an
amused look.

'Yeah. Vintage china. They've got this lovely floral pattern.
And look, this one. This cute village scene.' Zelda went across to
them and picked one up, bringing it over to show him.

'Hmm. Where d'ye get those?' he asked, his eyes twinkling.

'The charity shop in the village. Good size, too.'

'Aye. Well, they would have tae be. To accommodate all the
arses.' He laughed. 'Mind ye, arses weren't as big then as they
are now. Not in all cases, o' course.'

'The *arses*?' Zelda was mystified. 'What d'you mean?'

'I mean, they're chamber pots.'

'I don't know what that is.'

'Fer yer... number ones and number twos,' Hal suggested,
looking like he was searching for the politest term he could
think of. 'People used tae have them under the bed if they
needed to *go* in the night, back in the day. Before indoor
plumbing. Ah, dinnae worry. I'm sure they've been washed out
since then.' He dissolved into further gales of laughter. 'I bet

auld Tom in the shop couldnae believe his luck, gettin' rid o' these.'

'Hal. Are you *serious*?' Zelda was appalled.

'Aye. But they *are* nice things. And real china, like ye say. Dinnae worry, I'm sure they'll make very nice plant pots.'

'Oh, no. I... I posted on Instagram and everything.' She covered her eyes. 'But they're so pretty! How was I supposed to know?'

'It's not a big thing. Dinnae worry, hen.' He patted her on the arm, still grinning.

'But... Hal! They are literally pots where people used to *poop*!' Zelda started to giggle. 'And I've posted them on social media, being all like "hashtag vintage china, hashtag cottage makeover prettiness".'

'Well, maybe no one'll notice,' he suggested. 'Or, just own it. Change the post and say I told ye they're chamber pots and ye had no idea.'

'Oh, NO! I'm completely mortified!' Zelda cried, putting the pot down on the kitchen table.

'Maybe I shouldnae have said anythin'.' Hal grinned.

'No, you should.' Zelda poured hot water into the teapot. 'I'm just a dumb American, I guess.'

'You're no' dumb.' Hal shoved his hands in his pockets, giving her a sideways glance. 'I think ye've done a stonkin' job wi' the cottage. I'm just teasin' ye.'

'They're not chamber pots, then?' Zelda looked up, hopefully. 'Were you just making that all up?'

'Ach, no. I wasnae teasin' ye *that* much.' He shook his head. 'Ye might have a great eye for décor, but ye've got a lot tae learn aboot Scottish humour.'

'I guess I do.' Zelda sighed, and handed him a mug of tea. 'How about I stick to making things pretty, and you stick to telling the jokes?'

'Oh, gawd. That's an awfa' idea, Zelda. I'm even worse at

bein' funny than I am at makin' posters.' Hal took the mug, and their fingers touched for a moment.

'You make me laugh,' she said, quietly. Maybe she shouldn't have said anything. But it was true: she and Hal shared a sense of humour, and she loved it when they had fun together.

'Aye, well. We must be a couple o' dafties, then,' he said, softly, meeting her eyes with his deep blue gaze.

'I guess we are,' she said, and a long moment passed when neither of them said anything at all.

TWENTY-NINE

Zelda was carrying two takeaway coffees from Dotty at the inn to Fiona's shop when she saw the May Day party poster she and Hal had designed displayed in the butcher's window.

It looks good, she thought. She felt absurdly proud of all the work she and Hal were doing to organise the party – it was keeping her busy, but she knew the party was going to be amazing.

Zelda opened the door to Fiona's Fashions carefully, bottom first, so as not to spill the coffee.

Fiona took both takeaway cups from her and set them carefully on the shop counter. 'Hallo, Zelda!'

'Hi, Fiona. Excited about the party?' Zelda slumped into the easy chair next to the counter and sighed. She'd had a busy morning already, ordering the drinks from the local off-licence Hal had recommended. The sigh was because she was, if she was honest, kind of tired. But in a good way.

Hal had a plumber coming into the castle to repair a couple of the sinks, ahead of the whole village needing to use the bathrooms at the party. Apparently there were quite a few odd jobs that needed to be done to make sure the castle 'didnae fall down on anyone's heid while they're dancing,' as Hal put it. So, while Hal was sorting out the castle, Zelda was in charge of catering and a million other responsibilities.

'Aye, of course. So ye managed to persuade him, then?' Fiona took the lid off her coffee and blew on it.

'Yeah. I guess so.' Zelda took a sip of her coffee and made herself enjoy the fact that she was having a break. 'I think he wanted to do it. I guess he needed a bit of a push.'

'Well, I'm glad it's happenin'. In fact, I was thinkin' of puttin' a sign up in the windae, tellin' people they could get their glad rags here. I was thinkin' I could partner up with a dress hire place, an' then people can get ball dresses just for the night from me. What d'ye think?' Fiona looked hopeful that Zelda would approve of the idea.

'That's great! I'll give you the name of the place I rented those wedding dresses from: the ones I wore on the castle shoot.' Zelda thought for a moment. 'And you could maybe provide a fun experience for people getting their dresses here. Like, a glass of champagne, some cupcakes, that kind of thing. Make an event of it.'

'I love that!' Fiona grinned.

'Yeah. Look, I've been doing the drinks order for the party today. I'll just add in a few more bottles of champagne. I'm sure the Laird won't mind.' Zelda winked.

'You've got his credit card, aye? Seems like someone's got her feet under the table!' Fiona clucked appreciatively.

'Agh, Fiona. It's nothing like that. I'm just helping out.'

'Aye, I know. I'm just teasin'.' Fiona waggled her eyebrows suggestively. 'Still, he obviously likes ye. Tae trust ye with it all.'

'Well, I think he just needs the help. And I'm around to do it, that's all.' Zelda shrugged.

Her phone rang: it was Anna. 'Fiona, hun, I have to take this. D'you mind?' She looked up at Fiona, who nodded.

'Sure! I've got a stocktake tae do. Give me a shout when you're done.'

'Hi, Anna,' Zelda answered the call.

'Hi, Zelda. I just wanted to check in about the catering for the party.' Anna's low, friendly voice sounded as if she was somewhere busy. 'I'm with Hal just now and he's asking me about salmon for the party. What d'you think? I mean, it's very traditional, but you might not want that. We do farm it here, if you remember.'

'Oh, of course! Traditional all the way, Anna. Don't you think? I mean, it makes sense, right?' Zelda wanted the party to be the best one Loch Cameron had ever had, and she knew there was no point in trying to make it a New York party. This was going to be one hundred per cent Scotland, from the whisky cocktails to the traditional country dancing and definitely the locally sourced salmon.

'Great. I agree, I just thought I'd check. Are you happy for me to organise the rest of the food, with a traditional spread in mind? That'll include things like a cheese board, crackers, bridies, meat pies – that kind of thing.'

'Sure. Bridies?'

'Pastry crescents filled with beef and onion,' Anna explained.

'Sounds... warming.' Zelda laughed. 'Great, Anna. Whatever you think, really. You're the expert. I was thinking maybe we could do something with haggis, though. Like, something a little fancier than usual. Can you make finger food with haggis? Like, hors d'oeuvres, almost?' she added.

'I know what you mean. Yes, that's doable,' Anna agreed.

'Great. How's Hal?' Zelda was facing out of the shop window, looking at the high street outside. She could see the castle on the other side of the loch, looming over the village, and it made her think of him. The words were out of her mouth before she could stop them, and she cringed; there was no reason for her to be asking how Hal was. She saw him almost every day as it was. Anna was going to think she was some kind of idiot.

'Oh, he's fine.' Anna had a smile in her voice. 'I must say, he's been so cheery since all the party planning started. Anyone would think he was actually enjoying himself!'

'That's good. I was just... well, I don't know why I mentioned it, actually,' Zelda blustered awkwardly.

'Not to worry, hen. Listen, I'll catch up with you later. It's quite busy here!' Anna raised her voice: there was some kind of commotion in the background. 'See you soon, Zelda!'

'Cool. Catch you later!' Zelda ended the call.

Fiona returned to the shop floor with a printout in her hand. 'All okay?' she queried. 'Ye know, this stocktake's doin' ma heid in. I need a break an' I've only just started!' She stretched her arms above her head and then let them drop to her sides. 'How's things, anyway? I read ye column. I cannae believe I'm sittin' here with a *New Yorker* columnist!'

'It's going okay, I guess. The magazine likes it so far, and now that I'm helping organise this party, it fits in pretty well. They like the concept of me getting involved at the castle, you know? How does a modern Laird live now? Does he drink tea out of a golden tankard? Does he wear a kilt all the time? Are the beds made of swan feather eiderdowns, that kind of thing. I mean, the more I'm here, the more I realise that the castle's got bad plumbing, the roof's falling apart and it's full of mice. But the audience finds it all pretty romantic, whatever I say.'

'I saw your cottage renovation stuff on Instagram too.' Fiona picked up her coffee and leant against the counter. 'Ye've got such a good eye! Ye should come an' redecorate ma place. It's a cottage, like Gretchen's. Ah dinnae think it's been painted since Culloden.'

'Ha. Well, maybe, if I'm still around after I've finished it, and after the party.' Zelda smiled. 'I am really enjoying it, I have to admit. I've always been into interiors, but only as an amateur. I read the magazines, and I decorated my place in New York. But that was it until now.'

'Your follower numbers have gone mental in the last week or so, though.' Fiona sipped her coffee. 'And you get so many comments. I think people really love the whole thing about findin' bargains an' not payin' the earth for stuff.'

'Yeah. I have to say, that's really fun. Those websites where people list stuff free are amazing. You wouldn't believe what some people are getting rid of, usually just because they don't have room for it any more. I took some stuff to the tip last week, and I found this amazing painting under a pile of old flooring. I took it, cleaned it and now it's hanging in the bedroom. It's absolutely perfect.' Zelda finished her coffee. 'I'd actually love to get more into the interiors side of journalism. I mean, I've done a lot of arts, and they're kind of related. It's always been a bit of a dream of mine.'

'Then you should do it.' Fiona smiled at a customer who came in. 'Mornin', Jean! Those new jackets came in. To your right,' she called out.

'Well, it's not that easy, I guess. Lots of people would like to be an interior decoration journalist.' Zelda frowned.

'Aye, but ye are a journalist tae begin with, remember. An' ye've got this cottage renovation thing goin' on. Best way tae start, I'd say. You told me that, remember.'

'I did,' Zelda admitted. 'How's all that going, anyway?'

'Really good. I've been workin' on widenin' my social media presence like ye suggested. An' I put an advert in a couple o' local papers. Plus, look!' Fiona pointed to a new section of the shop she had labelled *Select Pieces*. There were a few well-chosen designer handbags on the shelves, and a tasteful rack of scarves and jewellery.

Zelda went over and inspected Fiona's choices. 'Hey, these are really nice.' She nodded approvingly, touching the silk scarves lightly and picking up one of the clutch bags to inspect it. 'Perfect for the older lady with a bigger budget, but also really nice for a local or a tourist looking for something special. I'd buy these.'

'Aye, me too. I hoped you'd approve.' Fiona looked bashful. 'Still sellin' wellies, jumpers an' waxed jackets, obviously. But it's nice tae have a mix o' things.'

'Sure. And I'll definitely hire a dress from you, for the May Day party. Hey, you know, Gretchen and me discovered this whole story about an ancestor of hers who had this illicit affair with a guy, back in the 1850s. She got pregnant, unmarried. But there's this letter from the guy to her about how he danced with her at the standing stones at May Day – you know the ones down on the beach from the castle?'

'Aye.' Fiona nodded.

'Yeah. So, that was when he fell in love with her, the letter says. Romantic, huh?'

'Och, aye. Sad, though. I can imagine the scandal something like that might cause. What happened to her?'

'I don't know exactly, I was going to try and research online for Gretch. But, yeah. I guess it wasn't okay to have babies if you weren't married, in those days.'

'Lord, no. Not a bit of it. I wouldnae be surprised if the poor lassie had tae move away. Or be victimised for the rest o' her life if she stayed.' Fiona shook her head.

'My mom was a single mother. It was hard for her even then – I mean, more financially than anything. She wasn't, like, ostracised by the community. I can't imagine what life was like for poor Alice,' Zelda said, thoughtfully.

'That's tough.' Fiona nodded. 'Still, your mum did an awesome job. I bet she's so proud of you.'

'Ah. Yeah. She passed, actually. But thanks. She was a really great lady.' Zelda sighed.

'Oh, darlin', I'm so sorry.' Fiona took her hand. 'When was it?'

'A few months ago. It's fine.'

'It isnae *fine*. It's okay tae be sad aboot it,' Fiona tutted.

'Well, I do miss her. I still have some of her clothes. I wear them sometimes. It's a way to feel close to her,' Zelda admitted. There had been a time when she hadn't wanted to mention her mom at all: it had been too raw. But, since she'd been in Loch Cameron, she had opened up a little, and it felt good to do so. It was still tough, and the tears still haunted the back of her throat when the subject of her mom came up. But she was at least able to talk about her a little more now, and that felt like progress.

'Sure.' Fiona nodded. 'Ye know, I'm so happy Hal's brought the May Day party back. It's fun, but it's also a way for us to all remember Maggie. His wife. Kindae the same thing.'

'Yeah, I can see that. Ryan told me about her. He said she was a really good friend.' Zelda nodded.

'Och, aye. She was a really bonny lassie. Kind. Funny. She always asked after yer family, always said hallo in the street.' Fiona clicked her fingers. 'Ye know, thinkin' aboot those letters ye found... I can ask my uncle if he knows anythin'. He's kindae a local historian. Just his hobby, now he's retired. But I can ask?'

'I love that! Fiona, you are a superstar.' Zelda beamed. 'I can text you everything I know, which isn't much. You know, the names and dates. I know Alice lived at the cottage on Queen's Point with her family. That's kinda it, though.'

'Uncle John's really intae Loch Cameron's history. I bet he'll come up wi' something,' Fiona assured her. She wrote a number down on the back of a blank till receipt roll, ripped the paper off and handed it to Zelda. 'This is his number. Drop him a line. An' it's a perfect thing tae write aboot in yer column.'

'Wow. Thanks, Fiona. That's so kind.' Zelda took the paper

and put it in her pocket. 'I hadn't even thought about writing about it in the column.' She frowned. 'A kind of mystery, you mean? Who was Alice? What happened to her baby?'

'Aye. But, ye ken, maybe somethin' else too. Aboot yer mum. What's it like bein' a single mum these days, in Alice's day... Ye could make a real thing of it.' Fiona shrugged. 'Yer the expert. I'm just bletherin' out loud.'

'I'm definitely not an expert when it comes to Scottish history. Or being a single mother.' Zelda thought about it. 'But I guess I grew up with my mom, and maybe Alice's baby didn't get to. It would kind of be cool to tell that story. If we could find out more. But this is also for Gretchen, you know? It's her family. I'd have to ask her permission to write about it.'

'Aye, definitely. You should ask her. But Uncle John's yer man for the diggin' around.'

Another customer came in, and Fiona went over to help them.

No time like the present, Zelda thought, and picked up her phone. She pressed Gretchen's number on the recent call list.

'Hey, Gretch,' she said, as Gretchen answered the phone. 'You know we were reading those letters? I'm wondering if I can ask you something about them.'

THIRTY

After chatting with Fiona, Zelda dropped into Ryan's bookshop. She noticed that he too had the May Day poster in his shop window.

'You're going, then?' She pointed at the poster. 'And, hi.'

'Hello, my sweet Audrey Hepburn,' Ryan drawled, looking up from where he was adding stickers to a pile of books on the shop counter. 'How are you this lovely morning? And... going to what?'

Zelda tapped the poster in the window. 'The big party. I'd like to take responsibility for that, by the way. I was the one who persuaded him to do it. And designed the poster.'

'Oh, right. Good job! Is there no end to your talents?' Ryan beamed at her. 'You look very pretty today, I might add.'

'Flattery will get you further than you think,' she flirted back a little.

'Oh! Good to know.' He grinned. 'But, as to the party, no, I probably won't go.' Ryan made a face. 'I put the poster up to show willing, you know. I mean, Hal is still my landlord. But, no. I don't think it'll be the same without Maggie.'

'Oh.' Zelda was disappointed. She was working really hard

to put the party together: it would be nice for Ryan to come. She'd even considered asking him to come as her date.

In the back of her mind, though, she was still having thoughts about Hal Cameron that she knew she shouldn't. She knew she was see-sawing between Ryan and Hal, and she was confused by her own feelings. Ryan was a fun-loving guy who was clear about the fact he liked her. If she was really honest with herself, she felt a deeper emotional and – yes – physical connection with Hal, but Hal was troubled, and she wasn't sure how he felt about her at all. And, as well as that, there was her inability to trust him.

'It'll be fun,' Zelda tried her best persuasive voice. 'I'm in charge of ordering the food and drink, so I can tell you there's gonna be no lack of good champagne. Or salmon. And Fiona's gonna get me an awesome dress.'

'Hmm. I can't deny that the thought of you in a low-cut ball dress isn't tempting.' Ryan gave her a naughty grin. 'But... I don't know. Let me think about it.'

'Okay. But you should come. Bury the hatchet with Hal,' she suggested.

'I think we're a long way beyond that. But I'll think about it. Okay?'

'Of course.' Zelda cast her eye over the new book releases shelf next to the shop window, knowing that things between Hal and Ryan were difficult. She didn't want to seem too pushy.

'So how's the column going?' Ryan came to stand next to her, adjusting the display a little.

'It's good, I think.' Zelda shot Ryan a smile. He looked very handsome, in a blazer with a T-shirt underneath and jeans. He wasn't a flashy dresser, but he did at least choose clothes that fit him well, unlike Hal Cameron, who generally looked like he got dressed in the dark. 'What's on your T-shirt?'

'Oh, it's an old one. Year 2000-ish Vivienne Westwood.' He

adjusted the blazer so that she could see the T shirt better. 'I believe it's what people call "vintage".'

'Ooh. That's cool.' Zelda feigned a mock-swoon. 'Did you buy it new?'

'I'd love to say that I was always in to fashion, but I'd be lying. I bought it online. Last week.' He looked slightly embarrassed.

'Last week?'

'Yeah. I might have been influenced by a certain person's interest in clothes.'

'Awww. That's so cute. Well, I approve.' Zelda grinned.

'Oh. Speak of the devil.' Ryan gestured at the street outside, where Hal Cameron was walking with a woman Zelda hadn't seen before. 'There's your pretend husband.'

'Ryan, I told you, that was just for the shoot. The model I'd booked didn't turn up.'

'I know, I know. I'm just pulling your leg.' Ryan nudged her.

'Who's that woman?' Zelda asked.

'Maybe he's got a new lady love.' Ryan picked at the remains of an old sticker on the glass door.

'Oh.' Zelda berated herself for the hollow feeling that had instantly appeared in her stomach at the prospect of Hal having a girlfriend. *Why? Why is that any of your business?* she asked herself, knowing there was an answer to that question, but it wasn't one she wanted to face up to right now.

Hal and the mystery woman were laughing about something, and looked very comfortable with each other. As they stopped to give way to an elderly woman on the street, Zelda noticed Hal placed his hand in the small of the woman's back.

'They look very cosy,' Ryan observed.

'I guess,' she replied, deliberately sounding offhand, but Zelda was wondering why Hal hadn't mentioned this woman to her. He hadn't said he was seeing anyone. Not that he had any duty to tell her, but they'd been spending quite a lot of time together recently.

She cast her mind back to the day at the nursery, when Hal had cut the pink rose just for her. There had been a definite moment between them – surely, she hadn't imagined that. She had thought of their time there together a lot in the days since, and felt a little warm whenever she recalled that quiet moment they'd shared. The rose was still in a tiny vase of water on her bedside table.

Seeing Hal with this woman sent an unexpected bolt of pain through her heart, and she turned away.

Zelda's phone lit up; it was Fiona's Uncle John. She'd only just texted him – *That was quick*, she thought. *I guess local history doesn't sleep in Loch Cameron.*

'Ah. I've got to take this. Bear with me.' She smiled apologetically at Ryan, trying to ignore the deeply inappropriate feeling in her heart. So what if Hal kissed someone? It was none of her business.

None. Of. Your. Business. Zelda. She lectured herself firmly.

'No problem. I'll make some coffee,' Ryan whispered, as Zelda answered the call.

'John, hi. Thanks so much for calling me back.'

Zelda turned back to the window as she spoke to Fiona's historian uncle, watching Hal and his mystery woman walk down the high street. Okay, they'd had a moment together. He'd given her a rose. Lairds probably handed out roses to American tourists on the regular, right? She was just getting overwhelmed by Loch Cameron and its annoyingly romantic ways: the sunrises and sunsets over the loch, turning it into a shimmering mirror of burnished gold; the droning of the bees in Gretchen's garden; the wildflowers and their remarkable scent that drifted into her bedroom at night.

Remember, you hate Scotland, she told herself. *There's nothing here but a father who didn't want you. Remember that.*

But then she thought, *that's kinda harsh*. It was as if she was answering her darker side, which had spent years reminding her that her dad had abandoned her, and had got stuck in a loop. *There are some good things here. Lots of good things. And good people.*

She focused back on the man on the other end of the phone.

'You're welcome, dear,' John said. 'Fiona gave you my number, did she?'

'Yeah. I was kinda interested in researching some family history, and she said you might help me out. I'm just visiting Scotland, but I was interested in something that happened with the Ross family, from Queen's Point,' Zelda explained.

'I can hear from your accent you're not from Loch Cameron.' John chuckled. 'Of course, dear. I'd be only too happy to help. Text me what you know, and what you want to know, and I'll see what I can do.'

John seemed very friendly. This was important, and she wanted to be able to do something nice for Gretchen, who had helped her so much since she'd got to Loch Cameron.

As she talked to John, she thought about what Gretchen had told her about Mary Queen of Scots. She thought about the legend that Mary, too, had met up with a lover secretly on the site of the cottage on Queen's Point. She wondered if it was true, or whether the legend was in fact a distorted reflection of another girl, much closer to home, and the scandal that befell her; a local girl with far less power and influence: Alice McQueen, who had loved the wrong man at the wrong time.

Yet, as she spoke to John, Zelda also couldn't get Hal Cameron and his mystery woman out of her mind. Who was she? She couldn't deny that she was attracted to the Laird, but if this new woman was a romantic attachment, it looked as though he was, almost certainly, the wrong man at the wrong time.

That was okay. Nothing had happened between them, and Zelda was a grown woman. Clearly, she had been right not to trust her feelings for Hal. This thought made her feel sadder still, even though she had proved herself right yet again. She was used to New York, where men stayed eligible bachelors for life, avoiding all suggestion of commitment. Zelda could choose not to get involved with Hal Cameron, a man who was clearly not interested in her.

So, why couldn't she stop thinking about the look in his eyes when he had handed her the rose?

THIRTY-ONE

YOU SAY BACKWATER, I SAY BOUTIQUE

By Zelda Hicks for *The New Yorker*

Use #zeldasscottishlife to share and comment

Preparations are go for the May Day bonfire party here in Loch Cameron, which is a Big Deal.

If you didn't know, May Day is the first of May. It's what they call a bank holiday in the UK, which means everyone gets the Monday nearest to the first May weekend off work – kind of like Labor Day weekend. As far as I can tell, for most Brits, bank holidays are nothing to do with banking, except that banks aren't open that day. Though, online banking is. In today's world of cyber currency, bank holidays feel like just another cute old British custom.

Anyway, May Day is a traditional festival which has its origins in the agricultural year. On May 1st, farmers would have bonfires to celebrate light and the sun and fire, and do things like drive their cows between two bonfires, hoping that the lucky smoke would give the cows health and the farmers blessings for the year ahead.

In Loch Cameron, it's an old tradition that, on May Day, the Laird throws a big party at the castle for everyone in the village. There's a bonfire, drinks, food and dancing, and I'm told that the Laird even recites some poetry.

Scottish poetry, of course. CAN YOU IMAGINE?? I can't actually wait.

In the lead-up to the party, my new friend Fiona McAllister at Fiona's Fashions, the only clothes shop in the village, is busy helping everyone choose a ball dress (or a cocktail dress – the dress code is pretty flexible, I believe) for the party. Just yesterday Fiona helped me choose a beautiful strapless red tartan gown that I LOVE.

Full disclosure: on the first day I visited Loch Cameron Castle, I had a moment imagining myself in a ball dress, overlooking the palatial castle gardens. Now, I'll never be part of the Scottish gentry, but a girl can dream, right? Even if the actual running of a Scottish estate is apparently (according to the Laird) tough and time-consuming.

And, a girl can have the dress, if not the title. Fiona tells me that the red tartan I chose is actually one of the tartans belonging to the Cameron clan. So, as a brunette, not only is red one of my colours, but it's also nice to be able to pay a small homage to the Laird and his clan with my outfit.

But, back to Fiona. Fiona's Fashions is a small but perfectly formed boutique in Loch Cameron where locals (and those further afield) can come to purchase a little glamour. Sure, Fiona also sells practical wear. She has to. This is Scotland, and not a Scottish city – I myself have had to avail myself of some walking boots and a few thick sweaters (or 'jumpers' as they say here; no idea where the jumping comes in).

(I have to admit that the boots are insanely comfy, by the way. I hate it, but it's true.)

Fiona herself is a true fashion entrepreneur. She started her shop after studying fashion at university with the help of a grant and a rent discount from the Laird, who is also the local landlord, and she's currently studying fashion merchandising too. Despite Loch Cameron's fairly remote location, Fiona is reaching out online to customers, as well as to other villages.

For my part, I'm always super keen to support young creatives. So, please follow Fiona's Instagram account below, and if you're ever in Scotland, then make a point of visiting her boutique for some truly original fashion finds. Fiona has a great eye, and since I've been here, she's given me some great ideas and turned me on to some amazing Scottish designers I didn't know about.

As we all know, new talent is our lifeblood, whether we're in theatre, publishing, fashion or the art world. And just because you live in a lochside village, it doesn't mean you haven't got something great to offer.

THIRTY-TWO

'So, you know what happened to Alice McQueen and her baby?'

Uncle John was sitting opposite Zelda in the cottage's small sitting room.

'Aye, lassie. And it's nice to meet you.' John sat on the sofa rather than the chair, having cast a nervous glance at the chaise longue when he came in. Zelda sat in Gretchen's hydrangea chair and poured tea from the teapot into two mugs.

Uncle John – Zelda thought she should probably think of him as 'John' – was perhaps in his mid to late fifties, dressed in the requisite Scotsman attire of brown corduroy trousers and a blue cotton shirt, since it was a warm evening. She thought he'd probably left a jumper or even a waterproof jacket in the car. He was a little red in the face, had a moustache and perspiration speckled his brow.

Zelda had told Gretchen that John was coming over with his findings that evening. However, it was Gretchen's canasta evening, which she said she couldn't possibly miss. 'It's the third in a tournament, dear,' she explained to Zelda on the phone. 'Mavis and I against David and Muriel. We've both won one and this is the decider. Mavis is apt to throw a fit and die if I cancel.'

'It's nice to meet you too. Fiona says you're really into family history. Ancestry,' Zelda added. 'Gretchen can't come over from the home tonight. But I'm going to tell her anything you tell me.'

'Right you are.' John accepted a mug of tea. 'Thank you, dear. And it's a pleasure to have a new project. I've researched most of the branches on my own family tree and my wife's, you see.'

'So is it a lot easier these days, what with the internet and everything? I guess in the old days, you'd have had to have gone to libraries, churches – that kind of thing?'

'Indeed, yes. Though sometimes it helps to do that sort of thing, too. In Loch Cameron, as is the case with some other regions where a Laird or Duke or other landowner holds a castle, they also keep records of the local area. Hal Cameron holds an impressive archive of the area – land records, official records kept by the previous Lairds and their estate managers – that's what used to be called "chamberlains". I've been up there once or twice before to find out details about this and that.'

'Did you consult the castle records about Alice?' Zelda pushed her fringe out of her eyes: she really needed a haircut but every time she walked over to the one salon in the village, it was still, apparently, shut. She realised, in retrospect, how lucky she'd been to find it open that one time ahead of her photoshoot at the castle.

It was like there was a weird local psychic arrangement where other people seemed to know when the salon would open, which wasn't necessarily the times on the sign on the door. She'd also called the number she'd found for the salon in a *Local Pages* magazine she'd found in the post at Gretchen's cottage, but no one ever answered the phone.

'Aye. Was most helpful, in fact.' John put his mug of tea

down and reached into a document case–type bag he'd brought with him. He laid some papers on the table as well as a laptop, which he opened and switched on. 'Shall we get started?'

'Yes, please.'

'So. You can see here, this is Gretchen Ross's family tree.' John pointed to the computer screen, which showed a diagram of the type Zelda had seen before. 'Here's Gretchen, her sister and her sister's husband. They had one child. Here you can see Gretchen's parents.' He pointed to two entries above Gretchen's name, labelled Jack and Mary Ross. 'You can see here also that Gretchen adopted a child. Sadly, she passed away not so long ago.'

'I had no idea! That's so sad,' Zelda frowned at the diagram. 'She never said anything.'

'Aye, well, she doesn't like to talk about it,' John shook his head. 'If she hasn't told you, then it's because it's probably difficult for her. She will, if she's ready.'

Zelda thought of the conversations she'd had with Gretchen: not once had her friend ever mentioned her own bereavement. Zelda felt sad that Gretchen hadn't opened up to her about it, but she wasn't about to head over to the care home and demand to know why. Grief was a difficult thing, and it affected everyone differently. Gretchen would tell her if she wanted to, in her own time.

'Now. The McQueens are linked to Gretchen's mother's side, but a few generations back,' John continued. 'Gretchen is a Ross. Mary Ross was Gretchen's mother, maiden name Smith. Evie Smith was her grandmother. Her great-grandmother was, according to the records I could find online, a Rosemary Stewart, and *her* mother was Alice Stewart née McQueen.' John followed the family tree with his finger. 'I found records at the castle of a McQueen family living here at the cottage about that time. The name Alastair McQueen is listed: I think that was Alice's father.'

'Alice had four children?' Zelda peered at the screen. 'The letters said she got pregnant from this Richard guy. Was that who she married?'

'No Richard McKelvie on the records related to Alice McQueen, but the castle records did show that there was a McKelvie family living in Loch Cameron at the same time as the McQueens.' John nodded. 'So I think we can assume that Richard was likely the son of the family.'

'And what about Alice's kids?'

'Well, she's listed as marrying one Donald Stewart, a farmer, in 1856, near Loch Awe. But look here.' John held out a piece of paper: a photocopy of an old document filled with almost unreadable handwriting in an old-fashioned pen and ink style.

'What am I looking at?' Zelda took the paper and frowned at it.

'This is the birth certificate for one May Stewart. Born a month before Donald and Alice were married. I'll wager May Stewart was Richard McKelvie and Alice's baby.'

'Wow. That would make sense. So, Alice married this farmer guy, and then she had three other children?'

'Yes. And one of them was Rosemary Stewart, who is Gretchen Ross's great-grandmother.' John nodded in satisfaction.

'Of course, with what we know now, we can say that any family tree branching off from May would need to be adjusted to incorporate Richard McKelvie as her biological father. But, honestly, goodness knows how many technical inaccuracies like mistaken parentage are included as fact in ancestry. In those times, it was seen as a sin to have a baby out of wedlock.'

'I know. It's so sad that Alice and Richard weren't allowed to be together. I wonder why Alice's father didn't just let her marry Richard, if that's what they wanted,' Zelda mused. 'And there might be members of the McKelvie family still around, maybe? Gretchen would be related to them – distantly, anyway.'

'We can't know about Alice's father's motivations, for sure. But the McQueens were likely religious, like many at that time. It wasn't unheard of for parents to send girls away when they got pregnant and pretend it hadn't happened. They might have told people that Alice went to help family elsewhere, or just pretended that she wasn't pregnant at all, and had gone to wed this Stewart fella. I don't think they would have thought it was fitting to let her marry a local boy when everyone knew they'd slept together first.' He paused, looking thoughtful. 'As to the McKelvies, I don't know of any in the village now. It would be interesting to find out.'

'I see.' Zelda sighed. 'And we have no way of knowing if Alice was happy with this Donald Stewart. I mean, I know she had three other babies, but that doesn't mean anything.'

'Quite. No birth control in those days, and it was normal to have a large family,' John agreed. 'All I can tell you is that Donald was significantly older than Alice. See, on their wedding certificate, it says he's a farmer, but that he's also forty-five. She was twenty at the time.'

'And I can't imagine that forty-five-year-old Donald the farmer was especially youthful in his outlook. It's not like today. Forty-five-year-olds are still struggling to settle down in New York.'

'I think you might be right there.' John picked up his tea and drank it. 'I suspect they made the best of it. But I doubt it was a love marriage.' He put the mug back on the table and brought out another piece of paper.

'This is another interesting thing. From the Laird's archive.' He passed the paper to Zelda. 'It's an entry from the chamberlain's journal. Like I said, the chamberlain was kind of like an estate manager is today. Looks after everything on a day-to-day basis for the Laird. In the 1850s, that was a guy called Philip Drury.'

'Right. So does Hal have an estate manager now?' Zelda took the piece of paper.

'No. He did, but I believe he's been without one for the past year or so. Not a job everyone wants to do.'

'Really? I can think of at least twenty people who'd jump at the chance to run a Scottish estate.' Zelda shook her head. 'And that's just from my apartment building back home.'

'Well, lots of people think they'd like to do something like that, but the reality is a little different from the romance, I'm afraid,' John said. 'I've helped Hal out on a few jobs over the years, and I can tell you he does most of the heavy lifting. If slates fall off the castle roof, he's the one who climbs up there and puts new ones on. It's Hal who does all the repairs: painting, electrics, plumbing. Nowadays, "Laird" is a code word for general labourer, most of the time.'

'Hmm. I guess it's kind of hard work,' Zelda acquiesced, remembering how Hal had run around checking everyone was okay on the night of the power cut. She also fought off a mental image of Hal, bare-chested and holding a drill. 'Anyway. What did Philip have to say about Alice?'

'Read it. It's quite illuminating.' John nodded at the paper in her hands.

'In the matter of Mistress Alice McQueen, Laird Cameron held a court at the castle on August 23rd, 1855. After hearing from Mr Alastair McQueen, tenant farmer, Laird Cameron decreed that, being ungodly and of unsound mind, Mistress McQueen be sent away to a place of her father's choosing, where she may not despoil the good reputation of her father further. A fine will also be applied to Mr Alastair McQueen for one year, payable to the Cameron Estate, sum to be agreed.' She looked up in amazement. 'Seriously?'

'I'm afraid so. It wasn't uncommon for Lairds to fine their

tenants for perceived wrongdoing then. The Laird is still the landlord to most here, but nowadays, of course, he doesn't impose fines for having babies out of wedlock. In fact, he refuses to rent the local properties out to external interests who would doubtless pay a lot more for them. Keeps the rents low, for locals, to ensure that the local businesses can stay afloat.'

'Yeah. That's great. But his ancestor was a pig,' Zelda fumed. 'Alice might not have got sent away if it wasn't for him.'

'It's hard to know, but yes. Possibly,' John mused.

'Does Hal know about this?'

'No. Well, not from me, anyway. He gave me access to the archive, but he had to be off somewhere. He left me to it, and I left the key with Anna when I was done.' John frowned.

'Well, he's gonna know. He has to take responsibility.' Zelda was angry. Alice's whole life had changed on the whim of Hal's powerful ancestor. It wasn't fair that a young woman's life could be ruined like that.

'Whatever you think best, dear.' John looked a little surprised. 'Is Hal responsible for what his ancestors did? I don't know the answer. Just asking the question.'

'I think he is. I mean, he didn't do that to Alice himself. And I know he's a good guy. But if anyone has responsibility... just to acknowledge what happened, you know? Or make reparation in some way. That person is Hal. He's the only person it could be.'

'I see what you mean, when you put it like that.' John looked thoughtful. 'Well, you should mention it to him. He's a reasonable fella, like you say.'

'I will.' Zelda was determined.

There was a slightly uncomfortable silence: she wondered if John thought she was being unreasonable. But, even if he did, she found she didn't really care. Some things were more important and, somehow, she'd ended up feeling responsible for Alice. There had to be something she could do to give Alice some kind of closure.

'These family trees are quite something.' John cleared his throat. 'They don't seem like much, when you first look at them. But they can be really quite... emotional.'

'Yeah. I get that.' Zelda stared at the laptop screen, lost in thought. 'I've never really thought that I might have one, you know? All this, with Alice – it's kind of triggering me thinking about my own family tree.' She knew that she was reacting strongly to Alice's story. Yes, it was sad, but it was also something that happened a long time ago, in a Scotland with a very different society than it had now.

If she was really honest with herself, perhaps her feelings of anger at the unfairness of Alice's story had something to do with the anger she still felt at her dad leaving her and her mom.

'Aye, it's interesting. Brings up a lot for people, sometimes,' John observed.

'I don't know anything about my dad's side of the family.' Zelda felt like she could trust John. He seemed kind, and he'd done all this work for Gretchen out of the goodness of his heart, apparently. 'He was – is – Scottish, actually. I'm not in touch with him, though.'

'Oh, how interesting! What was your father's surname?'

'Mackay. Robin Mackay.' It felt weird saying her father's name out loud: it had been such a long time since she had even acknowledged she had a father. In fact, when she'd mentioned it to Emery just before coming to Scotland in the first place, it had been the first time she'd told anyone in years.

Her father hadn't come to her mom's funeral. As far as Zelda was aware, he was still alive, but she supposed she wouldn't know if he had died.

'Mackay, eh? Big family. Still, if you had a date of birth and something else – were your parents married? Then I could likely trace the line.'

'They were married, yeah. They would have got married in America, though.'

'That's not a problem. These days, you can access records from other countries. There are some problem areas, like Germany in World War Two. A lot of lost records there.'

'Oh. Because of the Holocaust?' Zelda's heart clenched with sadness. 'That's so awful.'

'Aye. Terrible thing. All that lost history. Not lost. Destroyed on purpose. People still trying to reconstruct their family histories to this day.' John sighed. 'Shocking state of affairs. But Robin Mackay, I can probably do. If you want me to...'

Did she? Zelda didn't know. She thought about all the families who were desperate to connect to their ancestors but who were restricted from doing so because of persecution. They didn't have a choice, and probably yearned to know where they came from.

But Zelda had always refused to know. It was one small way that she could revenge herself on her father: by ignoring his existence and the whole of the Mackays' presence in the world. She had always been a Hicks, and her mom was her family.

But now, her mom was gone, and Zelda felt rootless. Her connection to family had been severed, and it was a lost, cold feeling.

Since she had been in Scotland, she'd had a nagging feeling: a strange kind of belonging. There was something about the land – the purple hills, the deep calm of Loch Cameron and the freshness of the air. It was difficult to describe, but Scotland felt like home, though it was a home she had never known.

'John, that's... that's so kind of you. Can I think about it and let you know?' Zelda didn't want to pour out her heart to this poor man who she'd only just met, and she needed time to think. Part of her was thinking, *Do this, do this, take this opportunity while you have it.* But the older, more familiar part of her was telling her that it would be a betrayal of her mom to follow up her dad now. Even just to know a little more about that side of her family, when she had always sworn not to.

She had loved – still loved – her mom so much. But it had been her own decision to cut herself off from her dad's side of the family. Her mom had never told her to do it. She had always said, *Do what feels right to you*. It had been Zelda's anger, her sense of abandonment, that had made her push her father away even more.

'Of course, dear. I'll leave these papers for you, and I can email you Gretchen's family tree.' John stood up, closing the laptop and putting it back in his bag. 'Nice to meet you, as I said. You're in Loch Cameron long?'

'I'm not sure. For now I'm taking a break here while I look for a new job back in New York.'

'Well, maybe your roots called you home,' John said. 'Funny how things happen, sometimes.'

'Maybe,' Zelda mused. 'Maybe it's just a coincidence.'

'Ah, well, dear – you know what they say. There are no coincidences. I'll leave you to enjoy the rest of your evening now. Thanks for the tea.'

'Thanks so much again, John. I know Gretchen will really appreciate all this.'

Zelda saw him out and watched him drive away up the dark, winding road around Queen's Point.

If there were no coincidences, then had the universe sent her to Loch Cameron? Why? To reconnect to her father? She wasn't ready to do that. But perhaps there was something in the idea of reconnecting to her roots.

Zelda stood in the doorway, watching the moon rise over the loch outside the cottage. She found herself thinking about *Rebecca*, the romance novel, again. In her column, she'd written about how the castle and the Laird somewhat reminded her of it, but that, after all, life wasn't a romance novel. Gretchen's life certainly hadn't been: John had told Zelda that Gretchen had adopted a child, who had died. She wondered when the adoption had taken place; she'd got the impression from Gretchen that she had never wanted children. And how old had Gretchen's adopted daughter been when she'd passed away?

She supposed no one would ever know if Mary Queen of Scots had also enjoyed a romantic tryst at the cottage. It was a nice idea, but the tale could have been the invention of someone trying to cover up the memory of what had really happened with Alice and Richard. It was feasible: how much easier to tell people that the rumour they'd heard was actually something far further back in history, and far less attached to their community. Nobody could be responsible for the lives of kings and queens. They were a law unto themselves. But a community could be responsible for ostracising a young girl.

Zelda pondered on the McQueen/Queen coincidence. Perhaps the legend about Mary Queen of Scots really *was* a village cover-up, intentional or not. The McQueen name was conveniently similar: perhaps it wouldn't have taken too much imagination to forget that Alice was a real girl, and not a queen, over time.

Perhaps, like Manderley, the moody old house in *Rebecca* that nursed dark secrets, the cottage at Queen's Point held something else. Not darkness, per se, but memories of lovers. Zelda imagined Richard McKelvie passing by the cottage as he said he did in his letters. She wondered how many times he had walked past, waiting for Alice to come out. And she wondered if the house held memories of Gretchen's daughter, too. So many of those must have been happy, even if some were also sad.

A breeze blew up from the loch, and Zelda wrapped her cardigan around her. She closed the door, not wanting to think about poor Gretchen's loss anymore, of the ghost of poor Richard McKelvie walking up and down Queen's Point forever.

She didn't believe in ghosts, in the usual definition of the word. But she wondered whether there might be ghosts of a different kind in old communities, where the families had lived alongside each other for so long. Many secrets would likely be buried beneath gardens, wedged between floorboards and plastered into walls.

Loch Cameron was a welcoming place, but Zelda could well believe that it held shadows too. And she wondered if anyone else knew about Alice, still – or whether her story had been buried in the foundations of the village.

THIRTY-THREE

Every time Zelda wiped another champagne flute, she thought about how the party was a few seconds closer than it had been before. She and Hal had been planning it for weeks now, and a part of her had thought it would never arrive.

There were only two days left until May Day, and the castle was in chaos. The bathrooms still needed to be fixed, one of the staircases needed mending, and Anna had been in the kitchen making pies and bridies for what seemed like days.

Eric, Dotty's husband from the inn, was on glass duty with her in the huge central hall of the castle. They had twenty boxes of hired glassware to go through, making sure it was clean and ready for use.

It's quite the experience, Zelda thought, *being inside this part of the castle.* The great hall was hung with muskets, swords and other old weaponry that, she supposed, the Camerons had once used in tribal wars. Large oil paintings in ornate gold frames hung everywhere – portraits of Hal's ancestors, many of whom shared Hal Cameron's intense blue eyes.

The hall also contained a variety of display cases holding valuable-looking vases and other trinkets. Zelda was particularly taken with a case filled with old photos in frames: black and white images looked back at her, of Scottish noblemen and their ladies with serious expressions; of greying men in formal wear and stiff-looking older women in cocktail dresses and hats. But some of the photos were jollier: there were some of groups of people at parties, laughing into the camera.

She was composing a column about the party in her mind, but she didn't quite have the angle for it yet. Plus, she wanted to weave in what she'd found out about Alice McQueen: if she could make a link from Alice to the modern-day Loch Cameron, and perhaps to women in general, then she knew she'd have a good story. But what did she really want to say?

She'd emailed Hal with the information John had given her a few days ago, but had no reply. She didn't know exactly what she wanted from Hal – a formal apology in the local newspaper? An acknowledgement to Gretchen that what his ancestor had done was wrong? It was difficult to know what was appropriate. But a reply to her email would have been nice, as a start. In fact, Zelda hadn't heard from Hal properly for a few days, which was odd. It made her feel a little stranded, emotionally; they'd been getting on so well, and they'd either spoken every day or been together at the castle or in the village, organising the party. The sudden silence, especially when the party was almost here, made her wonder if she had inadvertently done something wrong.

Perhaps her next column would be about men who didn't answer messages. She considered it briefly before reluctantly discarding the idea.

'I think it should all get done on time. As long as we all pull together,' Hal was saying as he walked in. Zelda looked down at the glass she was holding, not wanting to catch his eye. He was with the same woman she had seen him with from Ryan's bookshop the other day.

The woman was tall and slender, dark blonde and pretty in

a bland kind of way. She wore hiking boots, a rain mac and jeans, and her hair was held up in a ponytail.

Whoever this woman was, she looked as though she belonged in the castle: she had that perfect Scottish look, like she could take Finnegan, Hal's dog, out for a brisk hike up the hills at any moment, know the names of all the cows in all the boggy fields and roll up her sleeves to help out with a lame horse.

In fact, now that Zelda saw her up close, she realised the face was familiar. She'd seen this woman before – not just that time in the village, when Zelda had watched her and Hal walk along the high street – but she couldn't think where.

In contrast to Hal's guest, Zelda was wearing a pure white, full-skirted dress with low red strappy heels. She'd plaited her black hair and woven a red ribbon into the plait before pinning it up: overall, she thought her look was a kind of 1950s take on Heidi, which wasn't a bad thing at all.

She'd bought the dress from Fiona, having seen it in the window with some other new stock, and been powerless to resist. The shoes she'd found online while looking for a good bedside table for Gretchen's bedroom in the cottage, on an app where people sold vintage finds. There wasn't any particular need to dress up to be at the castle that day – she was only helping out, and in fact, she was already regretting the white dress, because she'd managed to get a long streak of dust on one side of it.

Seems like you still haven't learnt your lesson about practical clothes at the castle, Zelda girl, she thought, wryly. It was exactly what her mom would have told her, if she was there.

Finnegan raced in past Hal and the woman and gave Zelda a *hello* bark.

She knelt down and scratched his ears. 'Hello, boy. How are you? I haven't seen you for a while,' she murmured.

Finnegan licked her hand as if to say, *I know, I missed you!*

'Zelda, hallo.' Hal approached where she and Eric were arranging the glasses onto a long trestle table that had been covered with a length of red Cameron tartan. 'I... didnae know ye were goin' tae be here. Finnegan! Heel!'

'Oh, I just thought I'd come and help out,' Zelda replied, smoothly. 'And, don't worry, Finnegan's fine. We missed each other, didn't we?' She fussed over the dog again, to the spaniel's complete delight.

'Right. Eric. How's everythin' comin' along?' Hal cleared his throat and turned his attention to Dotty's husband, who nodded amiably.

'Aye, it should all be ready in time. Dotty and I've ordered up all the booze for ye. Should arrive this afternoon. An' Zelda's doin' a fine job helpin' me wi' the glasses.'

'Thank you both. May I introduce Bella, my guest for the party?' Hal introduced Zelda and Eric politely, though Zelda thought he seemed a little sheepish. 'Bella, Zelda helped me organise this shindig. She's here from New York on a... what? Sabbatical of some kind, aye?'

'Agh. Kinda. Flying by the seat of my drawers right now, not gonna lie.' Zelda shook Bella's hand. 'Great to meet you.'

'Ah, Zelda, I've heard so much about you,' Bella replied, in a tone that implied *maybe too much.*

'All glowing reviews, I hope?' Zelda grinned at Hal, who looked embarrassed and didn't reply.

Maybe not so glowing, she thought. Zelda stared at Bella's face, trying to place her. 'You know, I recognise you from somewhere. I've seen you before.'

'Possibly. I was in a celebrity magazine recently,' Bella replied, off-handedly.

'Oh, yes! That's it! You're the eligible heiress!' Zelda pointed triumphantly at Bella, who looked faintly alarmed. 'Sorry. In the magazine. That was the article. And Hal was the favourite of the possible suitors,' she remembered in a rush. 'Wow. Looks like they weren't wrong, for a change.'

'Indeed,' Bella cast her eyes to the ceiling. 'That was such a funny article.'

'So, have you known each other a long time?' Zelda asked.

'Oh, yes, a long time indeed. I'm an old friend of the family.' Bella laughed. 'Hal came to my fifth birthday party and took all his clothes off. It can make or break a relationship. Fortunately, it made ours.' She linked her arm through Hal's. 'We were boyfriend and girlfriend all through our teens. Then, Hal met Maggie, of course. God rest her soul.' Bella cast her eyes down piously.

'How sweet,' Zelda commented drily. 'I'm glad he seems to have got in the habit of keeping his clothes on. Although there is a party looming. Could be a crisis point.'

'I can assure ye everyone's safe from that particular party trick happenin' again,' Hal replied in a jolly tone, but Zelda could sense there was a thread of discomfort under his words. Was it what Bella had said, or was it the way that she had taken his arm, almost proprietorially? Zelda wondered how this old girlfriend reunion had come about. She was pretty sure Hal hadn't mentioned Bella to her.

None of your business, Zelda, she warned herself.

'Oh, Hal, by the way, I sent you an email about some local history I was researching – I don't know if you've had a chance to look at it, but it would be great to get a reply,' she said instead, taking the opportunity to make sure Hal didn't manage to avoid what she'd sent.

'Ah. Sorry. I've been busy. I'll look later.' He frowned.

'Okay' Zelda smiled, sensing an awkwardness between them.

'So, what did you think of the revamped castle website, Bella?' Zelda turned her attention to Bella.

'Oh, it's lovely! And the photos. What a good idea to put Hal in them!' Bella cooed. 'And at the last minute, too.'

'Well, fortunately that was kinda my job, before I got marooned here, anyway. When you're a journalist, you always have a plan B. Hal was my plan B. It worked out pretty well,' she answered smoothly.

'Oh, yes. All the pictures are lovely.' Bella squeezed Hal's arm. 'He's so handsome.'

Zelda noted that Bella didn't mention anything about her in the pictures.

I get it, lady, she thought. *Hal's yours, and you feel the need to stake your claim in public. Okay.*

'Well, I'm glad it's all worked out,' Zelda said. 'And I'm really looking forward to the party! I've never been to anything like this. I hear there's going to be something called a cay-lee?' She frowned as she pronounced it. 'That's a type of dance?'

'A ceilidh. That's the traditional dancing, yes,' Bella explained. 'Not one particular dance. There are a number of traditional steps. It's very high energy. Might not suit a city girl.' She laughed.

'Ah, that's okay, Bella.' Zelda smiled, sweetly. 'I think I'll be all right with a little dancing.'

'Hal told me you fell over outside and broke your wrist. You should be careful at the ceilidh,' Bella said. 'Oh, listen to me. I'm sure you'll be fine!' she added, looking awkward.

'No, I'll be careful, I promise. My cast came off last week,' Zelda made an awkward salute. *What was that?* she berated herself. *You don't have to salute the woman. She's not a Duchess.*

There was another brief, uncomfortable silence.

Hal cleared his throat. 'Anyway, we should be gettin' on. Thanks so much for the hard work, Eric. Zelda.' He nodded and turned away, Bella's arm still in his.

'Okay, take care!' Zelda called after them both.

Eric carried on polishing the glasses. Zelda sighed and picked up another one. She was still looking forward to the party, but she had to admit that the idea of Bella being Hal's date for the dance was going to take some of the shine off the whole affair.

A LETTER, A LOCH AND SOME VINTAGE LOUBOUTINS

By Zelda Hicks for *The New Yorker*

Use #zeldasscottishlife to share and comment

This week, I've been helping the village prepare for the May Day party at the castle. On Monday I made streamers, on Tuesday I helped build the bonfire, and yesterday I was on glass-polishing duty in the glorious great hall of Loch Cameron Castle.

I'm looking forward to learning some Scottish country dancing for the ceilidh, though I've been told I shouldn't wear heels for the event in case I fall over again. A fair point.

Anyway, when I haven't been scrubbing the castle in my pinny, I've also been helping out my landlady Gretchen research some of her fascinating family history.

Gretch is the person you'd get if you mixed the bookish, savage wit of Fran Leibowitz with Mrs Doubtfire. She worked in book publishing all her life, is staunchly single, plays a mean game of cards and she never met a biscuit she didn't like.

I've been staying at Gretch's darling old cottage in return for decorating it so that she can rent it out, now that she's moved into some sheltered accommodation. (She would like me to add here that this isn't because she's 'feeble' or 'lost her faculties' but because she decided to go somewhere she could have help on hand if needed, and she was sick of cooking for herself.)

At the cottage, I found a stack of old letters belonging to a former resident from the 1850s. With the help of Fiona's (remember, she runs the amazing fashion boutique here in Loch Cameron) uncle, John, we found out the sad story of Alice McQueen, a poor girl from the village who fell in love with the wrong guy at the wrong time, got pregnant and ended up being sent away to marry a guy much older than her in another town. Far enough away that her parents wouldn't be embarrassed by (what they thought of as) her indecorous behaviour, I guess.

I've been thinking about Alice a lot, and feeling sad for her. And I've been thinking about how our society can still demonise young women – especially those of lower economic status – for what they think of as 'improper' behaviour. Sure, we might not send our pregnant girls off to the other town anymore because their actions have shamed the family. But we do still judge young women all the time: for their clothes, for being loud/pretty/ugly or not loud, pretty or ugly enough. We judge young women for how many partners they have, if they have children outside marriage, for working and not working as moms, for breastfeeding or not breastfeeding, for being sexy or not being sexy.

Gretchen herself faced difficulties in her younger life, for not wanting to get married. She wanted a career and, in her words, she didn't want to wash some guy's socks for eternity. Amen to that.

Alice would have been able to stay with the father of her child in our times, but people might still have judged her. Some local might still call her a *sleekit hussy* if she lived in Loch Cameron today. Most people here are really nice, but there are gossips like there are anywhere.

So, at the May Day party, I'm going to dance in my heels – or maybe some flats, to be safe – have a few glasses of champagne, maybe even kiss some hot local guy – yes, there may be someone – and enjoy myself with the kind of wild abandon that this type of party deserves. And I'm going to do it for Alice, and hope that, somehow, she knows. And may I ask you all to raise a glass to Alice McQueen this May Day, and every girl like her. Because they all deserve our love and respect.

THIRTY-FOUR

That night, Zelda had a vivid dream.

In the dream, she was standing in front of a castle, but it wasn't Loch Cameron Castle. This was a small, ruined tangle of stones in a dark landscape. The dream felt ominous, as if something were about to jump out of the shadows at her at any moment.

In the dream, Zelda felt as though she knew this old place, but she couldn't remember what it was called. She walked around the ruined building, noticing its entrance, grown over by ivy, and the rooms, some of which were open to the elements, some of which were closed.

The light in the dream adjusted a little and Zelda could see that the castle stood in an overgrown field. In the field, there was a bull grazing. She walked away from the bull, fearing that it could charge her at any moment.

She walked up to the door of the castle and was about to step in when she heard the bull approaching her from behind. She looked over her shoulder in fear, expecting to see it charging with its horns. But, instead, it stood next to her and nuzzled her hand.

That was the end of the dream. She woke up in the middle of the night to the silence of Loch Cameron around her in place of the blankets she had pushed off the bed in her sleep. Cold, she pulled them off the floor and settled down to sleep again. Yet, she couldn't stop thinking about the castle.

———

'See, this is you, then your parents, reaching all the way back to Alice.' Zelda sat next to Gretchen at an outside table at her home for the elderly, showing her a printout of the family tree that John had researched. It was a clear, sunny morning, but Gretchen still sat with a fleece blanket over her legs. Both of them had a cappuccino from the onsite café, which, Zelda had to admit, was actually pretty nice.

'Oooh. What a thing.' Gretchen took the paper and peered at it through her reading glasses.

'Look, Gretchen, I hope you don't mind, but when John gave me the family tree, it also had your daughter on it,' Zelda said, finding the words difficult but knowing she had to say them anyway. 'I can understand that you didn't want to talk about it. I'm just saying, I know.'

'Ah. I see,' Gretchen tapped her fingers on the arm of her chair and looked away. 'I'm sorry... I just find it rather difficult to talk about her.' Her voice cracked a little. 'It's still rather raw.'

'Of course. I understand, and I'm not prying. I just happened to find out from this. That's all.' Zelda felt awful. She didn't know what else to say to Gretchen.

'I know you're not prying, dear. I'd never think that.' Gretchen looked back to Zelda and gave her a soft smile. 'My daughter – Stella – died a couple of years ago. Car accident. She was fifty.'

'I'm so sorry, Gretch,' Zelda took her hand.

'I know. Thank you.' Gretchen's eyes welled up with tears,

and she blinked them away furiously. 'Do you mind if we talk about Alice, now? I'd prefer it.'

'Okay. Sure. So, Alice had four children, in the end. Your family line came from her daughter Rosemary, who was the first child she had with this guy, Donald Stewart. But John thought that her first child would be the one who was actually Richard McKelvie's. Look at the date of birth and the marriage certificate. Too close.' Zelda passed Gretchen the papers John had left with her. She wanted to say something else about Stella, Gretchen's daughter, but she didn't know what. What could you ever say to someone who had lost a loved one? There was nothing that could make it better. Zelda knew that better than anyone.

'I see. Goodness.' Gretchen sighed, wiping her eyes. 'So, now we know what happened. She got sent away. Poor lassie. At least she made it back to the cottage when she was older. She must have kept Richard's letters for all that time. Honestly, I didn't know I had them. My mother must have been passed them, and hid them in that photo album. She was one for squirreling things away, it has to be said. I wonder if she knew anything of Alice.'

'Your mom never mentioned this whole thing to you?' Zelda asked.

'No. I knew nothing about it. Remarkable.'

'That's actually not all. The Laird at the time was pretty much responsible for hounding Alice out of the village, as was her father.' Zelda showed Gretchen the copy John had given her from Philip Drury's journal. 'I've emailed Hal about it, but I haven't had a reply. He needs to acknowledge what happened, at least. Say sorry to you.'

'Ah, Zelda. It was a very long time ago.' Gretchen sighed again. 'None of this is Hal's fault.'

'No, but he's the Laird here,' Zelda insisted. 'He has responsibility for the community. He knows that. And that includes the past.'

'Well, I hope you're not going to hound him about it, dear.' Gretchen gave her a fierce, gimlet-eyed look. 'Hal's helped me out a lot over the years. I count him as a friend. And I count you as one, too. So, just be polite.'

'Fine, fine, okay. Sorry, I know he's your friend. He's my friend too, I think. But, still,' Zelda grumbled.

'Manners are free,' Gretchen chastised her. 'Don't make Alice's troubles your own, either. It was a different time.' She broke off to wave at two gentlemen two tables away. 'Sam and Arthur. We play bridge sometimes.'

'Oh, right. Cool.' Zelda looked over at the two gentlemen in question, who were smiling away at Gretchen; one of them was adjusting his tie. Clearly, she was pretty popular here. 'But, still. I think Alice deserves some kind of justice.'

'I understand, and I agree. Let's see what Hal has to say on the matter.' Gretchen patted her hand.

'It's actually made me think about asking John to do my family tree,' Zelda confessed. The dream from the night before was playing on her mind. Instinctively, she felt that the broken-down old castle represented the Scottish side of her family: the Mackays. She had left that connection untended for so long – in fact, her whole life. She didn't necessarily want to reunite with her father and whatever other relatives there might have been, but she felt as though she did at least want to know where her dad had come from, and who had come before her.

'I see.' Gretchen nodded.

'It's my dad's side of the family. They were – are – Scottish. I dunno, Gretch. The whole time I've been here, I've had this kinda... urge... to connect to that side of my family. I mean, if only in terms of knowing more. I'm not sure I want to turn up on anyone's doorstep, demanding a hug, or anything.'

'Ha. I knew it!' Gretchen drummed on the table with both

hands. 'That first day we met, I thought, "Here's a girl who's lost her way." Or found her way here for a reason. I did say that to you, didn't I? That day when you turned up in the garden and I asked you in for tea.'

'You said maybe I would end up staying. And I did.'

'Hmph. Close enough. I must have thought the rest,' Gretchen tutted. 'Plus, you know, you do have a Scots look about you. Something about the eyes and cheeks. And that black hair. Pure Celt.'

'No one's ever mentioned that to me before,' Zelda replied, self-consciously wondering what Celtic cheeks were like.

'Well, that doesn't mean it's not obvious.' Gretchen waved her hand dismissively. 'Anyway. You should ask John, if he offered to do it.'

'I don't want to take advantage. He might just be being kind,' Zelda prevaricated.

'Nonsense. John's retired, he hasn't got anything else to do. Plus, he still owes me a favour.' Gretchen sniffed. 'Ask him. There. I've decided for you.'

'All right. I guess just having a family tree done won't hurt,' Zelda acquiesced.

'Exactly. You might want more, after, or you might not. But at least it's a start, eh?'

Zelda thought about her dream again, and the bull in the field that she had been so afraid of. Before she had woken up, it had become docile, even friendly. Perhaps that was a sign that she shouldn't be afraid of this, and that there might be some way to reconcile her feelings towards being a Mackay.

'It's a start,' Zelda agreed. 'And... all that stuff I told you about my mom. It kind of means something to me too, because of that. I'm aware it's not her family, and that she never reconciled with my dad or anything. It's just... I miss having something to be connected to, you know?' She sighed.

'I do know.' Gretchen nodded. 'You need roots. All yours

got pulled up. It's completely natural to want to know where your other ones grow, at least.'

Zelda felt tears forming in her eyes again, and she blinked them away. 'That's it,' she said. 'How did you get to be so wise, Gretch?' She wiped her eyes with the back of her hand.

'I'm old.' Gretchen shrugged. 'It happens to the best of us.'

THIRTY-FIVE

Enjoyed your column this week.

Zelda frowned at the message that had flashed up on her phone from Hal. She was sitting in Myrtle's cosy café, scanning various sites for jobs at her laptop. She had also just emailed John all the details she could remember about her dad's origins, plus her date of birth and her mom's. *Let's see what he comes up with*, she thought.

After her conversation with Gretchen about it all, Zelda had felt a little better about letting herself investigate her dad's side of the family. It didn't mean that she had to reconcile with anyone. But, as Gretchen said, it could give her some sense of her roots that were, currently, missing.

I didn't know you read it, she replied to Hal.

There was a pause before Hal answered.

Of course I do.

Not offended by my writing about social repression in Loch Cameron in the 1850s? she asked.

No, why would I be? he replied. *I wasn't alive then.*

Fair, she thought.

Did you read my email about Alice McQueen? she wrote.

There was another pause. Zelda looked back at the magazine and newspaper jobs website and filtered her results to 'Features Editor'. Nothing popped up. She sighed, and resisted the urge to give up looking for a job altogether.

Yes came the reply. Zelda waited for something else, but nothing did.

Myrtle appeared at her side and topped up her tea from a teapot.

'Any luck, dear?' she ventured. Today, she was wearing pink slacks and a white blouse with a black waistcoat on top and a pink floral scarf. Zelda thought again about the Molly Ringwald reference, but she wondered whether Myrtle would know who she was talking about.

'No.' Zelda sighed. 'Maybe I should just come here and work in the café with you, Myrtle.'

'Ah, that'd be grand, Zelda. But there're only four tables, remember. You'd not have much tae do.' Myrtle patted her shoulder.

Lovely to meet Bella the other day, Zelda wrote to Hal.

She hadn't mentioned anything to him after that day at the castle, but Bella had seemed a little off with her. Maybe she'd imagined it.

Yes, she enjoyed meeting you too, Hal replied.

Zelda had to admire his boring text style. It was all perfectly punctuated, for one thing – who used full stops in text messages? Plus, there were no emojis or pictures; nothing apart from full sentences. In fact, she found it quaintly charming – not that she would ever tell him that.

Yeah, right. She might as well have peed all over you, Zelda wanted to reply, but she restrained herself.

It would be nice to get to know her better, Zelda replied, instead. *Perhaps at the party.*

Yes, he replied.

It's fine, I get it. Now you and Bella are together, Zelda thought. *I just kinda wish I'd known before you walked into the castle with her on your arm like nothing had happened between us. I could have prepared myself.*

There was a pause, and another message from Hal flashed up on the screen.

I value your friendship, he wrote.

Zelda sighed.

Me too, she typed. What else could she say? She and Hal had flirted. They had chemistry. But there was nothing officially going on between them.

I think if you knew her, you'd like Bella, Hal replied.

I'm sure I will, Zelda answered, though she was hurt. There *had* been something between her and Hal: she hadn't imagined it. She knew they had both felt the crazy chemistry that seemed to bubble over when they were together. At the castle, at the stone circle, at the rose nursery, there had been so many moments when she had wondered whether anything was going to happen. Perhaps, in her heart of hearts, she had expected something to.

So, now Bella was suddenly on the scene, Zelda felt left out in the cold, and that made her sadder than she liked to admit.

It looked like Hal was replying something further: the dots scrolled on the screen for a long moment, but when he sent his message, it just said:

Okay. Looking forward to seeing you at the party.

Zelda stared at her phone, waiting for something more, but Hal had gone.

'Hey, gorgeous.' Ryan touched her shoulder from behind and made her jump.

'Jeez! You frightened me.' Zelda put her hand over her suddenly racing heart. 'Hi, Ryan. What're you doing here?'

'Lunch.' He sat down opposite her at the table. 'What about you?'

'Jobs. And tea, possibly leading to lunch,' Zelda admitted, looking over at the café counter where some of Myrtle's delicious-looking sandwiches sat behind the glass. On top of the counter, plates of millionaire's shortbread, huge oat cookies and rich-looking brownies sat under glass domes.

'May I join you?' Ryan asked.

'I think you have already,' Zelda retorted, but she wasn't cross at being interrupted. Quite frankly, she was ready for a break from job hunting.

'For lunch?' Ryan clarified. 'I can get something to go if you're busy.'

'No, it's cool. I need a break.' She sighed and closed her laptop. As she did so, she realised that Hal still hadn't answered her question about the email she'd sent him about Alice McQueen.

Damn, she thought. *I'll have to chase him up about it.* Plus, there were a number of party-related things they still had to talk over before the big event.

Zelda considered telling Ryan about Hal's ancestor and his judgement of Alice – and how Hal was refusing to talk about it – but she decided against it. Though she was cross with Hal, Ryan already disliked him so much that she knew it would just add more fuel to that particular fire. Something in her made Zelda hold the information back: it was still possible that Hal had a good reason for not responding – though she couldn't think what it might be.

'Have you met Bella... Hal's new girlfriend?' she asked Ryan, casually. She was curious to know what Ryan might think of her.

'I have, yeah. I thought that was her, when we saw them through the window that time. I mean, it was a while ago when we met. She visited Hal and Maggie some years back and we all had a drink at the inn one night. Maggie made me go. She was always trying to get Hal and me to be friends.' He made a face. 'I did it for her, obviously. But, yeah, Bella is one of those typical aristocratic girls. All private schools, horses and skiing.'

'Really?' Zelda finished the last dregs of her coffee. She wondered what Bella knew about Hal and Maggie. About what Ryan had said had happened at the end of Maggie's life, being imprisoned in her room. It had played on her mind since he'd told her, and she didn't like the thought of poor Maggie being alone, apart from Hal and a nurse, in her last days.

'Yeah. Why d'you ask?' Ryan glanced at Myrtle's specials board.

'Oh, no reason. She was acting kinda weird, when I met her. Possessive of Hal. Like, I got the impression she thought I was trying to get with him or something. Which I'm not, by the way,' Zelda added.

'I should hope not. I rather had ambitions in that area, so.' Ryan gave her a mock-smouldering look.

Zelda raised an eyebrow, but said nothing.

'Uh-oh,' Ryan muttered, and lowered his gaze. 'Don't look now, but they both just walked in.'

Zelda did look around and caught Bella's eye immediately.

'Oh. Hallo, Zelda. How nice to see you again,' Bella cooed.

'Hi, Bella.' Zelda smiled as warmly as she could. 'How are you? I like your jeans.'

'Oh. Thank you.' Bella stuck both hands in the pockets of her parka and looked awkward.

The café door opened again, and Hal walked in. Zelda noted he hadn't shaved for a while, and his scraggly beard was back; his heavy work trousers also had holes in them, and his jacket was muddy.

Clearly, Bella didn't care if Hal looked unkempt. They were both probably far too busy romping around the fields or clay pigeon shooting to care about clothes.

Not that style was the most important thing in life. If being in Loch Cameron had made Zelda realise anything – other than the fact that she loved tea and biscuits – it was that it was refreshing to live in a place where people weren't constantly analysing whether she was wearing the up-to-date season's clothes, shoes and accessories. Working and living inside the culture bubble in New York had been exhausting. She could see that now.

But Zelda would always love pretty dresses. In fact, clothes were a link back to her mom, and the dry-cleaning shop. It had been there that Zelda had been surrounded by the skirts, dresses, dinner jackets and all manner of other things that commuters would drop in, on their way in and out of Manhattan. Zelda's mom was such a renowned specialist, especially with the really delicate couture, that rich women from around New York also sent their ball dresses and evening dresses over for her to clean, often via a bored assistant who would wait as the young Zelda wrote out the receipt, and then hand over the dresses zipped in individual garment bags; they were often so heavy that Zelda almost dropped them.

'Oh. Hi, Hal.' It was strange, seeing him so soon after their text exchange. She hadn't figured on seeing either him or Bella; a quiet morning on her own was fast turning into an awkward lunchtime.

'Hallo, Zelda.' Hal gave her a polite nod. 'Bella's just been helpin' me organise the fireworks, you know, like we agreed. Thought we'd drop in for some lunch.'

'Fireworks. Right. Did you get them from the guy you were thinking of?' Zelda and Hal had discussed the duties for the week of the party in detail the last time she'd been up at the castle.

'Aye. Got a good deal. He's bringing them over to set up later.' Hal came over to Zelda's table, with Bella holding his arm slightly proprietorially.

'That's great, Hal. I can't wait to see them.' Zelda was feeling awkward with Bella there. She had in fact thought that she and Hal were going to look at the fireworks together. Was Bella taking over organising the party, and no one had told her?

No. Don't overreact, she thought. It all probably happened naturally – like he said. *Ah, I've got tae go and see a man about some fireworks now, lassie*, and Bella said, *Why don't I come with you?* That was it.

Be sensible, Zelda reminded herself. *You have a list of things you do actually need the Laird's opinion on.*

'Listen, Hal, while you're here, can I ask you about waiters and waitresses? I know we've got ten, but I'm not sure it's enough.' She picked up her phone, flicking onto her Notes app and casting her eye down the items on the page. She tried to ignore the disappointment she was feeling about – what? Losing Hal? *But you never had him*, she told herself.

'Sure.' Hal sat down at the table. 'Bella, why don't you go and order for us? I'll be right there,' he suggested.

'Right you are,' Bella said, giving Hal and Zelda a curious look before going to the counter. Ryan stood up and muttered something about lunch too, following Bella.

'So, yes, waiters. Do you think we need more?' Hal said, his leg brushing against Zelda's under the table as he shifted his weight. Zelda felt that now-familiar zip of electricity at the contact, but tried to ignore it.

Ryan and Bella seemed to be making polite chitchat at the counter. Myrtle served Bella some soup to take away and a couple of crusty rolls. Zelda could tell she was observing the dynamics between the group with her keen eye, but was of course too polite to get involved.

'Maybe a few more? Is there anyone you can think of who could fill in at the last minute?' Zelda glanced up at Hal and found he was gazing at her with an intense look.

'What? Oh. Right. Dotty and Eric have a lot o' grandchildren in their teens an' twenties. They helped out before. I can ask them,' Hal suggested. 'Nae bother.'

'Okay. Well, that left the fireworks, but you went today.' Zelda ticked the item off her list.

'Aye. It happened tae be on our way somewhere.' Hal looked slightly uncomfortable. 'I hope ye dinnae mind. It was a spur-o'-the-moment thing tae drop in, since we were in the area.'

'Of course I don't mind!' Zelda assured him, keeping her eyes on the list. 'Now, then, what else...' She trailed off, suddenly aware of the sound of raised voices.

'Hey! What's going on?' Hal frowned, getting up.

'Nothing. Let's go, Hal.' Bella reached out and took his arm. Myrtle put some paper bags on the counter, and Bella grabbed them.

'No. What is it? Did he say somethin' tae ye?' Hal looked at Ryan.

'We were just having a conversation. Nothing to do with you,' Ryan replied.

'Well, clearly it wasnae *just a conversation*. She looks upset,' Hal insisted. 'Bel? You okay?'

'I'm fine. Let's just go,' Bella repeated.

'If you must know, Bella and I were just talking about what a help Zelda's been to you in organising the party.' Ryan spread his hands out in an innocent gesture. 'But, as ever, you have to know everything. Are you going to try and control Bella, just like you tried to control Maggie?'

Hal turned to Ryan, glowering. 'What did ye just say? Keep my wife's name oot o' yer mouth,' he growled. All trace of his usual mild-mannered self had evaporated. 'Ye don't speak for Maggie and ye never did. Aye, she was kind tae everyone. But never think you knew her better than I did. She thought ye were a lost soul. She wanted to help ye. Yer friendship was based on pity, nothin' else.' Hal's eyes were blazing, and his face had flushed.

'She was my friend, Hal. You can convince yourself of whatever story suits you. But that's the truth. You couldn't deal with it then, and you still can't.' Ryan had raised his voice, standing his ground, but Zelda could see Hal's words had hurt. 'If she hadn't been so ill, she would have left you. You were too controlling. Everyone knows it.'

Hal grabbed Ryan by the collar and lifted him off the ground: he was probably a good six inches taller than Ryan and, while Ryan was slim and athletic, Hal was as tall and broad as a tree. 'Say that again!' he shouted. 'Don't you *dare*! Don't you *dare* talk about Maggie. Ever!'

'Hal! Stop it!' Zelda screamed, shocked that things had escalated this suddenly.

Hal released Ryan, scowling. Ryan put his hand to his throat. 'You'll regret that,' he said, in a low voice. 'I've got witnesses. You assaulted me.'

'I shouldnae have lost my temper and for that, I'm sorry.' Hal let out a deep breath, still seething. 'I shouldnae have touched ye. But I stand by what I said. Zelda, I'd advise ye to stay well clear of this liar,' he added.

'Don't tell me what to do, Hal,' Zelda snapped. 'You know you're in the wrong. Apologise to Ryan!'

'I've said everythin' I want tae,' he argued back. 'Don't get involved with this guy, Zelda. He's no' good to women. I wouldnae like tae see ye get hurt.'

Like you care about me, Zelda thought, her emotions rising quicker than she could push them down.

'My love life is none of your business, Hal,' Zelda shot back. 'Just like yours is none of mine.'

Hal held her gaze for a moment, looking like he wanted to reply, then nodded brusquely. 'Right.' He opened the café door. 'Bella. We're goin'.' And he strode out, with Bella right behind him.

'Oh my goodness. What's goin' on?' Myrtle came out from

behind the counter. 'I won't have violence in my café!' she admonished Ryan, who scowled at Hal's retreating back through the café door.

'It's okay, Myrtle. It's over,' Zelda pacified her. 'But I think we could both do with a coffee each. Maybe a little whisky in it, if you have any back there?'

'Aye, of course. For emergencies.' Myrtle looked concernedly at Ryan. 'Did he hurt ye, Ryan?'

'I'm fine,' Ryan snapped, then softened his tone. 'I'm sorry, Myrtle. Just a bit worked up. I'm okay, really. It was just an argument.'

'Aye, well. Ye should both apologise tae each other,' Myrtle muttered, shuffling back to the counter to make the coffee. 'Fightin' in ma café. As if ye were teenagers,' she huffed.

'Come on. Let's sit down.' Zelda pulled out Ryan's chair, feeling as though she was calming a wayward horse. 'You okay?'

'I'm fine. Sorry. That all got out of hand.' Ryan breathed out and covered his face with his hands. 'He just winds me up. He can't admit he was wrong about Maggie.' He shook his head.

'Well, you did say some awful things, too,' Zelda said. 'To be fair to Hal. He lost his wife, Ryan. I know what that's like. To lose someone you love so much.'

'Why should we be fair to Hal Cameron?' Ryan fixed her with a cold stare. Zelda wondered where her charming, sweet friend had gone. This was a different Ryan to the one she knew, and she wasn't sure she liked this version. 'He just assaulted me!'

'I know. Never mind.' Zelda thought it probably wasn't the time to get into it with Ryan about what he should and shouldn't have said. She also noticed that Ryan didn't ask her about her own bereavement. She thought of the way Hal had comforted her when they had shared their pain, up at the castle.

Instead, she thanked Myrtle for the drinks she'd brought over.

'I hope you're not intending to go to the party after that.' Ryan's tone was still icy.

'I don't know.' Zelda sighed. She had really been looking forward to the May Day celebrations, especially as she had been intending to write about the party for her column. But maybe it would be awkward now.

'You won't go, will you? If I can't?' Ryan took her hand across the table, his tone becoming warm again. 'It would mean a lot to me if you didn't. Solidarity and all that.'

'I've spent weeks working on it with Hal. I can't just not go.' Zelda was annoyed with Ryan for suddenly escalating what had been a subtle bit of nothing into a full-blown fight, putting her and Ryan on one side and Bella and Hal on the other. She didn't want that.

'We can do something nice instead. Go for a meal at the inn, and then maybe back to mine?' Ryan smiled and squeezed her hand. Like the flick of a switch, his easy charm had returned. 'We'll have our own party.'

Zelda didn't know what to think about that. Yes, a meal at the inn would be a nice way to spend the evening, but she had really been looking forward to the big event. She had so much invested in it.

'I don't know, Ryan. I'd still like to go,' she said, quietly.

'Don't you like me all of a sudden? I thought something was happening here. Hal attacked me just now!' Ryan protested. 'The cheek of the guy, trying to make trouble between us. He's just jealous.'

'Of course I like you,' Zelda replied, evenly. 'But I'm in charge of making my own decisions, thanks. And I hardly think he's jealous of us seeing each other. Why would he be?'

'I've seen the way he looks at you. All those hours together, up at the castle. Did nothing happen between you?' Ryan pouted.

'He's seeing Bella,' Zelda replied, shortly. 'That should be all the answer you need.'

Ryan gave her a searching look, but Zelda refused to say any more. There *had* been moments between her and Hal. Times when she thought they might have been close to kissing, and moments when she had felt very close to him. But, clearly, they hadn't meant anything to Hal, and they hadn't materialised into anything.

'Right, so.' Ryan stood up. 'Well, the invitation's open. Dinner with me, or hang out with Hal and Bella. Let me know what you decide.' He pulled on his jacket, and Zelda could see his feelings were hurt.

'Ryan...' Zelda called after him, but he had stormed out. 'Never mind,' she finished, watching the door close after him.

Zelda felt like she had come into the café with a relatively simple life and, in the brief span of an hour, everything had changed. Hal had looked like he wanted to kill Ryan just earlier. It hadn't been Ryan's fault that Hal had gone for him – physical violence was never the answer. But, Ryan had said some pretty hurtful things about Maggie, and Zelda knew he really hated Hal. It was almost like he was just looking for an excuse to lash out.

'Ye all right, lassie?' Myrtle patted her on the shoulder as she passed by. 'All happenin' today, aye?' she said, sympathetically.

'I'm okay. Thanks, Myrtle.' Zelda smiled, drinking some more of the coffee and then standing up. She'd had enough of all this drama for one day: for the moment, all she wanted to do now was go back to the cottage and read a book.

Ryan had been so good to her since she'd been in Loch Cameron. Even though today had turned into a strange series of events, she still enjoyed his company. Yes, he'd been cold just now, and said some unkind things to Hal. But Zelda understood why. Ryan was hurting. Hal was hurting. People said awful things to each other when they were sad. It didn't make you a bad person.

Zelda wasn't a hundred per cent sure about whether she would go to the party or not, but maybe the idea of dinner was the better, simpler option.

It was something to think about over a pot of herbal tea, under the covers in bed, Zelda decided. And, maybe one of Gretchen's old romance novels might have a message in it about what she should do. She smiled wanly at the thought. Was that where she was, now? Consulting romance novels in desperation for advice?

Zelda gave Myrtle a wave and left the café. As long as she didn't look at the copy of *Rebecca* that Hal had gifted her: that felt like it was asking for trouble. She doubted that Maxim de Winter or either of his wives had any good advice for this situation.

THIRTY-SIX

That night, Zelda dreamt of her mom.

In the dream, she and her mom stood together at the edge of Loch Cameron, looking into its dark, still water. Both of them wore ball dresses.

'You're the belle of the ball,' her mom told Zelda. Zelda replied that she wasn't going to the ball after all.

'But you have the dress,' her mom replied, and held Zelda's hand. 'I'm so proud of you,' she said, just before Zelda woke up, crying.

———

'Are ye sure ye dinnae want tae come to the party, hen? It's goin' tae be a good one, by all accounts.' Dotty, dressed in a full-length purple and black tartan ball dress, served Zelda a glass of white wine at the bar in the inn. 'I'm sure ye've got somethin' lovely ye could wear.'

'No, Dotty. I'm not coming. I'm meeting Ryan for dinner here,' Zelda replied. 'You have fun, though.'

She thought sadly about the red tartan ball dress hanging in her wardrobe, back at the cottage. She was even sadder about the fact that she had put so much work into the May Day party with Hal, and now she wasn't even getting to go to it. But, if she hadn't been sure about the party after the big argument at the café, then Hal's text the following evening had decided it.

I'll understand if you don't think it's appropriate to come to the party.

That was all he'd written. His usual text style was formal at best, but this was another level, Zelda had thought as she regarded her phone screen.

What did that mean, exactly? That he wanted her to come? That he didn't want her to come? Was he trying to tell her that he didn't expect her to come if it made her uncomfortable? Zelda couldn't tell.

Do you want me to come? she had replied, but hadn't got an answer. That had annoyed her.

If you're going to send inscrutable text messages, then at least follow up to clarify, she thought angrily.

She still hadn't received an answer, so she made a decision.

I think it's best if I don't come to the party, she wrote. *It's a real shame because we both worked so hard on it, but it feels kind of weird now. Hope it goes well.*

The problem she had now was what she would write about for her article. She'd been leading up to it in her posts so far, and sharing pictures of all the preparations on her Instagram account too. To suddenly fail to regale her readers with details of Scottish dancing, kilts and whisky cocktails would make it look like she'd made it all up.

'The Laird'll be disappointed not tae see you,' Dotty tutted.

'I'm sure he'll survive.' Zelda smiled, patiently. She thought about Hal in his full Scottish dress with a twinge of nostalgia. She had to admit, the shoot at the castle when she had worn the wedding dress and Hal had worn his full regalia had been quite something.

She had also *still* not had an answer from Hal to her email about Alice, and that annoyed her. Hal owed it to Alice to at least acknowledge what had happened. It irritated Zelda that Hal didn't understand how important this was to her – but how could he know? The story of Alice McQueen had become somehow emblematic to her, in a deep emotional sense. She related to Alice, not because she had experienced pregnancy or lost love, but perhaps because of the way that Alice had been unfairly treated by her father. Alice's father had sent her away, and Zelda's father had left her. In both cases, there was abandonment, and Zelda felt it keenly, like a knife in her heart, even after all these years.

'Aye, well, lassie, I'll leave ye the key. Everyone's goin' tae the castle.' Dotty sighed as she picked up a lilac wool wrap and headed out of the door. 'Have fun, dear. Just be careful o' that Ryan,' she added, almost as an afterthought. 'I heard about the big to-do between him and Hal.'

'That was fast.'

'Well, dear, Myrtle and I are very good friends.'

'Well, Hal lashed out. He would have punched Ryan, I think, if I hadn't been there.'

'Hmm. Not tae speak ill o' the lad, but it isnae like he doesnae deserve it.' Dotty sniffed. 'Ryan, I mean.'

'Why does he deserve to be punched? And why do I need to be careful of him?' Zelda turned around in her seat, frowning.

'Oh, he's a charmin' one. But that business wi' Mary Muir were pure shameful.' Dotty shook her head. 'I wouldnae like tae see a nice lassie like you get too involved wi' someone like him.'

'Dotty! You can't say something like that when you're about to walk out of the door!' Zelda protested. 'Who's Mary Muir?'

'Oh, have I no' mentioned this before?' Dotty gave Zelda a look that belied her 'forgetful older lady' act.

'You know you haven't, Dotty,' Zelda scolded her. 'Come on. Spill.'

'Ah. Well, far be it from me tae gossip,' Dotty lowered her voice confidentially, even though there was no one else in the bar, 'but Mary was a local girl. Much younger than him – barely twenty, I'd say. Innocent. Suffice to say, Ryan O'Connell had his way wi' the young thing and then cut her loose when he'd had his fill.'

'Oh. Well, that's unfortunate, but not the worst thing I've ever heard. Sometimes a clean break is the best thing.'

'Aye, lassie. But, thing was, she was in love wi' him. And he'd only been... usin' her. For you-know-what.' Dotty gave her a meaningful nod. 'Mary got a little bit obsessed. He'd broken her heart, poor lamb. One night, she was standin' outside his shop, watchin' him – he's got a flat upstairs, aye – as she couldnae keep away. Lorry came up the road. She must've been standin' in the road, because the lorry knocked her over.'

'Oh, no! What happened? Did she die?' Zelda's stomach felt like it had dropped into her feet.

'No. Broke her leg badly, though. She moved away, but I heard she still walks wi' a limp.' Dotty shook her head, frowning. 'Now, I know it was an accident. But she never wouldae been outside his flat if he hadnae treated her so badly. And, worse, when she was up at the hospital – and then when she came home – he never visited her.'

'Wow. That is... appalling.' Zelda was almost lost for words. 'Why didn't you tell me before?'

'Yer a grown woman, Zelda. An' ye were only stayin' a week, an' then a couple o' weeks. I didnae think it mattered. But if yer stayin' longer, ye should know what yer dealin' with.' Dotty pursed her mouth. 'Maybe he might say it was bad luck. Maybe we all make mistakes. But I dinnae trust that one as far as I could throw him, and neither should ye.' She patted her on the arm consolingly. 'An' when it comes to Hal Cameron, if he hit Ryan, or if he wanted tae, then I imagine he had a good reason. It takes a lot for Hal tae lose his temper, an' I've only ever seen it happen when he was defendin' someone.'

'Okay... thanks, Dotty.' Zelda nodded. 'I appreciate you letting me know.'

Everything that Dotty was saying made sense. Zelda knew, in her heart, that the fight had been more Ryan's fault than Hal's. And she had seen a changeability in Ryan a couple of times now, and dismissed it as nothing. But if what Dotty was saying was true, then Ryan wasn't someone she wanted to go to dinner with – much less back to his flat later. Zelda had no desire to be just another conquest for him or, worse, end up on the receiving end of his sudden coldness.

'Of course, dear.' Dotty arranged her wrap around her shoulders as Eric appeared next to her, looking very smart in his formal kilt and jacket. 'Sure ye don't want tae come with us? Still time tae change yer mind.'

Zelda thought about just leaving with Dotty and Eric: Ryan would get the message if he came and she wasn't at the inn. But she wanted to talk to him. She wanted to ask him about Mary Muir. She wanted to give him the chance to be honest.

'No, I'll be okay. I'll see you later.' She patted Dotty on the arm. 'Have a great time, both of you.'

Dotty handed Zelda the key to the inn, and Eric gave her a polite nod before they left, the door banging behind them. Zelda looked at her phone, noticing that she had an email. Perhaps Hal had finally replied to her about Alice McQueen.

She clicked on the email app on her phone, and opened the message. It was from Emery, not Hal.

She opened it while she waited for Ryan, feeling her heartbeat return to normal, but also feeling disappointed. She was still hoping for some kind of closure, and something from Hal that demonstrated he was the kind man she had thought he was would have gone a long way.

Darling, how's things in bonnie Scotland?

Loving the column.

However, should you still be looking for something back in the Big Apple, I'm at Home of Interiors now and they're looking for a new Features Ed. Naturally, I suggested you. They're good people, and the work culture is surprisingly non-toxic. Or, at least, so far. I took the liberty of sharing your column with them and they love all the castle stuff, and the cottage makeover. You'd be a great fit.

How's the Laird? No doubt you're dealing with a veritable legion of Scottish suitors but I rather liked him. Give the guy a chance, and give me a call too. It would be nice to hear your voice.

Much love, & everything crossed you want to come back and work with meeee,

Emery x

Despite Dotty's sudden revelation and her thoughts about Hal, Emery's email made Zelda gasp. *Home of Interiors* was a good magazine. She felt a surge of excitement. She'd always wanted to make the move into that space, but her experience had always been more in books, theatre and art. Plus, *The Village Receiver* was small potatoes. *Home of Interiors* was the big time.

A wave of relief rose up from Zelda's stomach. She hadn't realised she'd been holding so much stress about finding a new, full-time job, but of course it was there. She'd spent her whole working life feeling as though she was balanced on that tightrope of making ends meet, having enough to pay all the bills and never having anything in reserve to fall back on.

The *New Yorker* column paid well, but it still wasn't enough to live on, if she was going back to New York. Realistically, she knew she'd been avoiding facing up to reality, and that she couldn't stay in Loch Cameron forever.

Could she? Zelda had to admit that there had been moments where she had wanted to. But, now, what was there to stay for?

'Evening, gorgeous,' a voice whispered in her ear. Ryan wrapped his arms around her waist, having walked in quietly without her noticing.

Zelda jumped, almost falling off her bar stool. 'Jesus, Ryan! You scared me to death!' Zelda pulled away from his embrace.

'Sorry. Just couldn't resist.' Ryan drew her back to him, playfully, but she tugged her arm away.

'Stop it.'

'Hey. What's up?' He stepped back, seeming to sense that something was wrong. 'I thought we were all set for a lovely evening. I brought my A game.' He indicated his smart navy blazer and crisp white shirt underneath.

'I just had a very interesting conversation with Dotty,' Zelda said, standing up. 'That's what's up.'

'About what?' Ryan gave her that sheepish, affable rogue look that she'd found so charming before. 'Look... I'm a single guy living in a tiny village. People like to gossip. I bet I—'

'About Mary Muir,' Zelda interrupted him, watching his face.

Ryan's cheerful expression faded. 'Oh,' he said.

'Care to tell me what happened?' Zelda asked. 'Because, the way I heard it, you took what you wanted from that girl and she came off pretty bad from the whole thing.'

Alice McQueen, and now Mary Muir. Zelda wondered how many other young women had run afoul of Loch Cameron in some way. Ryan was obsessed with the idea that Hal had controlled his wife, Maggie, but the truth of it seemed more that Ryan, like so many men in Loch Cameron, had tried to control a young woman. And the young woman had suffered for it, just like Alice McQueen had when her father had made life-altering decisions for her.

'It's just gossip. I didn't do anything wrong.' A petulant look crossed Ryan's face. 'People don't know what happened between me and Mary.'

'Tell me, then. What did happen?' Zelda crossed her arms over her chest.

'I will. I promise. But let's get a drink and sit down first, shall we?' Ryan was trying to pacify her, and Zelda was not in the mood.

'No. Tell me right now.'

'Fine. Well, there's not much to tell. She was a nice girl. Too young for me, really. I admit I shouldn't have pursued it, but she was really sweet and she really wanted things to continue.'

'Ryan. That's not all that happened,' Zelda admonished him.

'Okay, what d'you want me to say? She got obsessed with me. How was I to know she was the bunny boiler type?' His voice had taken on a sulky tone that Zelda disliked immensely. 'She had an accident. It was her fault. She was stalking me. I should have pressed charges, but I didn't. I thought the best thing to do would be to leave her alone, so I did. If I'd visited her, it would have led her on.'

Bunny boiler? Oh, hell, no. Zelda felt a rush of righteous anger run through her body. She hated that phrase. 'Ryan. That is not what decent people do. She could have died!' Zelda was aghast.

'Well, she didn't,' he replied, mulishly. 'I stand by my actions. You don't know Mary. It was best that she thinks of me as the bad guy.'

'You *are* the bad guy, you idiot!' Zelda wanted to slap some sense into Ryan; she resisted the urge, and kept her hands by her sides. 'Anyone with a decent bone in their body would at least have gone to visit the girl after her accident. You could have had a mature conversation with her and explained that the relationship was over, but that there were no hard feelings. Or, as crazy as it may seem, you could have decided not to use a young girl for sex in the first place, and avoided dumping her unceremoniously when you'd had enough of her.'

'I'm sorry.' He sighed and put his head in his hands. 'But I don't understand why this is such an issue for you. I'd never hurt *you*, Zelda.'

'So I'm supposed to be happy about that? Jeez, Ryan. I thought you were a good guy.' Zelda shivered.

Ryan hugged her. 'Zelda. Please. I really like you. We've got a connection. Don't you feel it?'

Zelda didn't want to be hugged, but Ryan wouldn't let her go. She struggled inside his clasp. 'Ryan, let me go!' she cried out. She was furious about what Dotty had told her. She was furious that Ryan had acted like a perfect gentleman, making her think he would never be capable of using and discarding women in the way he had with Mary Muir.

She was furious that Ryan had made her like him.

At that moment, the door to the bar banged open again and Hal Cameron walked into the room. He was dressed in a slightly different red tartan kilt than the one he had worn in the photoshoot, with a black dress jacket, black waistcoat and a white shirt and cravat.

'Ah. Sorry tae interrupt,' he muttered. 'Dotty told me that ye might want tae come to the castle after all, Zelda. I've got the car outside. I was just pickin' up a few last things from the village, so if ye had changed yer mind an' wanted a lift...' he explained, his voice a monotone of disappointment. 'However, I can see you're busy, so...' He turned away.

Ryan, distracted by the Laird's entrance, released his arms from around Zelda.

'So nice of you to check in on Zelda. But we're just about to sit down for dinner, so she won't be able to make it after all,' he explained, smoothly. Zelda stepped away from him, amazed at the pleasant veneer he was able to drop over his features at a moment's notice.

'Is that right?' Hal looked Ryan up and down with a disdainful expression.

'No, it's very much not right.' Zelda looked around for her bag. 'Hal, if the offer's still open, I'd love to come to the party.'

'Oh. Of course.' Hal stood to one side of the hall, politely letting her pass. 'After ye.'

'Zelda. Don't be crazy. You haven't given me a chance to explain!' Ryan called after her. 'You don't want this guy, Zelda. You know what I told you about him.'

'I remember,' Zelda said to Ryan. 'But if you touch me again without my consent, I'll call the police.' She turned to Hal. 'Have I got five minutes to change if we go past the cottage?'

'Umm... sure.' Hal obviously wasn't sure what was going on, but he was also clearly not going to give Ryan the benefit of the doubt either. 'Ryan? I think the lady's made herself clear.'

He gestured towards the door, barring it as Ryan stepped forward as if to grab Zelda's arm. 'I wouldnae do that if I were you,' Hal growled, crossing his arms over his considerable chest.

'Fine. I'm going. You're making a big mistake, Zelda!' Ryan muttered. 'This could have been something good!'

Zelda watched Ryan barge past Hal and walk angrily down the street.

'What was that all aboot?' Hal gave her a quizzical look. 'And are you okay?'

'I'm fine. I'll tell you on the way.' Zelda sighed. She did remember what Ryan had told her about Hal, and about the last weeks of Maggie's life. She had never directly asked Hal about what Ryan claimed he had done, and now she was wondering if it was true at all.

THIRTY-SEVEN

In fact, it took Zelda twenty minutes rather than five to change into the tartan ball dress that was hanging on the front of her wardrobe in the cottage bedroom, hastily straighten her hair and quickly apply her makeup. However, when she appeared in the doorway of the cottage's living room, it was clear from Hal's expression that he really didn't mind waiting that extra fifteen minutes.

'You look... you're beautiful.' He stood up, reverentially.

'Thank you. I'm glad I get to wear this after all,' Zelda said, suddenly feeling shy. 'I got it from Fiona a week or so ago, and then when we all had that argument at the café, I was pretty disappointed I wasn't going to get to come to the party.'

'I wish I had a corsage to give ye,' Hal said. 'I just didnae think you were comin'.'

'I know.' Zelda sighed. 'I still wanted to, but then it was difficult because I thought you were mad at me.'

'I wasnae mad at ye. Didnae approve o' yer taste in men.' He gave her a serious look. 'He's no good, that one.'

'I know that now,' Zelda protested. 'Anyway, you sent me

that text. *I'll understand if you don't think it's appropriate to come to the party.'*

'I was just tryin' tae be nice. I didnae want ye to feel uncomfortable. But I wanted ye to come.'

'Why didn't you just say that?' Zelda shook her head.

'It was... difficult. I wasnae sure if I should.'

'Because of Bella? Surely she's going to be mad if I walk in with you?' Zelda adjusted the shoulder of her dress slightly.

The Laird cleared his throat. 'I wouldnae worry aboot Bella. She isnae comin' tae the party.'

'Why not?' Zelda was surprised. Hal and Bella had seemed so cosy when she'd seen them together. 'I thought you were seeing each other.'

'Hmm. No.' He frowned. 'We're just friends.'

'What? But you've been... spending time together. I saw you together, in the village,' Zelda explained. She thought back to that first day she'd seen Hal and Bella together: they'd been walking along together, talking and laughing, and Hal had put his hand protectively in the small of Bella's back. At the time, she had assumed they were together, because it was the kind of intimate gesture lovers made.

'Friends can spend time together,' Hal said, gently. 'We used tae go out, aye. She's been havin' a difficult time wi' the newspapers an' she wanted tae get away from it all for a bit, so I said she could stay. Just as friends. There's nothin' goin' on.'

'The newspapers?'

'Aye. They've been houndin' her lately. Ye saw that piece in the magazine aboot who she was goin' tae marry.'

'Oh, right. Yeah. I remember.' Zelda thought back to the magazine in Myrtle's café where she'd first seen the article about Bella.

'Aye. The pressure's kindae intense. She got really down aboot it, so I said she could hide out at the castle for a bit.'

'Oh. I had no idea.' Zelda felt awful for Bella. She understood what newspapers and magazines could be like. Even at *The Village Receiver*, she'd been at press events from time to time where the celebrity in question had been asked inappropriate questions and generally harassed.

'Aye. An' I have tae say, Bella feels a little protective of me since Maggie passed, an' I keep an eye out fer her too. Like brother an' sister, almost.' He paused. 'I told her I... had feelin's for ye. We've had some guid talks aboot it.'

Zelda looked up at him in surprise. 'You have feelings for me?'

'Aye. I wanted somethin' tae happen with ye. But ye were kinda seein' Ryan. It never seemed the right time.'

'*Hal.* We've spent weeks together, organising the party. We spent a day literally dressed in wedding outfits, pretending to kiss on the lawn.' Zelda had to laugh at the ridiculousness of the situation. 'What more did you want?'

'I know.' He hung his head. 'I shouldae kissed ye. I tried, that day when we were by the fireplace.'

'And Anna came in at the wrong moment. Yeah, that was bad timing.' Zelda laughed. 'So, what happened with Bella? She's not your date tonight after all?'

'She realised I was serious aboot ye, and she's a good enough friend to step aside so I could ask ye to come to the party.'

'Oh.' Zelda didn't know what to say.

'*Oh?* I've just bared my soul tae ye, Zelda.' Hal gave her a shy smile. 'Have ye nothin' else tae say?'

'Sorry. It's just all... kinda sudden. I always felt something between us. But you were so closed off. And grumpy,' she added. 'I never knew where I was with you. And then...' She broke off. *And then, Ryan made me think you were a controlling, hard-hearted bastard.*

'What?'

'Listen. I have to ask you something.'

If Ryan was a liar, could she rely on the rest of what he'd said to be true?

'Anythin'.' Hal looked concerned.

'Look. This isn't easy to ask. But Ryan told me that when Maggie was ill... before she passed, you shut her in that room with the pink velvet curtains. You didn't let her say goodbye to anyone. He said you imprisoned her.'

Hal looked aghast. 'What? You thought that was true? I wouldnae ever do that. I loved Maggie.'

'Well, I didn't know he was making it up. So there's no truth in that at all?'

''No' in the way he said! It's true that in the final couple of months, Maggie asked not tae see anyone else but me and the nurse I'd brought to live in. She didnae want anyone to see her in such a state.' Hal took a deep breath, his voice breaking. 'It was her decision, not mine. She made a livin' will. She'd decided more than a year before how she wanted to go. How she wanted tae do it. I was just obeyin' her wishes.' A tear ran down his cheek.

'Oh, Hal. I'm so sorry.'

'Honestly, I wouldae liked it if people could come and say goodbye at the end. But she was right. She was in no state for visitors.' Hal choked back a tear. 'Look at me. Big mess on the night o' the party.'

Zelda took his hand. 'It's my fault. I'm sorry for bringing it up. I should know better. I... I remember what it was like with my mom at the end. She was too weak to talk. To see anyone.' The emotion caught in her throat, but she took a deep breath and let it go.

'Naw, ye were right tae ask. And I'm so sorry, again, about you losin' your mother.' Hal wrapped her in a bear hug and held her tight. Zelda didn't think she had ever felt so protected and held before.

'Ryan was Maggie's friend. Maggie was always...' He

paused, still holding her, looking for the right words. 'She was always kinder than me. More accommodatin' with people. She could see his good side. But when that whole thing happened with Mary Muir, even Maggie couldnae overlook it.'

Zelda could have stayed in Hal's arms forever, but she stepped away gently. He took her hand instead.

'Oh, wow. So they weren't friends, then? When she died?' Zelda wondered if that had something to do with the reason Ryan was so negative about Hal.

'Maggie was still his friend. But they left it on a bad note, and I dinnae think he realised she wouldae forgiven him, in the end.'

'They had an argument? About Mary Muir?'

'Aye,' Hal nodded. 'Ryan confessed that he'd never really been serious about the poor lassie. She was so young, she didnae know what men like him were like. After Ryan broke it off wi' her... d'you know what happened?'

'Yes. She had the accident, and moved away.'

'Right. Well, she wrote tae Ryan after that. A letter a day, for months. Emails, texts. She was still besotted, but angry too. He brought some o' the letters to show Maggie. Maybe tae try and show her it wasnae all his fault, or somethin'.' Hal sighed. 'Anyway, by that time, Maggie was too bad to see anyone. So, I took the letters. I told Ryan I'd show her them, but she wouldnae been able tae read them. However, I know that Maggie wouldae forgiven him. That was just who she was.'

'What a sad story.' Zelda was still angry with Ryan, but she felt a little sorry for him too. Whoever he was and whatever he'd done, it did sound as though he had loved Maggie. And he had lost her, just like Hal had. 'He must have thought Maggie disapproved of him.'

'Aye.' Hal nodded. 'Ryan an' I'll never be friends now. But I do feel for the fella, if only because I know he was fond o' Maggie. She was fond o' him, too. I shouldae talked tae him.'

'There's still time,' Zelda said, softly. No matter what Ryan had done, he deserved to know that his friend hadn't died hating him.

'I guess.' Hal sighed.

'Hal? Why haven't you answered my email? About Alice McQueen?' Zelda asked, softly. She was still holding Hal's hand. He looked down and smiled, turning her hand over in his and placing it gently on his chest.

'I have a good reason, I promise,' he said. 'Can ye trust me a little longer? I promise I will talk to ye aboot it. Let's just enjoy the party first, aye?'

'All right.' Zelda looked up into his deep blue eyes.

'Listen,' Hal said, quietly. 'I didn't want ye to get involved wi' Ryan because I knew he wasnae good enough for ye. But, also, because...' He broke off.

'What?' Zelda breathed.

'Because I was jealous. I liked you from that first day, at the castle.' Hal kept her gaze. 'I like you. A lot.'

'I like you too, Hal.' Zelda's hand was still in his. She felt overwhelmed by his body next to hers; his warmth and solidity. The same electricity that had always hung like a mist between them filled her with excited longing. But it was her heart, more than anything, that felt suddenly open, raw and vulnerable.

'So where do we go from here?' she breathed.

'I've got tae get to the castle. I'm late.' Hal drew her to him. 'But first, I think we have time for a kiss.'

He met her lips gently, his strong arms encircling her waist. His lips were soft and warm, and he took his time, brushing her mouth with his.

A wave of electricity zinged through Zelda, connecting her head to her feet and resonating through her heart like a bell. She took in a deep breath, and let out a soft giggle, somewhere between nervousness and desire. She could feel Hal's mouth smiling as he kissed her.

'What's so funny?' he murmured, his beard brushing her chin. He kissed her again, gently, and Zelda felt as though her whole body was melting. He was so tall that she had to stand on her tiptoes to kiss him, until he picked her up and held her in his arms, her feet fully dangling above the floor.

'Nothing,' she whispered, pleasurably taken aback at being lifted off the floor. She kissed him back, more forcefully, and he made a sound somewhere between a low growl and a sigh. He murmured her name against her lips as the kiss grew deeper.

'Ach, Zelda. Ye don't know what you're doin' tae me,' he said, gently setting her back down on the floor.

She wrapped her arms around his neck, as far as she could reach, and drew him in for a last, sweet kiss. 'I do,' she whispered, as she kissed him tenderly. 'Believe me, I do.'

THIRTY-EIGHT

'When chapman billies leave the street,
And drouthy neebors neebors meet,
As market-days are wearing late,
And folk begin to tak the gate;
While we sit bousin, at the nappy,
And gettin fou and unco happy,
We think na on the lang Scots miles,
The mosses, waters, slaps, and stiles,
That lie between us and our hame,
Whare sits our sulky, sullen dame,
Gathering her brows like gathering storm,
Nursing her wrath to keep it warm.'

Zelda doubled her tartan wrap around her shoulders, shivering slightly as she watched Hal perform. Even though it was May, the nights were still cold in Loch Cameron and so she was grateful for the thick shawl Fiona had found for her that matched her dress.

Still, it wasn't just the night that was making her shiver.

As Hal recited the famous poem by Robert Burns, just as

Gretchen had told her that he would, he seemed to take on a totally different persona. Gone was the quiet, diffident Laird she had met when she had arrived at the castle. Gone too was his scruffy image: tonight, Hal was every inch the rightful head of the clan in his formal dress kilt, the silver buttons on his jacket gleaming in the firelight from the huge bonfire behind him. He was clean-shaven again, and his hair was newly cut. It really suited him much better short, showing off his chiselled bone structure.

Standing on a stage amid a series of tents in the grounds of the castle, Hal roared the poem aloud into the night. He stalked the stage, his words conjuring images of storms, magic and the wild ride of the witches, telling the tale of the unfortunate hero of the poem, Tam O'Shanter.

As she watched Hal perform, Zelda was also thinking about Emery's email. She knew a couple of people who were employed at *Home of Interiors* and she liked them: the magazine was known as a good place to work. She also loved the idea of working with Emery again.

However, Zelda had fallen a little in love with Loch Cameron while she'd been there on her extended stay. It would be difficult to leave all her new friends. And Hal's kiss had left her breathless. Why couldn't he have kissed her weeks ago? Why now, on the same night as she got a job offer on the other side of the world that she really couldn't turn down?

She looked up to see John on the other side of the stage, waving at her. She waved back, but he started edging his way towards her.

'Hallo, dear,' he panted, a little out of breath from pushing through the crowds by the time he got to her. 'Enjoying yourself?'

'Yes, it's great.' Zelda smiled, fighting an urge to find someone nearby with a tissue who could wipe John's sweaty brow.

'Ah, wonderful. Look, I won't keep you, but I just wanted to let you know I've emailed you your family tree,' John continued in a low voice. 'Very interesting, as it happens.'

'Oh! Thank you.' Zelda was surprised; she hadn't checked her email in the past couple of hours. John must have sent it just after she'd read Emery's message. 'Can I give you something for your time, John? I really appreciate you doing this for me.'

'No, not at all.' John looked pleased. 'Just tell me what you think, and let me know if you have any questions. There are things you could follow up, if you wanted. But it's very much up to you.'

'Okay.' Zelda was intrigued.

'Well. I should get back to my wife.' John pointed out a friendly looking lady in a long green tartan skirt with a matching shawl and a thick cream cable-knit jumper. 'I just wanted to let you know it was there.'

'All right. Thanks, John.' Zelda watched John push his way back through the crowd. She wanted to open up the email right then and there, but she was enjoying watching Hal too much. She decided to look at it the next day, when she'd be able to concentrate on it properly.

Dotty sidled up to Zelda at the side of the stage. 'Ye came, then.' She gave Zelda a shrewd look.

'Yeah.' Zelda gazed up at Hal as he commanded the small stage, his deep voice booming through the castle grounds. 'Where's Eric?'

'Gone tae get drinks. Good, eh? No' what ye expected?' She nodded in Hal's direction.

'Definitely not what I expected.' Zelda felt Hal's voice enchanting her as he spoke the old Scots dialect with ease.

'Still waters run deep.' Dotty nudged Zelda. 'He's a good man, the Laird, aye. Ye dinnae find a man like that every day.'

'I guess not.' Zelda shot Dotty a knowing look as Hal

finished his poem and the crowd cheered and whooped. 'You know, you're not as subtle as you think you are, Dotty. Just FYI.'

Dotty laughed. 'Aye, well. I've seen the way he looks at ye. Hal could do with a new lassie in his life. That's all I'm sayin',' she said, and mimed zipping her mouth shut. 'That's all. Finished. Kaput. I'm sayin' nothin' more.'

'I find that very hard to believe.'

'He came tae bring ye to the party personally. No one else arrived at the party with the Laird. That's all I'm sayin',' Dotty repeated.

Hal jumped off the stage and drained a glass of whisky that someone handed to him. 'To the stones!' he shouted, and the crowd roared in approval. Hal, approaching Zelda, bowed and held out his hand to her. 'May I ask the prettiest lady at the party to head the procession with me?' he asked formally, a grin on his face.

'You may.' Zelda curtsied and took his hand.

The crowd filed in behind them as they made their way down to the beach. Everyone was singing an old Gaelic song as they went, and some carried flaming torches.

'This is... quite something,' Zelda said, as they walked along. 'I'm pretty much lost for words.'

'That has tae be a first. No' lost fer words for yer column, though?' Hal gave her a twinkly look. 'I've read them all, ye know. I love yer writin'.'

'Thank you. I really enjoy writing it. And the readers are desperate to know what's going to happen tonight.'

'So am I,' he said, giving her a meaningful look. Zelda blushed, feeling like a schoolgirl.

'Ye should do more of it,' he added. 'The column, but also all the work you did with me on the castle. And at the cottage.' He caught her eye. 'Gretchen's been singin' yer praises.'

'Oh. That's good to hear.' Zelda grinned at a gang of young girls in tartan pinafore dresses as they ran past, wielding sparklers and screaming in delight. 'I've loved working on the interiors.'

She was still thinking about the new job offer.

'Well, ye've got a great eye. Bella thought so too,' he offered.

'Really?'

'Aye. She said she'd love some help doin' up her new place. If ye were interested.'

'*Bella* wants me to work with her?' Zelda laughed in disbelief.

'I told ye. She's a pussycat.'

'No, it's just that, until tonight, I thought she hated me.'

'Well, I guess you thought a lot of things that weren't true, until tonight.'

Jeez, you are beautiful, Zelda thought, watching his face.

There was a moment of silence between them as they walked past ancient hedgerows and the edge of the loch.

'How does all this compare to *Rebecca*? Better than their costume ball, eh?' Hal broke the silence, taking her hand. 'Oh. How's this wrist? All healed now?'

'It's fine.' Zelda felt a flutter of butterflies in her stomach as his hand touched hers. Neither of them had mentioned the kiss at the cottage, so far. 'My wrist, that is. Oh, this is all a million times better.'

'You really love that book, eh,' he said as they walked along. 'I still need tae find some way tae pay ye for yer hard work, settin' up the website, the photos an' all that. Seein' as I can't technically pay ye, bein' here as a tourist an' all that.'

'You gave me your grandmother's book. That was lovely.' Zelda treasured the lovely edition of *Rebecca*. It would always remind her of her time in Loch Cameron.

'Come on, Zelda. Ye put a lot o' effort in for me, an' I'm no' goin tae forget it. Anyway, I had an idea.'

'What?'

'I thought ye might like tae stay at the castle sometime.

Bring some friends, mebbe. I can pay for some flights from New York tae here an' put a party up for a week or two. As a thank ye.'

Zelda was taken aback. 'Wow. Hal, that's very generous. You don't need to do that.'

'I know I dinnae *need* tae. I want tae.' He squeezed her hand gently. 'Anyway, turns out I like New Yorkers.'

Zelda squeezed his hand back. 'Hal. That would be lovely. Thank you.'

'Very welcome.' Hal looked pleased.

'Listen.' She looked up at him. 'On the subject of New York... since we're talking about it.'

'Aye.' Hal guided her through a small coppice of trees, careful to avoid any stray tree roots that would trip them up.

'This is really bad timing, but I've been offered a job, back home. I think I'm going to take it. I've got to, really. Financially as well as anything else.'

'Oh. Of course. Congratulations! What's the job?' Hal looked a little disappointed, though she could tell he was trying to hide it.

'It's a Features Editor job at a homes and interiors magazine.' She waited as Hal opened a gate ahead of them, tying it back with a piece of rope so that the procession behind them could pass through it too. 'Apparently, they've been reading my column, following the cottage makeover, all that stuff. Emery recommended me.'

'That's brilliant!' Hal kissed her on the cheek. 'Well done. I know it musta been tricky for ye, losin' your job. Bein' adrift here, away from home. Ye'll be glad tae go back.' He cleared his throat.

'I will, but I know there's something here. Between us.' Zelda wrapped her shawl around her again as the beach opened up in front of them. Villagers raced ahead to place flaming torches around the beach and the standing stones, which had been draped with flowers, ready for the couples who wanted to pass through them to affirm their love or renew their vows.

'I'd like tae think there is somethin' worth pursuin'.' Hal stood to one side, taking Zelda's hand again and guiding her to a quiet spot on the beach while the villagers filed in. 'But I'm nae gonna stand in the way o' your career. It's too important. Come an' stay, with yer friends, like I say. That would be nice.'

'It would be very nice, Hal, but I want more than that. I want to see you more than for two weeks.'

The Laird stepped a little closer to her. 'I want tae see you too. Every day, if possible. But ye have yer career an' your life there. I respect that.'

'New York's a long way from Loch Cameron.' Zelda looked up at him. 'I mean... it's pretty hard to make long-distance relationships work. And that's a really long distance. But, on the other hand, magazine jobs come and go. And, I kinda feel like I belong in Loch Cameron. I've felt so adrift in New York since my mom passed.'

'Aye.' Hal nodded thoughtfully. There was a silence between them as the villagers filled up the beach, laughing and dancing to the Celtic tune being played by a group of musicians Hal had hired in for the evening. 'I get that.'

'I don't know what to do,' Zelda confessed. 'I want to stay. With you. But I also want to follow this opportunity.'

'Well, ye know, there is such a thing as planes. I could visit ye. Stay in a hotel. I can let Anna manage the castle awhile. See how it goes for a few weeks; then you could maybe come back here for a week or so. We'd take it from there.' He brushed her cheek with his fingers. 'Loch Cameron's no' goin' anywhere. If ye go back tae New York an' you miss it tae much, you know ye can always come back. The castle's always here for ye. An' if it's interiors ye want, I know of a whole village full o' auld cottages that need renovatin'. Not least the castle.'

'You'd do that? Spend weeks in New York, for me?' It was

hard to see in the dark, but Hal's eyes caught the flame of the torches from the beach. He stared intensely into her eyes and reached for her in the dark, his hand on her waist.

'Months. Years, if you wanted me to,' he breathed, drawing her close. 'If ye'll have me. We'll work it out. The important thing is that we'll be together.'

'Okay,' Zelda replied, her heart beating faster.

The villagers' song continued around them, the lilting Gaelic words weaving around them as Hal drew her in for a kiss in the shadows.

The kiss was deep and heady. Zelda wrapped her arms around Hal's neck, leaning in against him. His lips were full and soft, and they brushed against hers gently, and then with more intensity. She felt a fire ignite inside her at the feel of his arms that enclosed her in their strong grasp.

Zelda felt as though the whole world dimmed: there was nothing but her and Hal in that moment. She felt as though they could have been standing on the shore of the loch, a Laird and his Lady, at any time in the hundreds of years that the Camerons had ruled their clan.

The night was like a cloak, shrouding them in the history of Loch Cameron. The Gaelic song sung by the uplifted voices of the villagers wrapped around them like a blessing as Hal murmured in her ear. When she heard his words, she smiled, then nodded.

THIRTY-NINE

'I've organised a surprise for ye. Come on,' Hal murmured, as the kiss ended.

On the beach, the air smelt of the smoke from the oil-burning lamps some of the villagers had walked down with, and someone had also lit a bonfire. It was smaller than the one nearer the castle, but it still burned bright, casting an orange light on the flat water of the loch.

'What is it?' Zelda looked around her. Everything felt so magical. Loch Cameron was such a mercurial place: where a moody castle drenched in mist and rain could switch in a heartbeat to a sun-dappled haven; where you could find yourself standing hand in hand with the head of a Scottish clan on a firelit beach, your heart beating wildly at his touch.

A place where you could find parts of yourself you had never known.

Hal pointed to the standing stones, where Gretchen Ross was sitting in a wheelchair, a woolly blanket wrapped around her knees and a thick tartan cape around her shoulders.

'Gretchen!' Zelda ran over to her friend. 'I had no idea you'd be here!'

'Zelda Hicks! Enjoying your evening?' Gretchen beamed up at her. 'Surprise!'

'You're my surprise?' Zelda laughed. 'Well, it's very nice to see you. Are you okay? It's kinda cold.'

'Don't worry about me, my dear girl. Anna's been looking after me very well, and I may have been plied with a hot toddy or two.' Gretchen did, in fact, look a little sparkly eyed. 'I've been told that something important was happening that I had to be here for. Looking at your expression, though, I don't think you know what that is either.'

'I don't.' Zelda looked around at Hal. 'Hal? What's this important thing? Not that I'm not happy to see Gretch.'

'Well, I think we need a bit o' hush first,' Hal said, and climbed onto one of the long menhir stones that lay next to the two main standing ones on the beach. 'Can I have your attention please!' He raised his voice, calling out across the beach.

The hubbub continued: everyone had had a few drinks by now, and the dancing was in full swing.

'*Chlanna nan con thigibh a' so 's gheibh sibh feòil!*' Hal shouted, his voice resonating loudly along the beach. The crowd quietened.

Man alive, that was hot, Zelda thought. Standing there in his kilt, under the moonlight, Hal looked just as if he was about to lead his clan to war. The wind was even blowing his hair back in a sexy action-movie star kind of way.

If she'd had a fan, she would have tried to cool herself with it.

'Okay. Always nice to revive the old Cameron war cry.' Hal smiled. 'Thank you, everyone, for comin' along tonight in your finery to celebrate May Day. Ye all look absolutely stonkin'.' His voice carried across the crowd, who cheered. 'Right then. So, first, thank ye all again for makin' tonight's celebration so special. Maggie wouldae been so happy tae see ye all here.' He smiled at the crowd, who cheered. 'An' I want tae dedicate this party to her memory. God bless ye, Maggie.' He bowed his head for a moment, and the crowd replied by repeating her name, reverentially.

'So, tonight, we're goin tae make a new tradition as part o' the festivities. Aye.' He smiled down at some kids who were jumping up and down in excitement. 'Aye, it's excitin', eh? We're goin' tae commemorate someone special in our community. And this is a story that's only just come to my attention, courtesy of our recent visitor... some of you may know our very own New Yorker, Zelda Hicks. Give us a wave, Zelda.'

Zelda waved, mortified at being singled out in the crowd. What was this all about?

'Hallo, Zelda. Doesn't she look lovely tonight?' Hal blew her a kiss from where he stood, on top of the fallen menhir. There were a number of cheers and spirited wolf whistles, which made Zelda blush and laugh in equal measure.

'Now, then. Some o' you might know that Zelda's been stayin' up at Gretchen Ross's cottage on the Point. An' when she was there, she found some auld letters belongin' tae a relative o' Gretchen's. I believe it was her great-great-grandmother, aye?' Hal looked at Gretchen for confirmation.

'That's right, dear,' Gretchen replied.

'Right. Okay, so Gretchen's great-great-grandmother, Alice McQueen, had a bit o' a sorry story. She fell in love wi' a local lad, Richard McKelvie, on a May Day night in 1854. Alice and Richard danced through these very stones that night, an' maybe it was the auld magic, or maybe it was that they were twin souls, or whatever we think of these days, but they loved each other, an' Alice had a bairn.'

The gathered crowd *ahhh'd* in appreciation of the story.

'Aye. But, sadly, they were nae married, an' Alice's faither didnae approve of Richard either, so when he found out, he sent Alice away tae marry another fella up near Loch Awe. And Alice's bairn grew up with him as a faither, and Alice had three

other bairns. Then, many years later, her parents passed and
Alice and her family came back tae live at the cottage at
Queen's Point. Sadly, Richard had died by that time, so she was
never reunited wi' her lost love.'

There was a sigh from the crowd.

'So, in remembrance of Alice an' Richard, I've had their
initials carved here in the rock. This is where they first met, and
at least here we can remember them together,' Hal finished. He
stepped off the stone and held a torch to the side of the standing
stone, where Zelda and everyone else could see the initials *AM
& RM* entwined in each other in Celtic knotwork.

'This is something we're goin' tae do every May Day, from
now on,' Hal added, his voice ringing out across the beach still.
'I want us tae remember our ancestors. I cannae put right a lot o'
the things that might've been wrong in the past, but I can at
least do that.'

There was a loud cheer, and the villagers clustered around
the stones to see for themselves.

'Hal, that's so kind of you.' Gretchen wiped a tear from her
eye. 'I can only thank you from the bottom of my heart.'

'Not a bit o' it.' Hal crouched down in front of Gretchen's
wheelchair and handed her the torch. 'It's always been important to me that the Camerons look after the community here,
and when I read Zelda's story, I knew I had tae do somethin'.
My ancestor wouldae been at least partially responsible for
makin' Alice's life a misery at the time. It's the least I can do.'

'Zelda, did you know about this?' Gretchen asked, holding
her hand over her heart.

'I didn't know he was going to do this, no.' Zelda gazed at
the initials in the stone. 'Hal. This is... this is so beautiful.'

'I'm glad ye like it.' He looked away shyly, but Zelda could
see he was pleased. 'Make a nice end tae the story for the
column, maybe,' he added.

'Maybe. But it's so much more than that.' Zelda looked up

into those fierce blue eyes; the same intense blue Hal had inherited from the Lairds before him; the same eyes that looked down at Zelda from portrait upon portrait on the walls of the castle.

'Is it?' Hal murmured, stepping towards her and taking her in his arms. 'You're not just here for what ye can get out of this for the column, then? Not just a happy ending for the Laird and the New Yorker ye can write aboot?'

'Well, I *am* pretty invested in a happy ending right now,' Zelda said, leaning against his chest. 'But, no. I'm not just here for the column. I think you know that.'

She kissed him as the music started again, and the villagers started a new dance to another old tune. Dotty wheeled Gretchen to where some villagers stood at the edge of the dancing. The moon glittered on the water of Loch Cameron and the night breeze blew around them, but Zelda wasn't cold. She could never be cold in Hal Cameron's arms.

Breaking off their kiss, Hal took Zelda's hand.

'I could kiss you forever,' he said. 'But the Laird has responsibilities tonight. With his Lady, if you're willin'.'

'Of course,' she replied, enchanted by the night and the stars and the romance of it all, but mostly by Hal, who felt as simply *right* as anything had ever felt in her life.

Gravely, Hal led her to the front of a column of dancers that had formed on the beach. He bowed to the dancers, and Zelda followed his example. Fiona placed a flower crown on her head. Then, Hal Cameron, Laird of Loch Cameron, danced Zelda through and around the ancient standing stones, as everyone clapped and cheered.

FAMILY TREES AND ME: TRULY, MY SCOTTISH LIFE

By Zelda Hicks for *The New Yorker*

Use #zeldasscottishlife to share and comment

The May Day party was beautiful.

I almost didn't make it – I won't bore you with the details (though there was some high drama leading up to the big day) BUT – wow. Check out the pictures in this article to see Hal Cameron, the Laird of Loch Cameron, reciting traditional Scottish poetry, fireworks above the castle and, yes, that's me leading the villagers in a dance around the standing stones.

Loch Cameron knows how to party, y'all. I was absolutely blown away by the beauty of the evening: our lamplit procession through the castle gardens, walking through the woods in the glittering evening, hand-in-hand with the Laird (yes, THAT HAPPENED); and I've never tasted salmon as fresh.

The party was awesome. People were still dancing in the great hall at 2 a.m.; I found myself in a conga line of pensioners at 2.30 a.m.

But, what surprised and touched me the most at the party was the fact that the Laird had carved Alice McQueen's initials into one of the standing stones on the castle's private beach, along with her long-lost lover's. If you've been reading my column, you'll remember that Alice was the young woman who was sent away from the village for getting pregnant without being married.

Alice McQueen is also my friend and landlady Gretchen Ross's ancestor, and Gretchen was really touched to see that Hal had created that memorial for Alice on his own land, in acceptance of the fact that Alice wasn't supported by her community in the way that she should have been when she was alive.

This community failed her in her own time, but I think it's turned out to be a pretty awesome place now, filled with people who genuinely care about each other. I want to say thank you to Dotty, Myrtle, Fiona, John, Eric, Anna and everyone else who has made my stay so memorable and made me feel so welcome.

There's more to this story, though, and you'll have to forgive me for making this kinda personal now. But if you'd told me when I arrived in Loch Cameron that I would end up researching my own Scottish roots, I'd have told you to *get outta town*.

Yet, stranger things happen at sea, as they say here, and even stranger things happen when you decide to maroon yourself in a tiny Scottish village with one café, one butcher, one hairdresser (open two mornings a week: I still can't work out which ones) and one local historian, John.

John is Fiona's uncle. Fiona owns and runs the fashion boutique I told you about in a previous column. John is the one who found out what happened to Alice McQueen and her baby (if you've missed this, go back and read my other columns). And, when I told him that my dad is Scottish, he offered to research my family tree for me.

I know three things about my dad: 1. He is Scottish. 2. He left me and my mom when I was two, and 3. I didn't used to think I cared about him. Maybe I still don't. But maybe family isn't always that straightforward. Gretchen said to me a little while ago that we all need roots. Mine got pulled up when my mom died. So, it's completely natural to want to know where your other ones grow.

Since I've spent time in Loch Cameron, I've started to consider the fact that I could still know a little more about my family tree, and my origins on my father's side, without having to have a relationship with him. There are roots there.

I grew up in the Bronx with my mom. She did an awesome job as a single parent. We didn't have much, but I always had enough to eat and I was a happy kid. Yeah, I had to help Mom out in the dry-cleaning shop she'd inherited from her family, but that was okay. In a way, it gave me my passion for clothes, and I truly think it inspired me to break into journalism when I was older.

For the longest time – well, really, until I got to Loch Cameron – I refused to know anything about the Scottish side of my family. It felt like a betrayal of my mom and everything she had done for me. Despite him leaving us, we thrived. And so I vowed – yes, vowed! – that I would basically ignore his presence on earth forever more, as well as the presence of any family I might have on that side.

But, what if the rest of them are decent people? And, even if there's not a decent person among them for some reason, where are they from? Where do they live? Who are the people that came before?

After I thought about all this, I asked John to research what he could. And he told me some surprising things.

First, my dad was also an only child, and his dad died when he was six months old. So, he too grew up just with his mom. They lived in a tenement flat in Glasgow, in a pretty rundown neighbourhood. And I know that at some point he came to America and made a fortune on the stock market, which is when he met my mom. And he lost it all again promptly afterwards.

My grandmother, though, was born in Inverness. That's pretty far north in Scotland, and right in the middle of nowhere. I've seen some pictures, though: it's stunning. She was one of three kids and her mom and dad were farmers. Here's where it gets weird, though.

My great-grandparents lived in Loch Awe, not too far from Loch Cameron. Now, probably, you won't remember me mentioning Loch Awe before, but it did come up once before. And the eagle-eyed readers among you will remember that Loch Awe was the place where Alice McQueen got sent to when she fell pregnant with her baby by Richard McKelvie in 1855.

Yes. My ancestors come from the same town that Alice McQueen found herself in, all those years ago, when she was sent off by her dad to marry Donald Stewart. Not only that, they lived there for many generations, so there was likely an ancestor of mine living in Loch Awe at the same time as Alice got there.

This blows my mind. But it's all historical fact. I can show you the papers.

This column has been called 'My Scottish Life' from the start, but that's become something more than a slightly unimaginative title. Do I feel like I have reconnected to my roots? A little, yeah. I still don't want to reconnect with my dad, but I do want to visit Loch Awe and maybe even find the house where my family lived, if it's still standing.

And, as another thing, I may or may not have an actual Scottish Laird for a boyfriend too. Which is all very exciting, and also a long-distance disaster-in-waiting, right? Agh, I hope not. Don't tell anyone, but I kinda like him.

So, this is your Scottish correspondent Zelda Hicks bidding you all a very fond farewell. This will be my last column, as I've got a new job at an interiors magazine. However, if you follow me on Instagram, stay tuned for some more #castleinspo, #cottageinspo and some very smug posts about parties in castles and nights out in New York with a very hot Laird.

I want to say thank you to my mom, Karen Hicks, the best mom anyone could ever ask for. You taught me to be strong and resilient, but also taught me how to love. I lost you last year, and it's been so tough not having you in my corner. But being in Loch Cameron has helped me deal with your loss in a way I could never have predicted: by being accepted into a loving community, in the home of the father I never knew.

My mom once told me, remember what Maya Angelou said: *If you don't like something, change it. If you can't change it, change your attitude.* I changed my whole life in Loch Cameron, though I didn't do it on purpose. I also changed from being someone who thought love had abandoned her, to someone who found love when I wasn't looking for it.

So, I would also like to thank Hal Cameron, who truly has the biggest heart of anyone I've ever known, for his love. And I would like to thank the land of his ancestors and mine, too. Because it has begun to heal me. And for that, I am truly grateful.

A LETTER FROM KENNEDY

Hi! I hope you enjoyed *The Cottage by the Loch*. If you did enjoy it and want to keep up to date with all my latest releases, just sign up at the following link. Your email address will never be shared and you can unsubscribe at any time.

www.bookouture.com/kennedy-kerr

In creating Loch Cameron, I wanted to write about a welcoming community in a breathtaking and yet slightly remote location. I had already written about a little Cornish village in the Magpie Cove books, where characters often found themselves healing and reinventing their lives in ways they never thought possible. In Loch Cameron, the theme of healing continues, as does the theme of women supporting women, which is so important to me.

In *The Cottage by the Loch*, Zelda's mother has died, and she's within that first year of grief when, sometimes, even getting out of bed can be an uphill struggle. I've experienced that kind of momentous grief, and it knocks people hard. I wanted to write about someone coming through the worst of that experience, finding an unexpected shoulder to cry on with Hal, the (let's face it: very sexy) laird of Loch Cameron Castle, and being supported by the people around her. In Loch Cameron, people might have arguments and not always see eye to eye, but they have warm hearts and are always willing to help each other.

Zelda, in her turn, finds that she can play a role in supporting others: she helps Fiona with her business, and she becomes a friend to Gretchen Ross, who lets Zelda stay in the cottage while she's working out what to do with her life. Loch Cameron supports Zelda to find herself again after a terrible loss, and it ends with a community remembering another young woman from its past, who, perhaps, wasn't as fortunate.

I hope that Hal and Zelda's experiences of grief acts as an encouragement for you to talk to others, should this be happening to you or someone you know. As ever, talking is important, and being heard and loved is the most important thing of all.

With all my good thoughts,

Kennedy

facebook.com/kennedykerrauthor

twitter.com/kennedykerr5

instagram.com/kennedykerrauthor

ACKNOWLEDGEMENTS

The May Day celebration on May Day (1 May) is an old tradition in the British Isles that has been recovered in the present day, especially in Scotland. In Edinburgh, there is an annual May Day fire festival which inspired the celebrations at Loch Cameron Castle.

May Day is an ancient festival that celebrates the coming of the summer, celebrating the fertility of the land and a time when livestock would have been put out to pasture. Traditionally, bonfires were lit to give thanks for the light and the sun, and farmers sometimes drove their cattle around the fire so that they might be blessed by it for the year ahead. May Day was also a good time for couples to get married.

The Gaelic song that the Loch Cameron villagers sing at the May Day celebration might have been this one. In the nineteenth century, folklorist Alexander Carmichael (1832–1912), collected the Scottish Gaelic song '*Am Beannachadh Bealltain* (The May Day Blessing)' in his *Carmina Gadelica*, which he heard from a crofter in South Uist.

> Beannaich, a Thrianailt fhioir nach gann, (Bless,
>   O Threefold true and bountiful,)
> Mi fein, mo cheile agus mo chlann, (Myself, my
>   spouse and my children,)
> Mo chlann mhaoth's am mathair chaomh 'n an
>   ceann, (My tender children and their
>   beloved mother at their head,)

Air chlar chubhr nan raon, air airidh chaon nam
    beann, (On the fragrant plain, at the gay
    mountain sheiling,)
Air chlar chubhr nan raon, air airidh chaon nam
    beann. (On the fragrant plain, at the gay
    mountain sheiling.)

Gach ni na m' fhardaich, no ta 'na m' shealbh,
    (Everything within my dwelling or in my
    possession,)
Gach buar is barr, gach tan is tealbh, (All kine
    and crops, all flocks and corn,)
Bho Oidhche Shamhna chon Oidhche Bheallt,
    (From Hallow Eve to May Day Eve,)
Piseach maith, agus beannachd mallt, (With
    goodly progress and gentle blessing,)
Bho mhuir, gu muir, agus bun gach allt, (From
    sea to sea, and every river mouth,)
Bho thonn gu tonn, agus bonn gach steallt.
    (From wave to wave, and base of waterfall.)

Loch Cameron Castle and the village of Loch Cameron are
fictional, but I based the castle and surroundings partly on
Inveraray Castle, the seat of the Duke of Argyll, and the more
rugged Eilean Donan castle. Both are stunning and well worth a
visit.

Hal reads from Robert Burns' poem 'Tam O'Shanter' at the
party.

In the Cameron clan, a war cry was used that Hal shouts at
the May Day party: *Chlanna nan con thigibh a' so 's gheibh sibh
feòil!* Translates as 'Sons of the hounds come here and get flesh!'

The Camerons are a real Scottish clan, and were known in
history as fierce fighters – hence the war cry, and the grand hall
of Loch Cameron Castle being hung with so many weapons

(though this is also the case at Inveraray Castle). However, my fictitious Laird Hal Cameron is clearly more of a lover than a fighter. Additionally, my depictions of Hal Cameron, his castle and his family are in no way connected to the real Cameron family.

Printed in Great Britain
by Amazon